THE CABINET OF CURIOSITIES

36 TALES BRIEF & SINISTER

By Stefan Bachmann, Katherine Catmull,
Claire Legrand, Emma Trevayne

Illustrated in black-and-white by
Alexander Jansson

Greenwillow Books, *An Imprint of* HarperCollins*Publishers*

To our agents: David, Diana, Sara, and Brooks;
and to our editor, Virginia,
and
to the people, young and old, who go looking
for things that go bump in the night
—The Curators

The Cabinet of Curiosities: 36 Tales Brief and Sinister
Text copyright © 2013, 2014 by Stefan Bachmann; © 2013, 2014 by Katherine Catmull; © 2013, 2014 by Claire Legrand; © 2013, 2014 by Emma Trevayne
Illustrations copyright © 2014 by Alexander Jansson

The text of this book is set in Garamond. Book design by Sylvie Le Floc'h

Library of Congress Cataloging-in-Publication Data is available.
ISBN 978-0-06-233105-2 (hardback)—ISBN 978-0-06-231314-0 (pbk. ed.)

14 15 16 17 CG/RRDH 10 9 8 7 6 5 4 3 2 1
First Edition
Greenwillow Books

CONTENTS

Room Seven: Song

Drawer Eight: Fairy Tales

The Curators have selected the following four letters, all of them many years old, to give you a peek into the earliest days of the Cabinet: how it began in the mind of Curator Trevayne, some of the collecting adventures that followed, the building we constructed to house our collection—and the earliest version of the volume you hold in your hands.

Dear friends and intrepid explorers,

On my recent travels, while encountering some unique and wonderful artifacts, I was struck by an intriguing idea. Picture it, a strange, shivery collection of objects, each one telling its own dark and morbid tale. Whole rooms devoted to chosen themes, dark corners in which to hide our deepest mysteries.

The trouble, as you may well have guessed, is that maintaining such a collection alone seems like entirely too much work, not to mention that visitors could well get bored of only my particular tastes. Thus, friends, I turn to you.

You are all as keen to travel to lands unknown and bring back the oddities you find as I am. Do you care to join me, for the four of us to create a Cabinet of Curiosities (for this, in my head, is what we might call it) the likes of which has not yet been seen in this world or any other?

I eagerly await your replies,

E. Trevayne, hopeful Curator of the Cabinet of Curiosities

This letter is dated six months later, when the partnership was fully underway.

Dear Curators Bachmann, Catmull, and Trevayne,

You will not believe what transpired last night. I know,

I know: How many times have we begun correspondence to each other in this fashion? And yet somehow it manages to be true every time. Such is the life of intrepid curiosity-seekers, I suppose.

As you know, I've been exploring the lands west of us in hopes of adding something to my collection of malevolent music boxes. I recently came upon the Ratchet Wood, in which dwells a fearsome band of goblin-like creatures called grifters. According to the citizens of nearby Greybarrow, these grifters are not only bloodthirsty but also exist in a state of perpetual, unquenchable boredom, which I think you'll agree is a deadly combination. However, the grifters were rumored to be hoarding all manner of stolen charmed artifacts. Naturally, I had to investigate. Our shelves can always use a few more of those.

Considering what happened to me, you might expect me to say I wish that I had just left well enough alone, but if I hadn't investigated, I would not now be in possession of—well, perhaps I shouldn't write it down. This letter could be intercepted and used against us. It's quite possible I have made us a few enemies on this trip, my friends. A ravenous, forest-dwelling, full-of-existential-ennui band of enemies.

I suggest we consider adding a new guideline to our Excursion Manifesto: *Do not, however tempting it might be, poke sticks at sleeping grifters.*

Cautiously yet triumphantly,

Curator Legrand

P.S. Please have six ounces of finger-regrowth tonic prepared for when I arrive.

A particularly dramatic and still slightly fishy-smelling letter from Curator Bachmann, from around the same time:

To the Curators,

I write this from the belly of a sinking boat in a turpentine sea. I fear my letter will not reach you unless the bird is quick. But do not fret. I have a good brass tank of air, and a glass helmet with many rivets. The crew is doomed, yes, but what can be done? There is only *one* glass helmet and only one tank of air. They will be remembered, and it will be a good tale. All for the Cabinet, I suppose.

You will perhaps be wondering how I came to be in such a precarious predicament. Or perhaps you will not be. I know Curator Legrand has had much more deadly run-ins in the past, what with chasing a witch-girl and escaping flesh-eating gnomes. She will likely only shake her head at my possible drowning. But it was a tricky one to catch, this tale! Twisty and full of herrings, red and other colors. I followed the story many months, across countries laid out like bedroom quilts, through forests deep as time, into great, crumbling cities of luxury and lies. I followed the clues, scraps of words picked up from strangers in taverns, hints plucked from the snarling mouths of half-monsters in the alleys of Banzoo. They all led me to a boat, and the boat brought me to sea, and all was well until the whales came. I have the story, though. Now, I have the story. Here, I must finish. If the bird would only stop struggling! The water is up to my throat. The ink is going runny.

Farewell, my brave curators! In not too long I will return, and I will do so, I hope, with many more tales from the underside of the sea.

Ever-truly and with constant intrep—*(And here the ink becomes so runny and bad, and the page seems to have slipped into the water a bit, so the rest is quite indecipherable. Rest assured, though, that Curator Bachmann would have written a long and florid farewell and signed it all with his name had he not been in imminent peril of dying.)*

This letter from Curator Catmull, two years later, marks the completion of the building itself—and the beginning of what we now know as the Cabinet of Curiosities.

My dear Curators Three,

Work on our Cabinet should be complete any day. I have provided the workers with extra motivation by unleashing Curator Bachmann's marvelously disturbing collection of poisonous insects the size of puppies, two-headed snakes, and spikey bats. I just let them creep or wing about the place, here and there, you know, to take a bit of air and stretch their many, many, many legs. What jolly shouts I hear when the workers come across one!

Well, perhaps jolly is not quite the right word, but certainly very loud—and oh how much faster and louder it makes their hammers ring. I believe they are almost as eager for the work to be done as we are.

I think you'll be very pleased indeed when you see the building. Multiple high towers, my friends, with winding staircases. Narrow, dark hallways that sometimes lead where you mean to go and sometimes don't at all, at all. Cubbyholes filled with sharp yellow teeth, moaning and squeaking menageries, room upon room of objects and creatures caught behind glass—even a grand ballroom, which of course we won't use for balls but I think for all the unicorn skeletons, don't you? One of these days we'll take one alive! (If we haven't accidentally killed the last one—fingers crossed.)

I am especially delighted with the room dedicated to Unsettling Qualities of Light—also the one room that seems to be entirely empty, but which in fact contains . . . well, I don't have to tell *you* what it contains.

And yes, Curator Legrand! Your balloon idea was a superb

one, and the whole building can, if need be, travel across the skies and seas.

I have a little treat for you. I've been haunted by Curator Trevayne's brilliant idea of collecting not just the objects, but the stories behind the objects—the tales we were told by weeping families or terrified onlookers, or even our own collecting adventures. And so, as a little cabinet-warming treat, I have taken the liberty of printing up a collection of just a few of those stories.

I am holding one of the volumes in my hand right now. It pleases me to see each story pinned inside it, like a living butterfly pinned to a board and shut behind glass. Because stories are living things, you know.

I hope the book will please you, too.

Yours in all that is eldritch,

Curator Catmull

Drawer One: CAKE

Fellow Curators!

Apologies for the haste with which I write this—I simply must dash, for I've been invited to a tea party at which I've been promised the most wondrous variety of cake! I daresay you would all share my enthusiasm if you were here. It *is* cake, after all.

This leads me, however, to the point of this brief note. We've all heard tales of delectables that are not merely sugary confections. Pastries in which dark things have been mixed into the batter, or whipped up into delicious, deceptive icing. Should we perhaps devote a corner of our collection to this intriguing area of study?

If you write back, please do send that overindulgence potion? I suspect I may need it.

Yours,

Curator Trevayne

FAIRY CAKES

by Emma Trevayne

The fairies come in the night, leaving tiny footprints in the sugar and the flour.

The townspeople are always too tired after the day of baking to tidy up properly, sweep the floors, and wipe the countertops with a rag. A mess can wait.

But the fairies won't.

Everyone knows what happened the first time the fairies didn't get their cakes. It is, coincidentally, also the *last* time the fairies didn't get their cakes, and the stories are still told in shaking whispers, in lead-lined rooms, the only places the people can be sure they won't be overheard.

They come on a Tuesday, which is an odd sort of day all around, really, but most Tuesdays are not so very odd as the first Tuesday of February. For as long as anyone can remember, and far longer than that, the fairies have come on this day, and the snows always melt just in time to clear the pass through the mountains.

In the morning, the townspeople line the streets to wait for the deliveries. Fresh milk, and flour, sugar, and eggs wrapped in cotton, and honey from warm, distant lands where the bees are hard at work. The honey is especially important. No one speaks. No one even looks up. Eyes closed, they listen for the rumble of wheels over the broken road.

And on this morning, the sound never comes.

An hour passes, then another. Higher, higher, the sun creeps.

"They're not coming," says a voice. Quietly, but the whisper carries down the line, passed from neighbor to neighbor.

"Have to," says another. *"Have to."*

Everyone is thinking the same thing. Angry teeth and unbreakable, fluttering wings. The light fades and the shivers start, and the suggestion comes to check all the cupboards. At once the street is empty, the kitchens full of searching hands, thin and bony from winter. Little children are sent to bed, but they do not sleep, their fingertips caught by the dust on windowsills as they watch their mothers and fathers scurry to and from the town hall.

"It'll be all right," says a young girl to her younger

sister. Their noses press against the glass, tips growing cold
and red, until they have to wipe breath mist away with the
sleeves of their nightgowns.

"Promise?"

"I promise," says the older one, fingers crossed behind
her back.

On the wide countertop in the town hall, too much
wood shows between the meager gatherings, certainly not
enough to bake a cake for each one of the fairies, and no
honey at all.

Outside, the moon rises. The clock on the wall,
hammered into the lead with a heavy spike, chimes the
truth—there isn't enough time to get away.

There is no choice but to make do with what they
have. When all is said and done, a few dozen tiny cakes sit,
cooling, where there should be hundreds. One by one, the
townspeople slip back to their homes. They pull the little
children from the windows and tuck them into their beds,
planting kisses on foreheads. The girl and her sister curl
on their sides, huddling together for warmth, and they are
asleep when the humming begins.

Thousands upon thousands of wings block out the
moon and the mountains, the noise growing louder and
sharper as the fairies descend. Smiling, teeth bared, ready
for the feast that is their due. The town hall door stands

open; some fly inside, others land on the ground to run, cackling, over the floor.

And the cackles turn to screeching, inhuman cries.

Years later, the stories are told of what happened the *second* time the fairies didn't get their cakes. The girl is old, wrinkled, her sister only a little less so. In lead-lined rooms, they tell their children and grandchildren of the night the fairies went hungry. Of the sound that woke them from their beds and sent them back to the windows to watch as feathers flew and bloodcurdling screams tore the night apart.

They covered their eyes, and then their ears, and then tried to cover both at once. Crouched down, they waited, safe, for the fairies never harm little children. The screams finally stopped, and the humming grew distant, disappearing over the mountains into the dawn.

In the morning, feathers littered the broken road where the grown-ups had tried to protect themselves, even while knowing it was no use.

There was no blood. There were no bones. There was only silence, and then, slowly, whispers as the children met outside their houses. Older ones took smaller hands, promising, again, that it would be all right. They had watched their parents, and knew what to do on the next first Tuesday of February, and the one after that.

It would be all right.

Bravely, the children crept into the town hall. Crumbs littered the countertop, spat out by the fairies the moment they tasted the cakes, baked without honey. Splintered wood spoons lay strewn on the floor; mixing bowls sat dented because the fairies had used them for war drums.

In the last of the sugar and flour were tiny footprints, no bigger than a fingernail, from when the fairies had come in the night.

THE CAKE MADE OUT OF TEETH

by Claire Legrand

Henry Higginbotham was generally considered to be the worst child in the world, but even then, it's hard to say if he deserved what happened to him.

Do note the use of the word "generally" rather than "universally," for Henry's parents, as is often the case with horrible children, believed their son to be remarkable, precocious, and even *darling*.

For example, when Henry would not eat his supper of chicken and green beans, instead choosing to sit at the table hurling insults at his parents for a solid quarter of an hour and then proceeding to throw the green beans at their heads like darts, Mr. and Mrs. Higginbotham praised his stubborn spirit and fixed him a heaping platter of cookies instead.

When Henry was called to the principal's office

for bullying the third graders—pinning them to the blacktop during recess and pummeling them until he was satisfied, calling them nasty names that would have made even hardened criminals cover their ears—Mr. and Mrs. Higginbotham gave the school board a heap of money in exchange for "putting this *punishment* business behind us." They then congratulated Henry all the way home for inspiring the younger students with his physical prowess.

And when Henry threw an absolute raging fit the day of his eleventh birthday, declaring the birthday cake his mother had worked so hard to make "an ugly heap of eyeball pus," Mr. and Mrs. Higginbotham sent home the partygoers at once (who were only too glad to leave, having been bullied by Henry into attending) and took Henry into town for a new cake.

Of course—and this should not be surprising—not just any bakery would do. Not the bakery in the supermarket, and not the fancy bakery with all the cupcakes in the windows—but the little bakery far on the outskirts of town, in a neighborhood the Higginbothams did not normally frequent . . . *ah*. Henry pressed his face against the car window and smiled at the sight of the tiny rundown building with the faded lettering: **MR. HONEY'S HAPPY DELITES**.

Henry began thinking of all the ways he could make

fun of the unimpressive shop's proprietor, and his shriveled black heart leaped with glee.

"What a dump," said Henry. "We'll go here."

"But Henry," protested Mrs. Higginbotham, "don't you think it looks a bit shabby?"

Henry whirled on his mother, smiling when she shrank back from him. "What, do you think I'm blind, you idiot? I said we'll go here and *we'll go here*. I know what I want."

"Of course you do, son," said Mr. Higginbotham, glaring pointedly at his wife. "You know what's best."

Henry marched up to Mr. Honey's Happy Delites and let himself in, his parents hurrying to catch up. Inside the bakery, Henry stopped short, for the inside of the bakery and the outside of the bakery were, in a word, *incongruous*. Bright white tile covered the floor, warm lights blinked overhead, and displays of cakes, cupcakes, cookies, and pies sat behind pristine glass windows. Bright posters of laughing children at birthday parties and picnics and bowling alleys covered the walls. Some sort of cheery old-fashioned music came from a radio in the corner.

Henry scoffed, to cover his surprise. "*Wow*. This place is so . . . *cheesy*. What is this, 1950?"

At that moment, a man came out from the kitchen through a set of swinging doors and said, "Hello there. I'm Mr. Honey. How can I help you today?"

Now, Mr. Honey was a man so exceptionally handsome that even Henry felt a bit discombobulated. He had fair skin and fair hair and fair eyes and a wonderful smile that made Mrs. Higginbotham say to herself, "Well, my heavens," and blush a bright pink.

Henry saw the blush and felt furious. His mother was not supposed to think anyone handsome but Henry himself. So he marched up to Mr. Honey and slammed his fist against the cake displays with every screamed word:

"Give us a cake. *Now*."

Mr. and Mrs. Higginbotham rushed forward to gush about how delightfully *outspoken* their son was—and, perhaps, to more closely inspect Mr. Honey's handsome smile—but Mr. Honey ignored them. He had eyes only for Henry. You could say, in fact, that they were staring each other down, Henry with a fearsome scowl on his face (his most typical expression) and Mr. Honey with a broad smile.

"It's for his birthday," Mrs. Higginbotham explained. "The cake we gave him wasn't good enough."

"The cake *you* gave him," Mr. Higginbotham added sourly, eager to get back into Henry's good graces. "I told you we should have gone with a store-bought cake. Didn't I, Henry?"

"Oh, shut *up*, both of you." Henry was in top form. "Do you see what I have to put up with?"

Mr. Honey nodded, his smile a bit smaller now, and

his eyes a bit less kind. "Oh, yes. I see quite a lot. If you'll excuse me for one moment, I think I have just the thing."

When Mr. Honey returned from the kitchen, he held in his arms an astonishing cake. Not only was it enormous, but it looked *just like Henry*. Yes, a boy-shaped cake, from head to toe—from Henry's brown hair to his red high-top sneakers. His exact sneakers! In fact, the only thing about the cake Henry that was different from the real Henry was that cake Henry was . . . smiling.

Mr. and Mrs. Higginbotham found it unsettling to look at and stepped away.

Henry, however, was enamored. A cake, an entire cake, that looked just like him! It was, he decided, the perfect tribute. He wouldn't have to sit and look at stupid balloons or animals or other meaningless icing decorations while he ate. No, he would be able to look at *himself*, and was there anything in the world he liked to look at more than his own reflection? (There wasn't.)

"We'll take it," he said, looking up at Mr. Honey.

Mr. Honey smiled, but it did not reach his eyes. "Yes. I thought you might."

At first, everything seemed marvelous. As soon as the Higginbothams arrived back at home, Henry commanded his parents to set up a fresh table setting. They were, he told them, to sit there and watch while he ate a piece of cake, surrounded by his piles of presents.

"Maybe," Henry said, "if you're good, if I feel like it, I'll let you have some cake too."

Mr. Higginbotham smiled gratefully. "Oh, isn't that generous of you, Henry?"

"So generous," Mrs. Higginbotham agreed, though she wasn't sure she actually wanted any of that cake. It was, she thought, too disturbingly lifelike to be trusted.

She wasn't wrong.

"Where shall I start?" Henry lovingly inspected his cake, admiring the shape of his own arms and legs. "I suppose I'll start at the bottom and work my way up. Father, cut off the left foot. And hurry. I'm hungry."

Mr. Higginbotham sliced off cake Henry's left foot and slid it onto real Henry's plate, and the latter began to eat, and . . . oh. *Oh*. It was, without doubt, the best cake Henry had ever eaten. The icing melted on his tongue; the cake was moist and rich. But as Henry put the last bite of foot into his mouth, he noticed something strange; he paused mid-bite. His eyes went wide, and his face went green. He swallowed and began to scream.

"Something's eating me! Help me! Help, make it stop!"

For a moment, Mr. and Mrs. Higginbotham watched in stunned silence as their son fell to the floor, writhing and sobbing and clutching his left foot. What they did not yet know was that, though, *technically*, nothing was eating their son, he certainly *felt* like it was. All over his left foot, he felt the nibbling of teeth; they tore at his flesh, chomping, swallowing, grinding his foot bones into little bone granules. And Henry knew, instinctively, that the teeth he felt were his *own*.

"Make it stop!" Henry clawed at his own flesh, drawing bloody red marks across his skin, which, as you can imagine, did nothing to help the pain. "MAKE IT STOP MAKE THEM STOP MOMMY DADDY MAKE IT STOP!"

Now, Henry Higginbotham had not called his parents anything but their first names, scornfully, since the moment he was able to speak. So hearing him scream "Mommy" and "Daddy" shocked Mr. and Mrs. Higginbotham into action. They did everything they could to help Henry; they bandaged his foot, they forced medicine down his throat between his screams, they took him to the hospital to have him examined. But the bandages of course did nothing; and Henry threw the medicine right back up, in a sour, evil-smelling puddle; and the doctors could find nothing wrong with him.

"He's having a tantrum," they said. "Just let him cry it out." (The doctors were not, as most people in Berryton were not, the biggest fans of Henry Higginbotham.)

Helplessly, Mr. and Mrs. Higginbotham returned home and watched Henry scream and sob and bang his fists against his foot until he passed out. Mr. Higginbotham picked Henry up and put him to bed; Mrs. Higginbotham cleaned up the kitchen. Together, as Henry slept upstairs, they sat at the kitchen table in silence and stared at the one-footed cake.

The next day, Henry limped downstairs in a terrible temper.

"I'm hungry," he announced with his usual haughtiness (but he did eye the cake, wrapped up innocently on the countertop, with no small amount of suspicion).

Mrs. Higginbotham offered him a plate of eggs, and though Henry complained about their consistency, he gobbled them up. Perhaps he was eager to get the sugary aftertaste out of his mouth? But no sooner had he swallowed the last bite than it all came back up, in a most unsettling and foul-smelling pool of steaming black goop.

The Higginbothams looked at the black goop in dismay. Henry blinked. "But I'm *hungry*," he said, and Mrs. Higginbotham quickly toasted some bread, while Henry banged on the kitchen table with his knife and fork. But the toast was no good either; and neither was the waffle, the bowl of strawberries, the bowl of cereal. Every bit of food came back up stinking like rotten eggs, and each time, Henry became hungrier, and, worst of all, he began to crave a piece of cake. Yes, his foot still stung with the memory of all those invisible teeth eating him, and yes, he had had nightmares too unspeakable to write about, but he was *hungry*. And he knew only the cake would satisfy him.

So, Henry made a dive for it, dragging it off the countertop and into his lap. Mr. and Mrs. Higginbotham tried to stop him, but he flung them away with a *hiss*, and a terrible look in his eyes, and he began scooping the right foot of cake Henry into his mouth.

Mr. and Mrs. Higginbotham watched, horrified, as Henry finished eating his right foot and once again began to flail and thrash across the ground, shouting terrible things: "IT'S EATING MY FOOT, I'M EATING MY FOOT, I CAN FEEL THE TEETH, IT HURTS, IT *HURTS*!" He begged them to make it stop, but, of course, they could do nothing.

Nothing, but take him back to the place where the cake was made.

Mr. Honey was waiting for them, standing politely behind the counter of his shop in a fresh white apron.

"Now see here," Mr. Higginbotham said, slamming the cake down on the countertop. "You'd better explain yourself, sir."

"This cake is hurting our son," Mrs. Higginbotham said tearfully. "I don't understand it, but it *is*."

Henry, chomping and slobbering to himself at his father's side, made a wild-eyed leap for the cake, even though he was still crying.

"MORE CAKE," he said, clambering up onto the countertop. "No no no no. YES. MORE CAKE. Make it stop, oh, it hurts me!"

It was as though Henry was having a conversation with himself. Mr. and Mrs. Higginbotham backed away from him, huddling in the corner by the refrigerated ice cream cakes.

Mr. Honey stood and watched. "It's eating you alive," he said, "isn't it?"

Red-eyed, red-footed Henry looked up at Mr. Honey. "Yes. YES."

"Good." Mr. Honey's eyes flashed. "Horrible children deserve horrible cakes."

Then Mr. Honey smiled and turned to Henry's parents, and despite the fact that her son was rolling around on the floor screaming like a demon, Mrs. Higginbotham patted her hair smooth and Mr. Higginbotham puffed up his chest impressively.

"You should take him home," Mr. Honey said. "There isn't anything to do now but finish it."

"Now see here," Mr. Higginbotham said once more, "I'll call the police on you, I will. You can't just—you can't just *poison* someone and get away with it."

Mr. Honey smiled; it was not a nice smile; it could, in fact, be described as *bestial*. "The only poison in Henry is his own."

The Higginbothams left quickly after that, Mrs. Higginbotham wondering what she had ever seen in the handsome baker man, and Mr. Higginbotham sustaining a good number of bite marks from the wailing Henry.

Cake Henry stared at everyone, smiling, from the backseat.

To this day, the Higginbothams' neighbors trade gossip about what happened to the Higginbotham family that terrible week in August, when all they could hear from the Higginbotham house was Henry's unearthly screams.

"Maybe they're finally teaching him a lesson," said Mr. Bradhurst on Monday. "Brat's needed a good beating for years."

"Maybe he's decided he's not getting enough attention," suggested Mrs. White on Tuesday, "so he's moved on to constant screaming. You can't ignore screaming."

"Should someone call the police?" asked Mr. Rockwell on Wednesday.

No one called the police.

Quite a few of them, they shamefully (but not too shamefully) confessed some time afterward, had hoped something awful *was* happening to Henry Higginbotham—though none of them could have guessed how awful that something was.

At the end of that week, when all that was left of cake Henry was its smiling, red-cheeked head, the Higginbotham family gathered around it on the floor of the kitchen, for Henry could no longer sit up properly.

His entire body was red with teeth marks and blue with bruises. He had spent the week either miserable with hunger and craving cake, or devouring said cake and then feeling it, as it coursed through his body, devouring *him*. He had, like a wicked game of reverse Hangman, eaten his way through all of cake Henry . . . except for the head.

"This is it," Mr. Higginbotham said, exhausted. "Just one last helping, Henry, and this will all go away."

Mrs. Higginbotham was so tired, her head so filled with Henry's screams, that she felt a bit unstable. "Just . . . *eat it*, Henry. And hurry."

Henry, on the floor, dragged himself closer to the cake and looked at his parents with bleary, wild eyes. "Help me," he said, in a voice not entirely his own, and not entirely Mr. Honey's, but an unnatural blend of the two. It was deep and horrible and eager. "Help me eat it."

Mr. and Mrs. Higginbotham shared an uncertain look.

"HELP ME EAT IT. THIS IS YOUR FAULT. YOU MADE ME. HELP ME EAT IT. IDIOTS. STUPID. STUPID IDIOTS STUPID IDIOTS."

They did, fumbling for forks—as if forks mattered at such a time!—and when Henry—just Henry's voice, this time—screamed, "No! Wait! DON'T!" it was too late, for Mr. and Mrs. Higginbotham had already taken their first bites.

And Henry collapsed, mouth full of cake, screaming the loudest he had yet screamed. For now it was not only *his* teeth chomping through his skull and across his face, but also his *parents'* teeth, and there was something infinitely worse about that.

When it was finished, however, when the last bites had been swallowed and the cake platter licked ravenously clean by Mr. and Mrs. Higginbotham (who had, in the eating of cake Henry's head, discovered how *good* this cake was, how irresistibly sweet), Henry lay stone-still and cold on the floor, white as a sheet, his eyes open in shock.

And for a few minutes, Mr. and Mrs. Higginbotham thought he was dead.

(But of course, he wasn't dead. What a wasted effort that would have been.)

Mr. and Mrs. Higginbotham realized, as they stared at their possibly-dead son, that they weren't as devastated about it as they ought to have been, and this thought so completely disturbed them, that when Henry blinked awake at last, his parents vowed to make things different from that moment on. *How* they would make things different, they weren't sure. (But life, they would soon find out, would be much easier for them now that Henry had apparently lost all will to speak and instead devoted himself to peaceful, solitary tasks like bird-watching and organizing the spice cabinet.)

Mr. Higginbotham, however, did know one thing he would do, now that the frightening week had passed and he could think clearly once more. He picked up the phone and called the police, describing the odd bakery on the outskirts of town and how he suspected the proprietor, a "Mr. Honey," had sold his family a poisoned cake.

"See that he's put out of business, will you?" said Mr. Higginbotham authoritatively. "No man should be able to get away with something like that."

"Of course, Mr. Higginbotham, we'll start our investigation right away," said Sergeant Moseley at the police station, who had been taking notes.

Both men hung up, Mr. Higginbotham feeling quite good about how effectively he could get things done. Sergeant Moseley, who didn't care for the Higginbothams and their horrid son, begrudgingly started an investigation anyway, because the Higginbothams had recently helped finance the construction of the new city hall.

So, as Mr. and Mrs. Higginbotham carried their pale, speechless son to bed and tucked him in as they had always longed to do (and as he had never permitted them to do), Sergeant Moseley and his deputy drove to the outskirts of town and found the bakery, just as Mr. Higginbotham had described it . . . at least, on the outside.

Inside, however, the counter displays were crawling with moldy cakes, the kitchen was buzzing with flies, and the refrigerators held congealed, rotten pools of melted ice cream.

"There's no one here!" said the deputy, pushing back his cap. "And it stinks to high heaven."

"That Higginbotham's an idiot," muttered Sergeant Moseley, who had just found, on the floor behind the counter, an old stained apron. **MR. HONEY**, read the name tag, in swirling blue letters. It had obviously not been worn for years. "What is this, some kind of joke?"

THE OTHER HOUSE

by Stefan Bachmann

Two houses stand at No. 17, Farringdon High Street, behind the station tracks where the steam engines used to whistle and where the mushrooms grew tall as trees. One house you see, gray and cold, red drapes and only a single window lit. One house you don't see. One house you will never see.

I write this as a confession. I write this to speak of that other house—the one under the back stairs—and what happened to it, and what I did.

The stairs are still there. I hobbled down them just to be sure, while the nurse was sleeping. It is a dark, creaky flight, squeezed between the scullery and the back hall. It has a door under it leading into what may have once been a broom cupboard or a boiler room. You wouldn't know it now. You would never guess. I had it papered over years

ago in dull green stripes. Behind the door, that is where the other house stays. It is silent now, but when I was small and we had servants and maids for every little thing, the other house used to come out at night and I could hear it wheezing and clattering from all the way upstairs. It had *legs*, you see. Long, clickety legs like a spider's.

"Mother, there's another house under the stairs," I said to my mother once before bed, and she said, "Oh, how wonderful," and looked worried and hurried away.

I thought it was wonderful, too. One night, when I was feeling very brave, I left a crust of bread for it in the back hall and watched from between the spindles in the banister. I waited a long time before the little door under the stairs creaked open and the house scuttled out. It was like a dollhouse with four sharp metal legs and a turret. It went right up to where the piece of bread lay and seemed to tip forward, its joints scraping. If it were a dog, I would have thought it had sniffed the crust. It wasn't a dog, though, so I'm not sure what it did. Then it retreated through the door, leaving the bread untouched on the tiles.

It doesn't much fancy bread, I remember thinking. *I wonder what it does fancy. I wonder what it wants.*

For several nights I did the same thing, only with different foods. I tried a teaspoon of quince in a saucer. The house didn't eat it. I tried a single ripe gooseberry and a bit of pear. A great angry puff of smoke went up from the house's chimney when it investigated those and it immediately retreated under the stairs, slamming the little door behind it. It did not fancy gooseberries either.

I tried biscuits and snapped beans, a slice of plum pudding, and a bowl of curds. It investigated all of them, but it did not take any.

"Father, there's another house under the stairs," I said one day when he came back from the city, and he said, "What utter nonsense!" and had a talk with my mother, as if it was her fault.

Nonsense . . . Nonsense.

When I saw the house again, it seemed a bit darker and the windows were full of soot.

That evening, at dinner, I hid a sausage inside my napkin. Mother saw me, but she said nothing. Father saw, too. He said something.

"What is that for?" he demanded. "Why did you take that sausage?"

I said something about the other house, and how I wanted to catch it and open its roof and look at its insides, and how—

"There is no other house!" Father snapped. "There is *no such thing!*"

But there was! I knew there was!

That night, I slipped from my bed and padded down the back stairs. When I had settled myself behind the banister, I tossed the sausage into the hall. It struck the tiles with a sound like a slap. For a second nothing stirred. Then I felt a shudder under the stairs. The door opened a crack. Two long black legs uncurled, testing the tiles, testing the air. With a whir and clatter, the house shot out the door and fell upon the sausage in a frenzy of smoke and metal. I saw something, something so small I cannot be certain what it was, flicker out and snatch the sausage. That was when I knew I wanted to catch the house more than ever. I wanted to *open* it.

A few nights later I stole a small roast from the larder. The roast had a mottled white bone at one end, and to this I attached a length of twine. The twine I tied about my wrist. I laid the roast in the back hall. I sat up on the stairs. I leaned my head against the spindles, and thought about the house and all its secrets.

The other house came out after not very long. It was on the roast in a blink. The twine snapped tight around my wrist. The house began to drag at the roast, pulling and scrabbling, frantically trying to get it back under the stairs. I gasped, struggling to undo the twine, but it had pulled tight and was going tighter. My head slammed against the banister. The house pulled and pulled. The twine went tighter, tighter, and then I was thrown off balance and went tumbling down the stairs.

"Help!" I shrieked. "Father, Mother, *help me!*"

The spider-house was pulling me toward the door, right along with the roast. I squeaked over the tiles. Somewhere I heard doors open. Footsteps. Faces peering down at me, pale moons of befuddlement and indignation.

I wasn't moving. I was lying on the cold tiles. The roast was next to me, and the twine, and there were bruises on my arms and back.

"Mrs. Barrowstamp!" the housekeeper shouted. "Mr. Barrowstamp, your son!"

I got the most horrible lecture that night. It went on and on until I felt the words in my bones, and my head was full of them.

Nonsense, nonsense, nonsense.

I went to bed, and woke the next morning with it still ringing in my ears. Mother had cried, Father had shouted, the maids had whispered, and the housekeeper had shaken her head.

Nonsense, nonsense, nonsense. Someday you'll have to grow up.

And so I did. I stole a great big ham next. It was for

New Year's Eve. I think a servant was probably sacked because of it, but I didn't consider that then. From Father's glass cabinet I stole a syringe and a bottle of carbolic acid. I had heard what carbolic acid does. I wasn't innocent. The cold precision with which I went about all this shocks me now. I drew the acid into the syringe and injected the entire load into the ham.

As soon as everyone had gone to bed, I took the ham and laid it out on the tiles. Then I went up to my perch behind the banister and waited.

And waited.

And waited.

Nonsense, nonsense, nonsense.

I was almost ready to assume the problem had taken care of itself and I could go back to bed, when the door under the stairs opened. The other house stood there, swaying slightly on its spider legs, staring at the ham. It clicked over to it. It leaned down. The ham was already shriveling, drying into a thin twist of sinew. The house turned slowly. Its gable tilted up, and I might have sworn it was looking at me. Then it turned back to the ham and began to eat it, quietly. A spring popped from the tiled roof with the sound of a snapped wire. The house spasmed and jerked. It stopped eating and staggered around the newel post toward the foot of the stair. It began climbing the stairs, right up toward me, legs scrabbling for hold on the wood, as if desperately trying to reach me.

But when it was only two or three steps below me, it stopped. Through its little windows I could see people, tiny shadowy figures moving frantically this way and that. They had fingers and eyes and clothes on their backs. A woman ran to one of the windows and mashed her face against the panes. Her mouth was open in a silent shriek. She had been pretty once, like a painted doll. Now she was hideous, her face cracked and wicked eyed. I watched as the fumes engulfed her and ate her away.

I vaguely remember the house retreating, dragging itself back under the stairs. I think it must be there still, silent in the dark, spider legs curled around itself. I have not seen it since. I have not seen anything particularly interesting in the subsequent years, and I no longer believe there ever were mushrooms growing as tall as trees on Farringdon High Street.

My dear fellow Curators:

Just last month, while wandering through a high mountain forest made of fir trees and cold winds (*yes*— that adventure, and the crates should arrive soon), I came upon a tiny, weathered log cabin. Kneeling outside the cabin, gathering wild herbs, was a wiry old woman with wild, ice-white hair and cool, ice-blue eyes. As I stood listening to her tale, the sun sank behind the mountains till the sky was edged all round with blood. All the while, from inside the cabin floated a ghostly piano tune.

THE WOLF INSIDE

by Katherine Catmull

Once upon a time, a girl became a wolf. But this is not a werewolf story.

When Celia and her sister were tiny, their parents died, and they were sent to live with their aunt and uncle in the country.

"Live with" was one way to put it. Another way to put it was "work for, and slave for, and be starved and beaten half to death by."

The farm was near a forest, and the air was cool and sweet, fresh with fir trees, and the forest was full of animals and birds both ordinary and extraordinary. Sometimes at night, Celia and Maurie lay listening to the creatures' eerie calls. They longed to explore and play there.

But instead, they were kept inside, sewing hems on rough sheets, white thread on white fabric, over and over for hours. If their attention wandered out the window, their aunt would scream and shame them, or hit them hard on the back of the head. After a while, as they grew older, their heads stayed bent, even while they walked or ate, and their shoulders curved inward, as if to protect their fragile hearts.

Sometimes their aunt hired the girls out to work in a farmhouse a few miles away, tending babies and scrubbing floors and dusting while the owners were out. Although the work was miserable and the babies threw up a lot, the girls preferred this work to sewing, for three reasons.

First, the path to this other farmhouse led them through the gorgeous, mysterious woods.

Second, to be away from their aunt and uncle, no matter what they were doing, was paradise.

Above all, this farmhouse had a piano. It was only an old one, painted a dull midnight blue, with sticky, yellowing keys. But Maurie wanted more than anything to learn to play. Holding a baby in her left arm, she would practice chords with her right hand, then switch to play with her left hand.

But you make slow progress, practicing piano one hand at a time.

One morning, her aunt sent Celia alone to the other farmhouse with a heavy pail of milk from their cow, which she was to trade for more white cloth to sew. *White milk for white cloth,* she thought, her arm aching. *It's just like my life, one blank emptiness after another and another.* Head bent, she stopped to secure the pail more firmly, though it cut into her hand. If she spilled any milk—she didn't even want to think of the beating she would get, and probably Maurie, too, for no reason except her uncle's spite.

Just then, as she stood readjusting the pail, she heard something. It was a tiny, crying chorus, like a nest of heartbroken kittens. It seemed to be coming from some bushes that grew against a low, rocky hill to her left.

As well as she could with a pail, Celia ran toward the sound. She had always wanted a kitten, but of course had never been allowed one. Her uncle hated cats. After carefully setting down the pail, she dug into the bushes, then pushed beyond them, into a wide crack in the side of the rocks. She knelt down and looked inside.

Not kittens, was her first thought: *puppies!*

But then, remembering that she was in a forest, and in a den, her second thought: *No, not puppies. Wolves.*

Wolf cubs, more exactly. Seven newborn cubs, tumbling over each other, eyes sealed shut, mouths opening and closing hungrily, crying for milk.

And of course, Celia had a pail of milk with her. But if she lost even a drop of the milk, she'd be beaten.

The cubs mewled and cried, mouths opening, closing, little snouts seeking.

I'll take the beating, she resolved.

But first she paused. Celia was no fool. She looked carefully around her; she stood still and listened. But there was no sign of the mother wolf.

So Celia crawled into the den. She twisted up a handkerchief, soaking it in the milk, and gave it to each cub in turn to suck. And as she fed them, she fed herself as well—not with milk, but with something else. Some other much hungrier part of herself was nourished as she nourished those cubs.

It took a long time to feed seven little pups with a milk-soaked handkerchief, and by the time the milk was gone, it was growing dark. The wolf cubs were piled around and on top of her, fast asleep. Their warm little sides rose and fell, and they gave occasional small snorts or sighs. She knew it wasn't wise, but she was so warm and calm. Soon, she slept.

In the night, even before Celia's eyes opened, she inhaled a thick, doggy smell of damp fur, nothing like the sweet milky scent of the cubs. Hot, panting breath touched her cheek.

She opened her eyes just a crack: above her was a long red tongue, and curving yellow fangs, and a cold blue eye looking into hers.

Celia stopped breathing. Of course, she was afraid. But also, that she-wolf was the most glorious thing she had ever seen. *I am about to die,* she thought. *I'm glad it will be this way.*

But the wolf sniffed the empty milk pail, and the damp, twisted handkerchief. The wolf regarded her peaceful cubs. It seemed that she understood what Celia had done.

The wolf lay down, eyes still on the girl. A cub stirred, sensing her near, scrambled over his brothers and sisters to find a place at her belly, and began to drink. Soon all the cubs were at their mother's side, and Celia was alone.

She felt a terrible hunger, and a terrible loneliness. Despite the wolf's ice-blue eyes on her, in her misery she turned away from the happy, feeding family and fell asleep again.

In her dreams—was it a dream?—Celia thought she was a wolf cub. In her dreams, if it was a dream, she pushed through the mass of warm and breathing cub fur, all the small sighing animals, to take her place at the wolf mother's side.

In her dream, Celia fed.

If it was a dream—was it?

If it was a dream, then why, when she woke in the morning—alone, and cold, the wolves gone—then why did she feel no hunger at all?

And why, when she licked her lips, was there a taste of sweet, herby milk in her mouth?

Celia crawled from the den, blinking in the early light. Her clothes were covered with dirt and bits of fur. Her hair was a wild tangle of grass and bits of stick. She was heading home to a punishment worse than she could probably imagine.

And yet she had never felt more happy and alive in her life.

She felt full of fire. She felt loose and awake. Her shoulders no longer pulled down to protect her heart from insults and blows. They had fallen back, relaxed and alive.

She ran lightly through the forest, with grace and a new power, toward her sister. She ran, knowing she was an animal, and knowing she was free.

At the farmhouse, when her aunt raised a stick to strike her, Celia broke it in half. She strode into the house, filled a bag with bread and cheese, took Maurie by the hand, and walked back out.

"Where do you think you're going with that, you little thief?" cried her uncle. He raised a furious fist. "I'll make you sorrier than you've ever been."

"No, you will not," said Celia, calm, "or I will tear out your heart with my teeth." Stunned at her cold assurance, her uncle raised a fist to hit her—then stopped, his mouth open.

"Celia," said Maurie. "Your eyes." It was true. Celia's once shy and sad brown eyes were now an icy, inhuman blue.

"Do not try to stop us," she said to her aunt and uncle. "And do not follow us. If you do, I will burn this house to the ground, and you in it. I will do it with pleasure and without a second thought."

Their aunt and uncle stood openmouthed, fists upraised, but with no child to strike, as Celia and Maurie walked into the forest.

And that was that.

Of course, it wasn't easy for the sisters at first. They walked a long way through the forest, to be as far from their aunt and uncle as they could. When they ran out of the food, Celia scavenged berries and caught fish. They slept at night in hollow trees or up against mossy boulders. They had many adventures, and many scares, and then they came to a small and friendly town. Celia found work tending animals in the outdoors she loved. They rented a warm room in a boardinghouse, and the kind woman who ran it taught them to read and add. The boardinghouse had a piano, too, that Maurie could play any time, using both hands at once.

So you see, drinking the milk of the wolf did not turn Celia into a werewolf—not quite. But then again, perhaps her fur grew on the inside. Certainly her breath had grown hotter, and her movements more animal and loose. And of course, there were her new, ice-blue eyes.

But I think we all have a wolf inside us. If you feed yours, then it will feed you back. You'll know when it's happened, even if your eyes don't change. You'll know when your shoulders drop back, when your chin lifts high; when you run lightly and with grace; when you know you are an animal, and free.

Drawer Two: LOVE

Hello, dear Curators,

As I sifted through a box of half-burned valentines—part of a young woman's complicated cursing ritual, which went rather hideously wrong—a question came to me: Why do we celebrate love only with candy hearts and chocolate, roses and perfume?

Certainly, *one* side of love is as pink and sweet as candy hearts. That's the sweetness we reach for greedily, all our lives—from the comfort of the blankie to the softness of the teddy to the rapture when that special person finally laughs at one of our jokes.

But what about the other side? What about—when that teddy is taken away—the anguish, the rage, the childishly plotted revenge? What about the stab to the heart when that special person *doesn't* laugh but instead regards us like gum stuck to his or her shoe?

What about the way sometimes, in the history of love, a stab to the heart has turned into . . . well, a stab. To the heart.

Why don't we celebrate the dark side of love? It's almost as if most people try to pretend the dark side isn't there. It's hard to believe, but I sometimes suspect that not everyone rejoices in gloom and rage and shadows the way we Curators do.

To remedy that imbalance, here are four of our stories about love: love that is un-pink, un-sweet, and not nice at all.

MOTHERHOOD

by Stefan Bachmann

The woman pushing the stroller was tall and thin, and Amelia-Anne noticed her because her pants were a bit old-fashioned, like something out of an old cartoon. The woman's jacket was brown and lumpy. Her stroller was rickety. Amelia-Anne watched the thin woman's bell-bottoms drag over the ground, and then Amelia-Anne passed her and went to the park and played on the slides until she was tired.

The thin woman was back the next day. She pushed her stroller along with all the other moms, but none of them said hi to her. Amelia-Anne wondered why that was. When they were all at the playground, the other moms laughed and talked and loaded their babies into swings and bounced them and showed them off to one another.

The thin woman sat by herself, hugging her baby and speaking to it softly.

Amelia-Anne had to go to a birthday party the next day. She didn't really want to go, and her mom didn't want to take her. In fact, her parents had an argument about it, but Amelia-Anne was getting dressed so she didn't hear much of it. Her mom drove her to the party. There were presents and balloons and cupcakes with pink and blue frosting. The birthday girl, Ally, was turning seven and she wanted to be cool, so she had invited a bunch of fifth graders. Amelia-Anne thought that was dumb.

After the party, Amelia-Anne was going to walk home, but her mom insisted on coming in the car again to pick her up. All the other moms picked up their kids, too. Amelia-Anne thought that was nice, because it was getting cold.

Amelia-Anne's mom had arranged for her to meet Ally at the park and stay with her until Amelia-Anne's mom was done with work. Ally was sick, though, so Amelia-Anne decided she'd just wait at the park until her mom was done and go home then. She sat on her bench and started to draw with a red crayon on a big piece of paper. There weren't that many mothers in the park today, but the thin woman was there. She was looking around, clutching her baby. She saw

Amelia-Anne. She came over and sat next to Amelia-Anne.

"Hi," said Amelia-Anne, swinging her legs. Then she went back to drawing.

"Hello," said the thin woman. "Isn't my baby beautiful?"

Amelia-Anne looked at the baby. It looked like all babies, she thought. She went back to drawing.

"Isn't my baby fabulous?" the thin woman asked again. She hugged the baby.

Amelia-Anne thought it was a bit drooly and a bit chubby, but she didn't want to be rude, so she didn't say anything. She continued coloring, making a big red circle and drawing a red flower inside it.

The thin woman didn't seem to mind. "My baby's the most wonderful baby in the whole world," she said, and stroked her baby's head with her long fingers.

Amelia-Anne put a rake inside the red circle.

After a while the playground emptied. The sky turned gray and the leaves started to whirl. The other mothers had already gone home. Amelia-Anne headed home, too, but when she left, the thin woman was still on the bench, holding her baby and talking to it.

The next day, at the park, the sky was sunny and the birds were out, and so were the mothers. Their toddlers were stuffed into colorful sweaters and put into strollers or onto leashes so that they could crawl around. The thin woman was there. She was letting her baby crawl without a leash, but she was following it. Amelia-Anne watched them. The baby took about five crawl-shuffles for every one of the thin woman's long, long steps.

The baby went right up to one of the other mothers and looked up at her. The other mother saw and swooped up the baby, laughing. "Who's a little deary!" she said. "Whoooo's a little deary schnookums?"

The thin woman screamed. She screamed so loud that Amelia-Anne broke her crayon. Everyone on the playground froze. "Don't touch my baby!" the thin woman shrieked, and snatched the baby away from the other woman, who stood shocked and mortified.

The other mothers frowned and put their heads together. The mother who had picked up the thin woman's baby went away.

After a few minutes the playground calmed down again. Most of the mothers left. The thin woman let her baby stay on the ground, crawling as it pleased, and she followed it. Amelia-Anne went home.

The next day was dark and rainy, but Amelia-Anne went to the park anyway. Her mother had said, "Amelia-Anne, I don't want you going out by yourself," but Amelia-Anne had forgotten and had gone anyway. She went up the gravel lane to the playground and sat down on the bench. The wind gusted around her. She swung her legs. After a while the thin woman came, pushing her stroller. She saw Amelia-Anne and smiled and waved. Her hair was a bit mousy, Amelia-Anne thought. She needed extra-pomegranate conditioner. Amelia-Anne had seen extra-pomegranate conditioner on TV, and she was sure everyone with mousy hair needed it.

"Hello!" said the thin woman, and sat down next to her. She lifted the baby out of the stroller and set it on her knee.

"Hi," said Amelia-Anne. She didn't have her crayons with her today. She wished she did.

The wind blew around them.

"Isn't my baby the most wonderful baby in the whole world?" the thin woman asked.

Amelia-Anne sighed. She swung her legs. "What's your baby's name?" she asked. That was good. That was polite.

"I called him Max," the thin woman said.

"How old is he?"

"A few months." The thin woman bounced the baby gently. "Isn't he fabulous?"

"Don't you know *exactly* how old he is?" asked Amelia-Anne.

The thin woman looked at Amelia-Anne, smiling. "Isn't

he fabulous?" she asked again, and then the baby gurgled a big bubble of spit right out of his mouth, so Amelia-Anne said yes.

"I just love babies," the thin woman said, and Amelia-Anne couldn't be certain, but she thought the thin woman's eyes looked very dark right then. Very, very dark.

Amelia-Anne went home.

Amelia-Anne's mom wouldn't let her go to the playground the next day, or the day after, or the day after that. Finally, Amelia-Anne's mom said they could go, but only if Amelia-Anne's mom went along. So Amelia-Anne's mom did.

They sat on the bench. There were a few other mothers at the playground. The thin woman wasn't there. Amelia-Anne searched and searched for the brown coat and the long, long legs in their cartoon jeans, but she couldn't see them. Amelia-Anne's mom talked with some of the other moms. They kept looking over at their children, and at Amelia-Anne, too, as if they wanted to make sure Amelia-Anne didn't hear. Amelia-Anne didn't really care what they were talking about and she wished they would stop looking at her.

⇒ ⇒ ⇒

The next day, the thin woman wasn't at the park either. But that was the day that Amelia-Anne overheard her parents talking about the baby that had been stolen two weeks ago from its mother's grocery cart, and how no one knew where it was, and no one knew who had kidnapped it, and how there hadn't been a ransom note or anything. Police had been out looking for a crazy woman who might have done it, but they couldn't find her. They had been asking for clues. Amelia-Anne thought of the thin woman, clutching her baby, smiling. "I just love babies," she had said, so Amelia-Anne knew it couldn't have been her.

THE GRAVEYARD OF HEARTS

by Emma Trevayne

No matter how bright or warm the day, the graveyard was always a cold, foggy place. Fingers of shadow reached from headstone to headstone, brushing over dates long past, long forgotten.

Every week, Alice came with her mother. She wandered deep among the tombs and statues while her mother stayed at the edge to put flowers on those graves that bore their family's name.

"It's how we remind them that we still love them," said Alice's mother, and that was fair enough, but Alice always felt a chill in the graveyard.

The ground was soggy, sloshy from the recent rains, sucking at the soles of Alice's boots as she walked. By now, she had memorized almost all of the etchings on the stones, knew which residents had lived long lives and which had lived short ones. It was at old Mr. Fernsby's spot that she tripped.

Mud splattered everywhere. This would surely mean a bath later, but there was no point in worrying about the injustice now, not when Alice saw what had made her fall. Even covered in muck, the necklace was a pretty, delicate thing, clearly old. A filigreed heart hung from it by a tiny clasp.

Perhaps it had washed up, she thought, washed up on the bones of the last to wear it. It was a delicious, shivery idea.

"Time to go," Alice's mother called, and quickly Alice slipped the necklace into the pocket of her coat.

After dinner, Alice made sure her parents were occupied with their books before she fetched the necklace again, took it to the kitchen to rinse it clean under the tap. When it shone, all bronze and gold, she dried it carefully and slipped it around her neck.

Nothing happened. It was a disappointment, honestly, since *something* ought to happen when one put on old jewelry found in creepy graveyards, but Alice felt no different. She hid the necklace beneath her pajamas while she slept, and under her sweater at school the next day.

The following week, it was warmer in the graveyard. Not much. Possibly Alice was imagining it.

"Spring is coming," said her mother, hands full of

snowdrops, though the shadows still slithered around the headstones.

"I'm going for a walk," said Alice.

"Don't go far. I love you."

"I won't." Alice went off with a smile, eyes adjusting to the gloom. Against her chest, the little gold heart began to beat.

And the shadows were not just shadows anymore.

Deep, etched wrinkles marred the ghostly face of Mr. Fernsby as he sat on his own headstone, lips pursed in a whistle. Alice stood very still. There was Mrs. Culpepper, young and beautiful and translucent, drifting over the grass in her wedding dress. And Joseph Brown, who was shorter than Alice herself, skin bright with the fever that had taken him.

Alice wondered if she should be afraid, but she was not.

"You look pale." Alice's mother held her hand to Alice's forehead one morning the next week. "Would you like to stay home today?"

The filigreed heart thumped in time with Alice's pulse. "No," she said, throwing off the covers. She wanted to go to school so she could go to the graveyard after, to see if the ghosts were there again.

Muscles and bones aching, she tried to pay attention during math and science and art, trembling with cold. She thought of how cold the ghosts must feel, with no blood to warm them, and their bodies lying in the cold, hard earth. It made her feel a little better, and by the time her mother picked her up, Alice was shivering with excitement instead of a chill.

Inside the graveyard gates, the air was warm again, blissfully warm. Alice let go of her mother's hand. They were *everywhere,* so many more than the week before. Gaunt and bloody, old and young; tattered, rotting clothes hanging from pearl-gray limbs.

"Don't go far," said her mother, carrying a bunch of lilies of the valley right through Mrs. Dankworth, who had a friendly smile.

So her mother couldn't see them. But to Alice, the ghosts seemed so much more real, more solid than they had last week.

The metal heart jumped, twitched, beat against Alice's chest. A real, living thing. Old Mr. Fernsby adjusted his tie and touched Alice's arm with cool, dry fingers. Mrs. Culpepper whirled, arms spread, in her wedding dress.

That night, Alice fell asleep before she could even eat supper, she was so very tired. Still, the next day she waited until her mother was busy cleaning and sneaked from the house, growing more daring with every step toward the graveyard. In bone-brittle whispers, the ghosts told her their stories. Her great-great grandfather held her on his knee until she was so ill and exhausted she dragged herself home to bed, pretending, when her mother asked, that she had been there the whole time.

Against her chest, the heart was hot, too hot. She tried to pull it off, but it wouldn't come. The tiny clasp slipped through her hands. She tried to call for her mother, but her voice was silenced.

In the graveyard, they danced, warm and alive for the first time in many years, in centuries for some, as Alice lay in her bed. When Alice's mother came to check on her she flew into a panic, calling for Alice's father, for Alice was not in her bed. Was nowhere to be seen.

But Alice was there. As her parents rushed downstairs to see if she was perhaps in the living room, or the kitchen, Alice dragged herself up and over to the mirror above the chest of drawers.

Lit by the moonlight streaming through the windows, the faintest, ghostliest reflection of Alice shimmered, a tiny, filigreed heart around her neck.

DARK VALENTINE

by Katherine Catmull

People say love is life, is the great thing, makes the world go round, all that. It's a powerful thing, that's for sure. And it can lead you to some dark places. And I'm not talking about being sad when you break up, or whatever. I'm talking a lot darker than that.

This thing happened just a couple of years ago. I still think about it all the time. This boy I knew—he lived in your neighborhood, actually, on one of those streets named after a tree—this happened to a boy I knew. His parents are friends of mine, or they were at the time. They moved away, after all this happened, and no one around here hears from them anymore.

Jack was twelve years old, and he was in love with a girl named Mindy. Both of them were dark kids, dark hair and dark, serious eyes—him with a sweet smile that he only broke out once in a while, and her with a hilarious little frown and a determined walk. People who say you can't really be in love when you're twelve? They don't know what they're talking about. Those kids were crazy for each other, and tender of each other, and nothing came between them. She went to his cello recitals and he went to her soccer games; and every night, before they went to sleep, they would video-Skype from their computers to say good night.

But one day she got sick, and it was the bad kind of sickness, the kind that girls who are into tragedy do reports on in health class. The kind you don't get better from. The second time Mindy went into the hospital, her parents got her a smartphone, so that she could Skype and text with her friends—which mostly meant Skype and text with Jack, of course. And he sold his best comics, did extra chores, and begged his parents and aunts for early birthday money until he could get a smartphone, too. Just a used one, but it worked.

The last time Mindy was in the hospital, she and Jack Skyped and texted for hours every day. He fell way behind on his schoolwork, but his teachers knew, so they cut him some slack. She was in intensive care, so they wouldn't let non-family members visit. But at night Jack would sit on the edge of his bed, staring into the little screen, fingers texting away—or else staring at the grainy, moving Skype picture of her, sickly pale in the white sheets under the yellow hospital lights. Day and night he would talk to her softly, words no one could hear but her, and she would whisper back to him.

But of course, in the end, Mindy died. Most of the school came to her funeral. I went, too. They buried her with her soccer trophy, and her colored pencils—she was a really good artist, Mindy—and her bright purple phone, with the stickers on it from some band she liked, and the head of a unicorn with a flowing mane she had drawn herself with black Magic Marker.

I saw Jack at the funeral. He didn't walk past the coffin when his parents did. He sat in the very back corner, staring at the ground, holding his phone in two hands in front of him, staring at the empty black screen.

What happened next I found out about in pieces. Jack's parents had me over for dinner a couple of weeks after the funeral, after the kids were in bed. Jack had a little sister who was almost three, then—her name was Eleanor, but they called her Booshie for some reason I never quite got. Anyway, Booshie got out of bed that night, came wandering down in her pajamas with a smiley stuffed possum she liked. "Booshie!" said her mother. "Back to bed, young lady!"

"Mindy," Booshie said.

And the table got quiet.

"No Mindy," said her father. "Get back to bed now, Boosh."

"Mindy Jack's phone," said Booshie. Her parents looked at each other. "Mindy Jack talking," she added helpfully.

Her mom got up and kneeled down by Booshie. "You're having a dream, sweetheart," she said. "Come on, I'll take you to bed."

"No," said Boosh. "Mindy Jack! Where Mindy?"

("She loved Mindy," her dad murmured to me.)

"Honey, you didn't see Mindy," said her mom. "Jack's talking to someone else. Listen to me,"—and she held the kid gently by her little pajama'd arms—"don't make up stories about Mindy. Ever. You can't *ever* make up stories about Mindy, Boosh. Do you understand?"

She didn't yell it, her voice was calm, but Booshie must have picked up something in her tone, because she burst into tears and started shouting, "I sorry! I sorry!" Her mother scooped her up and took her upstairs. Jack's dad and I sat around in a weird silence for a while.

"How's Jack doing, after . . . everything?" I said, finally.

"Ehhh, not good. Not so great, really. Not good." We went back to staring at our plates.

And after that I started hearing stories about Jack,

from other parents in the neighborhood who heard stories from their kids. About him skipping classes, about him dropping out of orchestra. Sitting alone at lunch, typing furiously into his phone. Some kids even claimed they saw him sitting way out in the empty football field at lunch, leaning against the goalposts, holding the phone in front of his face and talking, all excited, like he was Skyping with someone.

"But he doesn't have any friends, my kid says, so who was he texting and Skyping with?" they'd say. "He never had any friends, really, but Mindy."

A few months after Mindy died, I had dinner with Jack's parents again. Their downstairs bathroom was broken, so I went upstairs. And at the top of the stairs, I heard the strangest thing: this voice, only it almost wasn't a voice—it was like a voice made of static. Whispery, jagged static that had somehow made itself into a *girl's voice*. "Love," the voice was saying. *SSshhhhh, hiss, zzt, szzshhhh:* Love.

It was coming from Jack's room, and his door was just cracked open. I walked up to the crack and peeked in. I know I shouldn't have, but that strange, staticky voice unnerved me.

Jack had his back to the door, so I could see the phone he was staring into. What I saw—it's hard to explain, how it hit me in the stomach, how it made me stumble back.

It was a face, I knew that. It was the face of a girl, but it was the wrong color, purplish and gray, and it was only . . . I don't know how to say it, but it was only pieces of a face. Or maybe the whole face was there, but some of the pieces were in the wrong place. A brown eye had slid down too close to the mouth. And the mouth was too wide, as if the lips were peeled back, exposing too much of the grinning gums.

And that voice, that whispering, hissing voice, saying "love, love." I stumbled back, I stumbled down the stairs. I told Jack's parents I wasn't feeling well, and I went home. And I tried to forget about it, tell myself I misheard, I missaw—though for the first few nights, that gray, grinning, lopsided face made it hard to sleep.

So we're almost at the end of this story, which is this. A few months later, I was out late, walking our dog. We'd been out to dinner and stayed later than we'd planned, so it was almost midnight.

I don't usually walk out beyond the Safeway, but the dog hadn't been out all day, and he wanted to keep going . . . and I forgot, to tell you the truth, I forgot what's out there. No streetlights, for one thing. No streetlights, but the yellowy light of a low full moon rising just over that little hill . . . that hill, that's part of the cemetery.

I'd forgotten I was walking past the cemetery.

And at just that moment, when the sight of rows of gravestones in the moonlight was making my skin go cold—just when I was telling myself not to be ridiculous, but still so wishing I were home—just at that moment, behind me, I heard it again. I heard that voice, that whispering, hissing, staticky voice.

I froze. My dog pulled back and whined. I turned around.

He emerged out of the darkness like he was made of darkness, trudging down the road, his shaggy head down, staring at a glowing screen.

"Jack," I said.

He looked up. He had changed since I'd seen him at Mindy's funeral. It wasn't just the moonlight. He was taller, and thinner, and his face was gray, and his eyes were huge and black in their dark circles.

"Jack," I said again.

"I was losing the signal," he said. I wasn't even sure he was talking to me. He seemed to be talking into the night, or over my shoulder, or to the moon. "I was losing the signal . . . I thought it was almost gone," he repeated. "But then I figured it out. It's way stronger out here." He smiled, a wide and unnatural smile. "It's way, way stronger out here."

"Jack," I said as he passed me. He started to run.

"Jack!" I shouted. "Come on, man, don't—" But he had already disappeared into the dark.

I should have followed him. I know I should have, or at least called his parents. I'll know that for the rest of my life. But I felt so cold all of a sudden, chilled right to the bone, and I turned around toward home and went straight to bed.

So anyway. That's the story. They found him the next morning. He was lying on her grave, facedown, and her grave was half dug up, as if he'd dug down with his bare hands. His fingernails were torn and bloody, and he'd actually managed to dig partway into the coffin lid. But he couldn't get through, I guess, and his hand was pressed flat against the wood, and he was dead.

And when they opened her coffin, her bony hand was pressed up flat against the wood, too.

And the weird thing was that when they found him, his phone was still on, was still hissing gray static, like an old TV—like something was still trying to get through.

So, love. It's not all pink hearts and flowers. It's not all *sweetness*, the way you might think, the way they try to make you feel like on Valentine's Day.

I guess that's all I wanted to say.

RED SHOES AND DOLL PARTS

by Claire Legrand

The story of Jackie and Mr. Jimmy is similar to that of the chicken and the egg.

Which came first?

Did Jackie start talking to Mr. Jimmy so much because the kids at school made fun of her and called her Wacky Jackie? Or did the kids at school start making fun of Jackie because all she ever did was talk to Mr. Jimmy?

No one really knows; not even Jackie knew.

But she thought she did.

She would get home from school and take Mr. Jimmy out of her backpack and sniffle over his cold, wooden head.

"Oh, Mr. Jimmy," she would say, crying into the mirror, which made things all the more awful, because she hated her uncontrollable hair and her pimples and how she looked like a string bean boy in her clothes, "why do they have to be so mean to me?"

And Mr. Jimmy would say something soothing like, "You shouldn't care so much about what they think, Jackie. Jackie, they're scum. Jackie, they're little creeps. I hate them so much. Don't you hate them?"

But Jackie would shake her head. "No. Hating's bad. Mom and Dad say so. You shouldn't hate people, Mr. Jimmy. Please don't." And then she'd put Mr. Jimmy away. He frightened her when he said things like that.

One day, though, it was the first warm day of spring, and Jackie had worn the prettiest sundress to school. It had polka dots and ruffled cap sleeves and a bright red belt. She had felt like an absolute princess, like a flower full of petals. But instead of everyone at school being impressed by Jackie's style, they had poked fun at her—for dressing up too much, for dressing too old-fashioned, for being able to see through her skirt, for trying to be so pretty when she obviously was so not.

Jackie ran all the way home from school and scuffed up her matching red shoes.

Her parents weren't home yet, and she was glad. No one should have to see her like this. No one but Mr. Jimmy. She hugged him tight and cried over his bright little blue suit.

"Oh Mr. Jimmy," she said at last, when she stopped crying enough to speak. Her voice was full of hiccups. "I do hate them. I *do* hate them."

Mr. Jimmy was quiet for a very long time. Then he said, "Oh? Is that really true?"

Jackie nodded fiercely. "I hate every single one of them."

"Then we should do something about it. Don't you think?"

Jackie wiped her eyes and stared. "What do you mean? What could we do?"

"Oh." And Mr. Jimmy, even though it shouldn't have been possible, seemed to smile. Not his painted-on smile, but one from deep inside himself. "I have lots of ideas. I've had lots of ideas for a very long time."

"What kind of ideas?"

"We could get back at them."

"But how?"

"Trust me, Jackie. Trust me. I have your best interests at heart. I love you, Jackie."

And poor Jackie, her face all red, smiled. "I love you, too, Mr. Jimmy. You're the best friend I have in the whole world."

"And I have been for a very long time."

"Why, yes."

"And I always will be. Your very best friend."

Jackie laughed. "Of course! Don't be silly."

"This isn't silly to me, Jackie."

There was that tone of voice that sometimes scared Jackie, the tone of voice Mr. Jimmy had when he talked about hating people. But Jackie was too tired from crying to care very much. So she put Mr. Jimmy on his stool and crawled into bed for a nap. It was exhausting to cry so much. She didn't even stop to take off her ruined red shoes. She nestled into her pillows and stared across the room at Mr. Jimmy's face until she fell asleep.

And Mr. Jimmy sat on his stool and stared back, which is the only thing ventriloquist dummies are supposed to be able to do.

But Mr. Jimmy was special. Jackie would have been the first to tell you that.

The next day, Jackie's parents heard a slight wooden clatter at the kitchen table and looked up from their cereal to see Jackie settling Mr. Jimmy onto her old booster seat, from when she was too little to reach the table on her own.

"Jackie," said Jackie's mom, "why is your doll at the kitchen table?"

Jackie's dad frowned and fiddled with his glasses. "Aren't you a little old for such things?"

"Don't listen to them, Jackie," Mr. Jimmy said through his bright white wooden teeth. "Things will be different from now on. People might not understand us, Jackie. They might not understand how much we love each other. But you and I understand, and that's enough. That's enough."

Jackie worked very hard to pretend like Mr. Jimmy hadn't said anything at all. She had figured out a long time ago that no one else could hear Mr. Jimmy but her. It made her feel special. It made her feel beautiful, like a thing that people wanted instead of a thing people teased, a thing people tripped in the hallways so she would drop all her books, a thing people pinched like she was some kind of ugly toy to be tortured.

"His name, *Mother*," Jackie burst out, her cheeks bright red, "is Mr. Jimmy. He's not a doll. He's my friend."

Her mother gasped at the meanness in Jackie's voice. Jackie's father stood up and tugged his shirt straight. "Now see here, Jackie-kins. . . ."

But Jackie didn't listen. She pushed her chair back so hard it crashed into the refrigerator. She grabbed Mr. Jimmy and cradled him against her chest as she ran out the door. She kicked the cat when it got in her way, and as the poor creature yowled and scrambled away, Mr. Jimmy laughed against her ear.

"Such a pretty girl, Jackie-kins," he said, and his breath was foul, but his lips were smooth. "We'll show them. We'll show them."

On the school bus that day, Jackie held Mr. Jimmy in the bookbag on her lap and fussed over him, petting his smooth, painted-on black hair, running her fingers down his smooth, painted-on suit jacket.

"You're so handsome, Mr. Jimmy," Jackie said dreamily, although she didn't say it as quietly as she thought she had, and a couple of boys nearby—Greg and Michael were their names—turned around to look and point and laugh.

"Me?" said Mr. Jimmy. "You think *I'm* handsome?"

In answer, Jackie kissed Mr. Jimmy's bright red lips.

"What are you saying to Mr. Jimmy today, Jackie?" said Greg. He had switched places with Mary, in the seat in front of Jackie's, so he could bend over the back of the seat and get right in Jackie's face. He was a handsome boy, and he had secretly always liked Jackie and was the one who pinched her the most when no one else was looking.

He didn't understand why Jackie preferred a doll to him.

"None of your business," Jackie said, turning toward the window.

Mr. Jimmy's bright blue eyes stared out of the open bookbag, right at Greg.

It made the deep, secret part of Greg—the same part that told him when he was in danger, or when someone was watching him—feel uneasy. But Greg wasn't good at reading the deep, secret part of himself, so he just got angry instead.

He grabbed Jackie's arm and twisted her around so she would look at him. Some of the other kids—Michael, and Mary, and Timothy and his sister Elizabeth—gathered around. The bus driver didn't care; the bus driver never cared.

"Let go of me," Jackie said miserably. She was not good at standing up to these people. When they treated her like this, she felt ten times smaller than she actually was. She felt squishable and dirty.

"No," said Greg. "Not until you tell me what you're saying to Mr. Jimmy."

"Mr. Jimmy!" Michael said in this high, fake-girl voice, and he batted his eyelashes and made kissy faces. "I *love* you, Mr. Jimmy!"

Mary laughed nervously. Timothy and Elizabeth watched with their mouths hanging open.

This went on for a while, and soon the whole bus was singing a song Greg had invented: "Jackie and Jimmy, sitting in a tree! One is a doll, and the other's a fre-eak!"

Mr. Jimmy was very calm in Jackie's lap. "I'll bite them. I will, darling Jackie. If you want me to."

"No," said Jackie, and her whole body was shaking. "We can't hurt them. It isn't right."

"But yesterday, Jackie, yesterday you said we could hurt them."

Jackie squeezed her eyes shut and put her hands over her ears, but that seemed to make Mr. Jimmy's voice even louder.

"Yesterday, Jackie, yesterday you said you loved me."

Jackie opened her eyes. Mr. Jimmy was very close to her. His eyes seemed alive; his mouth seemed wet. He smelled like something burning.

"I do love you, Mr. Jimmy," she said, wiping her tears.

Mr. Jimmy did not seem very sorry for her. His voice was cold and rattling. "Then *prove* it."

So Jackie stood up in the middle of the aisle, one fist clenched, the other holding her bookbag with Mr. Jimmy's head poking out of it.

"I'll tell you what Mr. Jimmy said," she announced, and the whole bus quieted because they thought *this* was going to be *good*.

"Shut up," Greg said, punching Michael, who couldn't stop laughing at his own mean jokes. "Wacky's got something to say."

"He told me," Jackie said, "that he wishes he was alive, so he could hurt you—every one of you—for being mean to me. He said he wishes he could make you cry. He said— he said—"

Jackie's bravery left her as quickly as it had come, and she sank back onto her seat, hugging Mr. Jimmy.

The other kids sat back down, too. They weren't laughing anymore. The deep, secret parts of themselves were screaming out warnings. It made their bellies feel funny and their skin turn cold.

That night, sirens filled the air of Jackie's neighborhood. She lay in bed, breathing hard under her covers. Her bedroom flashed red and blue. When she got up to peek out the window, she saw the ambulance and the police cars the next street over: Greg's street. And that house was Greg's house. And that broken window was Greg's window.

Was that body, on the stretcher, Greg's body?

"Mr. Jimmy," she whispered, "what did you do?"

He was there, at her feet, lying on the ground with his limbs askew. His cold wooden fingers touched her ankle.

"Just what you wanted me to do," he said kindly. "I did it so you didn't have to." And when Jackie went back to bed, she held Mr. Jimmy close under the covers. He whispered how much he loved her against her ear until she fell asleep.

⇆ ⇆ ⇆

"So horrible, what happened to that poor boy," said Jackie's mom at breakfast the next morning.

"I heard he's going to be all right, though," said Jackie's dad. "That's what I heard from the neighbors."

"What happened, exactly?"

"A nasty fall. Apparently, he fell right through his window."

Jackie was shoveling cereal into her mouth like a robot. Mr. Jimmy sat beside her.

Jackie's mom tried to ignore that smiling, frozen face. She had never liked that doll. She wished they had never visited that antique store that one, hot summer.

"Jackie," Jackie's mom said, "are you all right? You look terrible."

Jackie paused, a spoon of cereal halfway to her mouth, and glared at her mom. "Gee. Thanks."

"I mean it, sweetie." Her mother pressed a hand to her forehead. "You look like you didn't sleep at all. You have dark circles under your eyes. You're burning up."

"Maybe you should stay home from school," said Jackie's dad.

"No!" Jackie bolted up out of her chair. "I have to go to school."

"Poor thing," Jackie's mom said, concerned. "We've

been talking about little Greg too much, haven't we? Don't worry, Jackie-kins. Your friend will be all right."

"He's not my friend," Jackie said as she walked out of the kitchen with Mr. Jimmy dangling from her left hand.

"Did her voice sound funny to you, just then?" Jackie's dad said, after a moment.

Jackie's mom shrugged. Like most grown-ups, she had not listened to the deep, secret place inside herself for years. "I hope she's not getting a sore throat."

"He deserved what he got. He deserved what he got."

Jackie sat in the girl's restroom at lunchtime, Mr. Jimmy in her lap. The tile was cold against her skin.

"You shouldn't sit on the floor like this," Mr. Jimmy said. "It's probably covered with germs. You will get germs on your pretty legs."

"Are my legs pretty?" Jackie asked, feeling pleased.

"Of course. You know I think you're pretty, Jackie-kins."

Anger exploded inside Jackie. She threw Mr. Jimmy across the room. "Don't call me that!"

Mr. Jimmy did not break, but the sound of his wooden body careening across the floor was awful anyway. Jackie was horrified with herself. She ran to him and swept him up in her arms.

"Oh, Mr. Jimmy, I'm so sorry," she said, crying. "I didn't mean to hurt you."

"It's all right, Jackie," said Mr. Jimmy, very quiet.

"I just got so angry! Thinking about Greg. Thinking about the others."

"What about the others? That there are so many of them left? They are all the same, you know. They will just keep doing it, again and again, unless we get them first. They are making you angry and sad. They made you hurt me, just now."

"*Did* I hurt you?" Jackie's face ran wet with tears.

"You did. But I don't care, because I love you."

"You still love me." Jackie clutched him close. "You do, you *do*."

"Of course I do. But I feel a bit betrayed now, you understand."

Jackie nodded vigorously. "I understand, of course. You're right to feel that way. I was so terrible to you, throwing you like that."

"I know how you can make it up me."

"Anything for you."

Mr. Jimmy's fingers were cold on Jackie's neck, on Jackie's cheek. It made Jackie feel nice. "Anything?"

"*Anything.*"

It was Michael's house this time, which was close to Greg's—just across the street, in fact. All the children lived close together. All the children rode the same yellow bus.

It was two nights after Greg fell. Two nights later, and the neighborhood once again filled with sirens and flashing lights. There was another broken window. Michael had fallen, too, and this time they were not sure if he would be all right. Michael's family was richer; Michael's house was taller.

The police officers did not know what to make of the marks in the paint in Michael's bedroom. It was like something had dragged him, like he had dug his fingernails into the walls. The marks disturbed the police officers, but what disturbed them even more were the footprints.

Muddy footprints, in Michael's bedroom. Down the stairs, through the kitchen, and out the kitchen door. Into the backyard, down the sidewalk.

The footprints were easy to track. It had rained, earlier that very night. The world was wet and sloppy and quiet.

"They go through there," said one of the police officers to the others. She pointed down a garden path that led between two lovely clapboard houses—one white, one yellow. Flat gray stones marked with muddy brown footprints led into bushes and shadows. Sounds met the police officers' ears—sounds of wood crashing against a hard surface, sounds of someone crying, sounds of pain. A deep voice, and a high voice.

The police officers switched on their flashlights and hurried into the space between the houses.

"I couldn't stop him!" It was Jackie, crouching there in the mud, barefoot and still wearing her pajamas. Surrounding her were the parts of a doll—there, a wooden leg; there, a chubby little hand.

One of the police officers looked like he was going to say something, but he couldn't. He stepped back, away from Jackie, as if he wanted to run. There was something about the look in her eyes that sat horribly in his stomach.

"Okay, sweetie," said one of the other officers, crouching low, "just calm down."

"No! You don't understand!" Jackie backed away, trying to pick up all the shattered parts of Mr. Jimmy, but there were too many of them, and they fell onto the ground. She had destroyed him. She had beaten him to smithereens. "He said he needed my help, but I didn't know, I didn't think he would—I didn't think *I* would—"

Jackie stopped and looked up at them, at these men and women with their shining white lights. Behind them, Jackie's mom and dad came out of the house in their robes and slippers. Jackie's mom put her hands over her mouth.

"Grab her," instructed one of the police officers, "before she hurts herself."

"But she's just a little girl!" Jackie's mom cried.

The police officers took hold of Jackie's skinny arms and wrenched her out of the mud. She kicked and screamed; she bit at them. She hit them, and her hands scraped their cheeks, because her hands had bits of glass in them and splinters of wood.

"But I love him!" Jackie cried. One of the police officers picked her up, and Jackie reached back, kicking and clawing, struggling toward the pieces of Mr. Jimmy. "It was only because I love him! He told me to do it. He *told* me to!"

One blue eye stared back at her from the muddy ground. One blue eye above a shattered red smile.

The story of Jackie and Mr. Jimmy is similar to that of the chicken and the egg.

Which came first?

Did Mr. Jimmy come to life because Jackie loved him? Or did Jackie love him because he was alive?

Or maybe it was like the real answer to the chicken and the egg question:

What does it matter? The end result is the same: One loses its head; the other gets cracked open.

My dearest colleagues,

Oh, how I do love the old ones, as they are sometimes called. The fairy folk and their ilk. They are not always (or perhaps almost never!) as benevolent as one might wish, but that does make them decidedly more interesting, does it not? I have been mulling over the idea of a room filled with live examples, should we be able to catch some, but we currently don't have the space. Perhaps after a future expansion?

In particular, I would be terribly excited to get my hands on one type I'd never heard of until very recently. How I might trap it without risking all remains unclear, but it would make my success so much sweeter if I could manage it. My experiments are ongoing.

I shall be returning soon, and look forward to hearing the results of your expeditions.

Until then,

Cornelius Trevayne

FOOTPRINTS

by Emma Trevayne

Tabitha Turnbull first notices the footprints on Christmas morning and promptly forgets about them amid the excitement of presents and pancakes. Huge, fat snowflakes begin to drift past the windows, turning the whole world soft and dark and quiet.

The snow covers the footprints. By the time Tabitha remembers them, they're already gone.

Bitter cold settles in overnight, touching everything with frost fingers. Tree branches turn silver with ice, the pond at the bottom of the garden is as white as the moon.

"Wrap up warm," says Tabitha's older sister, Mary, who is always telling Tabitha what to do. This time, though, Tabitha listens, putting on her heaviest coat and a pair of ugly knitted mittens that match an equally ugly scarf and hat.

"Don't stay out too long," their father calls. "I'll drink all the hot chocolate if you do. *And* eat all the marshmallows."

"Don't tease them, George," says their mother. "But do come back before it gets dark, girls."

"We will," says Tabitha.

The snow is a perfect, smooth blanket. It's almost a shame to ruin it with their boots and sleds. There are no neighbors for a mile on either side of their little house, so Tabitha and Mary have the sledding hill to themselves. They race each other to the bottom on their sleds and see who can be first to climb back up.

Black clouds gather overhead, blocking out what little, watery sunlight there is. "Time to go," says Mary, shaking her head as Tabitha starts to trudge up the hill again. Cheeks pink, noses pinched red with cold, they head back toward the house, following their own footprints going the opposite way.

But theirs are not the only footprints.

"What made those?" Tabitha asks, pointing down at the tiny holes in the snow, running alongside the big, messy ones made by their boots. They hadn't been there when they went to the hill, she was sure of that.

"No idea. A bird, maybe."

They didn't look like the footprints of any bird Tabitha had ever seen, but, she supposes, she is not an expert on birds. She's careful not to disturb them, though. At the front door, the track disappears—the bird must have flown away.

Mugs of hot chocolate with marshmallows wait for them inside, and the warmth brings the feeling back to their lips and fingertips. The snow starts again, adding another inch to what was already there. It is, Tabitha's father says, the coldest, most miserable winter he can remember— which is a long time, because he's a grown-up and grown-ups are old—and there are still many weeks of it to come.

The next day, there are two sets of tiny footprints leading to the door. One minute the fresh snow is flat and perfect, and the next, when Tabitha looks up from her book and out the window, there they are.

"We should put food out for the birds," she says to her mother, who helps Tabitha find breadcrumbs and seeds and bacon rinds from breakfast.

That night, the wind whistles around the house and the branches of the tree outside Tabitha's window scratch along the bricks. Snowflakes hit the glass and sound like whispers.

In the morning, no less than ten tiny sets of footprints mark the snow leading right up to the front door.

"What *are* you?" Tabitha asks, very quietly. "*Where* are you?"

"Who are you talking to?"

"Nobody," says Tabitha, glaring at her sister because it's rude to eavesdrop. She doesn't tell Mary about the footprints, because Mary will still think birds made them, and she might tell their parents, who will think Tabitha is going crazy from being cooped up in the house during the bad weather.

Instead, she finds more food that will fit into little mouths, mouths the right size for a creature with teeny tiny feet. She turns up the heat, sure that the warmth is why they're coming. She plays board games with Mary and their parents and watches a movie, listening all the while for a clue.

"You don't have to hide in the walls," she says, alone in her room. "It's safe. You can come out." She doesn't know if they can hear her, or if they understand even if they *can* hear her, but she feels better having said it.

It's still pitch dark when she wakes. Her room is full of shifting shadows, perfectly ordinary things turned eerie and strange. Something moves. Tabitha turns her head. The wide-open eyes of an old doll stare right back at her.

Hundreds of footprints dot the snow outside. All coming into the house, not a single one leaving, as far as Tabitha can tell. All coming from the thicket of trees on the other side of the road. At least, there's usually a road, but right now Tabitha can't tell if it's there at all. It's just white, like everything else.

"I'm going out," she announces after waffles and orange juice. "I'll be back before dark."

Her father shakes his head. "Weather report's calling for a nasty blizzard, and I don't want you caught in that."

"I'll come back if it starts to snow," Tabitha says. She wants to follow the footprints, find where they came from.

"Wait a bit," says her mother. "Why don't you read a book?"

Even though it's daytime, Tabitha has to turn on a lamp to see the words. The sky outside is steel gray and ominous. The air smells of snow. Her father wanders around the house, checking drawers for batteries and candles.

The storm blows in after lunch, howling with fury, and all the lights go out. Tabitha and Mary and their parents huddle together in the living room, playing silly alphabet games by candlelight.

"I'll be glad when this winter's over," says Tabitha's father, not for the first time. "Nastiest one I can remember."

"Stop playing with the flashlight, Tabitha," says Mary "We need it to last."

Tabitha is just irritable enough not to listen. She hates this being cooped up, and she wants to be outside watching for the tiny-footed things, or seeing where they came from, or listening for them, just in case.

On and off she flicks the switch, and on again.

And then she stops.

It has a body of twigs and a head like a walnut.

And it is the last thing she sees.

A week later, the snow begins to melt. By the time anyone thinks to check on the family outside of town and discovers them dead, frozen in place, eyes wide and mouths open, the footprints are already gone.

Room Three: LUCK

Dearest colleagues,

As part of my continuing (and possibly futile) efforts to catalog and organize the second floor parlor, I have unearthed the following four stories, all of which deal with the topic of *luck*.

And speaking of luck—of the ill sort—apparently the jade scarabs Curator Catmull brought home from those catacombs in the Urals have been systematically pillaging our studies. I regret to inform you, Curator Bachmann, that the scarabs have consumed your stash of saltwater taffy from that mysterious island off the coast of New Jersey. I know this because I, of course, examined the scarabs' droppings and found them to smell most pungently of burned licorice (and I know that is your favorite variety). Try not to fret, however; I'm certain Father Theodore will happily send you more. It's the least he could do after you banished those restless spirits from his cemetery. (Although I must confess, I'm still not certain he didn't awaken the spirits himself for some dark purpose. But we have had this argument before.)

Thankfully these stories escaped the scarabs' appetite, so now I send them to all of you as a sort of cautionary measure. So much in our line of work depends on happy chance. Nevertheless, do think twice before yearning for a spot of good luck in your travels, for, as you will recall after rereading these tales, luck is not always what it appears to be.

With much affection (and not a few scarab bites),

Curator
Legrand

THE TIN MAN'S PRICE

by Claire Legrand

Mama always says we should never hurt each other, but Mama don't know nothin'.

She don't know about all the marks on my chest.

She don't know what Edie and I get up to in the attic these days.

She knows things are goin' real swell for us all of a sudden, but she don't know why.

I think Pa knows, but he won't tell.

I think it happened to Pa, too.

Edie's always wakin' me up in the middle of the night. We've always been opposite of the other. Like Edie don't sleep much and I can sleep through the end of the world, that's what Mama says. And Edie eats enough for ten people and I eat like a bird. We're opposites, Edie and me.

Miss Vickers at school says sometimes that happens with twins. One of you's this way and the other's that-a-way, and together you make up one person.

I like Edie, but I don't like us bein' twins. It's like we were supposed to be one person, but we got split up inside Mama and now we're two people. It's almost like one of us shouldn't be alive. Like one of us is a mistake.

So Edie wakes me up in the middle of the night and instead of goin' out on the roof to play cards like usual, she says, Someone's here, Tom. I know someone's here.

Someone's where? I say.

In the attic, she says.

How do you know?

I just got this feelin'.

Edie's always gettin' feelin's. Sometimes I think her feelin's are real, and sometimes I think she's lyin' just 'cause she gets bored and thinks our town's dull as mud.

How do you know someone's there, Edie?

I just know, why you gotta be such an idiot?

Well, I wish I wasn't an idiot, but everyone says I am so I shut up.

We go up to the attic. Pa keeps his old books up here, about geography and outer space and Egypt pyramids and irrigation. Sometimes Edie and me like to sit in the window and look through all these books. They're hard but we read 'em anyway. We like to do somethin' that Pa likes to do. We like to impress Pa. Pa don't say much, and Mama says thank god almighty for that, why'd you want a chatterbox around anyway?

There ain't no one up here Edie, I say, 'cause there ain't. Just dust and boxes and old clothes and Pa's books. Why you always playin' tricks?

It ain't no trick, says Edie. Her face looks stubborn, like Mama when she's on a tear.

I know I heard somethin', she says. I felt it.

'Cause I know Edie won't shut up about this till we do it, I say, Okay, let's look around then, and we do. Through the dust and boxes and old clothes. Out the window and on the roof. Under the loose floorboard where we hide our best stuff. Nothin'. Nobody.

I'm goin' back to bed you scaredy-cat, I say.

Wait, says Edie.

She's by the chest full of our old toys, the ones we're too big for now. She pulls out a tall round tin covered with pictures and letters I cain't read 'cause they're old and scratchy. It looks like the kinda thing you might could keep candy in.

I ain't never seen this tin before. It ain't one of our toys.

It must be heavy, 'cause Edie drops it and it hits her toe.

Ow, she says.

Then we hear it:

What're you children doing up here.

What're you children doing up here.

Why'd you wake me up.

Why'd you touch me.

Don't touch me.

DON'T TOUCH ME.

We should run, I guess, but we're too scared, so we just stand there starin' at the tin. It's shakin' on the floor. It's spinnin' faster and faster. Then the lid pops off.

It stinks at first.

Then it smells good.

I don't know what's comin' out of that tin, but it's dark and it's slimy like tar and it's silky and slow like molasses. It looks kinda like a person but kinda not.

I don't like it.

Hello, it says, and I guess it's smilin' but it's hard to tell 'cause its face is made up of globs and cracks. I apologize for yelling, it says, but you startled me, you see.

Who are you? Edie says. I wanna slap her for bein' so stupid. We should be runnin', Miss Smarty Pants, not talkin' to it. And they say I'm the dumb one.

I have many names, it says. But you can call me Luck. Because that's what I'm going to give you.

Good luck or bad luck? I say.

It looks at me. It blinks real slow. When it smiles, I feel sick to my stomach.

Good luck, of course, it says.

Edie crosses her arms. Oh, she thinks she's so smart. She's tryin' to be like Pa.

How much? she says. We don't got a lot of money here if that's what you want.

I have no need for money, Luck says. All you have to do is follow my instructions. It's quite simple.

What do you want us to do?

Luck blinks at Edie. It smacks its lips.

I want you to hurt your brother, it says.

Edie looks at me, at Luck, and back again.

What? I say. That's nuts. Edie, let's get out of here.

How much do I have to hurt him? Edie says. And what'll you give me for it?

We'll start out small, says Luck. A little hurt for a little luck.

Edie's thinkin' fast. I see that look on her face. I got a math test tomorrow, she says. And I ain't studied.

Luck smiles real big. A slap will do for that I think, he says.

Edie's eyes light up. Hang on, I say. But Edie's fast. She runs over and slaps me across my face. It hurts. I get mad and smack her right back, and it knocks her to the floor.

Oh, Luck says. Oh oh oh.

Then Luck shakes, and then it's not so slimy anymore. Like it figured out how to stand up straight. Now it looks more like a hole, just a hole in the attic where there should be wood and dust and boxes and now there's nothin' there instead, just a dark spot that almost looks like a person if you squint real hard.

That's good, Luck says. Thank you, darling ones. Now go to bed and when you wake up tomorrow you'll feel so much better than you did today.

I'll pass my math test? says Edie. You promised I would.

You'll make a perfect score, says Luck.

Then Edie says, And what about Tom? He hurt me, so he should get something too.

How clever of you, sweet girl, says Luck. Then it looks at me. What do you want, Tommy Tom Tom?

I don't feel right. This don't feel right. Edie's got a red spot on her cheek. My cheek smarts where her hand hit it.

But I got a math test too. And I need even more help than Edie does.

Idiot Tom. Edie the smart one.

Same here, I say. Math test. I want a perfect score.

Luck smiles. Its mouth drips. Then you shall have it.

≅ ≅ ≅

Our teachers don't believe us both gettin' perfect scores. Especially not me. They think we cheated so they're makin' me do my work on the board in front of everyone. And it's like my hand isn't my hand and my brain isn't my brain, and soon there's perfect algebra problems written all over that board. I didn't have to erase once.

At home Edie and I show our tests to Mama and she says she's so glad we finally started studyin' like we should. Now, if only we could peel potatoes faster, that'd be nice.

We show 'em to Pa too once he gets in from the fields.

He looks at us real strange.

How wonderful, he says.

We run upstairs before he says anything more. It's like he knows, and I don't want him to know. I got this feelin' he'd make Luck leave if he found out.

I don't want Luck to leave.

I like havin' Luck around.

I like it even though that night after Mama and Pa go to bed me and Edie go to the attic and pound on each other while Luck watches. Even though it leaves bruises all over Edie's arms and all over my chest. Even though it hurts so much I almost pass out and Edie starts to cry.

We don't stop. We'd do anything for Luck. We go for hours. We pound and bruise and slam and cut. It hurts it hurts but we don't stop.

Very good, Luck says. It's not as scary-lookin' tonight.
It looks more like a shadow than a blob or a hole. And
shadows ain't scary; they're just places where the light don't
reach.

Luck runs its hands through our hair. It makes me feel
even sicker, but I don't complain. I got a baseball game on
Friday and I wanna win. Make a double play. Hit a grand
slam. Not sit on the bench the whole time for once. And
Edie, she's got a softball game, and she wants a grand slam
too. Stupid Edie, always wantin' to be the same as me. Just
'cause we're twins don't mean we gotta be the same all the
time.

I wanna hurt her again.

Hurt and ye shall receive, says Luck. It's laughin' so I
guess somethin's funny but I don't know what it is.

One day Luck gets tired of watchin' us.

I want more, he says. I'm bored of you.

We could go into town, Edie says. She's cryin' because
I think I just broke her toe, but she won't say nothin' and
neither will I. We won both our games this weekend. We're
gettin' good grades for once. Amelia Simmons bought me
a milkshake at lunch. Everybody's lookin' at us different,
like we mean somethin'. Like we ain't just Tom and Edie,
those twins who live out on Hillside Farm, no sir. We're

Tom who gets hundreds on tests and Edie who hits grand slams.

Town, Luck says. He looks happy to hear that. He moves his head funny like a bird. And I've started callin' him a he because he looks more like a man now. He's still dark and fuzzy around the edges and sometimes when he blinks that tar drips out his eyelid, but he's mostly a man. He has a tall hat on, and he's skinnier even than me.

I should very much like to go to town, Luck says.

So we take him.

And the first person we see, Luck points and says, That one. Hurt that one.

We look. It's a girl from the junior high school walkin' her dog. I've seen her before but I don't know her name.

Edie frowns. But it's the middle of the day, she says. We cain't just go up and start punchin' her. Someone'll see.

Luck says, Not if we wait until she's somewhere hidden.

I don't like this, I say.

Oh. Oh no.

I didn't mean to.

It just came out.

Luck, don't be angry. Don't be angry, Luck.

I didn't mean it.

Luck looks at me long and hard. Edie looks at me even longer and harder.

Don't ruin this for me you idiot, Edie says. Don't make him mad. We need him.

I'm sorry, Luck, I say. I'll do it. We'll do it.

You had better, says Luck. Or I'll go somewhere else where my gifts are appreciated and then where you will be?

You'll be back in the rotten no-good place you came from, Edie says to me. You'll go back to stupid bad-grades on-the-bench idiot Tom. Livin' on a farm. Goin' nowhere. Is that what you want? Is that you want for us, Tom?

Tom, Luck says real soft. Tommy Tom Tom.

No, I say. That's not what I want.

So we follow the junior high girl through town and all the way to Thistledown Road, where it's quiet and the grass is high on either side.

We chase her down. She starts screamin' and we run even faster. She sets her dog on us and we dodge and the dog runs right into Luck's open arms and I don't see what happens to the dog after that.

I don't want to either.

We're runnin' faster than we've ever run before.

Isn't this great, Tom? Edie says. She's laughin' her head off. We're almost flyin', she says. We're like superheroes.

Ain't nothin' hero about it. Luck is right on our heels. I think Luck's helpin' us run this fast, tell the truth.

It ain't a good fast.

It's like runnin' from somethin' in a bad dream.

I guess it's like what the junior high girl feels with us gettin' closer and closer. We reach for her arms. We grab 'em. We pull hard.

It ain't her fault she cain't outrun us. She don't have Luck on her side.

We get home and eat dinner and go upstairs without sayin' a word to nobody. Mama don't notice cause she ran into Mrs. Jackson at the supermarket and there's a whole scandal about Mrs. Jackson's son runnin' off to the city or somesuch and Mama's happy as a clam about it. Finally somethin's happenin', she says, in this dull as mud town.

Pa watches me and Edie from across the table.

I don't like him lookin' at me.

It's like he knows.

It's like he saw us hit that girl. Just the one time is all it took for Luck to shiver and shake and roll around on the ground like he got an electric shock. When he stood back up, I could see his eyes real clear for the first time. They were dark and didn't have no white around 'em.

I don't like Luck's eyes.

Edie stood there twistin' her hands. Oh golly Luck, she said, we shouldn't'a done that. We shouldn't'a hurt that girl. She'll tell on us.

She didn't see you, said Luck. He smoothed down his coat. He dusted off his tall hat. He kicked dirt off his boots. All she saw, he said, was her fear.

Then he took our hands and led us home.

And now we're sittin' here across from Pa tryin' to choke down cornbread, and I swear he knows what we've done.

I almost say somethin'. I cain't help it. This ain't right.

It ain't right it ain't right.

IT AIN'T RIGHT IT AIN'T—

Edie kicks me under the table.

Stupid Tom. Stupid idiot Tom.

I shut up. I don't say nothin'.

I ain't stupid idiot Tom with the smart sister no more. Not with Luck around.

So I don't act like it.

At first when I wake up that night I think it's Edie comin' to get me 'cause Luck said when he brought us home before dinner, he said, Darling children I want you to come up and see me tonight.

But we just hurt that girl for you, I said. Ain't that enough for today?

Luck touched my arm. He squeezed tight till I couldn't breathe.

It's never enough, he said.

But it ain't Edie wakin' me up. It's Pa.

Hurry, he says. Follow me.

Where're we goin'?

To the attic.

I stop cold. Why?

'Cause I know what's goin' on and it's gonna stop tonight.

Pa, ain't nothin'—

I ain't an idiot, Tom, and you ain't either.

But I am an idiot, I say. Ain't no use lyin'. I ain't a good liar. Edie's the one who's good at lyin'.

I need Luck, I say. We're at the attic door. Pa's holdin' the cross from above the supper table like a gun.

I ain't no good without him, I say.

I'm cryin'.

No you got that wrong, Pa says. He leans down so I can see him. His face got crisscrossed lines all over it. He looks tired, but his eyes don't.

You're a good boy, Pa says. He holds me tight.

Where's Edie?

She ain't comin' with us.

Why?

'Cause she ain't strong enough. Ain't her fault. You could'a been the weak one just as easy.

I'm the mistake twin, I say. I'm still cryin' 'cause that's what idiots do. I shouldn't be alive.

That's right, says a voice.

It's Luck.

You shouldn't be alive, he says.

The attic door flies open.

Pa holds out his cross in front of us. He's got it in one hand and me in the other. He rushes into the attic.

Somethin's screamin':

You again.

You you you.

Not again.

Get that away from me.

GET IT AWAY.

PUT IT DOWN.

No, Pa says. I ain't puttin' it down.

He grabs that heavy tin Edie dropped, the one Luck lived inside. It's so heavy Pa can barely lift it. Maybe with two hands he could lift it but he cain't let go of that cross. I know that without even askin'.

Tom, he says, help me get it outside.

So much screamin' and so much wind. Books and clothes and boxes flyin' all over the attic. There's a kind of dark in here so thick it's like drinkin' cement.

But we lift it together, me and Pa, and we get it outside.

Luck follows us, and there's dirt flyin' in our eyes and the ground's shakin' under our feet, but if I look out into the fields it's calm like springtime. It's a good thing we didn't stay in the attic. We might've brought the whole house down.

I guess Pa knows that.

How'd you know Pa? I say. How'd you know what we done?

It happened to me too. He has to shout it 'cause Luck is screamin' nasty words so loud I cain't hardly think.

When? I say.

When I was a boy. Luck found me too.

You should'a gotten rid of it, I say. So me and Edie couldn't find it. This tin, we found it with our toys.

That's the thing, Pa says.

He looks at me.

I did get rid of it, Tom.

TOM. TOM. TOMMY TOM TOM.

WHERE WILL YOU BE WITHOUT ME TOM.

Don't listen, Pa says, real calm. We're by the creek now. He's got the tin in one hand and the cross in the other and he's tryin' to bring 'em together like magnets that just won't go. There's sweat on his forehead and his muscles are big like mine'll never be, I just know it.

YOU'RE RIGHT TOM, says Luck. He don't look

like a man no more. He's all kinds of slime and glob. He's crawlin' on the ground. His hat ain't a hat no more. It's just a tall, tall head. YOU'LL NEVER BE AS STRONG AS YOUR PA.

YOU'RE NOTHING WITHOUT ME.

YOUR SISTER COULD MAYBE DO IT. SHE'S SMART ENOUGH. SHE'S PRETTY ENOUGH. SHE COULD MAKE IT WITHOUT ME.

Don't listen to it, says Pa. He's sweatin' hard. He cain't hardly breathe. It ain't nothin' but tricks and lies, he says. Luck ain't real. Luck don't last.

DON'T LISTEN TO IT, Luck says. He drips black on my feet. He's real close now. DON'T LISTEN TO IT.

I NEED YOU AND YOU NEED ME.

WITHOUT ME YOU'RE NOTHING.

Then Pa says, Okay Tom. Okay now.

And I say to Luck, You got that backward. And I'm cryin' but I just don't care.

And Pa slams his hands together, cross to tin.

And Luck shrinks into a smokin' black piece of somethin' burnt.

And flies into the tin.

And the lid slams closed.

⤜ ⤜ ⤜

With Luck gone everything's quiet again. There's crickets in the grass and a coyote out somewhere by the foothills. And there's me and Pa starin' at the tin on the ground like it's this thing you don't want to touch 'cause if you do it'll blow you to bits.

What'll we do with it? I say.

What'll we do without it? What'll we do without Luck? That's the question I really feel like askin', but I know I probably shouldn't. I think of all the things I done. I wonder if Pa done those things too when he was a boy. I wonder if anybody ever called him idiot or thought he was the dumb one.

After a while Pa says, We'll bury it. Far from here. Farther'n' I did the first time. Deeper too.

We're walkin' back to the house now, me and Pa. We grab two shovels from the barn.

Me and Pa.

Not Edie. Not Mama. And Pa's lookin' at me like I ain't a boy no more. Real proud, he looks like.

I bet you didn't count on that did you, Luck? I bet you didn't see that comin'.

You thought I was nothin' without you.

You was wrong.

I sling the shovel on my shoulder just like Pa does.

I liked havin' Luck around, I say. It was nice.

I know, he says. I did too.

What'll we do without it? What if we never get it again?

There. I said it. I know it's shameful but I said it.

Well, says Pa. Well. Then he says, We'll go to sleep.

We'll wake up in the mornin', he says.

And then we'll get back to work.

JOHNNY KNOCKERS
by Stefan Bachmann

The *Misselkree* was nineteen days at sea when Johnny Knockers came aboard.

The crew had just dragged up a long black whale, had sliced it open fin to fluke, and then there he was, lying still as could be, staring up through the bloody cleft.

He was little more than bones. His skin had been bleached white by the whale's stomach liquids. All his hair had fallen out.

Hooks and paring blades clattered to the deck when the whalers saw him. They jerked back, growling into their beards, wiping the blood off on their rough woolen sweaters.

"Is he breathing? Oh, crikey, he's breathing. . . . "

"He's been swallowed," one of them said, a sailor named Crickets. "Swallowed alive, like in 'em old stories."

"Let's throw him back," Eli, the cabin boy, suggested, but they were a thousand leagues from the nearest lighthouse, a hundred fathoms above the nearest ship. It would have been murder. Murder was unlucky.

So the whalers kept him.

He had forgotten how to walk, but they lifted him from the whale's carcass and brought him belowdecks. He was slippery as a fish, all knobby elbows and slimy legs.

They propped him up by the iron cookstove, fed him broth with laudanum and whiskey. At first the broth dribbled down his chin, but then he swallowed, and all the men gathered around him let up a shout.

They tried to teach him how to stand next, and how to speak. They asked him tricky questions about oceans and winds to see if he might be a whaler like them. They tried to learn his name. He never spoke a word. He never even looked at them.

"We'll call you Johnny Knockers, then," they said. "Because those knees knock like a drum." And they all laughed.

That night, the clouds heaped against a stiff wind. An air of anticipation settled among the hammocks and the narrow galleys belowdecks. Was Johnny Knockers a gift from the sea? Or a curse. . . The whalers locked him in the brig just in case, slouched on a bucket next to the cold stove.

≕ ≕ ≕

Whaling was good the next day. The water chopped, deep and dark, and a great beast of a whale was caught in the first hour of the watch, which was a rare thing and a lucky one. The men rolled up their chains and stowed the harpoons, and even the lookout was allowed to come in and sit the rest of the day out of the wind. Everyone was given an extra ration of whiskey. Everyone except Eli. He was barely fourteen, and not a proper whaler, and so he was given a spoon and a bowl of stew and told to go feed Johnny Knockers.

Eli went to him, scowling. He sat down on a stool next to Johnny Knockers and began shoveling stew into the pale man's mouth, so hard that the spoon clanked against his gray teeth. Johnny Knockers did not protest. He did not move at all, just stared into the dark corner like he could see something there, something endless and sad.

Eli stopped. He was such a piteous-looking thing, Johnny Knockers, so bony and haunted looking.

Eli spooned slower. "All right," he said. "I didn't mean it about throwing you back, yeh? We was afraid is all. You're a right frightening chap to look at."

Johnny Knockers said nothing. He did not swallow. The broth dripped down his throat, and Eli was almost sure he could hear it collecting in a puddle in the man's belly.

He spooned the broth in silence. Then he said, "I don't suppose you'd tell where you came from? Where your home's at? D'you even remember?"

The whalers had tried to find out. They had searched Johnny's garment (a shred of bleached cloth, stiff with salt), but all they had found was a long tooth on a leather cord hanging around his neck, and black scribbles on one arm in some foreign writing. "What language is that?" they had asked, but he hadn't told them.

And he did not tell Eli. He did not look up. His pale blue eyes were fixed on the floor planks now, worn smooth and glimmering.

Eli listened to the whalers, merry and loud in the next room.

"I'm from Suffolk," Eli said. "Suffolk by the Sea."

Spoon, wait, spoon, wait.

"Have you been there? If you haven't, you're not missing anything. It's a gloomy place. A nasty place, right up next to the water. Not as bad as this, though."

And somehow, though Johnny Knockers never moved, Eli felt that Johnny Knockers agreed with him.

That night, a storm struck, vicious and screaming, all lightning and waves and a white wind that rushed in the sails. A rope snapped. One of the harpoon stations was lost to the sea. But the men were fresh off the victory of the morning's catch, and so it was shrugged off as nothing.

Eli got the job of feeding Johnny Knockers again the next day. He grumbled loudly about it in front of the whalers, which confused the cook, because that morning Eli had waited for everyone to leave and had begged him for the job.

Eli took the bowl of stew and sat down by Johnny Knockers.

Again he spooned in silence. Then he said stoutly, "I'm not always going to be a whaler. In fact, not sure I like it much. Hauling all day, cutting and slicing and shoveling. It's right horrid." Then, with a furtive glance into the dank brig, he said, "One day I'm going to be a shoemaker."

Johnny Knockers said nothing, and Eli didn't mind. "I'm going back to Suffolk when I'm older and have got enough money. There's a girl there named Lizzie. I gave Liz a tin of taffy before I went, and she gave me a ribbon." His fingers unlooped a slip of cloth from one of his buttonholes. The weather had faded the blue to gray. "What, d'you think o' that, Johnny Knockers? Sound like a plan? Sound like a good thing?"

Eli would have gone on, but then feet hammered the deck above. Shouts split the air.

"They'll be needing me," he said, and left the remainder of the stew next to Johnny Knockers's feet. Eli did not see, but Johnny's eyes moved a bit as he turned to go, just a flick, and it made a sound inside Johnny's skull like a fingernail snagging.

Whaling had never been better, but no one spoke that night as they clambered into their hammocks. Rations were going bad. The tack was beginning to turn green, and the meat for the stew was rancid. The cook had found spiny crabs swarming the larder like spiders. The whalers were becoming grumbly and lead-footed. And yet none of them wanted to turn back.

That morning, a great big beast had been spotted going north, and all the whalers wanted the *Misselkree* to press on, despite there being nothing but rancid stew and tack to eat, and no fresh anything. The whaling was good, and the whalers were convinced they were still on a streak of luck.

As for Johnny Knockers, no one really wanted to go near the bony figure by the stove, and so Eli had to feed him permanently, which was all right with Eli.

He liked talking. He liked telling someone things, and he didn't mind not getting any answers. In fact, it was almost better that way. Even after the cook had gone to his hammock and the whalers were snoring in their hammocks, Eli murmured to Johnny Knockers in the dark, told him of Lizzie and how she was very poor and so was Eli, and how neither of them minded. He told of the house far inland that he wanted to buy in a year or ten. Just a short jaunt from the town, Eli said, a short jaunt that a buggy and an old horse could manage nicely. And no more of the sea. No more fear of drowning, black water creeping over pale faces, filling your nose and then your lungs. You didn't drown on a dirt road. You didn't drown in a buggy.

The crabs had left the larder and had begun snapping at the men's toes as they slept. Barnacles were found on the inside of barrels, which was unheard of. The food was worse than ever. But the whales came steadily, one a day, at least, and they were becoming ever larger. Soon the *Misselkree* would be full to bursting. It was a large whaler, and they had room for many barrels of blubber, but there was only so much space, and only so many barrels.

"Perhaps it's him," Crickets said one night to the other whalers as he scraped the puffs of green fungus off his tack. "Johnny Knockers. It's like he's luring them. The whales."

No one agreed at first, but slowly they came to an

understanding: whatever was happening around them had to be due to unfortunate weather and bad planning and a no-good blarsted tack-and-flour merchant back in Liverpool. Whaling had never been this good, whales never so foolish. And Johnny Knockers was very good luck indeed.

He's like a lure, Crickets kept repeating, and so they made him into one.

At the crack of dawn they dragged him from his place by the stove, up onto the deck. A coil of rope was brought.

"Stop!" Eli yelled when he saw what they were doing, but the whalers pushed him aside. They tied Johnny to the mast, tight, so that he wouldn't flop about.

"Shut yer trap, boy," Crickets said when Eli kept up the racket. "It's more blubber in the barrel, for you, too."

A whale came very soon. Its tail slid up out of the water. Then its head, very close to the ship. Johnny Knockers saw it. His eyes took on a sickly, desperate glaze. He began to strain, pushing against the ropes.

"Stop!" Eli cried again, but no one listened.

When the first harpoon struck the whale, the shriek that came from Johnny's throat was ghastly. The beast began to struggle suddenly, where before it had been calm. It thrashed and Johnny Knockers did, too, his voice screeching up and up. The harpoons rained over the side of the ship. For an instant the water was stained red.

When the whale was at last dead and the men were scooping the pearly fat from under its ink-blue skin, only then did Johnny Knockers stop screaming. He went limp again. Eventually they dragged him belowdecks, and Eli sat next to him, trying to feed him, because it was the only thing he could think to do, but Johnny didn't eat. He sat staring into nothing, and Eli felt sure his eyes were full of hate.

The whalers went to their hammocks, tired and coughing, but not Eli. He stayed with Johnny.

The hours crept past. Eli dozed. And then, deep in the night, when the only sound was the creak of timbers and the lap of waves and the snores of the men, a hand crept forward and gripped Eli's arm. He sat up with a start. The hand was wet. Johnny Knockers had not been in the water for days, but somehow his skin was still slippery, as if the water were oozing out of his pores. He fixed Eli with a wide-eyed stare, and Eli stared back.

The cook woke at one point to empty the chamber pot and saw them silhouetted by the stove, the boy and bone-thin Johnny Knockers. Later, when asked, he could not for the life of him remember if it had been Eli whispering . . . or Johnny Knockers.

≅ ≅ ≅

The next morning dawned cold and blue. Only two sailors were up when Eli came on deck and wrapped his arms in chains and plunged himself into the sea. He sank like a stone before anyone could reach him, before anyone could even shout.

The whalers held a service for him on the windy deck. Ashes to ashes, brine to brine. The captain read from the ship's damp and battered Bible. They had to shorten it a bit because a humpback had been sighted, very close by, floating calm as you like toward the *Misselkree*.

The hold was filled beyond anything the *Misselkree* had ever managed before, barrel upon barrel of blubber, but there was still one corner left. One last corner with space for a few more barrels. The food was rotting, the men were sick, but it would only take one more whale.

They tied Johnny Knockers to the mast again, to speed things up. One last whale and they would turn toward home. Back to port, and alehouses, and enough money to live at least until Christmas for those who drank, fairly well until June for those who didn't.

It was about noon by the time a tiny whale approached the ship. Johnny Knockers did not thrash or scream this time. He looked at the whale darkly, and just before it came within range of the men's harpoons, it turned and folded back into the ocean. The men cursed and shouted after it. They had been looking forward to the journey back. They dragged Johnny Knockers below and threw him to the floor.

Another whale came not too long afterward. They killed it and filled the last of the barrels. They felt very pleased with themselves as they vomited over the side of the ship.

That night, a whaler named Smithy died of dysentery. Several others were too sick to move. But they were headed home now, headed to port and a year of comfort.

"What an expedition," said Crickets as the men huddled in their hammocks. "What a lucky expedition." And everyone agreed.

The whales came in the night. Thirteen, fourteen, fifteen, surrounding the *Misselkree*. The night was black, the air still and cold, and the men barely stirred as the waves from the whales' fins began to buffet the sides of the ship. They started gently, became stronger. Then the whales struck, headfirst on all sides, and the men woke with weak shouts.

Leaks sprang. A porthole burst, splashing Crickets in the face.

The men staggered to their feet. They hobbled on deck in their undershirts, lanterns swinging, tiny fireflies in a great black ocean. The whales struck again, again. The hull buckled. Men were thrown from their feet. And then the *Misselkree* split, right down the middle, with a deafening *crack*. She sank quickly—ten seconds, and she was gone—and all the little fireflies winked out.

And just before the last of her slipped under the waves, Johnny Knockers stepped off into the gurgling water. He did not sink. A whale's head rose up, a black monolith, blacker than the night, and a deep, hollow sound echoed out of its belly. The whale opened its mouth. And Johnny Knockers flopped in, curling into the dark and the red like a child in a womb.

Far away, a boy struggled up a rocky shore, dragging himself over the stones. He was paler than he had been, just bones. His hair was not as thick as a fortnight ago, and his eyes were somewhat sunken. A ribbon was looped through his buttonhole. Only the faintest threads showed that it had been blue once.

He would live years yet, Eli—forty, fifty, and he would find roads and travel them, to Lizzie and shoe shops and houses on heaths.

Not the men on the *Misselkree*. They lay at the bottom of the sea in a boat full of blubber. Not all the luck in the world could have saved them. And neither had the whales.

THE CIRCUS

by Emma Trevayne

They said I was found in an eggshell. That a witch sailed to sea in the shell to whip up a storm that would smash the boats to ribbons on the rocks, and when the shell came back to land, there was I, curled inside.

That's what they *said.* Rubbish, of course, but in our line of work, an interesting story was as important as the clothes on your back. Maybe more important.

And it's true I was always lucky, right from a tiny thing, always first to find stones with holes in their middles when we cleared the ground for the tents, or see a cat the color of midnight. Lucky Luke, they called me.

I was seven, possibly eight. Not knowing exactly my birthday on account of the eggshell, it was difficult to say for sure, but that sounds about right. Seven or eight, and there was so much glittering, thrilling fun to be had, ducking under the juggler's clubs, spitting water back at the elephants. Waiting for the moment when everyone had taken their seats and the whole tent held its breath . . .

"Welcome, welcome!" Mr. Scully, the ringmaster, would cry. The towns changed—some big, some small, at the edges of lakes or swaddled by mountains—but this was always the same. And then I would be wheeled out in a special box, and the magician would saw me clean in two.

Not *truly*. But it looked for all the world as if he had.

On one particular day, the animals were tired and grizzly, and the rest of us soaked through from a week's worth of rain. "Are we there yet?" I asked. I remember this quite clearly.

"Nearly, Lucky Luke!" roared Scully, trying very hard to smile beneath his drooping, dripping mustache. Beside me, the fortune-teller made a sign to ward off evil spirits.

We turned down a dirt road walled on both sides with trees tall as hills. Somewhere behind my little nest of blankets the lion roared; the tamer rattled his chains.

Nightfall had come at breakfast time, so dark it was in the shade of those trees. Leaves rustled, and whatever tiny points of light broke through seemed more like stars than daylight. The trees kept the rain off, however. That was something.

It felt an age that we traveled that dark road, peering ahead for any sign of it ending, and when it did, trees giving way to open space and a large town of wood and brick, it was as abrupt and surprising as a miracle. As finding a penny beside your shoe the moment you happen to look down.

"Everybody out!"

Everyone has a job in the circus. In truth, everyone has twenty-seven jobs, all part of a well-oiled mechanism. The acrobats climbed atop the wagons to grasp tent pegs with their toes. The magicians vanished burlap sacks as soon as they were emptied. I wriggled through the small spaces, ran jackrabbit quick between the carts and the tent, delivering hammers and ribbons, sandwiches and balloons.

With a sweeping arm, Scully donned his top hat and crossed the muddy field to the town. I remember this quite clearly, too, though I could not now say why it made such an impression. He always went to issue a formal invitation, as if the people hadn't watched our arrival through their windows.

The circus had come to town, and oh, wouldn't they come that very evening to see what wonders the Big Top held?

Of course they would come. They always came, to stamp their feet and clap their hands and hiss like snakes.

Only later, much later, did I realize I hadn't found a single stone with a hole in it, or seen a cat hunting for field mice. I was too busy helping the tumblers with their spangles, tying knots in the trapeze ropes, fetching buckets of sawdust and rainwater.

The tent was full to bursting. I sneaked out and away, far enough that I could see how grand it was, great stripes lit up with torches against the backdrop of that deep, black forest.

"Luke!"

"Here!" I ran back, back to Maximilian the Magician, who was ready to tuck me into the box so he might cut me in two again.

"In you go, then."

It was dark as a bruise inside the box, but I wasn't afraid. No need for that. Done it a hundred times, hadn't I?

The tent was dark, too. I couldn't see, but I knew it was always dark as I was wheeled to the edge of the ring. Dark and quiet enough to hear a pin drop. The band silent, Scully in his waistcoat and top hat waiting, waiting until the townsfolk couldn't stay still for another moment.

And then the lights would burst to life, and the band would start to play, and Scully would welcome everyone, and the show would finally, finally begin.

Just another moment, that's all. Squashed inside my box, I knew it would only take another moment.

That's when the whistle came. A low, mournful whistle that brought goose bumps to my skin. A trombone made a noise like a cat under the wheel of a cart. Glass shattered.

"Lights!" Scully ordered.

Maximilian flicked the box latches with fingers that made the whole thing shake. I tumbled out, heart thudding, as the ring of torches flared on our fearful faces. High up on the ladders, Ivan and Cassandra dropped their trapezes and put their hands to their mouths. Juliette's cards did not foresee this, but she shuffled them anyway.

"Who was that," Scully whispered, gazing about the tent. "Who whistled?"

No one said a word.

He looked terrifying, terrible, inhuman with his wide mustache and goggling eyes. "It is horrendous luck to whistle in a circus tent, you know. Let us not get off on such a wrong foot, my friends. Who was it?" he asked again.

Still, no one answered. Bunch of cowards, I thought then. Bunch of stinking cowards.

Scully gave a last look around the tent. "All right. Welcome, welcome."

The smashed mirror was swept, trapezes were retrieved,

latches closed on the box to lock me back inside. For the first time, I was afraid as the sword sliced the air, but the trick went off without a hitch. And as for the rest, if our hands shook a little more, if our feet were not so steady that evening, who was to notice?

We would not stay another night; that was decided the instant the tent had cleared out. Pack up first thing, be on our way to somewhere more hospitable.

But in the morning, the wheels stuck so fast in the mud that not even the elephants could pull them free.

That afternoon, bored, restless, Cassandra set up a tightrope between two trees, and Ivan wasn't quick enough to catch her when she fell.

Sulky and starving, the lion seemed to feel the tamer was taking too long to bring his dinner. A single scream disturbed the sunset; blood stained the ground.

By nightfall, we were all huddled in a single wagon, Juliette's cards promising death, and death, and death again.

I don't suppose I'll ever know who knocked the candle, and I am the only one left to think of it.

I was always lucky. Found in an eggshell, the first to spot four-leafed clovers and shooting stars.

The only one to wake as the flames licked and crackled over dry wood and moth-eaten blankets. My screams trapped in my throat, my hands weak. No one stirred when I shook them.

Jackrabbit quick, I ran. Into the woods, dark, dank, safe. From behind a tree I saw the fire spread down the chain of wagons, heard the lion roar, the elephants stamp their feet and toss their heads, strong enough to break their chains and run free.

But there was no saving the circus.

With knocking knees I approached, edging closer to a sight too terrible to look at and too terrible to look away.

Part of my magic box survived, charred wood held together by silver hinges, surrounded by a pile of spangles and ash. A beautiful, brightly colored bird, like fire itself, flew down to perch on it.

It turned a beady eye on me, and then on the rising sun. And it began to whistle, sounding for all the world like a man.

LUCKY, LUCKY GIRL

by Katherine Catmull

Isn't Simran a lucky girl?

When she wants something—when she wants something quite badly—well, then, somehow, something lovely always happens—and she gets it!

Like that awfully hot day when she *really* wanted ice cream, and she heard the truck, but she didn't have any money. But then—oh, it was *so* lucky—the ice cream truck broke down just outside her house. All the ice cream was melting, so the ice cream man shouted, "Free ice cream! Free ice cream for everyone!" And she got as much ice cream as she wanted!

Isn't that *lucky*?

Or another time, she wanted a particular pair of shoes in pale blue leather. But her mother said they were ridiculously expensive, and she wouldn't spend that kind of money on her own shoes, let alone a child's.

Simran's mother was a little *unlucky* just after she said that: she must have bitten too hard into her cheese sandwich, because her tooth broke off, right in the front of her mouth—which was awfully painful, and awfully ugly, too, until she could get it fixed.

But later that same day, Simran had the *best* luck. A woman had bought those exact same shoes, just in Simran's size, for her own daughter. The woman had saved and saved for months to buy the shoes, because she knew her daughter had her heart set on them for her birthday. But—lucky for Simran!—something must have distracted the woman, because she left the package on the roof of her car. When she drove past Simran's house, the shoes fell right into Simran's yard, and the woman drove on, never knowing.

How lucky is *that*?

Or: in sixth grade, Simran liked this boy Jeremy. But he was the most popular boy in school—the cutest, and the funniest, and the best soccer player—and he never noticed her; you know how that goes. Well: Jeremy was in a dreadful car accident. That wasn't very lucky for *him*, because he broke both legs. But it was very, very lucky for Simran, because he was in a wheelchair for many months afterward. No more soccer for Jeremy! And after a while all his cute, popular friends got tired of sitting around with him, and they ran off to play soccer or ride bikes to the mall. Then Simran had Jeremy alllllll to herself.

Wasn't that totally lucky?

Now poor little Emily: she was not so lucky. Back in second grade, their class play was "Sleeping Beauty." Simran wanted to play Sleeping Beauty herself, of course—but instead, she was cast as Sleeping Beauty's mother, a boring role where she only had one line ("Oh! How long have I been asleep?": blah) and wore a stupid costume made out of a paper grocery bag with jewels drawn on it in crayon.

Emily, with her sky-blue eyes and so-pretty long black hair—she got to play Sleeping Beauty and wear a real-looking diamond tiara and a long blue dress that matched her eyes. So Simran asked Emily, very, very nicely, if she would trade roles with her.

But Emily said, "No."

That same day, Emily ran into some very, very bad luck indeed. Something dreadful happened to her—no one knows exactly what, but it must have been quite bad, and quite terrifying. She was missing for three days. And when she reappeared, her black hair had turned pure white, and her blue eyes had emptied, and she couldn't stop trembling for three days more.

Emily would never say what had happened. In fact, that was way back in second grade, and Emily has not said a single word since the day she disappeared—not a single, solitary word.

It's pretty sad, really.

On the bright side, Simran got to play Sleeping Beauty after all. Lucky, huh?

It's funny, actually, when you think about it. Simran's friends aren't lucky at all. Her family isn't so lucky, either, and neither are her neighbors—sometimes they're pretty *unlucky*, actually. It's almost like Simran uses up all the luck in her part of the world!

Like one time the man next door came over to complain about Simran's cat going to the bathroom in his children's sandbox. It wasn't the cat's fault—a sandbox looks like a litter box to a cat!—but the neighbor *refused* to understand that and said mean things about calling Animal Control if it happened one more time.

But he never got a chance to call Animal Control, because that night, his house very unluckily caught fire and burned to the ground. The family got out okay—well, except for the dad. He was blinded in the fire. He never saw again.

That was definitely some bad luck for him. But, well: maybe he won't be so mean next time.

(They never did rebuild that house, and now Simran's cat uses the ashes of their whole house as a litter box. Which is a *little* funny, as Simran would be the first to point out.)

Another time, Simran's little sister, when she was only four, was watching some dumb baby show right when Simran wanted to watch Animal Planet. Simran told her very nicely that she had to change the channel, but her sister kicked up an unpleasant, screamy fuss. Her sister might have met some bad luck right then—it's *quite* bad luck to scream around Simran, who doesn't like screaming at all—but just then, their dad came in and swooped Simran's sister away.

He took the little girl into his room and shut the door. He talked to her in that quiet-but-super-upset voice that parents use to tell small children to stay away from fire or not run into traffic. He said: "Look at me. No: *look* at me, and listen. *Never* argue with Simran. Never, ever, ever argue with Simran. Do you understand me, honey? Say that you understand me. Just do whatever she says."

Her father thought Simran couldn't hear him through the door. She could, though. She was standing right outside, and she heard every word.

But it didn't make Simran angry. It made her smile to herself, and nod.

So maybe Simran's dad was a little lucky, after all.

It's funny that the people around Simran—her family, her neighbors, and Jeremy, and Emily, and that little girl who got no birthday present—they were not lucky at all. More the opposite, really! Like that poor ice cream man, who lost his whole inventory that day, and had no money to replace it, and couldn't buy food for his family: he wasn't lucky. Come to think of it, all those people were very, very *unlucky*.

But it's okay, because Simran's always lucky. When Simran wants something, what she wants comes to her— one way or another. So her luck sort of makes up for everyone else's bad luck, at least in her opinion.

Isn't she a lucky, *lucky* girl?

My Friends,

On my latest visit to the Royal Library of the Kings of the Hidden World, I was fortunate enough to have tea with the Fourth King himself. I was most surprised by his invitation, as the Fourth King is notoriously reclusive. But apparently he also harbors a secret fascination for tales from the Known World. As you can imagine, this fact, were it to be revealed, would be most embarrassing for the king. He is supposed to be concerned only with the Hidden World, not with the mundanities of the Known.

Nevertheless, the king's fascination remains (and I trust I don't need to ask you to keep this piece of information to yourselves?). While perusing Known libraries, and disguised as a middle school principal, the Fourth King uncovered a most fascinating story. When he brought it up during our tea, I immediately understood why he had summoned me.

This story—about a group of girls and a terrible tragedy that befalls one of them—seems at first glance to take place in the Known world. But then something happens. Something that, in both my and the king's opinions, hints at something Hidden. Something that should not ever have stepped into the Known world.

But it did.

This is the story, as best I can piece it together, of the girl who, most unhappily for her, got in its way.

A bit bemusedly, and with salutations from the king,

Curator
Legrand

JUST A LITTLE GRAVEYARD GAME

by Claire Legrand

Chapter I
(In Which the Players Are Introduced)

Emily Partridge was the queen of Dale Reynolds Middle School.

She was the kind of girl who could make anything happen at any given time because she had contacts in every social group, from the band kids to the basketball players to the science geeks to the preppy student council types. It was kind of like a middle school mafia. If you were one of Emily's contacts, you were part of Emily's Family, and to be part of the Family was to be one of a privileged few. The really cool thing about Emily, though, even cooler than her power, was that she didn't flaunt it. It wasn't something she lorded over everyone. It's just that there has to be someone in charge, and Emily was the kind of person to be in charge of things.

Ana Lopez was Emily's best friend.

They had been best friends since kindergarten, and they went everywhere together. Somehow they always had the exact same class schedule. Everyone guessed this was because Emily sucked up to the counselors. She kept the school staff in her pocket like a ring of keys, to be taken out and used whenever she encountered a locked door. But no one said anything about this sucking up, and whether or not it was fair. To speak against Emily was to take your social life into your own hands. Emily had eyes everywhere, and those eyes were Ana. She was a bold, brash, artistic enforcer. She wore funky shirts and starred in all the school plays. You didn't mess with Ana, but you wanted to be her. There was no one Emily loved more.

Tara and Theresa Flemington were twins.

Strategically, they were good choices for Emily to include in her inner circle. Tara was eighth grade class president and Theresa was captain of the volleyball team: a politician and an athlete. Tara was the most organized person who had ever lived. Theresa was cute and fun, and she would probably have been the most popular girl at school, were it not for Emily already having claimed that position.

Under Emily's tutelage, these four girls ruled benevolently. They weren't mean girls; they saw themselves as guides. They mediated disputes, comforted people suffering through breakups, and made sure the right people got elected to the student council. It was for the greater good.

Quinn Murphy was the new girl.

Lucky for her, she arrived at Dale Reynolds Middle School around the same time Emily was itching to add another person to her team. The minute Emily laid eyes on Quinn Murphy, she realized her potential. Quinn was quiet, but she wasn't shy. She just didn't consider many people worth talking to. When she did speak, though, everyone listened, because she knew everything, and it was kind of like being in the presence of Einstein or Mozart: you knew you were around someone special, so you sure did shut up and pay attention. She was probably the smartest person to ever walk the halls of that school.

Emily snatched her up on her first day. It was practical to have a scholar on your side.

"We have a proposition for you," said Emily. She, Ana, Tara, and Theresa sat in front of Quinn beneath the stairwell in the southwest corner of the first floor. Quinn felt a little like she was about to be interrogated, but she was smart enough to just say, "Okay. Shoot."

"I'll keep this brief. At this school, I'm in charge."

Quinn raised her eyebrows. "Isn't the principal in charge?"

"Officially. But not really, not where it counts. Anyway, this is Ana, Tara, Theresa. And as you know, I'm Emily. We run the place. And we'd like you to be part of our group."

"What would that involve?"

Emily explained how, if the social structure of Dale Reynolds were a pyramid, she would be at the top. Ana, Tara, Theresa—and Quinn, if she so chose—would be just beneath her, overseeing everything. She explained their mediation, personal, and political duties.

Quinn considered the proposal. On the one hand, she would probably be too busy studying to participate in . . . whatever this was. Then again, *whatever this was* would admit her to the most powerful social group on campus. Quinn was a logical girl.

"Fine," she said. "I accept."

Emily shook her hand and grinned. "Great. But before I can officially welcome you, we need to have an initiation."

Chapter II
(In Which the Players Gather)

The girls met at Emily's house the Friday after Quinn arrived at school. Emily was not one to waste time, and Tara had jumped at the chance to organize an initiation slumber party.

When Quinn's dad dropped her off, Tara was standing in the kitchen checking their supplies against her inventory, which she kept on a clipboard: seltzer water, board games, movies, pizza coupons, snacks—edamame for Ana, cheese puffs for everyone else (Ana was grossed out by artificial flavoring).

"Hi," said Quinn, still embarrassed by how excited her dad had been for her to be going to a slumber party the first week at her new school. She hoped her embarrassment didn't show. "Is anyone else here?"

"Of course. And you're two minutes late." Tara smiled, tapping her pencil against her clipboard. "But don't worry, you'll get used to being on time."

Everyone piled into the kitchen, and for a few hours it was such a typical slumber party (at least, according to what Quinn knew about slumber parties, which was based entirely on academic research and not experience) that Quinn felt a little disappointed. Mrs. Partridge ordered them pepperoni and veggie pizzas, and they watched

Ferris Bueller's Day Off and *Sixteen Candles* because Ana was obsessed with eighties movies and wanted to make sure Quinn knew it.

It wasn't until Mr. and Mrs. Partridge went up to bed and the girls settled onto the living room floor in their sleeping bags that things changed.

They were all talking and giggling, and Quinn felt kind of nauseated from too many cheese puffs, but she was too happy to care. It seemed like a fairy tale, that someone who wasn't great at making friends could have made four powerful new friends so easily.

Emily rolled over with a businesslike expression on her face. Immediately, Ana, Tara, and Theresa fell silent, waiting. Quinn was puzzled. She watched as Emily moved about the house, making sure her parents and baby brother were all asleep.

"All's clear," Emily finally said, and as if on cue, Theresa pulled out a bag from under the sofa. Tara clipped another list onto her clipboard and started checking the bag's items.

Quinn felt a small thrill skip along her arms. "Is this my initiation?"

"Not here. Are you crazy?" Emily took Quinn by the hand. "We're going out."

"Now? But it's after midnight."

"We couldn't initiate you in daylight. That's no fun."

"It isn't? Why not?"

"Don't sound so scared!" Emily slung an arm around her shoulders. "It's not like we're gonna hurt you. We're just gonna play a game."

"A game?"

"A graveyard game," said Ana, smirking.

"We've all done it." Theresa smiled. "It's really no big deal. But it's tradition."

"You can back out, if you want." Emily's eyes were wide and innocent.

"No!" Quinn whispered. "No. That's okay. I'll do it."

Emily grinned. "I knew I was right to pick you. This is going to be *so* fun."

Chapter III
(In Which a Game Begins)

Birchwood Cemetery sat near the center of town, surrounded by an iron fence. The gates were locked, but there was a spot on the back side hidden by draping vines, where an old tree stump provided sufficient height to propel oneself over the fence.

Thus, Emily, Ana, Tara, Theresa, and Quinn snuck into the graveyard.

"Ugh, I think this place gets creepier every time we do this," said Theresa, crossing her arms over her chest.

Ana wore a Cheshire Cat grin. "You mean, it gets more awesome every time we do this."

Emily was all business. "Do you know the story about Old Man Winthrop, Quinn? I bet you don't, being new to the area."

Somehow, Quinn had missed this story when conducting her pre-move research. "No, I don't."

"Well, it's a long story, but basically there was this old couple who used to live on Oak Lane—"

"Right over there!" Ana pointed beyond the graveyard fence at a nearby street. "See that blue house with the black roof?"

"—*Anyway*. So Mrs. Winthrop died a long time ago, when she was really young, under mysterious circumstances."

Quinn gulped. "They don't know how she died?"

"Well, they couldn't find her body. At first. Her husband, Mr. Winthrop, went nuts after she died, shut himself up in that house and never came out. Had everything delivered, even his groceries. No one ever saw him again."

"That's terrible."

"Right? Anyway, so after he died, his family went to clean out the house and get rid of his stuff and whatever, and guess what they found buried out back?"

Quinn didn't want to guess.

"Mrs. Winthrop's bones!" Ana rushed at Quinn, shoving her hard in the back. Quinn yelped, but Theresa caught her.

"Ana, don't be a jerk," said Theresa. "It's scary enough out here already."

"Wimp."

"Jerk."

"You need an insult thesaurus."

"Guys." Emily held up a hand, commanding silence. The girls obeyed, and Quinn looked on in admiration. "Anyway, so they think Mr. Winthrop went nuts way before his wife died. They think he killed her and buried her body in the garden."

Tara, who had been setting everything up, came over and brushed off her hands. "It's ready."

Emily led Quinn toward a tomb made of white marble. Lit candles stood on the concrete in front of it, set up in four points, like a compass. A five-pointed star in a circle had been drawn in chalk on the tomb door.

"What's that?" whispered Quinn, even though she could guess.

"The Winthrop tomb," said Emily. "They were super rich, obviously. Both Mr. and Mrs. Winthrop were buried here."

"Together?"

Ana nodded gleefully. "Yup. Talk about drama."

"The legend is," Emily went on, "that their spirits live inside the tomb, constantly trying to kill each other. Because Old Man Winthrop is crazy and Mrs. Winthrop wants revenge."

"They say no one can stay inside the tomb for five minutes without getting caught in their spiritual war."

Quinn took a step back. "No. No *way.*"

"Oh, come on." Ana rolled her eyes. "We've all done it. It's just a stupid legend."

"Are you ready yet?" Tara kept checking her phone. "We're already behind schedule."

Quinn found herself being guided toward the tomb door, which Ana and Theresa pried open together. "What's that drawing on the door?"

"It's a protective sign," says Tara. "So nothing can hurt you while you're inside."

"Not that anything will," said Emily. "But it's tradition, you know?"

Quinn stared inside the Winthrops' tomb. The open doorway looked like a giant black mouth. Along the walls lay two lidded stone drawers. Coffins. She swallowed hard.

"Come *on.*" Ana blew out an impatient breath. "Or do you want to stand out here all night?"

Theresa squeezed Quinn's hand. "It's okay. Just five minutes and then we can go home and watch another movie or something."

"We *believe* in you," said Emily, and the ferocious sincerity in her voice filled Quinn with pride, despite her creeping sense of dread.

These girls had chosen her, out of all the girls at Dale Reynolds. That meant something. They prized her intelligence; they considered her worthy.

She turned and walked inside the tomb, and stood in silence as the girls pulled the door shut behind her.

Chapter IV
(In Which Quinn Breaks Tradition)

Quinn stood in the dark, concentrating on taking long, measured breaths. Hyperventilation was a real danger here, so she wanted to fight it for as long as possible.

Pride warmed her heart, buoying her. She could hear the girls laughing and talking outside, and she felt a great sense of peace with the world, a sense that her existence finally had a purpose. Her life before now seemed to have served to bring her here, to this exact moment, with these girls, in this tomb—proving herself, becoming part of something bigger than one measly old genius Quinn.

As she stood there, floating in the bubble of her own happiness, inspiration struck her.

What if she did something different? What if she set herself apart from the girls who had been initiated before her? That would impress Emily; that would impress all of them. Maybe it would even catapult Quinn to a senior position within the group.

She walked toward one of the stone coffins, her fingers resting on the cold lid. For a moment, she hesitated. But then she remembered the protective sign drawn on the tomb's door, and she heard Theresa's distinctive laugh.

She would do it. Wouldn't Emily be impressed when she opened the tomb door and saw Quinn standing there, bold as brass, not only inside the Winthrop tomb, but with the Winthrops' coffins open on either side of her?

She would become a legend herself, and not just for her brains, but for her courage.

Quinn grasped the first lid's metal handle, and lifted and dragged with all her might.

ᴐᴐ ᴐᴐ ᴐᴐ

Chapter V
(In Which Things Go Horribly Wrong, But No One Can Do Anything About It)

Tara was the first one to notice.

She stood closest to the tomb, glancing at her phone and sighing to herself. She appreciated the idea of initiation, but it always fell to her to organize such events, and she was bored of being the event planner. Didn't anyone realize she was only organized because no one else would do it, and without organization, everyone in the world would sleep in until four o'clock like Theresa would do every day if she could get away with it? It wasn't as though Tara *liked* carrying around a clipboard all the time.

Then she heard it: a crash from inside the tomb.

She turned to the door, frowning. "Guys?"

"I'm just saying"—that was Ana—"that Ms. Bower should totally cast Dylan Berry as the lead in the end-of-the-year play. If she wants the play to fail miserably, that is."

Emily waved her hand. "Oh, calm down. I'll talk to Bower."

"Even *you* can't convince Bower to change her mind. She's like a battleship."

"Just watch me."

Then there was a second crash, louder than the first. It silenced everyone in time to hear Quinn start screaming.

The girls rushed to the tomb.

"Quinn?" Emily yelled. "Quinn, what's wrong?"

"Get me out!" Someone was pounding on the other side of the tomb's door—Quinn, desperate. Quinn, sobbing. "Please, open the doors, OPEN THE DOORS!"

More crashes from inside the tomb—great creaks and groans; gibberish words, whispered high and fierce; something sharp and metallic scraping against stone; through it all, Quinn's screams.

"Oh my God." Theresa started crying, backing away from the tomb with her hands over her mouth. "What's happening?"

Ana and Emily pulled on the door, but it wouldn't budge. All the girls tried, four at once, shoving and pulling, kicking and pounding, but it was no use.

"Help me!" A scrabbling noise from inside the tomb made it sound like Quinn was clawing at the ground, clawing at the door. "Open the door, open the door!"

Emily staggered back, eyes wide. She was in shock. "What—I don't understand. . . ."

"It's Old Man Winthrop," Ana growled, pushing everyone aside to pound on the door. "He must have woken up. Leave her alone, you murderer!"

"Are you *crazy?*" Tara said. She was trying to dial 911 and comfort her sister at the same time, but her hands were shaking. "There was probably some lunatic in there, hiding out, and we didn't notice before we shut her in."

"Oh, because that's better!"

Something heavy slammed against the door, knocking dirt from the tomb's roof onto the girls' heads. The something heavy slammed over and over, and with each blow, Theresa started crying harder. Emily sank to the ground.

The tomb shook, and a force threw the girls back onto the ground. Quinn's screams turned into a sound that none of the girls would ever forget, no matter how hard they tried. Then, the screams stopped.

The graveyard was silent, except for the sounds of a bird landing on a tree branch overhead, and four girls crying over melting candles.

Epilogue
(In Which the Door Is Opened, But Too Late)

When the police arrived and forced open the tomb, they found nothing—no Quinn—nothing except for the peacefully decomposing remains of Mr. and Mrs. Winthrop, undisturbed in their coffins, though the lids were gone, and a fine white dust coated everything. Tracks ran down the dust-coated wall and across the dust-coated floor—ten tracks that looked horribly like the tracks of ten grasping fingers.

The tracks ended at a fresh crack in the floor. The crack stretched down the middle of the tomb, from wall to wall, as though something from deep underground had forced apart the stone, and then, having gotten what it wanted, slid back down into the earth and pulled the floor shut behind it.

Drawer Four: TRICKS

My dear Curators,

I have come ashore, only half dead, one-quarter alive, and one quarter something else (the nature of which I am not quite sure of myself). I am writing to remind you of the little box in the fifth-story hallway containing a medallion, a blue eyeball, an old police tape, and a jackknife, as well as four sheets of folded paper. Open with greatest care, especially the papers.

Curator Bachmann

TRANSCRIPT: INFORMATION PROVIDED BY AN ELEVEN-YEAR-OLD MALE, TWO WEEKS AFTER THE INCIDENT

by Katherine Catmull

It's my fault. It was because of me. I'm sorry, I'm so sorry.

Just tell me again what happened. Let's just start from the beginning.

It was just a game. Just war, we were playing war, in that field between the school and the woods. It's so perfect for war, it has these high weeds to hide in, and mounds to climb, and big rocks like boulders you can lay behind.

And right in the middle is this old, dead tree, this creepy tree with twisty dark dead arms going in all directions. You can climb it and see the whole field.

How did it all start?

Allison wanted to play that day. She hadn't wanted to play in a million years, but that day she said she was bored of what she was reading. I was so psyched. I hated her not playing. She's one of those people that when she's around, suddenly whatever stupid thing you were doing seems so cool and hilarious and great. I've known her since kindergarten, and she was always so cool like that.

But now we're eleven, and, whatever. She doesn't play with us so much anymore. But this day she was bored of what she was reading, and she came out to play war with me and Tom, like we used to.

It was one against all, no teams, and right away she grabbed the best spot, which is this mound by the dead tree. We didn't even flip for it—she just ran over and called it, and when I said, "*So* not fair," she only laughed.

So I was sort of mad about that. She didn't play with us for six months, and then she grabs the best position, just like she always did, like she could just come back and do that. *And* she called being America in the war.

That made you angry.

Well, not like *angry*, but just kind of mad. Anyway, so I took the second-best place, a higher mound, but not near the tree. And Tom took the edge of the woods—which is actually pretty good, except you have to keep running so far back and forth. Tom's a good runner, though.

I still don't understand how she—

It was me, I did it. I mean—but not on purpose that it would end so bad! I was only just playing a trick on her, because of being a little mad.

The thing about that mound that makes it so perfect, besides being by the dead oak, is that there's this hole in it, so you can crawl inside. Well, I guess you guys know that now.

Yes.

We used to play that it was the opening of a cave, when we were little, even though really the hole doesn't go back very far. Still, when you're inside, no one can get at you. It's the best spot for war.

My trick was that I waited in the weeds on my stomach until I saw her crawl into the hole. I know her, she always does that first, she loves it in there. Then I waved Tom over, and did that motion of "Be super quiet."

And then me and Tom moved this big rock in front of the opening, so that she couldn't get out. We weren't trying to hurt her, I swear we weren't. We left a crack for air and everything. We just wanted to scare her—or I did. I wanted to get her back.

Anyway. That rock was heavy, we had to lean on it and push with our legs. But the ground slants down toward the mound, so at the last second it just rolled into place perfectly, like it wanted to go there. Allison's strong, but we knew there was no way she could roll it out herself, especially from on her stomach inside the cave.

How long did you leave her there?

We were just going to leave her for a minute, I swear, just to scare her, just to get her back for taking the best place and calling being America and never wanting to play anymore. But she got so mad when she realized—she started yelling at us, using pretty bad words. So then we couldn't let her out right away, or it would be like we gave in.

It was kind of hot that day, so we just leaned against the rock and waited for a breeze, and waited for her to stop yelling.

And did she stop?

She didn't stop exactly. It was more like . . . the yelling changed. Because at first she was mad, but then she got suddenly so quiet, it was more like she was talking to herself. I thought it might be a trick she was playing back on us. I put my ear up to the crack to listen. And I could hear her voice, like *arguing*. I heard her say, "Stop it, *don't*," a couple of times. I thought she was totally messing with us.

But also, it was sort of working. I did start to feel really creeped out.

And then all of a sudden she started screaming. And it didn't sound like a trick kind of screaming. It sounded real.

Like something was hurting her? Was she in pain?

I don't know. Maybe. But more like she was really, really scared. She sounded so scared that it scared us. We started pushing at the boulder. But it was a lot harder now. It had rolled down so easy, but moving it up—and plus she was screaming these terrible screams, screaming for us to move the rock. And we were yelling, "We are, we're trying, we're *trying*, just wait!"

What happened then?

Then she stopped screaming. And it was so weirdly quiet, but me and Tom kept talking to her, saying "Almost, Ally, we almost got it," like that. And finally we pushed the stupid boulder out of the way.

And she wasn't there.

And there's no way she could not be there. We've all been in that tiny cave a million times, since we were little. Back then we could fit two of us at a time, but we can't do that anymore—the rock narrows down to nothing. I mean, where could she go?

But she was gone. Both of us stuck our heads in to be sure. And I said, "Do you think it's like a trick? Is she tricking us?" But Tom didn't answer. He looked like he was going to throw up. He said, "I'm gonna get someone," and took off running. He's fast.

Tom brought his parents to the location of the occurrence, correct? And they called us.

Yeah, I guess. I don't know.

So Tom went to get adults. And what did you do?

I went in. I know it sounds stupid. But I still thought she might be tricking us back.

I went in, I crawled in on my stomach, and—and it was different. It was really different. Where the cave used to end, it didn't end anymore. It got taller and wider, instead of smaller and tighter. And it went down and down and down.

This is the part that's difficult for us to believe. Because we sent someone in—

I know.

And the cave doesn't go back more than a few feet. After that, it's solid rock.

Okay. I know. That's what it always was before. But I don't know what else to say. That day, it kept going, and it went down. And I went down with it, to find Allison.

The walls and ceiling and floor were all dirt. I could see that, because there was this cold pale light, like moonlight. Only there wasn't any moon, because I was underground, so I don't know where that light came from.

And things were growing from the dirt of the walls and floor and ceiling. All around me, on all sides of me, were these little green stems, and they were sort of gently waving and *twisting* in the air, and reaching for me, like grabbing at my shirt and pants. It was disgusting. It was the most disgusting thing I ever felt. But I kept walking, and the ones that grabbed me ripped out of the walls and floors while I walked, but I kept walking down.

And then the passage got wider, and taller. And—I don't know why I looked up, I must have heard something? I don't know. But for some reason I looked up, and I saw what I thought for a minute was a tree hanging down. I thought it was that old dead tree, but hanging upside down.

Then I saw that it was roots. It was the roots of that dead oak, and I was underneath them now.

And then—this is the bad part.

Okay. It's okay.

And then I saw something tangled up in the roots that wasn't roots at all. Up above me, pulled up tight against the earth, something was wrapped up in the roots like a moth in a spider's web. And it was Allison. It was Allison, and she was—I know this sounds dumb, but it was like she was becoming part of the tree. Like the tree was *absorbing* her. These long snaky roots, all green and dark, wrapped around her, under her arms, around her neck, around her legs. Her mouth was open and—

You can stop if you like. Here's a tissue.

No, listen, please just listen. Her mouth was open. And this long, snaky root was growing *out of her mouth.*

All right. Calm down. Just take a minute and calm down.

That wasn't the worst part, though! The worst part was

that she didn't look dead. She should have been dead, but she looked alive. Her eyes moved, I swear they did. The rest of her was all wrapped and cocooned in those roots and vines, and her mouth—but her eyes moved, and they looked at me. And the look in her eye, the way her eyes were. I can't sleep because my brain keeps thinking about it, and—

Your parents should have a doctor prescribe some medications for that.

I can't sleep because I ran. I didn't stay and try to save her. I saw her eyes looking at me, and I got so scared, and I ran. I ran back up that long, steep dirt passage, and the little green vines grabbed at me, and I just ran.

I know I already told you guys all this. And I know you don't believe me.

I wouldn't say—

Stop, wait. I came here because I have to tell you one other thing.

My parents basically won't let me out of the house since this happened. But last night really late, I sneaked out of the house. Or I guess it was early this morning. I just went out the window, I had to go back, I thought I might try— Anyway. When I got to the field it was just being dawn, that gray light and all. But someone had filled up the cave entrance with cement.

We did that. It was a public safety issue.

It's horrible you did that. I wish you'd let me in one more time. I wish so hard that you would. But I guess you wouldn't.

No. We wouldn't.

I freaked out when I saw that it was blocked. I just sat down hard against that horrible tree. And then I saw something.

This is the thing, this is the main thing I wanted to say. That tree, that dead tree—it has little buds on it now. Every creepy twisty black finger of every creepy dead black branch, they all have these tiny curling greeny-gold leaves now.

That tree was *dead*. That tree was dead for years. Since I was in, like, first grade, it hasn't had a single leaf.

Now that tree is full of leaves, all those different colors of green. That tree is alive again. And I know it's her. It's Allison. That tree *ate* Allison, to make itself alive again. Only she *isn't dead*. She's still alive down there, because her being alive is making the tree alive. And I think she's going to *stay* alive, as long as the tree is alive. And you filled the hole up with *cement*, so she can't ever get out, and we have to do something, we have to dig that tree up, or *blow* it up, or burn it down, we have to—

Calm down, son. Just calm—can I get some help here? Will someone call his parents, please? Calm down, would you—Steve, turn that off.

QUICKSILVER AND THE STRANGER

by Claire Legrand

Nobody in the town of Willow-on-the-River knew Quicksilver's real name, or where she came from, or who her family was.

All they knew was that she was eleven years old (she proclaimed this, loudly and often, after outfoxing someone who should have known better), that she had an unbecoming piggish nose, and that she had hair as gray as a crone's. So she was known as Quicksilver, for her hair and for her cunning, for there had never been a girl with so slippery a nature. Many called her Quix for short. They hissed it like snakes when she managed to trick them and laughed it wryly when she managed to trick others.

Quicksilver. Quixxx.

They knew to keep special watch on sour apples and religious artifacts, for canny Quix had a weakness for the former and a fascination with the latter. They knew she lived on the rooftops when the weather was nice and in the ditches when it wasn't, for then she could cover herself with mud and sticks and pretend to be a poor hapless urchin. Someone would take pity on her, and then before they knew it, she had picked their pockets and slipped away, hooting.

You might think the Riverlings would have learned, eventually, not to trust even the most pitiful-looking urchin, but the Riverlings are kind folk, and Quicksilver was a master of disguise.

She was also utterly alone in the world, and she was fine with that.

But then came a particular autumn day, when Quicksilver awoke to a shadow on her face and a whisper on the wind.

The shadow was far away—on the edge of town, while Quicksilver was high in the church belfry, sleeping barefoot and easy as a bird in a tree. But still she felt the shadow on her cheek like the touch of winter, and shivered in her sleep.

The whisper on the wind, though, was worse. It said her name, her real name, the name that nobody but she herself knew.

Anastazia, said the wind.

Quicksilver awoke, and nearly tumbled onto the roof.

Anastazia.

She blinked, rubbed her eyes, and searched the town below for the shadow she had felt. Or had it, and the voice, been only a dream?

Ah, no, they had not. For there, at the crooked bridge that marked the way into town, stood a hunched dark figure with bright red hair, and though it was far away, Quicksilver knew it was staring right at her.

Quicksilver watched this dark stranger for a long time as it hobbled into town and patted children on their heads and gave them treats. She watched as the stranger bartered for a space in the town marketplace and sat on a tall stool. And sat, and sat.

Riverlings began approaching the stranger, slowly. Quicksilver squinted at them from her perch on the belfry but couldn't see anything worth seeing. She was too high up. She paced, tossing coins between her hands. She wanted to go and see what this figure was all about.

But she was afraid.

For ever since the stranger arrived, the voice on the wind, saying her name, had continued:

Anastazia. Anastazia.

No one but Quicksilver knew that was her true name, and yet she felt, somehow, that this voice on the wind belonged to the stranger down below, and that the stranger was here for her. She didn't know what that meant, but it gave her a peculiar feeling in her stomach.

Finally, she was too curious to resist. She pounded her fist against the belfry's stone, angry that this stranger had already gotten the best of her, making her do something she would rather not do. She clambered across the rooftops until she was right above the stranger, in the shadow of a teetering chimney.

A small crowd had begun to gather around the stranger, for the stranger was doing magic—street magic, of course, not true magic. True magic, Quicksilver knew, as did everyone, had long ago bled from the world. But this magic of card tricks and disappearing coins was useful enough—*sleight of hand* was the term. Illusions, and misdirection. Quicksilver knew of such things, instinctively; she used them every day. They were as much a part of her as her blood and her bones. But she had always wondered if she could do more than simple street tricks, something grander. Perhaps she could learn it here, from this magic-doing stranger. Perhaps, perhaps . . .

With a great, clumsy crash, not-so-canny Quix pitched off the roof and into the stranger's lap. She had been leaning out too far from the chimney and lost her footing.

The crowd roared with laughter. Never had they seen their own surefooted Quix have such a fall! So too did the dark stranger with the bright red hair—although the crowd's laughter was loud, and the stranger's laughter was silent and wormed its way into Quicksilver's throat like a bad smell. The stranger's long bony fingers curled around Quicksilver's dirty legs.

"Little girl," said the stranger, "have you hurt yourself?"

Quicksilver leaped down and dusted herself off.

"I never get hurt!" she said, and she sounded ferocious and angry, but inside she was more afraid than ever. She could not tell whether this stranger was man or woman. Its red hair was unnaturally bright, a color not found in

Willow-on-the-River; its face was so old and lined that flaky white skin fell from the corners of its mouth and eyelids as it spoke.

"Fair enough." The stranger shrugged and went back to its business of pulling jackrabbits out of old shoes and whistling tunes that called birds to its arms like a scarecrow, from head to fingers.

The marketplace of Riverlings applauded and cheered, and tossed copper coins.

Jealous Quix paced and scowled and muttered insulting things under her breath that made a young mother nearby cover her children's ears. But while Quicksilver muttered and scowled and paced, she also watched. She watched the stranger's fingers, so frail and yet so sure, spinning tricks out of old cloths and rickety buckets and seemingly ordinary well water. She watched those crumbling white hands pull fresh, fully grown flowers out of cracks in the marketplace cobblestones.

Once, the stranger snapped, and the crowd gasped, for the movement cut open the stranger's right thumb in a tiny spray of blood. A shower of sparks rained down and transformed in midair to cover everyone in white feathers.

Quicksilver plucked a feather from her shoulder and sniffed it. It smelled of burned things, and she was the only one to notice that the stranger's blood dried almost as quickly as it appeared, and turned to ash that fell to the street.

The show lasted well into the night, and when the last sleepy child had been herded to bed, Quicksilver was finally alone with the stranger. For a long time, they stared at each other. The stranger fiddled with a necklace it wore, a dirty, knobby thing that might have once been gold.

Then the stranger said quietly, "I'm better than you, little swindler. I am a magician. You are just a thief."

Was that a cracking, splintering smile on the stranger's puckered face? Was that a challenging gleam in the bleary, watery old eyes?

Proud Quix thought so. Just a thief, indeed. She put up her chin. "You are no magician. There is no magic left in the world. You're just playing tricks."

"Ah, but perhaps," said the stranger, "I have not shown you all of my tricks, Anastazia."

Hearing her name—not on the wind, but in a real, true voice—took Quicksilver's breath away. She could not speak for a long time. Then she said, "Teach me."

The stranger coughed up crusty yellow bits that spotted its collar. "Teach you what?"

Quicksilver frowned. She would have to say it, then; the stranger would make her. "How to do . . . *magic* . . . like you do." Quicksilver blushed to say such a silly thing.

The stranger was quiet for so long that Quicksilver thought perhaps the old rotting lump of a thing had died.

Then the stranger said, "I will do it, if you will answer my greatest riddle. I will even," the stranger said, leaning closer, "give you three tries to do it. Three chances, one riddle, endless tricks."

"Magic," Quicksilver teased, proud of her own cleverness, "not tricks. Remember? You just said."

The stranger seemed to smile. It looked painful, but pleased. "As you say."

They slapped hands in agreement, and Quicksilver yawned. Even eleven-year-old master thieves are still eleven years old and grow tired after such a long day. And Quicksilver had much to think about.

"Well," she said, tossing her coins about impressively, "good night, then."

The stranger grabbed her wrist, stopping her, and that twisting grip hurt. The necklace swung heavily from the stranger's neck. On that neck, Quicksilver saw angry red marks where the necklace's chain typically rested.

"But you must answer my riddle," the stranger rumbled. "Tonight is your first try."

Quicksilver stamped her foot. "But I'm tired tonight! I will try tomorrow."

"Tonight. I am impatient, and you should have known

better than to agree to a bargain without first setting your own rules."

The stranger had a point, and sly Quix had been the one outfoxed for once. It was not a pleasant feeling.

"Fine." She hopped on a small fence opposite the stranger and made an ugly face. "What is the riddle?"

The stranger spoke swiftly. "How do I know your true name, Anastazia?"

That was it? That was the riddle? Part of Quicksilver felt glad; that was not the mind-twisting riddle she had expected.

But another part of Quicksilver shivered at the stranger's voice, so hungry and old and dark.

A possible answer came to her mind—too easy an answer, but she was tired. "You used your magic," she said, "to find it in my mind."

"Bah!" The stranger spat, shoving Quicksilver off her fence and to the ground. When the stranger moved, a stink followed it, a stink of unwashed skin and countless years. "Magic, to do such things? That was a stupid answer. You didn't take any time to think about it." The stranger glared at Quicksilver, rubbing its necklace with finger and thumb. "How disappointing."

Quicksilver leaped to her feet, gray hair flying everywhere like a lion's mane. If anyone else had insulted her like that, she would have done something truly nasty to them—but the stranger was truly nasty, so Quicksilver said, "Fine. *Fine.* I'll try again tomorrow."

"Two more chances," the stranger growled as Quicksilver scrambled up the roof and away. "Two more chances, stupid thief. Tiny, stupid, precious thief."

Quicksilver barely heard those last few words, but she did hear them, and thought them odd, and sat awake for a long time beside the cold, silent church bells, thinking.

The next day was cold and pale. Quicksilver stole an old coat trimmed in fur from a traveler at the inn. She wrapped herself in it and sat on the roof above the stranger, watching another day of the stranger's art—puppets moving on their lonesome, with no hands to guide them, and snow falling out of a sunny sky. She watched the stranger pick pockets without ever moving from its stool, and saw a man so bewitched he thought the stranger was a beautiful woman, and said so, and planted a kiss on those chalky white lips.

That made the crowd of Riverlings roar with laughter. They slapped knees and wiped away laughing tears, and led the poor confused man to the tavern for supper.

Quicksilver watched it all, focusing on the stranger's bright red hair, listening to the croaking voice that was neither man's nor woman's. She paid such close attention that her head hurt, and her eyes watered, and her body ached with stiffness.

Finally, Quicksilver jumped down, silent as a cat, and hurried to the stranger's side.

The stranger counted copper coins, chuckling. They gleamed red in the light of the setting sun. The necklace the stranger wore also gleamed, despite its coat of filth.

"Well?" said the stranger, without looking up. "Do you have an answer for me, stupid thief?"

Stupid thief. Ah, but the stranger had said *precious thief* the night before, and the words had stirred something lonely and forgotten in Quicksilver's hard little heart. At first she hadn't realized what it was, and then, sometime during the night, she had started to wonder, and this whole day she had wondered, and now she knew. She knew. It had to be the answer, this wondrous, terrible thought.

"I do," she said, and she smiled, and it was not the smile of outfoxing someone, but a real, honest smile. "You are one of my parents, my mother or my father, and you've come to find me at last."

After Quicksilver's first answer, the stranger had been angry and disappointed. Now, the stranger seemed simply tired. Its shoulders slumped with sadness.

"No, child," the stranger said at last. "I am not either of your parents. Your parents left you at the doorstep of

St. Agatha's and never looked back."

Quicksilver remembered that place, the tiny convent with the dark roof and the darker rooms. She had run away from the silent, stern sisters as soon as she was strong enough, but one thing the sisters had taught her was the beauty of prayer and faith, and she had never forgotten it. The statue of St. Agatha, which Quicksilver kept in her pocket, was the only thing she had ever felt guilty about stealing.

She held it now, her fist tight around it in her coat.

She would not cry in front of this stranger, who looked so suddenly sad.

"You ugly thing," Quicksilver said. "You ugly, horrible thing. You made me think you were. . . . "

The stranger blinked slowly at her. "Did I?"

Of course, the stranger had not made lonely Quix think anything. She had done it for herself, letting herself hope, letting herself wish for a family, for the first time in ages.

"One more chance," the stranger said, after a moment. "One more chance, and then either we are done, or we are just beginning. So go. Sleep."

To keep from crying, Quicksilver grabbed a fistful of dirt and flung it at the stranger's face, and then she raced up to the rooftops, alone.

⇒ ⇒ ⇒

Quicksilver did not sleep, though she needed it, and it was a good thing, for her exhaustion allowed her to see things more clearly.

All the next day, she paced on the roof, and when the crowds came and went, and it was evening, and the stranger sat alone on its stool, scratching its bright red head, Quicksilver climbed down and stood tall, though she was more afraid than ever.

For she had found the answer to the stranger's riddle.

The stranger raised tangled eyebrows. "Well? This is your last chance, thiefling. What is your answer?"

Quicksilver remembered all the times she had thought herself brave and clever before, and realized how silly that had been. She breathed in and out. She stared at the stranger's necklace, instead of at the stranger's eyes.

"You are me," she said. "That is how you know my name."

Though Quicksilver had spoken softly, the words seemed to ring in Willow-on-the-River's tiny brown marketplace. She held her breath. She counted the seconds, trying to be patient.

At last, the stranger's mouth grew into a smile that stretched its skin tight like worn leather, across yellowed teeth and black gums. Quicksilver looked for her own face in that folded-over skin and couldn't find it, and that was the scariest thing of all.

"Aye, child," said the stranger. "I am you."

And as the stranger spoke, telling Quicksilver stories that only Quicksilver could know—stories of St. Agatha's, of the other orphans poking fun at her head of thick gray hair, of her escape and travels on the road afterward— crafty Quix felt a bit like she was floating above her own body. She had thought it was the right answer, but still, to hear proof was another thing.

"But how?" she whispered.

At that, the stranger's eyes turned sharp and narrow, lit up in a new way. "You wanted me to show you my magic."

"Yes. I did."

"And I said I would, if you answered my greatest riddle."

Quicksilver drew her stolen coat tighter about her body. "We slapped hands on it."

"Aye. Then so be it done, at last." The stranger took a long, slow breath, and then, before Quicksilver knew what was happening, the stranger was on her feet, pressing her necklace into Quicksilver's sweaty hands, breathing sour breath on Quicksilver's wide-eyed face.

"Then have it," this strange, redheaded Quicksilver said. She seemed sorry for something, but also joyous, and determined. "Have it, and go."

"Go where?" Quicksilver started to say, but the

necklace was growing hot in her hands, so hot that it burned her. She tried to drop it, but she couldn't. The necklace was dissolving into her skin; golden light swirled brightly around her.

Through it, Quicksilver saw the stranger fading away, sighing, her eyes closed. The stranger shed first her dark cloak, then her bright red hair, and then her skin itself, like a tired bird shedding old feathers. She was a shriveled husk of a thing. A skeleton. A mirage.

The gold clouding Quicksilver's vision became too thick to see beyond.

Quick-tongued Quix thought, "Funny, for a girl named Quicksilver to die in a sea of gold."

But Quicksilver was not dead. Not that night.

Not ever, really.

But she did not know that yet.

When Quicksilver next opened her eyes, she sensed without even looking around that she was no longer in Willow-on-the-River, but somewhere entirely new.

She knew this because when she breathed, she nearly choked. The air stung her lungs and burned her insides. It was too thick, too full of energy, too different.

She did not know, in that moment, that she was breathing in air laced with magic.

She did not realize that the land she had found herself in was old, much older than the land of the kindly Riverfolk.

She did not understand why the people here sported hair in all manner of outlandish colors—blue as electric as storms, and green as bright as springtime, and red. Red as bright as a stranger's hair.

Red as was Quicksilver's hair, now.

She saw it in the reflection of a still pond. Somehow, this was the most unsettling thing of all, that her hair had lost its gray and was now this fiery red. For what is a person, without a name, and what kind of name is Quicksilver, for a girl with red hair?

"Why has my hair changed color?" she wondered. "And where has the necklace gone? That stranger's necklace?" She paused, afraid, looking around at this world glowing with so many colors that her eyes hurt to look at it. "My necklace."

She did not understand any of this.

But she would understand it soon.

Soon, she would understand that she had come to a time before her own, when magic still lived in the world and the people prayed to different gods.

Soon, she would begin traveling, as she had done before, and she would learn real magic, and the poor street tricks she had always performed to survive would seem like dusty memories in the corners of her mind.

Soon, she would take up her true name and become Anastazia once again, and everyone from the poorest thiefling to the richest king would come to her, seeking the cleverness of her magic.

And later, many lifetimes later, when much of the world had changed and grown dimmer, and much of its magic bled away, she would stumble upon a dirty, knobby necklace in the far north of the world. She would hold it and laugh, and be glad, for this meant that her story was both almost over and close to beginning again. Old Anastazia, cleverest witch, would put the necklace over her head and she would not take it off, not for many years, not even when it rubbed sores on her chalky white skin.

And she would keep an eye out, in those frail days, for a small girl with limbs like a fox, nose like a pig, and hair gray as a crone's in winter.

For, like the necklace she wore, Anastazia Quicksilver was a circle, and so was the world, and so was everything, though few ever realized it. It was a grand game, the thorniest of tricks, and no one played it better than she.

PLUM BOY AND THE DEAD MAN

by Stefan Bachmann

A black tree leans over the rocky road from Harrypatch to Winthrop—a monstrous tree, thick and warped like a rotting blood vessel. Its branches whirl into the sky, strands of ink in frozen water. The countryside all around is bare, and the fields stretch for miles, and this is the only tree in sight, as if it has frightened all the other trees away. A length of rope is knotted through its crown, back and forth and crisscrossing, and one bit of the rope hangs down, and from it hangs a man—a thief, they say, and a murderer. And now look! A little boy is coming up the road. He is rich as a too-ripe plum, and round like one, too, and he has little toothpick legs and a jaunty green cap.

He stalks along, swinging a half-sized walking stick made just for him, staring at the darkening sky with large watery eyes. He sees the tree, and he sees something

191

hanging in it but he does not understand what. Only when he is directly below it does he see that it is a man, and the man is dead.

Plum Boy startles. He clutches at his hat and his knees knock together.

Slowly, very slowly, he begins to edge around the ugly tree, pressing himself to the far side of the road. And now he is past it and hurrying on.

And this is when the dead man calls out:

"You," he cries very softly from his dead, dry throat. "You? Come here a moment?"

The boy lets out a shriek and breaks into a proper run. But he is clumsy and he trips, and wriggling onto his back, he stares up in terror at the tree and the hanged man.

"Don't run," the dead man says very gently. He is hanging with his back toward Plum Boy, but there is no one else in the fields and no one on the road, and Plum Boy is sure it was the dead man who had spoken.

"Who are you?" Plum Boy squeaks. And then, because he does not want to sound afraid, he says, "Why are you hanging in a tree? You might startle someone. Come down at once." Because Plum Boy thinks the dead man is playing a game. And perhaps the dead man is. . .

"I wish I could," the dead man says, turning slowly on the end of the rope. "But I'm afraid I am quite incapable."

Plum Boy stands quickly and brushes the dust from his velvet breeches. He eyes the corpse suspiciously. "It's a trick," says Plum Boy, but his voice shakes. "Come—come *down!*" He stamps his foot.

The dead man has turned a half-circle. He is facing Plum Boy now. His head is cricked over the noose, his eyes empty. He is smiling, because there is nothing else he can do; he has no lips anymore.

"Alas," the dead man says. He sounds unbearably sad. "I cannot. But come and sit down a while at the bottom of my tree. . . . Come and speak with me."

Plum Boy gapes at him. The dead man *sounded* kind, but there were maggots on his cheeks.

"No," says Plum Boy. "I'm going now."

"Oh, do not leave me! Do not go! It is so lonely here."

But Plum Boy is a cruel boy. He does not feel sorry for the dead man, even though it *is* lonely there. The fields are nothing but bare, wretched humps all the way to the horizon. Night is coming. All Plum Boy thinks, however, is that he would prefer the dead man to be very desperate if Plum Boy is going to speak to him. . . . Plum Boy stuffs his fingers in his pockets and hunches his shoulders.

"No," he says again. "They hanged you for something. You're a criminal. You deserve to be lonely, that's my opinion."

The dead man continues to smile. His teeth are very

white. In life they must have never grown yellow with cane sugar and tobacco like those of Plum Boy's parents and indeed of Plum Boy himself. The dead man begins to turn away from Plum Boy again, the rope creaking.

"You seem to think a very great deal of your opinion," the dead man says softly.

"Of course I do. My father says everyone ought to have opinions or they'll be wobbly as pudding."

"But what if your opinion is not true?"

Plum Boy thinks that is a very odd idea. He spins and begins to walk again, for good this time. At least, he *pretends* it is for good, but he simply wants the dead man to beg.

And the dead man does. "No, please!" he cries after Plum Boy. "Just tell me a few little things. What is your name? What is happening in the world these days? Is the tree still blooming in the square in Harrypatch? Tell me anything, so that I can think on it while I hang here."

The dead man cannot move, but it is almost as if he is struggling to twist back toward Plum Boy.

Plum Boy sighs. He shakes his head slowly. Then he returns to the tree and pulls out a large, flowery handkerchief that has been soaked in lavender water and covers his entire face with it.

"All right," he says dramatically. "But I don't want to look at you, because you're so ugly. I live in Winthrop, in a big house that is nicer than all the other houses, and I have a mother and father and four sisters and three brothers and my mother owns the bakery and the pie shop and the coffeehouse, too."

"How grand," the dead man says. "And what month is it? And what is the weather like? And what is in your pockets. And what is your name?"

Plum Boy realizes the dead man must be very nearly blind.

"It is April. Spring," says Plum Boy. He begins digging in his pockets, almost eagerly. A jackknife comes out, a bit of string and some sticky, nasty, yellow toffees. He lists them to the dead man. "I have a wind-up horse, too," says Plum Boy, "but I forgot to bring it."

And then Plum Boy straightens suddenly. The handkerchief slips from his face, but he does not catch it. "You asked me my name twice."

The dead man hangs from his rope, smiling.

"I'm sick of your questions," Plum Boy says, stuffing everything back in his pockets. "Why did they hang you?"

"Oh," says the dead man. "That is a very long, sad story."

"Well, you can leave out all the boring bits and the sad bits and only tell me the horrible crimes."

"But those are the most important parts," the dead man says. "The boring bits and the sad bits. . ."

"I don't want to know them. Did you kill someone? Was it very gruesome?"

"It was very gruesome," says the dead man. "Seven people from the farms, seven people on the forest floor, and they had no eyes and no teeth, but I did not do it. I was an herb brewer then, and I lived far from the town, but the magistrate said I was the murderer, and everyone was certain they agreed with him. They made their opinions so quick, in an instant, but their opinions were strong as stone. And so they hanged me here. Who is the magistrate these days? Is it still old Master Penniman? And what is your name?"

Plum Boy stares up at the tree. The sun is going down. It is an odd picture, a round boy and an ugly tree and a strange dead person, stamped in black against the bloody red sun.

"William," says Plum Boy. "That's my name."

"And who is the magistrate?" The dead man's voice sounds precisely the same as it had the first time he had asked the question, kind and a tiny bit wheedling, as if he does not realize he is asking it again. As if he does not care. "Who is the magistrate?"

Plum Boy peers up curiously. The handkerchief is blowing away up the road. He does not notice.

"It *is* still Master Penniman," Plum Boy says slowly. "He's my father."

"Ah." The dead man stares down at Plum Boy, still grinning, and the red glint of the setting sun is in his cold, blank eyes. And for the first time Plum Boy notices that the dead man has iron at his wrists and at his ankles and making an X across his ribs. He is *caged* in it. But it cannot stop him anymore.

"That is your name then," the dead man whispers. "William Penniman."

There is an odd brush of wind that flies around Plum Boy's ankles and pulls at his cap. And then Plum Boy feels very strange, very light. . . .

Plum Boy's eyes are dim as old wicks. He feels dull and heavy, and he is watching a little figure walking away up the road, as if through haze.

At first Plum Boy thinks he has been robbed. My jacket! He thinks. The little imbecile in the road is wearing my jacket and holding my half-sized walking stick and my lovely green cap!

And then the figure turns to face him. . . .

With a slither of fear, Plum Boy realizes that he is high up, staring down, and below him is his own smug face and watery blue eyes.

He tries to shout, but all he can do is smile.

The boy in the road smiles back. There is a jackknife in

his pocket, and he lifts it out and swings it between thumb and forefinger, back and forth, back and forth.

Then, with a little laugh, the new Plum Boy wheels and skips away down the road, and the night wind spins around the old Plum Boy and the black tree, and turns him on the gibbet, and he must look to the north, though he does not want to look that way.

He decides in an instant: he doesn't like the view at all.

GENEROUSLY DONATED BY

by Emma Trevayne

It is 1:17 in the afternoon, and you are bored. Who cares about mummies and old statues and broken bowls someone found in the dirt, anyway? Not even a whole bowl. Your feet drag, and once again Mrs. Webster's voice calls, "Keep up, everyone; remember to stay with your buddy!"

Her voice echoes around the drafty museum, and Sabrina Linklater is most definitely *not* your buddy. She smells like cotton candy and she doesn't like you. You know this because she's told you every day since you were both five, so it's just your luck to be stuck with her now.

"We're going to see a very special exhibit," says Mrs. Webster, which means nothing; she's said this about all of them, all day, and your feet hurt. Nobody listened this morning when you insisted these shoes pinch your toes, because they were too busy trying to make you eat horrible slimy oatmeal and reminding you to remember your bag for the field trip.

This room is dim, and cool, like the others have been. Spotlights bounce off glass cases and the walls seem to swallow every noise, turning voices down to whispers. A few other visitors are wandering around, stopping in front of each piece before slipping through the swathes of shadow to pop up at the next thing to see.

It's the statue that makes you pause. There's nothing special about it—in fact, it is another boring thing, just a figure of a small man, cast in white stone.

It looks exactly the same as it did in the last room.

And the room before that.

Which is cheating, really, isn't it? The museum should try to put different things in all the exhibits, or there's no point to traipsing through the entire building. Then maybe your shoes wouldn't be squashing your feet so much. You're certain you have a blister, just there, on the outside of your left pinky toe.

But you move toward the statue. The air in the room smells funny, like the second before a lightning strike in the heat of summer. Slotted neatly between two of the statue's fingers is a small card:

Puck, or Robin Goodfellow
England, c. 1808
Mythical trickster and nature sprite
Artist: Unknown
Generously donated by Mr. Alistair Harbuckle

Boring. You turn, and a tiny sound breaks the hush that smothers everything else, including Sabrina Linklater's whiny voice and Adam Beech's constant questions.

Scrape. Scrape. You've made that sound before, striking two rocks together to start a fire—which, you can say with authority, absolutely never works.

Scrape. Scrape.

Scraaaaaape.

You whirl back. The statue is perfectly still, and looks no different except it must be like that famous painting because its eyes seem to follow you. The hairs prickle on the back of your neck.

"This way, kids," says Mrs. Webster. You can barely hear her.

"That statue is weird," you say when Sabrina reluctantly falls into step beside you.

"You're an idiot," she answers.

⊒ ⊒ ⊒

The next room is filled with bones and ghosts of the dinosaurs and grinning skulls with hollow eyes peering down from overhead. This is more interesting than half an old dinner plate or an ancient chess set, and you move up close to read the names on the little cards.

Scrape, scraaaape.

The statue is in the corner, glowing white in the shadows, stone frozen and smiling, its finger crooked, beckoning you. Nobody is watching. Your buddy—ha-ha—is way over there, exclaiming over something that would once have had huge, leathery wings. Mrs. Webster is leaning against a pillar, her hair falling loose from its pins.

The outline of a door scratches itself onto the wall beside Puck, or Robin Goodfellow, mythical trickster.

This is *not* boring. Your heart beats faster, and you check again that no one is watching. Just for a minute, that's all, and then you'll go back to looking at the bones, but the statue chose *you,* not stinking Sabrina or annoying Adam Beech, and this is very, very interesting.

"In here?" you ask, and it doesn't even feel silly to be speaking to a piece of stone, however humanlike it suddenly seems to be.

Scrape. Nod. Scrape.

You push on the wall. It's cool, but not cold, smooth, but not perfectly, and it gives way without a creak, a doorway just large enough to pass through.

Into a forest. A square, room-shaped forest, but a forest. The sunlight from the ceiling is warm on your face, the earth soft underfoot. It smells like it just rained, fresh and clean. Fat bumblebees buzz lazily in a cluster of snowdrops. The air is tinged with green so rich and sweet you can taste it. Birds twitter, something scuttles away, unseen. The nearest tree is thick, branches gnarled like an old man's hands, and carved into its trunk are the words:

Forest

Elsewhere, c. The Year of the Mocking Mirrors

Generously donated by Lord and Lady Hummingbird-Glass

It is real, the bark rough as bark should be, catching your fingertips when you trace each one of the letters. Fallen twigs snap as you step deeper into the trees.

At the far side of the forest, between two trees growing right from the walls, another door stands an inch ajar. One more room won't hurt. This forest room is a clever trick of the museum's, and maybe the next exhibit will give you a clue as to how it works.

This is what you tell yourself.

But the next room is empty. A dull, gray box.

You begin to laugh. Laugh so hard your eyes water and your belly hurts and you fall to your knees, holding your sides as if the air is tickling you.

"Help!" you gasp. "Stop!"

No one comes. It's up to you to crawl, cackling, to the next door, and the instant you're through the laughter dies, smothered by the weight of thousands of eyes, watching, paired up in jars, in rows and rows on shelves. Green and blue and brown, floating in water—or something like it.

Eyes

Everywhere, c. The Beginning of Time—Who Knows?

Generously donated by: please see individual labels

Scraaaape.

You jump.

"Would you care to make a donation?" the statue asks. He's still holding the sign with his name on it in one hand. In the other is an empty jar with *your* name on it. And a spoon. "Yours are lovely."

"You mean, these are—?" And there is nowhere in the room that's far enough away.

Scrape, scrape.

"Do I have to?"

"Oh, no. It's not required. Please, enjoy your stay. There is always one who is bored."

The watch on your wrist has stopped. Perhaps it's time to go back. You look up and the statue is gone.

So is the door back to the laughing room.

A tingle crawls slowly down your spine. That thud is your heartbeat. Thud. Thud-thud. *Thudthudthud.*

From inside their jars, the eyes follow you as you walk, then run the length of the room. Through a new door and into a room of music boxes, each playing a different tune. And another full of spiders, all spindly light legs that skate over you through the next four rooms, rooms you don't see because you hate spiders most of all. In the one after that, it's snowing. And a room of ghosts, cold and dark, generously donated by . . . everyone. The next room makes you scream as you tumble.

For it has no floor. It is only sky. *Generously donated by . . .* and a gust of wind blows the rest of the letters to nothing, tossing you this way and that, blowing you through a hole in the blue to land on a hard, bruising floor.

This has become, perhaps, a little too interesting.

"Hello?" you call. "I need to go! They'll be missing me! They'll be wondering where I am!"

No one answers.

"Puck?"

There is no scrape of stone. Only laughter. Distant laughter.

"This isn't funny now! I need to get back!"

Laughter, laughter, laughter.

You grit your teeth and look around. This room might be the strangest, most wonderful and terrible of all, for it is yours. Everything as you left it this morning, in the shoes that pinch, belly full of slimy oatmeal.

The sweater you hate is at the back of the closet. The secret thing you don't tell anyone about is under the bed.

It can't be.

Outside the window, the sky is pink and orange, the first stars glinting at the edge of the sunset.

You can't have been gone that long. They're all going to be so furious. Maybe they've even called the police, desperate to find you.

You sit on your bed. Feel the lump in the mattress that's exactly where it always is. Read the plaque on the bedside table that is the only unusual thing, and stop when you get to your parents' names.

Generously donated by . . . No, no, no.

"Is this all because I was bored?"

Scrape.

"Mostly it's because I am," says the statue. He snaps his fingers, two doors appear. "One of these will lead you back out," the statue says. "One will keep you here. If you go through either, you cannot return to this particular room, even if you stay."

Flutter, flutter, thud. Your heart beats. "Is this a trick?"

"Yes. No. Possibly."

And he disappears again.

The doors are identical, down to the knots in the wood, the polished brass doorknobs. No way to tell them apart, so which do you choose? How *can* you choose?

You close your eyes.

Reach.

Feel the round doorknob, cool against your hand, perfectly smooth.

The draft as you pull it open.

And you smell . . . cotton candy.

"*There* you are," says Sabrina Linklater. "You're a terrible buddy. I don't like you."

Mrs. Webster is still leaning against the wall, her hair loose from its pins. The rest of the class is clearly tired of the dinosaur bones. The statue stands in the corner, and you wonder if the donation from Mr. Alistair Harbuckle wasn't the biggest trick of all.

The watch on your wrist ticks away, working just fine.

It is 1:43 in the afternoon. And you are not bored.

My dear Curators,

I cannot tell you how I came by this story. Not because I don't remember, but because *no one* remembers. You see, this story has not happened yet. Suffice it to say that getting it involved climbing into a small wooden cupboard that claimed to have the ability to take one far into the past and farther into the future. And further suffice it to say that what I witnessed there was not pleasant at all. I have burned the cupboard subsequently. We can only hope the things it showed me were lies. . . .

Curator Bachmann

THE HIVE

by Stefan Bachmann

One morning, Jacky Turner woke to find himself alone. His parents were gone. His little sister was gone. The apartment was dark as the underside of a blanket. Jacky's window was covered with a heavy steel plate.

Jacky wandered out of his bedroom, down the short hallway, his bare feet squeaking on the shiny floor.

"Mom?" he called. "Dad?"

He went to the kitchen first. It was hard to see in the gloom, but the counters were filthy. Dirty dishes were stacked in the sink. Dirty dishes were never stacked in the sink when his parents were home. Jacky went to the office and his parents' bedroom. All empty. All dark.

Usually Jacky's dad would be calling for Jacky to bring him the mail right about now. Then he would ruffle Jacky's hair and say, "Thanks for being such a sport."

Not today. Jacky's dad was gone.

Jacky tried the windows in the living room. They were covered in steel plates, too. The window opened, but on the other side of the glass were the plates, and they didn't budge. They let in only tiny seams of sunlight, and tiny drafts of air.

Jacky tried the light switches. He tried to turn on the TV and see if maybe there was a hurricane. Nothing worked.

He went to the front door. It was hammered closed with nineteen long, black nails.

At first Jacky was only a little bit scared. He went back to the kitchen and ate all the strawberry granola, then all the Peanut Butter Puffs, and then he spooned all the whipped topping into his mouth and pretended he was a rabid dog. For snack time, he found a blue bottle filled with French vanilla coffee creamer and poured it over his granola instead of milk. He didn't remember ever having French vanilla coffee creamer. His mom never bought it. Weird.

After snack time Jacky was sick. Then he got up and began to wander around the apartment again.

He was a little more scared now. It was a school day. Jacky was probably late. He went to look at the clock on the wall.

The clock had stopped.

He tried his computer. It didn't turn on. His games

didn't work, and his computer didn't work. His books worked, but he couldn't read in the dark. Everything was too quiet. He didn't even hear traffic from the street.

Suddenly it was not cool at all.

He went to the phone next to the TV and picked it up. It was a cordless phone. It worked. He punched in his Mom's cell number. He'd had to memorize it when he was smaller in case he was kidnapped.

He waited, listening to the *beeep . . . beeep . . . beeep*. He watched the blinking red light.

The beeping stopped. The red light turned to a steady, flat glow, like a tiny, staring eye.

Static. Jacky heard static on the other side. The call had gone through.

"Hello?" Jacky said, walking into the middle of the living room. "Mom? Can you hear me? Mom?"

The static continued.

"It's super fuzzy. Mom, where are you? Are you on the subway?"

Jacky squinted at the little screen on the phone. It wasn't his mom's number. It was a series of X's.

The static continued, droning on and on.

"Mom?" Jacky was starting to feel really sick. He could still taste the coffee creamer and it was gross now, plastic-y and fake.

Sssssss went the phone.

Sssssssssssss.

And suddenly: *"Jacky."* Just a whisper, like blip, super fast.

Jacky froze. "Mom?" he said.

Behind him, in the hallway, he thought he glimpsed something, a slither of silver, down in the dark. He pivoted, squinting up the hallway. There was nothing there.

Sssssssssss went the phone against his ear.

"Mom!" Jacky shouted. "Mom, can you hear me? I'm in the apartment and all the windows are covered and——"

Jacky saw the slither again, wire thin, streaking along the wall. And all at once, "Jacky," clear as real life, right in his ear.

Jacky's heart lurched. He almost dropped the phone.

It wasn't his mom's voice. It was a flat, metallic voice, mixed with the electric fuzz of the static.

"Jacky," it said again. "Jacky . . . Jacky . . . Jacky." Always the same tone, blank and insistent.

He hung up the phone, staring around him. The phone didn't hang up. The speaker clicked on. "Jacky . . . Jacky . . . Jacky." It echoed through the whole apartment, loud.

"Jacky . . . Jacky . . . Jacky."

Jacky ran to the door, pounded on it. "Mom? Mr. Wheeler? *Dad!*"

"Jacky . . . Jacky . . . Jacky," went the phone, blaring through the whole apartment.

Jacky spun away from the door. He ran to the phone and grabbed it again. *"WHAT."*

The phone shut up for a second.

Only for a second: "Go to the window, Jacky," it said. "Go to the window and open it."

"Why?" asked Jacky.

Static. Again. Almost a minute this time. Then, "You're a very important boy, Jacky Turner. You have a very important job."

"What— Who are you? Who is this?"

"Go to the window, Jacky. Go to the window and open it."

"What if I don't?"

"Go to the window. Go to the window or you'll be sorry."

The voice never changed, but something about it made Jacky shiver.

"No," said Jacky. "Where's my mom? And where's Dad? I'm going to call the police."

"I am the police," the voice said. "And I'm Mom and Dad, too."

"What?"

"Go to the window, Jacky."

This time, Jacky went.

"Now open the window."

"I can't," Jacky said. "It's blocked."

"Yes, you can. You can open it. You know how."

And suddenly Jacky realized he *did* know how. Somewhere, like a foggy memory, he saw the steel plates and he heard screaming and he saw bolts spinning, drilling lightning fast into the wall.

He began to work at the bolts. He twisted and twisted. And then the last bolt came loose. The steel plate fell away from the window, plummeted into the street far below.

Jacky's heart froze.

There was a machine in front of the window. Hovering. It was huge. And swirling around it were a thousand metal tentacles.

"Hello, Jacky," the machine said, and it had the exact same voice as the telephone. Metallic, flat. "Thank you for letting us in."

Jacky screamed, but it was too late. Tentacles, thin as wires, were snaking out of the machine, sliding around Jacky.

"You're the last boy on earth," the machine said. "The last human. Don't you remember? You barricaded yourself in your apartment. After the triangles fell from the sky. After your parents started acting strange and speaking in sharp languages. You got the hammer and nailed the door closed. All that's gone, though. The memory wipe was in the coffee creamer."

The machine opened its maw and another tentacle slid out, so thin, a hair, small enough to slip through a seam, under a steel plate, through a window.

The tentacle slid over Jacky's face. Then the machine let out a shriek, and Jacky was drawn out of the window, over the street below, hoisted up by the steely, snaking arms.

"Welcome, Jacky," a voice said, cold, monotonous. And then his mom's voice, and then his dad's, and his little sister's voice, too. All the voices of the world, all speaking at once: "Thanks for being such a sport."

In the apartment, the static on the phone cut off. *Sssss-Jacky-sssss,* then nothing.

Drawer Five: FLOWERS

My dearest colleagues,

I've heard tell of the bitter, howling winds and snows that are rattling the windows of our precious Cabinet, but even as I write I have happened upon a strange and beautiful land where it is always spring. The flowers, my lovelies, the flowers! One of them nearly bit my foot off yesterday, and it was only my affinity to such plants that kept my toes at a nice number ten! (Well, all right, nine and a half, but discussing that matter still makes my right foot twinge in remembered horror.)

I am sending back several species—carefully packed, naturally—so that you may see the flowers that have entranced me so on this little expedition. It is my hope that they will form the cornerstone of a new collection.

With deepest affection,

Cornelia Trevayne

THE IRON ROSE

by Katherine Catmull

This happened on an island kingdom, a long time ago, although not so long ago that everyone has forgotten. I have not forgotten.

On this island stood a bright and flourishing city. Around the elegant palace flowed broad streets full of cheerful people buying and selling fish and shoes and toys and bread and other pleasant things. Near the western edge, the soil was rich, and farmers grew vegetables and herbs.

In the center of the island was a forest, and in the center of the forest was an unusual flower. Some flowers grow in the deep woods, you know, no matter how scant the sun. Deep purple violets, creamy foamflower—they can grow among shadows and dappling light.

And deep in this wood, among the bleeding heart and

monkeyflower, among the baneberry and sweet-after-death, grew a flower that needed no sun at all: a flower made of iron.

"Grew" isn't quite the right word, of course. It had been planted there, long ago, an iron-gray rose in full blossom. Each of its hundred petals was carved in thin and curving metal, and its iron stem bent gracefully, and its thorns were sharp and precise as tiny daggers.

In spring, when the real flowers were just budding, the Iron Rose stood among them, tall and complete. In summer, when the real flowers blossomed out full, the Iron Rose stood unchanged. In autumn, when the real flowers bent low, faces crumpling into death, the Iron Rose stood strong.

And yet the Iron Rose had its own seasons. Spring rains brought the Season of Glistening Like Wet Black Ink Against the Last Snow; then came the Season of Rust, which flaked off in pretty patterns, and floated on the wind like pollen; and then the loveliest season, the Season of Jewels, when every ice-coated leaf, petal, and thorn became silver and diamond.

And like a real flower, the Iron Rose had its own perfume, or sort of perfume: a warm, metallic scent, like the taste of blood in your mouth.

One late summer day, a woman walked through the

woods, swinging a stick in front of her to clear her path. She was a writer of stories, and writers like to walk. She wasn't thinking about the flowers, and she had murdered or maimed scores of them in her irritable passage.

But then her stick clanged against something metallic and hard.

That's unexpected, deep in a forest. So the woman looked down, and saw it—the Iron Rose, unchanging among the blooming and fading forest flowers. She knelt to look closer. The craftsmanship was flawless. The emperor would pay splendidly in gold for this.

Careful of the thorns, she tugged at the rose, and it came up as easily as a piece of grass. Holding it gingerly, arm outstretched, she walked home, daydreaming about what the gold might buy her—a voyage to Alexandria? a new roof?—and marveling at the rose's extraordinary, intricate craftsmanship. Why, it was almost as if it had been made by magic.

In fact, the Iron Rose *had* been made by magic, the magic of a very great magician, and a very wicked one. He was so wicked that the emperor, who was a nice if unimaginative man, had many years before banished him from the island kingdom.

But banishment is not always the best weapon against badness. For example: You are no sooner told that you may not have a cookie when a cookie is all you can think of, and it becomes the most gorgeous and desirable thing there is. Where before you might have had one cookie, now you find yourself sneaking off with seven.

Before he left the island, the wicked magician had made and planted the Iron Rose. It stood in the forest like a time bomb, slowly tick-tick-ticking off the years, until someone found it, as he knew they would, and took it to the emperor, as he knew they would, for he had made this flower the most gorgeous and desirable object ever seen on the island.

It certainly looked gorgeous and desirable to the emperor, who paid the writer all the gold she had imagined and quite a bit more, in order to possess that Iron Rose.

But I think the emperor must have had a cold that day, because he did not notice its faint perfume of blood.

For a while, that was that. The emperor displayed the Iron Rose in a silver vase in his treasure room, and he visited it often—though less often as the weeks went by, as something about its sharp iron petals and even sharper thorns unnerved him.

Then one day, a few months later, as a maid dusted the Iron Rose, a noise startled her. It was only one of the emperor's cats, leaping off a suit of armor. Only a cat: but still the startled maid's hand struck against an iron thorn, which pierced her finger—just as the magician had known it would do, somehow, some way, to someone.

"Ah!" cried the maid, because it hurt surprisingly much. She held up her finger, saw it welling with red.

Three drops of blood fell onto the Iron Rose.

The dark gray metal softened. Its color deepened, first to something like black, then to something like red. The chief housekeeper, who had come running at the maid's cry, watched the transformation with her. Yes, no question: the iron was reddening before her eyes. Imagine a black-and-white photo turning into color.

But that wasn't all: the iron was softening, becoming more delicate, more vulnerable, more alive. It was no longer an Iron Rose, but a real flower, red and glorious, at the height of its beauty. It was a real rose now, in every way but one: it retained its faint, metallic, bloody perfume.

Word made its way to the emperor, who soon stood before the flower with the maid and chief housekeeper and all his counselors, marveling and exclaiming and having the maid tell the story of how it had happened again and again.

Then the emperor and his counselors and servants all went to bed.

The next morning, there were two roses.

The morning maid called the chief housekeeper, who

called the chief counselor, who called the chief gardener, but no one had an explanation. They decided not to mention it to the emperor.

The next morning, four roses crowded the silver vase. The maid laughed out loud. This time they did tell the emperor, who wondered in astonishment whether someone was playing a practical joke. A watch was set up, which watched all night and saw nothing.

But the guards must have fallen asleep, though they swore they had not, for the next morning, there were eight roses. These new roses spilled on the table and floor. The emperor said sharply, "Take them outside."

You can perhaps guess what happened. The next morning, on the scrap of lawn where the eight roses had been tossed, were sixteen roses. The morning after that, there were thirty-two.

"Well, I like roses," said the emperor, defiantly.

The next morning, there were sixty-four roses.

As a boy, the emperor had never paid close attention to his mathematics lessons, but his chief counselor had. He understood that a daily doubling of the roses might have quite serious consequences. "We must destroy those roses," he told the emperor.

The emperor shrugged. "I don't care," he said. "I don't like them anymore. Whatever you think."

The counselor ordered the chief gardener to poison the roses with the strongest weed killers he had.

The next morning, there were 128 roses.

The counselor ordered the gardener to dig a hole and bury the evil red flowers.

The next morning, on the lawn around the empty hole, lay 256 roses.

The counselor ordered the gardener to build a bonfire and burn the roses until nothing remained but ashes.

The next morning, there were 512 roses. The scrap of lawn where they had been thrown was now ankle-deep in thorny, blood-red flowers.

I will allow you to imagine for yourself how it went over the next two weeks. Despite all their efforts, the roses doubled and redoubled, like the fury of a banished magician. By the twenty-fifth day, over 167,000 roses filled the palace. The people of the island, who had at first been charmed by the sight of red roses spilling from the palace windows—it must be a sign of favor from the gods!— were less pleased to see roses scattered through the streets as well. Besides, they were growing slightly ill from that strange, sickening perfume.

Three days later, over a million roses choked the city streets. People stayed in their houses, because to wade outside was to have your legs torn open by thorns.

The next day, roses carpeted the crops on the western side of the island, smothering them.

The emperor now sat miserably in his palace's highest tower, crowded among his counselors and servants. People began to panic, to discuss abandoning their island. But it was trading season, and the fish were running, and most of the ships were gone. The few small pleasure crafts left on the island were now buried under tons of thorny flowers.

From the emperor's high tower, with frantically waving semaphore flags, they tried to call back the last big ship to leave—a passenger ship on its way to Alexandria. No one on the ship noticed the tiny, distant flag—except one passenger, a writer of stories. But she couldn't read semaphore, and turned back to her guidebook.

It was lucky—by which I mean, our world was lucky—that the sea was there to stop the roses. They spilled out onto the beaches and filled the shallows, and great rafts of them floated out hundreds of yards. But eventually the salt water poisoned and discouraged them enough that they stopped doubling, and they began to die.

Or perhaps the magician's anger was finally sated.

When the trading vessels and fishing boats returned, they found an island buried under a mound of dead and dying roses. The forests, grasses, and people underneath were crushed, and smothered, and dead. Bodies were discovered bound down by thorns, mouths stuffed with fat red blossoms.

The boats left quickly, and no one visited the island again for many years. The kingdom was abandoned. Even today, it is rarely visited. When travelers do stop there, they find a ghost island, populated only by skeletons wrapped in thorns. The broad streets and narrow forest paths alike are piled with dry, dusty petals. And everywhere lingers a faint perfume of blood.

THE GARDEN FULL OF BAD THINGS

by Claire Legrand

The dog lives in the backyard of a yellow house.

Beside his yellow house is a gray house, and behind the gray house is a garden. The garden is overgrown, and sends the perfume of flowers up and down the street, and sometimes also the smell of sweet rot.

The dog is a small dog, white and twitchy, and he has been trained well. He sits on a stool in his backyard and watches the garden day and night. It isn't his job. No one told him to do it, but he is a dog and has a sense of duty he can't shake.

His humans bring him inside on occasion, but the dog will sit at the door and whine and howl and scratch and destroy the carpets until they let him back outside. He feels so guilty about this that it has given him chronic indigestion, for his humans are perfectly good humans and don't deserve such disloyalty. See? Even now, they demonstrate their kindness. They are bringing him a bowl of the special kibble prescribed by the veterinarian. It is supposed to be good for dogs with stomach problems. They set the bowl down beside the dog's stool. They pat him on the head.

"I suppose he must really like it out here," says one of the humans.

"Maybe it reminds him of his wild ancestors," suggests the other.

Neither of them says what they're thinking, because they don't want to hurt the dog's feelings. What they are thinking is that ever since they moved into this house, the dog has been acting strangely. They wonder for a moment if the house is haunted, or if the soil is contaminated, or some other such thing that a dog might sense and a human cannot. Then they laugh to themselves and go back inside.

The dog's heart breaks. He wants to go inside with them and lay his head on their feet and sleep on the foot of their bed. But he is a dog, and he has a duty. The gray house's garden is not right. The gray house's garden is full of bad things.

The gray house's garden is full of flowers that whisper and growl and entice. They are angry flowers. They are greedy flowers. But most of all, they are hungry. It has been several days since their last meal, and the dog knows they will try again soon. As always, he will try and stop them. He never stops to think that he will fail, even though he always does. For he is a dog, and he is full of hope.

So the dog settles on his stool and waits.

The dog's name is Rabbit.

Rabbit wakes up in the middle of the night because he hears footsteps on the sidewalk. The footsteps are quick and uneven, like the owner of the feet is in a hurry but also unwell.

Rabbit knows that sound. He has heard it many times. He jumps off his stool and races toward the fence of his yard. There are many layers of sound in a dog's world, and sometimes they can be hard to pick apart. For example, right now the dog is hearing the spider crawl through the grass and the owl waking up in the woods behind his house. He can hear his humans breathing as they sleep and he can hear a rain cloud turning over in the sky.

He can hear many things, but none of them are as loud as the sounds from the gray house's garden. They are the sounds of immediate danger, so they are like thunder in Rabbit's ears.

They are the sounds of the garden waking up. They are the sounds of the flowers whispering to each other and calling to the footsteps on the sidewalk.

Rabbit slips under the fence, through a hole he dug long ago and has cleverly disguised with an empty flowerpot. He sees the owner of the footsteps, and he whimpers.

It is a child. It is a boy in his pajamas and slippers, and he smells like old baseball gloves and dirty socks, which is paradise to Rabbit's nose. But Rabbit is not distracted. Rabbit is a very good dog.

He rushes toward the boy, his nails clicking on the sidewalk. He puts himself directly in the boy's path and barks.

The boy skids to a halt. His eyes are wild and white. His smile is uneven and loopy. "What do you want?" he asks Rabbit. "You're in my way."

Rabbit does everything he knows how to do. He runs back and forth between the boy and the gate that leads to the gray house's garden. He growls at the gate. He runs at the boy, trying to push him away.

The boy gets angry. "Go away," he says, and he jumps over Rabbit, and Rabbit despairs. If only he weren't such a *little* dog. If only he were a Rottweiler or a German shepherd or even a Labrador. But he is only a tiny white mutt of a dog with big pointy ears that gave him his name.

He chases after the boy. The boy's hands are on the gate! Rabbit bites his pant leg and tugs and tugs. The boy turns, growling, and his face has transformed. It is sick with the garden's power.

"I have to go to them!" says the boy, and he kicks Rabbit away, hard.

Rabbit yelps. The wind is knocked out of him. He watches from the sidewalk as the boy opens the gate and slips inside. He hears the boy's sigh of relief once his slippers hit the soft wet dirt. Rabbit knows the boy's nose is not sensitive enough to detect the scent of bones that wafts up from the dirt when the boy steps on it. The boy's ears are not sensitive enough to distinguish the squelch of dirt wet with water from the squelch of dirt wet with blood.

Rabbit howls and howls, but the flowers only laugh at him. The daffodils bobbing in clumps on either side of the gate, the morning glories winding around the gate's iron spikes—they are all laughing at him.

You're too late, they say. Their voices are ugly. Their petals form wicked mouths, and their tongues are dark. When they breathe, the air fills with the scents of hair and fingernails and screams. For to a dog, even a scream has a flavor. *You're too late, Rabbit.*

Rabbit shakes. He hates it when they say that. For he is always too late, isn't he? And too small, and not smart enough.

So he sits and watches as the vines wrap around the boy's legs and pull him down. He watches as the boy sighs and smiles and laughs, because this is just what he wanted. He wanted to come to the flowers. He heard the flowers calling him, and their voices were so beautiful. Rabbit hears the boy whispering it to himself: "So beautiful. So beautiful. Hello. Hello." The boy is talking to the flowers as if they are old friends.

Their leaves burrow into his skin, and still he smiles. Their blossoms bend over him like heads, and their black tongues unfurl, and still he laughs.

It isn't until the orchids latch on to his face, smothering him, that he begins to scream.

Rabbit makes himself watch, though he does grant himself the small mercy of putting his paws over his ears.

The next day, Rabbit doesn't eat. He noses at his kibble and sits under his stool. He does not deserve to sit on his favorite stool today. He can smell the boy's body as the flowers bleed it and chew it and pull it slowly into the ground. He can hear the flowers celebrating, hissing and laughing and complimenting each other.

They are very loud this morning. Children are their favorite, after all. *Children,* Rabbit often hears them saying, *are the sweetest meat.*

Rabbit's humans leave for work. Rabbit can no longer listen to the flowers gloat and belch and clean the blood from their petals. He is beside himself with shame. He wanders through his backyard, whimpering. The poor boy, he thinks. The poor boy with his baseball gloves and his smelly socks. What will his parents think?

At the edge of the backyard is a fence, and beyond that fence is a field of tall grasses and some woods. Rabbit digs under the fence and comes out into the field on the other side and howls quietly to himself. He will continue to wander forever, he thinks. He will wander away until he finds somewhere he can actually be useful, or perhaps until he dies. Perhaps, he thinks forlornly, dying would be best. A dog who cannot help humans is no dog at all.

But then he hears footsteps crashing through the grasses. The footsteps are coming from the direction of the woods. Rabbit thinks this is curious, for he has never heard anything in these woods except for foxes and birds and snails.

Then he sees the girl. She is as young as the dead boy was. She is wearing a dress that is torn and dirty. She has a wild face and wild eyes, and her hair is full of mud and twigs. She does not move like a human. She moves like an animal, darting this way and that.

She runs toward the gray house's garden. She is confused. She does not know where she is going.

Rabbit follows her, barking. He does not stop to think

how strange this girl looks, or that he has decided to wander off and die. For he is a dog, and when it comes right down to it, he will forget his own problems and do the right thing. He runs and barks and thinks that he will bite the girl's leg if he has to. A bite from a small dog named Rabbit will be better than getting eaten by flowers.

But the girl stops. She stares at him. She kneels down in the dirt and begins to talk to him, but she does not talk like other humans do. She talks in growls and clicks like an animal, and Rabbit understands her perfectly. He sits back on his haunches and cannot help but wag his tail. This girl is a strange one. He likes this girl.

"You're saying," says the girl, clicking and growling, her eyes wide, "that the flowers in that garden eat people?"

"Yes," says Rabbit, barking. It is a serious moment but he nevertheless has trouble stopping himself from licking her face. He has never talked with a human before, and it brings him a joy not unlike the joy that comes from getting his belly scratched. "Yes, that is what I'm saying. The flowers talk to people. They trick them inside, and then they eat them. They like children best of all."

"How do you know this?"

"I hear them talking to each other."

"Ah." The girl nods. "I didn't know dogs could understand flowers. But it makes sense."

"Does it?"

"Of course. Dogs hear and smell and understand things much better than humans do, don't they?"

"Much better indeed," Rabbit says gravely.

The girl looks at Rabbit, and then looks around, and then pulls a thorn from her skirt. "Where are we? Could you please tell me?"

Rabbit does not understand. "What do you mean? This is the world. We are in it."

"But it's our world, isn't it? Not theirs?"

"Who are you talking about?"

"This is the world where the sky is blue and the stars come out at night and things are all facing right side up?"

Rabbit tilts his head. "Apparently the sky is blue. That's what the humans say. And roses are red. They say that, too."

"Yes." The girl's face is strange now. "Roses are always red."

Rabbit has been so distracted that he doesn't notice it until now: "You smell funny. You smell not quite right."

"I've been . . . away," the girl says. She looks at the ground. She smells afraid. "I have been far away, in a place where the sky is black and the stars are falling and everything is upside-down."

"Well, you are here now. My name is Rabbit."

"A dog named Rabbit." The girl frowns. "What nonsense. My name is Alice."

When Alice says her name, Rabbit hears the flowers in the gray house's garden stop gloating and boasting. He hears them turn their heads. He feels their silence and their fear.

That, he thinks, is odd. The flowers have never been afraid before.

"You should go home," says Rabbit. He growls, because he thinks that will frighten her away. "It is not safe here. The garden, the flowers, they will hurt you. You are a child, and they will want to eat you. Go. Run away. Go now."

Alice looks at the garden through her muddy hair. She looks angry. "They like children best of all, do they?"

Rabbit hears the flowers bending closer to listen. He hears them licking their lips. He hears the clacks of their throats full of teeth. "Yes!" Rabbit is becoming afraid for Alice. He yaps and yips and runs around her feet in circles. "You must leave! Oh, hurry, before it is too late!"

"Rabbit." Alice picks him up. He stares into her dirty face. "I swore I would never go there again, once I got out this time. I swore it. But I think that I must. Because I think I know of a way to destroy this garden, these flowers that eat children, and if I know of a way, I must do it even if it scares me, mustn't I?"

"What do you mean, go back there?" This time Rabbit does lick Alice's face, because that is the best way he knows to help a frightened human. "You mean to the upside-down world?"

"Yes. If I go back there, and I return with a great weapon, a weapon that can destroy that garden and those flowers, will you help me do it?"

Rabbit stops wagging his tail, because he understands this to be a solemn moment. "I will."

"It will be frightening," Alice whispers. She is not looking at him. She is looking away, back at the woods. Rabbit is not sure if she is talking about fighting the flowers, or returning to the upside-down world. And he is not sure if she is actually all that frightened. Her emotions are confusing.

"All important things are frightening," says Rabbit.

Alice nods. "Yes. Yes, you are of course quite right. Will you come with me and wait outside while I'm inside?"

That does not make sense to Rabbit, but he will of course follow her anywhere, this wild girl who talks like an animal, who smells like one and has been to an upside-down world. She seems more like a dog than a human, this Alice. Rabbit likes that. He trots beside her into the woods. They reach an ugly tree with a giant hole in its trunk. The air here smells strange, like Alice does. Rabbit puts his head on her bare feet and waits patiently while Alice cries beside the tree. She is scared, but she is also brave. It is a feeling Rabbit can understand.

Alice dries her tears on her muddy skirt. "This is the last time I will ever go back, *ever*," she says, but Rabbit knows it is a lie. He can hear it in her voice. He can feel it in her heartbeat.

Alice climbs into the hole in the tree. She screams, and disappears. Rabbit sits in front of the tree, and whines, and waits.

When Alice comes back, she is even dirtier than before. She smells like salt water and metal and old stone. There are feathers in her hair, and her skirt has a belt now, and in the belt is a knife.

Rabbit jumps up and Alice holds him in her arms and shakes. She holds him too tightly, but Rabbit is happy to be useful again, and he is quiet until Alice stops shaking.

"Well?" says Rabbit. "Do you have it? Do you have the way to destroy the garden?"

"I have *a* way," Alice says. Her voice is scratchy and tired and frightening. "It is probably not *the* way, and it might not be someone *else's* way, but it is *my* way."

"I understand. *My* way was to try and scare away the humans before they got inside the garden. But I don't think that was the *best* way. But it was the *Rabbit* way."

Alice looks at him with a funny expression on her face. "You are a strange dog."

"And you are a strange child, but I like you."

Alice smiles. It is the first time she has smiled in months, but not even Rabbit can know that.

"What is the great weapon?" Rabbit asks.

Alice sets him down and holds out her hand. In her hand is a seed. It is a large seed, and angry looking. It is black and red and spiky. It has left tiny bites on Alice's palm.

"In some places," Alice whispers, "there are flowers even worse than child-eating flowers."

Rabbit whimpers. He senses he is close to things too big and important for one small white dog to handle. "You mean, in the upside-down world?"

Alice nods. "And this is a seed of one of them. And we are to plant it in that garden, and let it grow and destroy the others."

Rabbit is ecstatic. He jumps out of Alice's arms and rolls around in the dirt. As usual, his joy is quick and gets the best of him. But then he thinks of something. "But if these flowers are even worse than child-eating flowers, and we plant these even worse flowers, won't the garden become even more dangerous?"

Alice looks back at the tree. She is still a child, but she seems much older than she was when Rabbit first met her. "No," she says. "It will not. It will be a beautiful, tame garden for as long as this world is a world, and everyone will come to admire it, but it will never hurt anyone. We made a deal."

Rabbit does not know who Alice is talking about. He does not want to know. He has no interest in this upside-down world that sounds so dangerous. He hopes there are no dogs there, but he somewhat vindictively hopes there are cats.

At the gate of the gray house's garden, Rabbit is ready. He is growling to make himself feel fierce. Alice is beside him. They have a plan. Alice is beside him and her hand is on the gate's latch, and in her other hand is the angry black-and-red seed.

The flowers are watching them. Their petal faces are watching the gate. They are hissing and spitting. They are beckoning and laughing. *Alice. Alice. Alice and Rabbit. Try it. Just try it. We are not afraid of a girl and a Rabbit.*

But they are afraid. Rabbit can sense that.

Alice looks down at him. "Are you ready?"

Rabbit wags his tail, and Alice smiles but also looks sad.

"You are a good dog," she says, and Rabbit's happiness overwhelms him. He almost turns over to show Alice his belly and request a nice scratch. But then Alice is opening the gate, and they are running.

It is Alice's job to plant the seed. It is Rabbit's job to protect her while she plants it.

He runs as fast as his tiny white legs can carry him. Lilies snap at him. Vines wrap themselves around his legs. Tiger lilies throw themselves at him, petals crashing into the ground. The petals smell like blood, and they attach to his coat like suckers. They hurt, but Rabbit does not stop. They will not stop him, these shrieking flowers that smell like dead children. He is a small dog, and he is too fast. Too fast for them to touch and too small for them to catch.

Alice is digging. Petunias are swarming over her feet and up her legs, and their voices are small and high like children's voices. *Such a sweet girl, Alice is*, they sing. Alice is crying, but she is brave. Alice slashes at vines with her knife. And Rabbit is tearing at the flowers with his teeth and his claws, ripping them to pieces. There is blood on his white coat, but he doesn't mind. Helping is what a dog does best, and he is happy.

"There!" Alice cries, and slams her fist onto the dirt. She has planted the seed. Her hands are covered in blood and mud and thorns. She finds Rabbit. He is choking in a bed of violets. They fill his mouth and his nose and his ears, and he is afraid, but then he sees Alice. She is crying and ripping the flowers from him, and then he is in her arms. She is saying, "Good dog, such a very, very good dog," and Rabbit is wagging his tail even though he is hurting. Alice is running out of the garden, and he is in her arms.

The flowers are screaming.

Rabbit opens his eyes and sees it happening. The garden is thrashing and crashing. The garden is drowning under the weight of something new.

They are roses.

They are red roses, bushes of them, towers of them, and they do not speak but they do have teeth. They smother the other flowers so they cannot breathe. They rip the other flowers from the ground and tear their roots to shreds. Even though it is dark, and even though Rabbit sees the world in gray and only knows what color his humans say things are, he knows that these roses are red. They are redder than blood. They are dripping red.

When it is finished, the roses poke their heads over the fence and whisper, *Alice, dearest girl, dearest Alice. We did what you said. Now you do what you said. Dearest darling Alice.*

"Alice." Rabbit is whimpering. He wants to say thank you, but Alice is hugging him too tightly. She is setting him on the porch of his house. She is ringing the doorbell and knocking on the door. She is crying and plucking the thorns from Rabbit's coat. He feels that she is afraid and sad, but also that she is happy.

He hears his humans inside. They are waking; they are hurrying down the stairs.

"Alice," Rabbit tries to say again, "what did you say you would do? What deal did you make?"

But then the door is opening and his humans are exclaiming things. They are afraid for him. Rabbit knows he will be all right, and he tries to tell them this by licking their hands. They are calling the veterinarian, and they are carrying him to the car. Rabbit feels their love so deeply that he almost doesn't see her:

Alice, climbing over the fence and running through the field toward the woods. He hears her crying and he hears her laughing. He feels it when she climbs inside the tree. He smells her fear when she screams, and he smells it when she jumps, and he understands now what Alice said she would do. He understands that this time, the jump is forever.

MABEL MAVELIA
by Stefan Bachmann

There were six things Mabel Mavelia could not abide. The first was toast; the second was tea; the third was parakeets, all sorts; the fourth was her father; the fifth was her mother; and the sixth was the great, tall house on Curliblue Street, in which they had made her live. She hated that one most of all. By way of rebellion, she had locked herself in the attic.

She had been fighting with her mother. The fight had begun in the dining room, escalated in the stairwell, and had exploded into a frightful burst of screaming in the third-story hallway.

"Why can't we go *back*?" Mabel had shrieked. "I don't like it here! I don't want to live here, and why do we only do what you and Father want? What about me?"

"Oh, oh," Mabel's mother had said, coming after her, her

great silk bustles dragging. She was rather breathless, and she kept wringing her hands and reaching out toward Mabel, as if she could not decide which gesture might be more useful. "Don't cry, please don't cry. I know the City isn't what you're used to, but...well, if you would only give it some time—"

"I don't want to give it time; I want to leave."

Then Mabel had dashed up the attic stairs and had come upon a little door. Mabel had never seen the door before—the Mavelias had only just moved into the house on Curliblue Street—but there was a key already in the lock, and so Mabel had snatched it, waited until her mother was only steps away, and then had screamed and slammed the door with great gusto and twisted the key twice 'round.

"I'm not coming down, and I'm not opening the door, ever," she shouted at the door. "Also, I hate you."

Now, Mabel Mavelia was a strange child. She was sickly and pale, like salt, but sharper, and her gray eyes were so huge in her thin little face that she looked to be in a perpetual state of bewilderment. She was not a bewildered child, though. No, Mabel knew exactly what she wanted, or thought she did, and she knew exactly what she hated, or thought she did. She hated her parents and she hated the house on Curliblue Street.

She stared about the attic, her hands clenched at her sides. It was an ugly room, she decided, squeezed under the eaves. There was a window with four frosty panes in the roof, a desk, and a wooden chair without a cushion. The wallpaper was yellow.

Mabel frowned and went to the chair and sat down. She listened for a sound from the other side of the door, but there wasn't one. Her mother had already left, murmuring and smoothing her curls.

Mabel turned her frown to the window. Chimneys and gables stretched away as far as the eye could see, hills and valleys and forests of rooftops, rolling on forever. The sky was a gray swirl overhead, like a windstorm about to descend. Mabel hoped a windstorm *would* descend. She hoped it would sweep the City up and fling it into a dustbin and the dustbin would go to an incinerator and . . . and Mabel would escape suddenly and miraculously and everyone else would become victims of the conflagration.

Give it time, Mabel thought bitterly. She didn't want to give it time. She didn't know anyone in Curliblue Street. The people were all tall and gaunt and gray faced to her, and the City was vast and anonymous, and her new school was full of sallow-faced children who stared at her like cows. Or like her dolls. She always put her dolls in the corner when they looked at her like that, but it was not allowed to put other children in corners.

Far, far below, in the nice part of the house with its red drapes and bric-a-brac, Mabel thought she heard movement—the clink of silverware, laughter and conversation. Dinner, perhaps, going on without her. For an instant, the sounds made her sad. And then they made her angry. They shouldn't be talking and eating without her. It wasn't fair. They should be sad, too, sad about living in this horrid city, sad about living on Curliblue Street. She rapped her knuckles on the desk.

The sound echoed in the room like a pistol crack. Mabel jerked a little in her chair. She peered over her shoulder. It was perhaps not a very good place to be, she realized. The room was very small. The yellow wallpaper was very hideous. Evening was creeping across the city outside, and it was becoming quite gloomy.

Mabel looked about, huge eyes darting. She wasn't afraid, she told herself. She was going to stay up here until her parents begged her to come down again. "We'll bring you back to Heretofore, darling! Whatever you want, only please come down!"

But her parents did not come up, and so Mabel hated them more with every passing second.

It began to get very dark in the attic. Almost pitch-black. The only light came from the four small panes in the roof.

Mabel got up to pace. She wasn't about to leave. But it was getting *so* very dark. She circled the room. She felt the wind tickling across the roof tiles like spiders' legs.

She ran her hand over the yellow wallpaper. It was rough and old and rather nasty. She tugged at a rip in it. A long strip of it came away in her hand. And then she saw that there was no wall behind it. No boards or plaster. There was nothing. Emptiness.

Or not.

Behind the thin layer of yellow wallpaper was another room. It was rather dark and gloomy, too, but Mabel could just make out the glass roof of a conservatory, and much foliage and flowers. She hadn't known there was a conservatory in the house on Curliblue Street. It was just like her parents, not telling her the good parts.

A puff of warm air flew into Mabel's face, thick air, heavy with damp and earthy smells. It blew back her hair. Then Mabel slipped through the gash in the wallpaper and wandered forward.

Above her, dim flickering lights sprang to life along the ceiling. She saw that the space was in fact vast, and that the flowers stretched on for what seemed like forever. They were very odd to look at. Some were brightly colored, others gray like rotting meat, and there were little contraptions darting in the shadows as well, little mechanical hands to pat the soil, and little glass tubes to measure the fertilizer, and little chicken-footed watering cans to water the roots.

She stooped in front of a flower shaped like begging

hands and sniffed it. She thought it smelled of laziness. She went on to the next one, a rose with a human eye at the middle. She squinted into it suspiciously. . . .

And then, all at once, a little boy stepped from behind a particularly large potted fern and stared at her.

Mabel stood up quickly. She stared back at him. Her face twitched a little bit. She didn't like the look of that boy. He was younger than she was, and yet he had a tiresomely clever, self-satisfied face and golden curls that would take Mabel hours to put up. Mabel thought he looked rather haughty.

"What are you doing here?" she demanded. "What's your name?"

The boy said nothing for a second. Then he moved away suddenly, darting among the plants. "Mr. Pittance," he called, and laughed.

"You're not old enough to be a Mr. Anything," Mabel snapped. It was odd enough that there was a conservatory she had not known about, but now there was a haughty little boy, too? She really could not abide children who made a show of themselves. She would have to add that to her list.

"Am I not?" the boy asked. And just before he disappeared behind the thick trunk of a tree, he looked at her, an odd sparkle in his eye.

Mabel watched the boy carefully. When he passed close by again, Mabel made a move to catch him. "What is this place?"

she asked, running after him. "Tell me at once. Am I in the next house over? Did I cross the partition wall by accident?"

"No. It is still your house."

Oh, good, Mabel thought. "Well, in that case, what are you doing in our attic? Are you a thief? Does Mother know you're in our greenhouse?"

"*Your* greenhouse?" The boy popped up from behind a pot and peered at her. "It isn't yours."

"Yes, it is. It's in my attic."

"It's my skin garden."

"No, it isn't, it's—" Mabel stopped short. "Your what?"

"My skin garden," the boy repeated. He stood and lifted a silver watering can labeled "Self-Pity" and laid its spout gently against the roots of a plant. Purple liquid dribbled out, and the dirt drank it thirstily.

"What—" Mabel cleared her throat. "What's a skin garden?" It would have been nicer to continue quarreling, but she was curious, too. What *was* this place?

"It is where I plant things," the boy said.

"What do you plant?" Mabel glanced around her, at the leaves and up at the ceiling. The night pressed against the glass above. She wondered if her parents would come looking for her now.

"Oh, I plant everything," the boy said. "Kisses, and faces, and words, and sorrows, and bits of fingernails, and flakes of skin. Drops of tears, and blots of ink, and horrid mistakes, and mortifying secrets."

Mabel squinted at him. It seemed very fanciful.

"It's my job," the boy went on. "I make them grow."

"You're not old enough to have a job. And no one wants their mortifying secret to grow anyway. What a stupid sort of job." She hoped that would wipe the smugness from the little boy's face. She was suddenly glad her father had a dull, respectable place at a bank. Perhaps she could throw that at the boy shortly.

"But surely they do," the boy said, wandering away. "Why would they keep them if they did not want them to grow?"

"Keep what? No one keeps their bits of fingernails."

"But they grow, don't they?"

Mabel frowned at the boy's back. "I don't know what you're talking about. Does Fath— does Mr. Mavelia pay you?"

"No."

"So you steal these things? You live in our attic, and then you steal things!"

"You said no one keeps their fingernails anyway."

Mabel chased after him. She'd had quite enough now. Everything the boy said made a tiny, flitting bit of sense, and then none at all. Well, Mabel decided to be just as annoying to the little boy as he was to her.

"I bet you don't make much money. What happens

once they've grown? The plants. What's the point?"

"Well," the boy said. "Everyone has a flower, and—"

"Everyone in the world? Here? In my attic?"

"Don't interrupt. Everyone has a flower, and I simply make the flower grow the way they want it to."

"Oh." Mabel thought for a second. "And what would happen if you cut them? What would happen if you took those scissors there"—she stabbed a finger at a pair of silver shears lying on a chair nearby—"and snipped them all down and made them into a bouquet?"

"What odd thoughts children have," the boy said, but he did not answer her question, which made Mabel even more curious and more angry.

He glanced at her, then, and his face was all amusement. "Here," he said, and opened a little box. "I see you don't understand at all. You may watch me."

From the box he took three small objects. One appeared to be a handful of words, like printer's blocks. Another was a few ribbons of musical notes. And the last was a pearl, black as a dead man's heart.

"See here? I have three things from this house. Your mother read a book, and I do believe it will stay with her many years. And here is the song your father heard the other day on Fangdiddy Street. There was a Gypsy boy with a three-string violin, and the sound of it touched your father's heart like a knife. And here are the words you told your parents, yesterday over breakfast."

Mabel saw the blob of black, like a spider, wriggling, trying to escape across the boy's hand.

"You're going to plant that?" she asked. She didn't know which words they were, but they probably weren't very good ones.

"Yes."

"Why? No, don't. I don't want you to."

"Too late."

The boy went to a flower and dropped the blob into its roots. It sank in slowly, but then all at once, and was gone, and the flower drooped a little bit.

"Was that my flower?" Mabel flew to his side. "Was that me?" She felt a bit panic-stricken, though she couldn't say why.

The flower was frayed and gloomy around the edges. Mabel's first thought was to be insulted. But then she saw the center of the flower. It was red—a lovely, rich red. It made Mabel happy to see it. She stood there in her white dress and smiled a little bit. "It's very nice," she said softly.

"Hmm," the boy said. "It's not much to look at. The petals need work." He turned away. It was a simple motion, perhaps not even intended to be cruel, but it stung Mabel. She frowned at his back. He was such a short thing. She wanted to clobber him.

"Do you have a flower?" she asked suddenly.

"Of course!" The boy's face lit up. "Come, let me show you."

He took Mabel by the hand and drew her toward the far end of the skin garden, to a glass dome veined with a filigree of wires. Under it was a single marble pot, and in the pot was the most magnificent flower Mabel had ever seen.

"That's yours," she stated, and she said it in a flat way because the instant she saw it she was overcome with a terrible, wriggling envy. The boy's flower was far prettier than hers. Its petals were blue, speckled with gold, and its leaves were such a dark green that they were almost black, glossy and smooth as eels. At the flower's center was a glittering poof of golden pollen, like a brooch pinning a marvelous bow.

The boy walked around it proudly.

Mabel stared at him, and then at the flower. She looked sullen, but behind her great dull eyes, Mabel Mavelia's mind was clicking like a typewriter. She could not *stand* the boy. Not right then. His nose was in the air, and he had such a perfect know-it-all face, and she hated his careful garden, and she hated that he had a job even though he was just a baby, and she hated everything.

Before she knew what she was doing, Mabel had run back to the chair with the silver shears, snatched them up, and was charging toward the great flower with all her might. She saw the boy's eyes widen. Her mouth pressed itself into a thin line. She came to the flower . . . And she snipped it right through the center.

It was like cutting a snake in half. The skin was thick, and as soon as the blades bit through it, a wash of red liquid oozed out, dark and slow.

Mabel turned, breathless, smiling in triumph. . . .

But the boy was just standing there, a look of abject terror on his pale face. He raised a hand, as if to grasp Mabel, as if to stop her. And then the flower fell, its petals tickling Mabel's neck. The boy fell, too. He had been cut clean in half.

Mabel's glee turned to fear. The boy did not have bones and blood inside him. He had many little birds and little music notes and little hopes and dreams, glimmering like stars. And when he fell they all dissipated, flying into the skin garden and vanishing among the leaves.

Mabel dropped the shears. They clattered to the floor. She spun, as if she were afraid someone might have seen her. The flower continued to ooze. She heard noises, voices calling her, and something inside her snapped. She picked up the two empty halves of the boy and dragged them to the nearest patch of dirt. She laid him in the soft earth. The flower's ooze was all over her, on her hands and face, but she did not notice it. She scrabbled and dug. She patted dirt over the boy's eyes and tried to cover him with leaves, and when he was as deep as she could hide him, she fled through the garden, under the glass mullioned roofs, past plant after plant that seemed to grasp at her as she went. She came to the wallpaper, slashed through it. She found the key to the attic door, unlocked it, and flew down the stairs.

Her mother spotted her in the hallway, her little sash disappearing into her bedroom.

"Mabel, dear?" her mother called, but Mabel didn't stop. She was too busy trying to wipe the plant's blood from the front of her white pinafore, but it wouldn't go, and she couldn't hide it.

Upstairs, behind the little door, behind the yellow wallpaper, Mabel's flower stretched its roots into the dirt toward a pale hand buried there. The hand had begun to grow roots, too, from its fingertips and from under its nails. The finger roots met the flower roots. Slowly, they began to twist around each other.

The next morning Mabel woke with a start. She'd had such a terrible dream. Her heart was still heavy with it, heavy as a stone. She got up and walked about her room. It was regular, hideous, she thought, with its silly paintings and its silly fireplace. And then she remembered the boy and the dirt closing over his staring eyes. She hurried upstairs and peered into the little attic. It looked quite harmless. The yellow wallpaper was slashed, but there were only boards behind it now.

"Mr. Pittance," she called. "Mr. Pittance?" And then, quietly: "I suppose I'm sorry. I did not want to, but I was so angry with you! Please don't be dead!"

But if there was a skin garden on the other side of the wall, it did not show itself, and Mabel did not know whether to be relieved or terrified. If there was a skin garden, there was also a beautiful flower with gold-speckled leaves lying on the floor with a chopped stem, and a little boy with golden hair, buried in the earth together with a pair of shears. And if there wasn't . . .

Mabel shuddered. She looked out the window. She went to it and sat down. It was all just a dream. It had to be. She watched the milkmen and the ice men and the automobiles clogging the streets, and watched the smoke rise from the chimney forests, and it was all so deliciously normal that it convinced her she had done nothing wrong. She had only dreamed it.

She went downstairs and ate breakfast with her parents.

Dinnertime in the Mavelia household was salad. Mr. Mavelia had become taken by a new craze, which was to eat only salads and drink prune juice for as long as was

humanly possible. Mabel's mother approved of this craze.
Mabel did not.

Dinner was served by the maid. She brought in the
tureens, three silver dishes with silver domes. She laid them
on the table, one for Father, one for Mother . . .

Mabel got hers, a specially sized little dome, with a glass
of water, and a glass of prune juice, black as gutter water.

The maid lifted Mabel's dome with a flourish. And for
an instant, Mabel thought there was a hand on the bed
of salad inside, a pale hand reaching out of the puff of
lettuce and onions. Mabel gagged. She tipped from her
chair, about to be sick.

"Mabel!" her mother exclaimed, and rushed her
upstairs, and so Mabel was sick upstairs instead of
downstairs.

Mabel woke that night, ice-cold. She had heard a sound,
and it was not a good sound. Slowly, her eyes adjusted to
the darkness.

Something was hovering over her bed. A monstrous
plant, its long, thorny limbs coiling and snaking, black in
the night. It had come in through the doorway, and Mabel
could see its hide glistening in the hall and all the way up
the attic stair. And in the plant, skewered on its thorns, was
the boy, Mr. Pittance.

"Go away!" Mabel shrieked. "Leave me alone! I did not mean to! I did not want to!"

"Oh, you *did* want to," the boy said, and his angelic face was no longer kind. "You planted me in the skin garden; well, come and pick the fruit that grew." And here he held out his hand, and in it was what looked like an apple, only it wasn't an apple; it was a bloody, beating heart.

Mabel leaped from her bed. She took up the lamp and lit it with trembling fingers and hurled it at the boy and the writhing vines. They burst into flames. So did the drapes. The smoke came fast and thick, and then the screams, and Mabel was bundled out into the freezing street, coughing and crying.

The house on Curliblue Street burned to the ground. Mabel's parents took her to see a series of doctors. They thought it necessary. Because whenever Mabel looked up or down or anywhere at all, she saw plants climbing the walls of her schoolroom, or filling the streets and choking the City, and the flowers in Pimlico Park always had little mouths with little red tongues, and Mabel could not eat vegetables or fruits because they turned to golden hair in her mouth. She became ill. And then, when she had been like this for several years and her parents had sent her to an asylum for the mentally distressed, she found a little room under the roof, with a little window looking onto the moors. The wallpaper in the room was yellow, ripped and clawed.

"Mr. Pittance!" she shrieked at the wallpaper. "I'm so sorry, Mr. Pittance! I'm so terribly sorry!"

Mr. Pittance came out of the wall then. He was just as young as he had been years ago. His hair was golden, and his face was pale and knowing and smug. The only difference was that he had great big stitches across his midsection, and a knotted, gnarled wound.

"Mr. Pittance," Mabel sobbed, dropping to his feet. "I *am* sorry. I *am*."

The boy wandered into the room, smiling. It was neither a kind smile nor a cruel one. "Oh, but I never doubted you were sorry," he said. "It was simply too late then. Too late to pull up the roots."

And he took her tears and he took her scars and planted them in the skin garden. They grew into a pretty, velvety flower, not as tall as her old one, but much hardier, a gray flower with a purple heart. Mabel got better. In fact, she became quite merry after that, and whenever new, sad inmates came to the asylum, Mabel knew just how to cheer them up. But when her parents came to visit, they did not let her out. They never let her out.

My friends,

It is with much trepidation that I send you this letter and the attached tale of terror and torment.

I was most disturbed when I uncovered the story you are about to read, of a girl who, through a series of circumstances I'm still not certain were accidental, came to possess an item of ancient and horrible power. The sister of the girl in question told me the tale, though her telling was disjointed at best and took many long hours. Truly, this interview tried even my considerable patience. For you see, this poor girl was so affected by what had happened to her sister that she is . . . my friends, she is not entirely well. Not anymore.

Thankfully, after a bit of searching through the sisters' home—which has now been abandoned and is having trouble finding new owners in the wake of what happened—I found a diary. It appears to have been kept by the victim herself.

I am currently in search of the object around which this girl's story centers. Apparently shortly after the incident, both girl and object disappeared. We are dealing with old magic here, my friends. I fear the world will not be safe until we have this item safely in our custody.

Cautiously, and with great affection (for who knows when we will next meet?),

Curator
Legrand

MIRROR, MIRROR

by Claire Legrand

June 9

Dear Diary,

I guess I'll start writing in you. Or whatever. I should probably just dump you in the garbage, to be honest.

God, this is so old-fashioned. Mom is so old-fashioned. Would it have been *so hard* to get me a phone for my birthday? I mean, I don't ask for much. Becca has had a phone for seriously, I think, like, two years now. Since we were *ten*. And now I'm twelve and practically in high school and I still don't have a phone???

(Okay, so I have one more year in middle school. Plus this summer and next summer. But when you think about my whole life so far, one year isn't that long.)

Daphne says I'm being ungrateful. She can be so *insufferable*. Yeah, insufferable. Yeah, Daphne, I DO

READ IN FACT. Ugh. Big sisters are the worst. I feel like since I don't make good grades like she does, she assumes I'm an idiot. I'm not an idiot. I JUST DON'T LIKE SCHOOL.

I'm bored with this.

BYEEEEEE

June 10

Dear Diary,

I guess you're wondering what my name is. Mom says I should treat you like a friend. She says I'm supposed to tell you all the stuff I don't feel comfortable saying to everyone else. She says you're supposed to be my "safe place."

MAJOR EYE ROLL

Anyway my name is Reagan.

R for Rebel

E for Extra-amazing

A for Awesome

G for G-L-A-M-O-R-O-U-S

A for Artist

N for NOSY (according to Daphne, and Daphne, if you read this ever, consider yourself DEAD. MEAT.)

You're still lame, Diary.

REAGAN OUT

June 11

Dear Diary,

UGH. UGH UGH UGH.

I am so mad right now.

I just want to stay home and watch TV because it's crazy hot outside, but Mom's making me go antiquing with her today. ANTIQUING. I guess the technical definition of antiquing is when you visit a bunch of antique stores and shop around, but *my* definition of antiquing is being stuck with my weird old-fashioned mom for *hours* inside buildings that smell like OLD PEOPLE and MOLDY SHOES while she shops for, like, I don't even know— dolls and music boxes and old clothes that should be burned and RECORDS??? Who listens to RECORDS anymore??

She's calling me from the car right now. Oh my God, I want to bang my head against the wall.

REAGAN OUT (probably foreverrr UGH)

June 12

Dear Diary,

So, yesterday Mom and I went antiquing, and I thought it was going to be the worst thing in the world. And it was, for the most part. I think the old bearded guy who owns Nostalgia has a crush on Mom. It's pretty horrifying.

But you won't believe it: I actually found something in all that junk worth keeping.

I'll try to describe it for you because this is seriously the coolest mirror I've ever seen. I know, I know—a mirror? WHAT can be so cool about a mirror? But I don't know. This one reminds me of something a princess would have in her dressing room. And not a lame princess with a ball gown and a Prince Charming. A rebellious princess with tattoos and short purple hair. She still likes crowns (WHO DOESN'T??) but she hates tea parties and fancy hats. Everyone thinks she's hopeless but she's NOT. She just doesn't like being a princess.

So this mirror: it's oval-shaped and long and HEAVY. I have a hard time lifting it by myself. The frame is black and funky. I think it's made out of iron? And even though we got it at an antique store, it's pretty clean and doesn't have any scratches on it or anything.

I guess the last owner took really good care of it.

Dad helped me hang it up across from my bed. He was all like, "A black mirror? Really? Isn't it kind of, uh, Goth? Is that right? I mean, it's so mean-looking."

Dad is so oblivious. It's kind of funny.

Sarcastically, artistically, ravishingly,

REAGAN

P.S. Also, I don't know what it is about this mirror, but I look *really good* in it. It makes me look . . . I don't know. I usually hate looking in mirrors. But I don't hate looking in this one.

June 13
Dear Diary,

Okay, so the weirdest thing happened to me this morning.

I was sleeping in because HELLO, IT'S SUMMER. I shouldn't HAVE to get up at 8 in the morning to go antiquing, or to the grocery store, or to the gym. Thanks, Mom. Thanks for being the single most annoying creature on the planet.

This morning, though, she wasn't her usual annoying self, and I got to sleep in until 10. BLISS. HEAVEN. PERFECTION.

But the weird thing was, it wasn't my alarm clock that woke me up, and it wasn't Daphne blasting her stupid hipster music either. It was someone talking to me—from INSIDE MY ROOM.

I know, it sounds crazy. I feel like the biggest dork ever for writing that. But it's true. I guess I could have imagined it? Maybe it was something left over from a dream. Like an echo. But I could have SWORN I heard people whispering, even though when I searched my room, I couldn't find anybody.

I know what I heard, though. They were saying my name. They said they were bored and they wanted me to come closer.

That's all I heard. That's it. And the more I think about it, the less I like it.

Confused but at least well-rested today *ahem*MOMgetthehintplease*ahem*,

REAGAN

June 13 (LATER)

Dear Diary,

I don't even know what

Okay. Wait.

C-A-L-M. D-O-W-N.

It's the middle of the night. I have EVERY FREAKING LIGHT ON in my room. Because a few minutes ago, I got out of bed to get a drink of water. When I came back to my room and crawled into bed, I looked across the room at my new mirror.

I mean, it's hanging *right there* on the opposite wall. I can't not look at it. But I wasn't *looking* at it like trying to inspect it or anything. I just glanced at it.

There's someone

~~There's someone in my mirror~~

Whatever.

Mirrors are only supposed to show reflections. They aren't supposed to show you . . .

Forget I said anything.

GOOD NIGHT.

REAGAN

June 14

Dear Diary,

~~I didn't sleep well last night. I couldn't get back to sleep after I saw that person in~~

I didn't sleep well last night. I don't know what to think, except that I nearly gave Mom a heart attack when I walked into the kitchen at 7:00 a.m. and started making myself toast. She just sat there at the kitchen table with her coffee mug halfway to her lips, staring at me.

I'm in the car right now. Mom's running into the cleaners to pick up some clothes. I'm sitting here, waiting.

It's hot outside, but I like it. It makes me feel safe. ~~Things can't hurt you in the sunlight.~~

LATER:

Okay, forget what I said earlier in this entry. Okay? Just forget it.

I was just seeing things last night. OBVIOUSLY. You

know how sometimes you get stuff in your eyes at night, and those weird floating colors that fly away when you focus on them? They're weird light residue in your retinas or something. I looked it up once. I think that's right anyway.

WHATEVER. The point is, things look different and shadows shift around . . . it was just that.

Mom's taking me to get a smoothie. I think she's flipping out that I've spent all day with her of my own free will.

I told her I'm feeling generous. Whatever THAT means. Ugh, I'm starting to sound like Daphne.

REAGAN

June 15

Dear Diary,

Forget what I said. Forget EVERYTHING I said. For real this time.

It's the middle of the night. I'm sitting on the floor in front of my mirror. I'm trying to write as quickly as possible so I don't know if I'll be able to read this when I wake up in the morning but

I wasn't seeing things. I wasn't imagining things.

There are people inside my mirror. And they're talking to me.

You might think people living inside a mirror would be freaky or evil. I did at first. But they're not. They're actually really nice.

(OH MY GOD I AM INSANE SITTING HERE WRITING ABOUT NICE PEOPLE LIVING IN A MIRROR)

I feel like laughing because this is NUTS but I don't want to wake up Daphne in the next room. It's not that I want to be nice to her (NO WAY). It's just that the people in my mirror say I shouldn't wake up anyone else because no one else will be able to see them.

I'm the only one who can. I'm special.

LATER:

We've been sitting here talking, me and the . . . the I don't know. The people in my mirror. The mirror people.

There are four of them. Sometimes three, sometimes five. A boy, three girls, an old woman.

I'm trying to write as quickly as I can and get everything down because I don't want to wake up and realize this was all a dream. I want this to be real.

(I AM SERIOUSLY INSANE)

But really: The old woman is nice. She's knitting something, and I can't tell what it is because the images in the mirror are kind of blurry. But I know whatever she's knitting is pretty. I can just tell.

The three girls are so nice to me. They're beautiful, too. One has blond hair, one has red hair, one has straight shiny black hair. They

They

I'm crying. Why am I crying?

Because they're talking to me like they don't think I'm hopeless.

Because they're being friendlier than most people are. Except for Mom and Dad, but parents don't count.

I am such a loser.

The people in my mirror don't think so. The old woman is knitting something for me, and the three girls are talking about how they wish I could come visit them, and if I did, they'd give me such a great makeover. Not a LAME makeover, like frilly and girly and froo-froo. No way. They were DISGUSTED at the thought. They say girly frilly ANYTHING is the dumbest of the dumb. They said they would dye my hair purple. They said they would give me a short cut that would look great on a magazine cover. They said they would pierce my ears and my nose, and

The boy in the mirror thinks I'm cute.

Ohmygodohmygod.

He's staring at me like he's not lying, either. And when I look closer at my reflection, I get it.

I'm blushing. My hair is brown and shiny. I can hardly see that pimple on my chin.

He's saying, "You're so cute, Reagan." He's blushing. I'M BLUSHING.

LATER:

We've been talking for hours. Just about anything I want. ANYTHING I WANT. Not Daphne, not my parents, not stupid pointless school.

It seems like the people in my mirror are getting sharper. At first they were blurry, but now they're not so much anymore. When I ask them about it, they say they don't know what I'm talking about, and they sound so sad to be trapped in my mirror that I don't argue.

I don't want them to go away.

ACTUALLY GLAMOROUS REAGAN

(the boy in my mirror said I was, so Derek from science class last year can go JUMP OFF A CLIFF)

June 16

Dear Diary,

There are more people in my mirror tonight. A whole crowd of them.

I didn't sleep last night, and I've decided not to sleep tonight either. We have more important things to do.

The old woman must have been working all day while I

was out with Mom because whatever she's knitting is a lot bigger now. I ask her about it but she winks at me and says it's a surprise.

The girls tell me I've never looked prettier than I do right now. They say lack of sleep agrees with me, and you know what? I think they're RIGHT. I've always been a night owl but NOOOOOO everyone says I have to go to bed when I'm not tired and get up in the MORNING and I HATE MORNINGS!!!!

And no one talks to me like I'm anything interesting.

No one takes me seriously.

No one thinks I'm anything but a giant walking pimple. No one does any of these things except the people in my mirror, and . . . I feel stupid. I am stupid. How can I be talking to people in my mirror? THIS DOESN'T MAKE ANY SENSE.

I feel so weird. Mybrainisdumbmybrainisdumb

~~I AM AN AWKWARD LUMP.~~

The boy in my mirror made me cross that last line out. He says it upset him because he doesn't think I'm awkward or a lump.

He's asking me if he can show me something. He's smiling at me. I guess I'll let him. One sec.

LATER:

He showed me something

He showed me something *beautiful.*

He showed me a meadow full of wildflowers. A great big pond full of fish. A tree with a swing tied to the biggest branch. A tree house up in the leaves.

The girls showed me something too: A HUMONGOUS house with one of those fancy curving staircases and a bedroom that was ohmygod SO much bigger than mine. It had a huge bed and a HUGE TV, and it looked like somebody was about to have THE. MOST. EPIC. sleepover of all time. I saw pizza boxes and a Ouija board (I love those btw but GUESS WHO won't let me have one?? Uh-huh) and neon green nail polish and a stack of scary movies.

One of the new people in my mirror, this guy with a tux on, he showed me a beautiful museum full of sculptures and paintings and . . .

A is for ARTIST

That'll be me someday JUST YOU WAIT

I told Tux Man that. He smiled and said he thinks I'll be a great artist. He can tell by looking at my hands. They're beautiful hands, he says. I've never thought of my hands as anything much. They're kind of pudgy and I bite my fingernails constantly.

Tux Man says he wishes he could touch my hands. Not sure why???

The old woman just told him to keep quiet. Her knitting needles are clicking like CA-RAZY.

REAGAN, ARTISTE MAGNIFIQUE

June 17

Dear Diary,

~~I'm afraid~~

I'm pretending like everything's fine. I don't want them to see what I'm writing. Somehow they always know.

HOW DO THEY KNOW???

I asked the people in my mirror what these places they're showing me are all about. They didn't answer so I kept asking over and over, like what I sometimes do to Daphne to annoy her:

"Whataretheseplacesyou'reshowingme whatarethese-placesyou'reshowingme whatarethey whatarethey WHA-TARETHEY HUH HUH HUH??"

It was a joke, you know. Like poking Daphne over and over until she freaks. They reacted the same way Daphne does. They yelled at me.

They told me to BE QUIET STUPID GIRL. They yelled it, all at the same time. They turned on me and rushed at the glass.

After that, their shapes in the mirror got blurry and smoky, blending together until I couldn't tell what was the boy and what was Tux Man and what was the old woman's knitting needles.

The shapes blended together into one giant dark shape. It was a man. I think. Maybe a woman.

Maybe a ~~creature?~~

I don't know. It's still there, whatever it is, staring at me. It's dark all over. I can't tell if it has a face.

I don't like this.

I don't know where my friends in the mirror are. I finally just now got up the guts to ask the dark . . . WHATEVER IT IS, and it didn't answer me.

It just stared. I mean, I can't see eyes anywhere on it— ANYWHERE—but I still know.

LATER:

It's still staring. I've been in bed for an hour and it's still watching me.

~~I feel like it's getting closer.~~

~~I don't like this.~~

~~I DON'T LIKE THIS.~~

LATER:

Maybe I can wake up Daphne. But she'll think I'm so stupid. She won't believe me. Maybe she won't be able to SEE it.

It's staring at me. I swear to God it's getting bigger.

⇉ ⇉ ⇉

June 18

Dear Diary,

The thing in the mirror spoke to me.

It said, "I WANT TO SHOW YOU SOMETHING, LITTLE GIRL."

And because I'm an idiot, I said, "I'm not little. I'm freaking twelve years old."

Mistake.

It reached out an arm—it reached out an arm—IT REACHED OUT AN ARM

The arm came out of the mirror.

It was a dark, slimy, smoky arm that wiggled. It wouldn't stop moving. I think it might

I think I think I felt worms or . . . I don't know what it was, I don't know!

It pressed my face against the mirror, and it showed me—

The boy. He was in the treehouse. He was being dragged across a wooden floor. His fingernails scraped against the wood, but that didn't slow him down as he flew toward

The three girls: In that G-L-A-M-O-R-O-U-S bedroom, being dragged across the carpet toward

Tux Man, in the museum: falling UP THE STAIRS somehow, being dragged UP THE STAIRS by nothing, by a shadow, by darkness, toward

The mirror.

THE MIRROR

MY MIRROR

MY MIRROR

June 19

Dear Diary,

I've got to destroy it.

I'm not sleeping. The thing in the mirror won't let me sleep. It's the boy and the three girls and Tux Man and the old woman and hundreds of others, all mixed into this giant dark shape with a giant dark mouth. Hundreds of giant dark voices and they won't SHUT UP.

LITTLE GIRL LITTLE GIRL COME ON IN

LITTLE GIRL LITTLE GIRL R-E-A-G-A-N

That's what they're saying. They're singing it over and over.

I've got to destroy it.

DO YOU HEAR THAT? I'M GONNA HAMMER YOU TO PIECES. I'M GONNA SHATTER YOUR GLASS.

I'm not going ANYWHERE.

LATER:

It didn't work. Omg it didn't work. How can a mirror not break?? I pounded on it with a hammer from the basement. I pounded on the glass over and over and over.

I don't understand why I don't

June 20

Dear Diary,

I woke up Daphne and Mom and Dad when I was trying to break the mirror last night.

I think they think I'm I-N-S-A-N-E.

Maybe I am. Maybe I really truly am. Because when they came into my room, they just saw a plain old mirror on the wall. I pointed at the dark thing in the glass and they looked at me like I was crazy.

I asked them YOU CAN'T SEE IT??

They said oh sweetie you had a bad dream it's okay

Daphne said what a little freakazoid. So I ran at her and started swinging the hammer at HER.

I'm grounded. They won't let me leave the house. I'm stuck here in my bedroom with

Him. It???

I can't stop crying, but no one will listen.

I can't stop shaking, but no one else sees what I see.

LATER:

I see the old woman. She's holding something in her hands. I see now what it is. She's holding it up for me to see.

Why am I writing right now why am I not screaming and crying and running for my life. My hand is shaking. I'm crying and telling them to stop but they won't. I'm telling the old woman to put it away but she won't.

She's holding ME. She's knitted a new ME. A rag doll ME, staring out at ME from inside the mirror.

She's holding mirror-ME in her lap, rocking ME, singing ME songs. And I SWEAR I AM NOT CRAZY but when she touches mirror-ME's hair, real-ME can feel it. I can feel her hands in my hair

I've got to get rid of it. I've got to throw it away.

I'LL THROW YOU OFF A BRIDGE, YOU FREAK MIRROR

Diary it's back.

Diary help me.

Diary I pulled it off the wall and the nail ripped a hole in the wall and my parents are going to kill me. Diary I dragged the mirror down the stairs and I felt the people inside the mirror pulling at my hands and feet as I dragged it down the street. Diary the neighbors saw me and I bet they called my parents because HERE IS THIS CRAZY GIRL DRAGGING A MIRROR DOWN THE STREET AND CRYING HER EYES OUT because the mirror is full of people who want her inside the glass with them.

Diary I threw it off the bridge into the creek and watched it get sucked up by the water. But Diary I'm back in my room and the mirror was so heavy that now my hands have blisters and my skin is all scraped up FROM WHAT?? FROM THEM, FROM THEM INSIDE, GRABBING AT ME.

And Diary it's back. It's back up on the wall. It's hanging there, and THEY are inside, and I can't get to the door because I'm too afraid. All I can do is write because someone has to know.

THE MIRROR DID THIS. Mom, Dad, stupid Daphne: It was the mirror. I'm sorry I'm sorry. IT WAS THE MIRROR. GET RID OF IT.

Don't let ANYONE else get it.

I can't scream. I can't MOVE except to write. Something's holding me down. It's cold and it smells.

Diary can you hear me? CAN ANYONE HEAR ME??

They're crawling out of the mirror. OUT OF THE MIRROR. They're on the floor. They're like snakes or I don't know they're like they look like they smell like they sound like they're going to hurt me

The boy being dragged, the girls being dragged, Tux Man being dragged, the rag-doll ME

WHY CAN'T I MOVE?? wrongwrongwrong

Diary! DIARY. Someone help me I can't move. I can't SomeonehelpmeSOMEONEHELPMESOMEONE HELPME

Drawer Six: TRAVEL

Hello dear Curators,

Surely no one knows better than we the deliciously miserable perils of travel. So often I have planned a trip from the comfort of my quarters, surrounded by maps and suitcases, only to find myself a few days later stranded somewhere equatorial, without a penny of the local currency, facing down a family of spiders the size of compact cars. Ah, how it warms my heart to remember.

Because we spend so much of each year traveling the weirder parts of the globe, collecting our objects and stories, we are sturdier travelers than most. When I remember how Curator Trevayne thought nothing of having to strangle, bare-handed, an enraged ghoul infesting her Alpine cabin; or how Curator Legrand slept comfortably on the back of a furious north wind; or Curator Bachmann's weeks wedged underground, recording the whispered conversations of eighteenth-century corpses— it's quite extraordinary to think there are those who feel ill-used if a hotel does not carry their favorite breakfast cereal.

So these four travel stories are for those less-experienced travelers, perhaps still at home with their guidebooks, innocent and happy, all unaware of what awaits them when they step outside their doors.

THE TROUBLE WITH THE GHOUL

by Stefan Bachmann

It is late July, and Nanny and Jane and Paris and I, though I am very small, are taking the steamer from Belmont, across a chugging blue sea, to a little white town on the coast. This is the first time I am going. Well, it isn't *really*, but I don't remember the other times; this is my first time going where I am clever enough to know about it, so I'm quite excited.

The steamer whistles and shears ahead, through water that sparkles very brightly. I wave at Mama and Father on the shore, and so does Paris, and Jane and Nanny take out handkerchiefs and wave those.

I'm afraid I've mostly forgotten about the other summers I went. I only remember bits and pieces of them, like everything inside my head is a glass and I dropped it. I remember the glossy mango leaves, and dripping lemonade pitchers, and sitting on a step and digging my toes into the hot, dry dust. I remember someone being scolded. But it is all terribly indistinct. It doesn't matter. Last year, quite without me noticing, I shot up like a little plant, and now I am very clever. I can do additions, and I can speak long sentences and not become confused. This summer, when I go to the white town on the coast, I am determined to remember everything.

We are staying with a Mistress Frobisher, who owns a pretty house a small ways outside of the white town, about a mile from the sea. We had to take a wagon to get there, and Nanny's trunk opened when the farmer loaded it up and all her clothes fell into the road. It made everyone laugh, except Nanny. The house, I noted when we arrived, had a red roof and whitewashed walls and blue, sunbaked shutters. We have only one neighbor, though there are other, similar white cottages scattered along the road leading toward the town.

Mistress Frobisher is a very proper, buttoned-up sort of lady. She is a friend of Mama's, I think, though she is not a friend of ours. I don't know why she is Mother's friend. Perhaps because she has such a nice house. When we arrived, she straightaway gave us a list of rules:

Don't be too long in the sun, or you'll get sunburn.

Don't touch scorpions or bees or anything with teeth.

Don't track dust into the house.

Don't scream or speak too loudly.

And *certainly* don't wander by yourself. Not in the tall grass, or in the road. Not anywhere.

I noticed Jane and Paris glancing at each other at that, and smirking, and I glanced and smirked, too, but they didn't look at me.

I met Jintzy on my third day after arriving at the white town by the sea.

I had decided to wander by myself, which of course was number five on the list of things I was not allowed to do. We were in a hot part of the country, and Nanny had warned us that there were snakes in the brush, and large spiders, and possibly lions. But I was tired of sitting about on the front step and waiting for Paris and Jane to do something interesting, and since I am six now, I went off behind the house when no one was looking and hurried away into the canopy of green and leaves at the edge of the back garden.

I wandered for quite a while. I passed a little gurgle of a brook, climbed over great boulders, went ever deeper into the green woods. The air buzzed with insects, and the leaves were huge as giants' faces. The trunks of the trees did not only have bark on them like they did back home, but were also wrapped with snaking vines and clumped with mushrooms. I saw a lizard, and it saw me and blinked. And then I came to a field. There was a cottage in the field. It was a plain stone cottage with plants climbing the crooked walls. A woman was out front, tending to a patch of a garden. She was dressed in bright, flow-y clothes and she had a scarf wrapped around her head, like a turban. Her stockings were very colorful, red and orange and purple, with plenty of frills and bobbles. I thought she looked wonderful. She was singing to herself, very prettily, in a high, piercing voice:

Rosa, Rosa, lived by the sea
Alone in a cottage built for three.
She never sang and she never danced.
She wouldn't say why, and I know she can't.

Rosa, Rosa, sat in the dark
And gnashed her teeth and broke her heart.
She never ate, and when she did
It was air and shadows and things she hid.

Rosa, Rosa, come away quick
They'll catch you, they'll catch you and beat you with sticks.
Live in the shadows or die in the sun.
Eat seventy pastries, it's better than none.

But Rosa, Rosa stayed by the sea
And they came, and they caught her; they broke her knees. . . .

Now Rosa lives in a new house by the sea.
It's white and it's lovely, 's got forty-three keys.
It has so many toys, and it's so much fun.
But the cottage is built just for one.

I suppose whoever wrote the words to that song was silly, but I liked the sound of it. The melody was sad, and it curled in the air like silver silk.

I wandered closer.

The woman did not see me. She worked away, plucking beans from soft green tendrils and poking about in the dirt with her stick, and all in such a lively happy way, like everything was her friend. She continued to sing, now something about a cloud and a sailboat and cockroaches. And then, all at once, a large, hairy animal rounded the corner of the cottage. It spotted me, standing in the field. It was a dog, and it began to bark.

My heart leaped right into my throat and I turned tail fast as I could and fled back to the trees. I did not stop until I was sure the dog was not following me. Then I crept back to the edge of the woods and peered through the leaves at the cottage.

The colorful woman was still working in her patch,

picking beans, poking with her stick. . . . But although she was very far away I was almost sure she was smiling to herself, a small, secret smile.

I got a little bit lost on the way home. I walked through those hot green leaves, on and on until I came to a river. It was not the gurgling brook I had encountered earlier. It was very wide, and I had to cross it on some strange, knuckly logs that moved and shifted under my weight. I found the road again shortly afterward. All would have been well, except Mistress Frobisher was cross when I got back. She had been fretting. So had Nanny. They thought I might have been eaten by crocodiles, the sillies. They both seem to be quite unaware that I have grown up.

I told Nanny and Mistress Frobisher about the cottage and the lovely, colorful woman, tending the garden patch.

I didn't think anything of telling them; I suppose I thought that if Nanny and Mistress Frobisher knew I had been near people and houses they would be less frightened, but it was not so. Nanny and Mistress Frobisher exchanged hard, quick glances, and then Mistress Frobisher took hold of my arm very cruelly and said, "You must never go there again. Wicked child."

I began to cry when she said it, though I didn't want to. I tried to twist away. "Why not?" I asked.

"It's Jintzy's place. You must never go there."

And then Nanny asked "Why not?" too, and this time Mistress Frobisher had a better answer:

"Much speculation over that woman," said Mistress Frobisher, wagging her finger. "Much speculation. One time, as I was walking that way, collecting—well, collecting things, I saw a *goat* in the window of her house! A *goat,* looking right at me, saucy as you like!"

I did not tell Nanny or Mistress Frobisher that the only window I had seen was on the left side of the house, half-hidden behind a twisted, bushy tree, and that Mistress Frobisher would practically have had to press herself to the wall to see in. I said nothing at all.

Today Mistress Frobisher took Paris and me to the town to see a collection of performers throw things about in the dusty square. Jane and Nanny stayed behind at the cottage because Jane was complaining of dizziness and nervousness.

We set off just after tea. Paris had run ahead a little way. I was with Mistress Frobisher and she was holding my hand. She thinks I am still a baby, I know it.

We were about halfway to the town, walking under the arching boughs of some trees when we met Jintzy on the road. She was coming from the opposite direction, and it was the first time I had seen her up close. From a distance she had already looked tall and lovely, but up close she was simply magical.

She was like a fairy queen, or a princess out of a storybook. She had a strange, beautiful face, and her eyes were very bright, as if there were bits of stars in them. Her hair was tied up in a scarf, and as she came up the road toward us, her colored sashes swished in the summer breeze.

"Hello, Mistress Frobisher!" Jintzy called out. She smiled at Mistress Frobisher and then at me, and I thought she smiled at me best.

"Hello," said Mistress Frobisher stiffly. We paused.

And then Jintzy fixed her flashing eyes on me and clapped her hands together and exclaimed, "Who have we here? What a darling little person!"

"I'm actually six," I corrected her gravely.

"Of course you are." Jintzy's eyes crinkled at the corners. "Silly me." And then she dropped down in the road in front of me and whispered in my ear, "In fact, I shouldn't wonder if your cow is a bit jealous of you, now that you are six. You must be very careful not to let her know."

"My *cow*?" I said, pulling away, aghast and giggling both at once. "What d'you—"

"Shhh." Jintzy put her fingers to her lips. Her eyes were laughing, and I was laughing, too, but when I looked up at

Mistress Frobisher, her mouth was like an iron pincer, shut tight.

I stopped laughing. For a moment there was only the chirp of birds. Then Mistress Frobisher said, "Come along, child," sharp as a pin, and pulled me away from Jintzy. But Mistress Frobisher did not start walking. She simply clutched at me, and we stood in the road, very still.

"Well," Jintzy said, standing and brushing the dirt from her green-and-purple knees. "Good day to you, Mistress Frobisher. And you." Jintzy smiled at me. Then she went on down the road, soft-footed in the puddles and the moss, stockings flashing in the sunlight.

Mistress Frobisher and I stood there a while longer. I looked up at her, confused. She was squeezing my hand very hard.

Finally she gasped, "Those *stockings!*" and tut-tutted, and pulled me on down the road, so sharply that I protested.

Today there is a carousel by the sea and we each have a little stub of ticket to go. I'm practically bursting with anticipation for it all. I have never been on a carousel before. Well, I have, but I was a baby then.

Jane, Paris, and I all set off in a giggling, skipping gaggle, like a bunch of geese. We are the color of geese, too, in our white linens and stockings, starched and stiff as new paper.

We ran up the dusty road, far ahead of Nanny and Mistress Frobisher.

"You'll never catch me!" shouted Paris. "I'm the fastest."

"No, you're simply the loudest," said Jane. And then they put their heads together and began whispering to each other and laughing.

I watched, a few steps behind. I did not know what they were saying, but I wanted to be a part of it. I decided to say something scandalous: "Jintzy called Mistress Frobisher a *cow*."

I said it loudly, because I wanted to be sure they heard the first time, but I did not realize that Mistress Frobisher and Nanny had caught up quite a lot since we had stopped running. I realized it very quickly, however, and turned and looked up at Mistress Frobisher's stern face, and then down at my shoes.

Mistress Frobisher said nothing. She stared at me, her mouth like the iron pincers again. Then she said, "On with you. Get to the sea," and we children went running up the road as quick as we could. When we rounded a bend, out of sight of Nanny and Mistress Frobisher, Paris cuffed me for saying nonsense in front of grown-ups.

The carousel was grand. For several minutes after the incident with Mistress Frobisher, and after Paris cuffed me, I felt sure the day would be spoiled and that I would be forced to pout for the rest of it. But then Paris, who is such a jolly-jolly, laughed and pinched my arm, and said, "Oh, come now, she *is* a cow; you just mustn't say it so loudly or she'll begin to suspect," and I laughed and joined Jane and Paris and rode the carousel four times around, which made me quite proud.

One of the little boys fell off, but he was just a baby. *I* didn't fall off. I held on very tightly, and that made me even prouder.

On the way home from the carousel, something dreadful happened. Nanny had taken off her shoes to sit with her feet in the sea and she had not buttoned them up all the way for the journey home. And then, as she was walking, she twisted her ankle in the rut on the side of the road and because her boots were very loose, she broke it, the ankle, with a sound like a snapping twig. She screamed very loudly. We children stopped, startled, and were very concerned for her. Mistress Frobisher soothed her and tutted and ran to the nearest house to ask for a buggy and a donkey or a mule of some sort.

She came back with Mr. Brock.

He leaped down into the ditch and tried to help Nanny up, and that was when I saw there was blood on Nanny's shoe and on her stocking.

I stepped a little closer to Paris.

"What the bl—" started Mr. Brock, and Mistress Frobisher gave him a warning scowl and jerked her head in our direction, because she did not want him to curse in front of us.

"Look at it," he grumbled into his beard. "Look what she stepped in. It's a small cage!"

And it was. Nanny's foot had slipped down the side of the rut and gotten caught in a little cage, and the wires had caught on her skin.

We were still trying to grasp this, and what it meant, when I saw Jintzy, ambling up the road. She was wearing green stockings today, with little brass bells jingling up their sides, and she had a ring of flowers in her hair and a basket on her arm.

"Oh dear!" she said, when she saw Nanny crying and screaming in the ditch. Jintzy dropped her basket and ran toward our little group.

We children made room for her right away. But Mistress Frobisher hissed like a cat, and Mr. Brock growled and said, "We don't want your help here; keep going."

And so Jintzy did. She gave us children a quick, sad smile, like she was sorry Mr. Brock was such an oaf, and gathered up her basket and all the things that had fallen out of it, and went on down the road without a word.

ꙍ ꙍ ꙍ

"Too much strangeness," Mistress Frobisher said to our neighbor over the fence that evening. The light was golden and hazy. Nanny was in the kitchen, her foot up and a cold cloth on her forehead. Paris and Jane were writing letters home. I was playing in the acacia tree, and I don't think Mistress Frobisher knew I was there.

"That wicked woman," she was saying. "It's her doing, no doubt about it."

I wondered what wicked woman they were talking about. Wicked people were very interesting.

"I heard she catches little animals with those cages. And what does she do with them, I wonder. It's anyone's guess. Imagine if a child should fall in. Living in that cottage all by herself. With a *goat*. There's something wrong with that one."

"Aye," the neighbor agreed.

"First Jane and then Nanny and then your wife, only days afterward, falling down a hole and skewering her hands."

"She fell down the hole in Barmsalid—" the neighbor began, but Mistress Frobisher said, "It simply *can't* be coincidence. It's too much!"

I watched them both very closely through the knobby branches, and I listened very sharply. But then they started talking of children and the price of coffee and it became rather dull.

I shrugged and left the acacia tree and went and played elsewhere.

At dinner, Jintzy was brought up again, this time by Jane. She said, "Jintzy was in our yard today. I was out reading by the orange tree and she passed me and said it was a shortcut to the road and she hoped I didn't mind. I said of course I didn't."

I scowled at Jane. I would have preferred it if *I* had been in the garden then, and that Jintzy had asked *me*. But I had hardly any time to think about it, because Mistress Frobisher sat straight up in her chair and screeched, "Good heavens, child, you didn't! Strangers on our property? What were you thinking?"

Then I was glad Jane had met her instead of me.

"Jintzy's practically our neighbor," Paris said reasonably, trying to help out Jane, who was beginning to fumble. "She's not exactly a stranger."

But Mistress Frobisher would have none of it. "No! She is a dreadful creature, and everyone agrees. The neighbors and half the town. Laila Ishkeri said Jintzy might well be throwing curses at folk, making people ill and making them hurt." She nodded at Nanny's foot, which was still very swollen. "Of course, she doesn't do it directly. Not in plain sight. She's far too clever for that. But Mirka down the road said there was a shadow on her window one night, and there's been talk of creeping things in the town." Mistress Frobisher narrowed her eyes and when she spoke the next words, her mouth was red and wet, like a wound: "If she comes again, tell her to put on some reasonable shoes and to take the road like everyone else. It simply doesn't do to be nice to certain people."

I thought that very interesting. After a moment of silence, I said, "I like Jintzy."

"No, you *don't!*" screamed Mrs. Frobisher. "You're just a child. You haven't learned anything yet, and you don't know how the world works."

I thought this very insulting. I was six. I knew about a lot of things, like additions and carousels, and I wasn't like that baby who had fallen off. I hated Mistress Frobisher quite a lot just then.

It was Saturday when it happened, and I had not been expecting it at all. I was helping Nanny shell peas in the kitchen. Her ankle was up on a chair. And then I heard it: "A ghoul!" came the shout through the window, faint and dull, but coming closer. "A ghoul in the town hall!"

I sat up so fast I may have bumped Nanny's ankle chair, because she gave a yelp.

"What?" I demanded. I hurried quick to the window.

People were in the road, running toward the town. The neighbor woman was stumbling out of her house, tying down her bonnet, and others in the road wore no bonnets at all and looked quite disheveled and in a great hurry. It was a bright, hot day. Someone, I couldn't see who, kept screaming, "Ghoul! Ghoul! Ghoul in the town hall!"

I did not know what a ghoul was, though I had heard them mentioned in vague terms in stories. In a flash, I had unlatched the window and was on my tiptoes, leaning out.

"A what?" I screamed at the passing people. "What's a ghoul?" But just then I saw Mistress Frobisher in the crowd, her face gray and determined, like a soldier off to war. When she saw me, she said, "Stay with Nanny, child. Stay inside!" And then she went on with everyone else.

"Nanny, what is a ghoul?" I asked, hurrying back to her side. "What *is* it?"

Nanny was distracted. She kept glancing at the window, and picking at the same peapod over and over. "Oh, it's a dreadful, terrible thing," she said, her eyes darting. "It's born of shadows and witchcraft, I heard. It eats the dead, eats their bones and eats their hearts."

Immediately I thought of the conversation I had overheard in the acacia tree, of the shadows in the town and the creeping things. I thought of Jintzy, and what Mistress

Frobisher had been saying about her being a witch. I hoped it wasn't Jintzy's ghoul. I hoped she was all right in her little cottage behind the woods.

But even if it *was* Jintzy's ghoul, I had to see it for myself. I was six.

I waited until Nanny had turned her head and then fled right out of the kitchen and out the front door. Then I was off, my feet kicking up scuds of dust from the road.

I came to the town quickly. The houses looked bare and empty. No one was out. I raced into the square. It was there I found the townsfolk, crowds of them, jostling and screaming in front of the government hall.

"What is it?" I shouted, worming under arms and around legs. "Where's the ghoul?"

I saw Paris, standing to the side. "Have you seen it?" I said breathlessly, running up. "Have you seen the ghoul?"

"Yes!" Paris exclaimed, turning to see me. "At least, I think I did. Oh, it's dreadful. You can't even imagine. It has so many arms and legs, and they have too many joints, and it has three heads. One's lovely, and one's sleeping, and one's squished like a cabbage, and the skin is green and rotting, and it has so many teeth!"

Paris would have said more, but just then the crowd surged forward and we were separated. I was bounced about until my head felt quite numb. I kept hearing,

"How dreadful! Oh, I do hope they kill it! Oh, look!" And while I *tried* to look, everyone else was much taller, and so I only heard. Dreadful shrieks were coming from the town hall, through the open door. The sound bounced up the white fronts of the buildings and echoed inside the church bells.

Someone shouted, "Be gone! Be gone, evil creature!"

And then I heard a gasp, and everyone—all the tall people—went stock-still.

"The ghoul has been transformed! It has taken on the shape of one of the townsfolk!" shouted the voice, and it took me several seconds to realize the voice was Mistress Frobisher's.

"Who?" whispered the crowd. "Who did it change into?"

"That *woman!*" came the answer. "That Jintzy from behind the woods!"

And that was when pandemonium broke out in all earnest. The crowd pushed me right into the government hall, and I saw Jintzy for a split second, or what looked like Jintzy, only her hair was disheveled and there were bruises on her arms. I saw her bright stockings flashing. I did not see her eyes. They were closed, perhaps in pain. And then one of the ladies caught me and dragged me out again, saying, "Good gracious, come away from here. The ghoul might enchant you straight out of your senses."

I was delivered back to the cottage. Everything seemed

dry as a husk. The sun beat down, unbearably hot now. The screams died away.

Later that evening Mistress Frobisher said that the ghoul had been dealt with and had been buried with iron and salt and a stake through its wicked heart, that it would not disturb these parts again. And what a vile creature it was, taking on the form of a citizen.

Everyone breathed a great sigh of relief as we sat down to our peas and pheasant stew. But I couldn't eat, and I still thought it was too hot, and my collar scratched, and all I wanted to do was go to my room and lie on my bed, though I couldn't say why.

Just before she brought us to the kitchen for our baths, Nanny turned to Mistress Frobisher and said, "Rosa, hand me the lamp, won't you?"

I never saw Jintzy after that. The few times I slipped away from Nanny and Mistress Frobisher and went to her cottage, it looked quite empty and desolate, and the garden had grown wild, and the half-hidden window had disappeared entirely behind the twisted, bushy tree. I wondered often if Jintzy had moved away due to the trouble with the ghoul.

CLICKETY-CLACK

by Emma Trevayne

Lush green leaves with sawtooth edges brush the top of the skeleton train.

It comes from nowhere, and goes there, too, speeding by in the night, billows of steam rising to join the clouds.

And the tracks go *clickety-clack*.

Little Stevie March waits in the crook of a bend, just past the old stone bridge that is slowly crumbling into the water below. Hearing the stories is never the same as seeing for yourself. So he sits, scarf tied against the cold, nibbling the cheese he filched from the kitchen on his way out, closing the door so quietly no one else in the house so much as rolled over in their beds.

He hears something—but it's only a rabbit—*hopefully* a rabbit—wandering through the bushes. A yawn nearly splits his face in two, and his eyelids grow heavy.

But there . . . there it is.

Clickety-clack. Clickety-clack.

Quickly, he scrambles to the edge of the tracks. The wind comes whistling down a tunnel of trees and makes him shiver.

Black as soot, dusty, rusty, the skeleton train rounds the bend. The windows of every carriage glow, the light flickering across the trees. For a single breath, he thinks of turning away, it's coming so awfully fast, and one mistake will leave him a smear on the grass that will rot away with the end of summer.

But he jumps, fingers closing around metal handholds, cold and rough with age. Gasping, thrashing, kicking, he hoists himself to the platform between two carriages and stands still as the world rushes past.

Then he opens the door.

The skeletons are dancing to violins played with bony hands. All of them are grinning. Goblets of wine— hopefully wine—slosh with the rocking of the train.

"A flesh-child!" cries a skeleton, pointing. It has no fingernails. "Welcome, flesh-child! Join the dance!"

"Yes, join us!" cheer the others.

And when they talk, their jaws go *clickety-clack.*

The train is like no train Stevie has ever been on, not the ones to the city or to visit the aunt his mother doesn't like but won't say so. Real crystal chandeliers swing from the ceiling. Plush purple velvet covers the seats, but no one is sitting.

"Tell us your name, flesh-child," says a skeleton, wrapping bleached-bone fingers around his wrist, pulling him into the throng of ribs and elbows. A single long, blond lock of hair clings to her skull, just below her forehead. The ragged remains of what was surely once a pretty dress drip from her shoulders.

"Stevie," he says, laughing because the stories were true. Really true! "Stevie March, ma'am."

"No need for manners here, Stevie child, but you must dance, for we are the stuff of night and dreams, and the moment is gone all too soon!"

They spin and twirl, smiling toothlessly, snapping their fingers to the beat. *Clickety-clack.*

Mountains and oceans and the square shadows of sleeping towns whiz past outside, undisturbed by the passage of the skeleton train. Word must spread to the other carriages, for soon this one is packed so full Stevie can hear bones scraping and he has to repeat his name over and over for the newcomers.

Stevie slips, quick as a fish, through the dancers and winds his way through now-empty carriages, past tables full of empty goblets and plates of strawberry tarts and paté.

The soles of his shoes squash food into the lovely rug, fallen there because of course the skeletons can't really *eat* it. Perhaps they can't even taste it.

"A flesh-child!" comes the familiar cry when he steps into the cab at the very front of the train. A navy-blue coat with brass buttons is fastened tightly over this one's ribs, a smart cap with a peaked brim perched jauntily atop a skull round and smooth and thin as an eggshell. "To what do we owe the honor of a visit?"

"I'm Stevie. I heard the stories and wanted to see for myself."

"Aaaah. Pleasure to make your acquaintance. And do we live up to the tales?"

"It's even better. No one told me about the dancing or the violins or the food."

The skeleton grins. Well, he was grinning anyway, but it seems to Stevie that the smile widens, just a bit. "We know how to enjoy ourselves here on the skeleton train, for what is the point, if not fun and revelry?"

"You have fun here?" asks Stevie.

"Of the very best kind!" Ahead, the sky is pink with the first flush of dawn. The skeleton's shoulders fall ever so slightly. "But morning always comes," he says, the words hissing through the spaces once filled by teeth.

"Why does morning matter?" Stevie asks. The cab is quiet. Under the floor, the tracks go *clickety-clack*.

"You'll see. Go back to the party, little Stevie."

The party is still a chaos of bones, of rattling laughter and merry jokes. Squeezed by a window, Stevie watches the sun rise over a lake edged with weeping willows. The skeleton with the lock of blond hair sits beside him, her cold, smooth hand on top of Stevie's warm one.

"My daughter wakes up early," she says, staring at him through empty eye sockets.

"Oh?" It's an odd thing to tell him, but it's best to be polite. "Do you miss her?"

She doesn't answer.

She simply fades away.

Rays of light stream through the windows, and Stevie is alone. He's never heard this part of the story, but they are all gone. He walks up and down the carriages, looking in vain for any skeletons left on the skeleton train.

The chandeliers blow out, the violins are silent. Outside, there are no towns or mountains, no rivers or bridges. Only a blank whiteness, as if the clouds have fallen all around the train.

Clickety-clack. Clickety-clack. Clickety-clack. The train chugs on, rocking gently back and forth. It's cold on the skeleton train without the music and the laughter. It's lonely without the dancing. It's strange without the land rushing past the windows.

But the seats are still very plush and soft, and Stevie curls up in the corner of one, hugging knees to chest and trying not to wonder what happens next, or to think about his parents waking from their warm bed to find him gone.

"Flesh-child. Flesh-child." Thin fingers curl around Stevie's arm to shake him awake. "It's about time you went home, isn't it?"

Stevie blinks. The train is clean, tables crammed with

goblets freshly filled. The sky is dark. The violins await.

"*Can* I go back?"

The chandelier's light bounces off brass buttons thick and round as coins. "Of course you may, now that you know the truth. Go back, and do not forget to dream of us. Stand between the carriages and I'll slow it down, unless you want to go before your time."

"Thank you."

In the tiny vestibule between compartments, the wind howls, the tracks are loud. The train slows to a crawl, and as Stevie prepares to jump, the music begins to play.

He lands heavily on a bank of grass and rolls down, down, into the river with a splash. The skeleton train is already out of sight, but just ahead is the old bridge, its stones crumbling into the water.

Soaking wet, shaking from the chill, Stevie drags himself out of the river and up toward the road. What a sight he'll be when he gets home, though perhaps that doesn't matter now. He wraps his arms about himself for warmth, but his teeth still chatter.

Clickety-clack.

RED RAGING SUN

by Katherine Catmull

It's too hot here. You should come to this place in winter, when you'd be happy it's warm. Not in summer; it's way too hot. But Dad said *Affordable* and Mom said *Adventure*, so we're here. We've been here almost a week.

I don't like it here. The dirt is yellow on the empty paths that run from the jungle to the beach. The dirt glows hot and yellow back up to the hot yellow sun.

There's an ocean, but the water's hot, and when the sun's out the beach is too hot to walk on barefoot. The sea breeze feels more like walking past an open dryer, the wind is so hot and damp. The sun is so bright on the water, it gives you a headache.

At night it's cooler, with better breezes, salty and fishy and dark. When the sun goes down, everybody—not the local people, but the vacation people, like us—everybody walks down to the beach, and we build a bonfire, and we sit around it. It's the best part of the day, when the sun is gone. The fire is like the sun, but all packaged up and neat, surrounded by rocks, so it can't jump out and get you.

I like to sit on the warm sand in the dark, just outside the circle of light, watching the fire, listening to the laughing. It's nice. Mom and Dad sound happy, happier than at home. The three of us walk back singing to the cabin—Mom calls it an eco-cabin, which means no glass in the windows, and no doors in the doorways, and a roof made of dry grass. It's like sleeping outside. Mom and Dad have the bed, and I'm in a hammock by the window, facing the jungle. I swing to sleep like in a rocking boat.

But later that night I wake up, because someone is talking. A light is flashing all around the room like a scared bird. For a second, before I wake up all the way, I think somehow police are in our room, arresting us.

Then I see that it's Dad. He's sitting straight up in bed, shining a flashlight all around, all wild. When the light catches his face by accident, I see he's sweating.

Monkeys, says Dad. His voice is shaking. He's saying: *There were monkeys in here, did you see? Did you see them? I swear, just a second ago, these long-armed . . . They must have been monkeys. . . . I swear they were here.*

And all the time Mom is saying *Shhh, shhh,* and *Bad*

dream, and *Honey, maybe you shouldn't have had that margarita.* All very soft—she's trying not to wake me up. That's nice of her.

The flashlight goes out, *click*. In a while, I hear their breathing go long and soft again.

But I don't go back to sleep.

Because for just a second, just for one second, while that yellow light flew around our cabin, I saw something. I did. I saw something long-armed and long-tailed swing

over me in the dark, out the window and into the jungle.

I only saw for a second. I don't know what it was.

But it didn't look like a monkey to me.

I'm not hungry for breakfast that morning, and I walk on the beach away from other people. The sun hangs over the sea, burning at me.

In the afternoons we always nap, but I have a bad dream, that there's an animal in the room with us but I can't quite see it, only hear its heavy tail dragging along the floor. When I wake up, the cabin smells wrong, a dirty, snaky smell. Mom and Dad are still asleep.

I can't stay in the cabin with that smell, so I go for walk. I start at the beach, but it's way too hot, even with flip-flops. The rubber's melting under my feet. So I start walking back.

But you're not supposed to go into the jungle, because of snakes or something. Mom made a big deal out of that, and asked me did I understand and did I promise.

Now I'm standing there on the dirt road. I can't decide what to do. A pale green lizard, only much bigger than the lizards at home, turns its face to me. Its eyes are half open, something pulses at its throat.

Oh: the ruins, I think. I'll go there.

The ruins are mostly huge piles of gray stone, lots of thousands of years old. But in some of the piles you can see the shapes of the buildings they were, see the steps leading up to broken temples at the top. I'm not supposed to go to the ruins, either, actually. But it's not as definite as the jungle. Dad was actually all disappointed—he thought it looked archeological or something. But the people who run this place said *It needs repairs, and reinforcements; it's not safe to climb on.* They said how last year a little girl ignored the warnings and fell, and died.

But I'm not going to be stupid and climb on the stones. I'm just going to look around.

As I walk past him, the lizard turns its head to watch me.

I walk for a few minutes. The sound of the waves is nice. But it's so hot, my head is hurting, and my eyes are squinched up against the brightness. My shirt sticks to my body.

But walking is good. The sun will go down soon. I start to relax. Just a bad dream.

When I'm almost at the ruins, all of a sudden, there's a dog. There's nothing around here, I don't know where it came from. It's not a huge dog, but it comes up to my knees. It has slick brown hair, peeling off in patches to show gray-and-purple skin below, and its eyes are blue and round and blind. At least I think it's blind. It stares just over my head, barking hard, growling in its throat.

Hurt, it sounds like it's saying. *Hurt, hurt, hurt.*

The dog walks in front of me on the road for a while, walking backward, facing me, barking *HURT, HURT, HURT*, like it's trying to stop me. But I stay brave, I keep walking, and after a while the dog gives up. I walk through the door of a chain-link fence that's just hanging there, broken, and into the ruins.

The ruins have their back to the jungle. It's like the jungle made them, kind of, then pushed them out: *Here. I made this for you. Come in, come in.*

That's a dumb thought, but it's what it looks like.

The sun shines hard on the huge blocks of gray stone. They crowd everywhere, you have to sort of pick your way through. Even just one block is taller than my head, and one of the old . . . buildings, I guess is what they are, the one that's still mostly there, is really tall. A zillion steps are running up the side. That girl who died must have climbed up there and fallen.

It's quiet here, a weird kind of quiet, no birds or insects at all. And it's so hot, the heat is like a fever or a warning, but I don't know what the warning says.

Hurt, hurt. Hurt hurt hurt.

My parents might be awake by now. I should go see.

But I don't go see. I keep walking through the stone blocks and towers, the huge piles of stone.

Now a shadow passes across me. A bird? But it's too

big for a bird. I look up. The sky is squinty empty blue.

But then—what was that, out of the corner of my eye? Not a bird, but more like something on one of the stones above me. Something running.

And then behind me—I whip around fast. I can hear a ripple of running feet, high on that one pile of gray stone.

And now that, there—out of the corner of my eye— it's gone now, but it seemed like a leg, almost a human leg, but also it had—a tail?

A monkey?

But it's not a monkey. No monkey has a tail so thick, so heavy, swishing across the stone like a thick, pale green snake.

I should go. It's time to go. My heart is beating really fast, and I turn back—but I'm not sure where I am now, where the gate is. The stones are so high, and I'm all turned around. I start one way, then turn back and try another.

A skittering sound above me, nails on stone.

I start running. I don't know where I'm going, but I know I have to run.

But I started running too late. When I round a corner, they are waiting for me, and their hands are on me.

Their hands are scaly with long, sharp nails. Their teeth are pointed and long, and their mouths are open in horrible smiles. Like they're glad to see me. One of them is holding a cup, like a wineglass, but carved out of the same old stone as the ruins. They hold me, and they force my mouth open, and they pour something burning down my throat.

In a minute, in less than a minute, I can't move at all. I can't even close my eyes.

With green, long-nailed hands, they lift me high above their heads. They take me to the steps, and they begin to climb.

My mind is going so fast, so fast in my still body. I see that they were waiting for someone to come. If it had not been me, it would have been someone else. Maybe my mom or dad, come here looking for me. Maybe just some other tourist kid, dumb enough to wander in here.

I think of that as they bear me gently in their long-nailed hands, their thick-muscled arms holding me high above their heads, as if I were weightless. Weightless, paralyzed, and my blood going so fast with fear that it makes everything perfectly, exactly clear. I think: At least it won't be someone else.

Green, long-toed, long-nailed feet climb the stone steps, and the indentations in the stone match their feet exactly. How many thousands of years have they been doing this?

It's getting late. The sun is going down, it's looking

straight at me now, and its face is red with anger. Why is the sun angry with me?

Shining, scaly arms lift me high, high, so the sun can see me. The long-nailed hands begin to turn me toward the empty air. The sky darkens around the red, raging sun.

I think of my parents, and I feel so sad. I can't move my face to cry, but tears leak out and fall far, far to the ground below. In my mind, I can see the search party. I can hear the screams of the ones who find me first. They'll say I fell, like that little girl. They'll say they told me not to go to this place, that I must have climbed up on the rocks and lost my footing, and fallen.

But that can't be right, my mother will say. She will say, *Too good, too smart.* She will say, *It can't be, it can't,* as my father cries, big gasping sobs.

And the other vacationers will say, *Shhh, shhh: the old rock crumbled, and the child fell.*

But they'll be wrong, I think. I want to shout it, but I can't shout, but I want to shout: I didn't fall, I didn't fall.

I am thinking that, I am thinking all of that, as I fall, as I fall, as I fall.

My dear Curators,

As I was going to St. Ives,
I met a man with seven . . .

   Well, he did not have seven knives, or seven kittens, or any of that nursery rhyme nonsense, but he did have a tale for me, concerning two very odd towns and the feud that nearly destroyed them both.

Curator Bachmann

TALE OF TWO TOWNS

by Stefan Bachmann

"It's decided then," said Bobby Clattertank, and hunched his shoulders against the wind and dug his hands into his pockets. "All the parents and all the grown-ups, and all the old people, too, must be brought to the very top of Mizzling Cliff and be pushed into the sea." And the other children nodded gravely and had to agree that yes, that was what had to be done.

It was a strange scene, the group of solemn-eyed children standing together on the cliff top. Had someone passed by on that blustery day, he almost certainly would have wondered if there was an asylum for delinquent children nearby from which they had all escaped. He would wonder whether someone would come and catch them soon, before they put their dreadful plans into action. It would almost certainly never have crossed his mind that all the parents and the grown-ups and the old people *deserved* to be brought to the very tip of Mizzling Cliff and be pushed into the sea.

But they did.

The trouble had started many months before, in a country that was all green and blue—green fields and blue sky. Dark, stormy blue sky.

The country sat beside a great ocean, and though most of the population lived in farmhouses and hamlets deep among the rolling hills, some braved the wind and waves and sharp salty air of the cliffs.

Two, in fact.

Two towns.

The towns were called Moss and Bucket, and they were not so very different really, even though they appeared to be. They were perched facing each other across a great divide, under which the sea chopped and waved. Bucket was built of good, strong houses, with curled slate roofs like wizard hats. Moss was a huddle of wattle-and-daub cottages with wooden shutters, but it was not so bad either. Bucket had cobbled streets and iron-wheeled vehicles. Moss had dirt roads, rutted and old. Bucket smelled of buckets, and Moss smelled of moss.

The population of the two towns did not *look* different

either, no more than most folks. It could be argued that in Moss, the people were a little rougher in the face due to the stronger winds on their side of the cliffs. It could be said that in Bucket, everyone was slightly taller and had, due to recent developments, evolved slightly longer noses, which they employed almost solely to look down upon the people of Moss. But in general they appeared very much the same.

There was one difference, though—the people of Bucket had, several years ago, developed a sort of bucket that had thin metal legs and could carry itself, and this they had sold all over the country. They had become wealthy. They wore fine woolen clothes now, with bits of purple and green velvet. They taught themselves dainty manners.

The people of Moss didn't do any of that. The people of Moss bred snails and goats and collected a cheap sort of moss that grew on the cliff faces, which had a strange sort of smell that could be used to make particularly noisy babies sleep calmly. They were the same as they had been for hundreds of years, and they were rather poor but they were happy that way.

And so that was how it was until, one day, the storm struck.

First came the wind, slashing over Bucket with the power of a hurricane and blowing an entire wagonload of self-carrying buckets into the sea. It blew on toward Moss and tore at the flimsy roofs and the wooden shutters.

Then followed the wave. It was the tallest wave anyone had ever seen.

A family of Bucketers looked through their thick glass windows with terrified eyes, saw it rising as tall as the cliffs, taller in fact, a tidal wave. A family in Moss saw it, too, and cowered under the thatched roof of their attic as the wind screamed through the unglazed windows.

And then the wave flew over the cliffs and shattered.

It was a dreadful day in Bucket. It was a worse day in Moss.

For while Bucket had its solid houses with foundations that stabbed right into the skin of the earth, Moss had poorer dwellings, and a great many of them dripped into the ocean along with the wave. Many lives were lost that day, and when the wave was gone those that were alive lay in the mud and screamed.

The next morning, the mayor of Bucket went across the cliffs to Moss to assess the damage. He came upon the mayor of Moss just outside of the town. He looked down his long, thin nose at the Moss mayor and said, "Goodness, what a mess."

The mayor of Bucket had brought his son with him. The mayor of Moss had a daughter with him. The Bucket boy tried to look down his nose at the Moss girl the way he had been taught, but they were both the same height so it was no use. They had to make do with looking each other in the eye, seriously, as their fathers spoke.

"It could have been averted," the Bucket father was saying, walking about importantly and kicking at the rubble. "It *should* have been. Look at our town! Look at our strong houses and our thick glass and our chimneys. It is all still there. Half your town has been washed into the sea."

"It is very sad," agreed the Moss mayor, and he wouldn't look at the Bucket mayor.

"I do hope you'll learn something from it," said the Bucket mayor. He took his son by the hand, about to turn back. "You ought to be more like us."

Now it is starting. Oh dear. The Moss mayor drew himself up and puffed out his chest. He said, "I wouldn't want to be like you if you were the king of the moon. How dare you?" and his daughter said to the Moss boy, "Yes, how *dare* you?" though the Bucket boy had said nothing at all.

And the Bucket mayor insisted, "I'm simply stating the facts," but facts are not important when one's pride has been damaged, or when one doesn't believe in facts. They argued for a while longer, their voices becoming louder and louder, and their children looking more and more anxious.

And then the Moss mayor and the Bucket mayor parted ways, one muttering under his breath, the other looking down his long nose and shaking his head.

That was the beginning.

The next morning the people of Bucket, resplendent in their woolen clothes and velvet ribbons, held a meeting, and the mayor told them what he had seen in Moss, the sad sights and mourning people, and the people of Bucket passed a law then and there that had something to do with making the Mossers less likely to die.

When news of this law reached the Mossers, they were not pleased at all.

"It is for the best!" the Bucketers reasoned. "You are hurting yourselves with your backward ways! You are being foolish and lazy." But the Mossers did not want to be reasoned with by these pompous people who thought they could boss them about. Because though the Mossers *were* perhaps a bit lazier and less ambitious than the Bucketers, they did not see themselves the way the Bucketers did. They only saw that the Bucketers had so much food they became fat, and had so much money they forgot what it was like to be hungry, and did not even notice the sunken-eyed beggars on their streets.

And so they fought, the two towns. At first it was only little nudges, like sharp elbows to a bony back. A Mosser would come to the Bucket side of the cliffs with a present for the mayor, and the present would in fact be a cake full of ring worms, which would crawl up the mayor's nose.

The Bucket mayor would then go to Moss and pat the hungry Mosser children on their heads, but he had little nets of lice in his hands and so the next day Moss was infested with the raisin-black insects, and all the mothers were shearing their children's heads like sheep.

It went on and on like this, on and on and on. After a while, fists were employed instead of cakes and lice. Teeth were knocked out. Then pitchforks were stabbed into unfortunate places, and people began to die.

"No!" the Bucket mayor would shout, bellowing full into the Moss mayor's face. "You are not allowed to be this way. You are not allowed to think that. You are not allowed to refuse our help. It is harmful." And then he would knock the other mayor over the head.

And then the Mosser would say: "Who made you king of anything? We will do as we please, and we will do as we have been doing for one hundred years, and a hundred years more." And the Moss mayor would knock the Bucket mayor back.

It would have been funny were it not for the way Bucket began to look somewhat windblown and desolate because everyone was too busy fighting to tend to the self-carrying bucket factories. It would have been funny were it not for the bodies piling up behind the coffin makers.

And all the while the children of the two towns watched. They watched as their homes grew shabbier and shabbier, and their cupboards emptier. In Moss, the children tried to keep the goats alive and the snails well, but it was very hard without the help of the grown-ups.

And one day—a dark, blustery day when the sky was deep and blue, and the sea was flat and gray—the children of the towns met on the cliffs. Their parents were fighting, as usual. The Bucket children were sick with ring worms, which were still curling in their stomachs. The Moss children were itching with the lice. They all stood in a huddle on the cliffs and spoke to one another for many hours, while in the towns all the parents and the grown-ups, and all the old people, too, fought and did not notice that their children were gone.

And after a while, Bobby Clattertank ducked his head against the wind and dug his hands into his pockets and said, "It's decided then. All the parents, and all the grown-ups, and all the old people, too, must be brought to the very top of Mizzling Cliff and be pushed into the sea." And the other children nodded gravely and had to agree that yes, that was what had to be done.

The children of Bucket and Moss went about their business methodically, with chilly-fingered precision. They returned to their towns in twos and threes. The children of Moss took all the remaining moss from the barrels and gathered the slime from their snails and churned them together into a pulp. The children of Bucket released all the self-carrying buckets that had been standing abandoned for so long and sent them running along the cliffs to the other town. In Moss, the children filled the buckets with the mixture, and the buckets went everywhere, every cottage and tent and great wizard-hat house, until the streets were ringing with the sound of their little metal feet. The grown-ups were too busy fighting to notice. They did not notice as their children answered the doors to the tap of buckets. They did not hear the slop of snail slime and cliff moss in the tea their children brought them. They did not notice how very quickly they fell asleep.

And when they were all snoring soundly, all across the two towns, the children took them one by one and hoisted them to the top of Mizzling Cliff and tipped them over the edge.

The grown-ups fell quietly, their clothes fluttering like wings, and then slipped into the sea. When the last two, the Moss mayor and the Bucket mayor, were tipped over the cliff, the children went back to their houses.

⇒ ⇒ ⇒

Many years passed, and they were not better years. It did not take long before the people of Moss and the people of Bucket began to fight again. A Bucket boy married a Moss girl, and since Moss was now quite wealthy from its Moss-water invention (which it sold to doctors and unhappy people) and Bucket had become quite poor, having dropped all the people who knew how to construct self-carrying buckets off Mizzling Cliff, the people of Moss resented the lowly union. Fighting ensued. Pitchforks and lice and ring worms were put to use vigorously.

It would have gone on like this forever, except for one person, one day: while walking along the cliffs, a Moss girl met a child from Bucket. The child was in front of his family's house, squishing snails with his toes. The mother was watching from the doorway, and she smirked as the Moss girl approached. Her fingers twitched, brushing a small bag of lice. She would pat the girl's head when she was close enough, and the girl would be bald by tomorrow morning.

But the Moss girl came to the child first, and when she saw all the squashed snails at the boy's feet, she almost shouted at him. She almost slapped him and shouted, "You mustn't do that! The poor snails!"

Only she didn't. She stopped herself, and instead she

made her voice very gentle and very kind, and she said, "You know, if you were a snail, you wouldn't like to be squished. Supposing we're all like little snails and we don't know it, and one day someone decides to squish us with his toes. Wouldn't that be awful?"

And the Moss girl sat down beside the Bucket child and they made a little wall out of mud and dirt and herded the rain snails along the top with gentle prods from a twig. The mother watched from the doorway, her eyes wide. Then she went back inside and dropped her net of lice in the dirty laundry water.

And everything was a bit better after that, for everyone.

Room Seven: SONG

Oh, my fellow Curators!

I am terribly pleased to inform you that I have a bit of most excellent news: I have uncovered a new room in the Cabinet! I know this might startle you, but it is indeed true.

An entirely new room. Joy of joys! Horror of horrors!

At first I thought that perhaps the darkside weavers had grown bored of playing tricks on the neighbors and had decided to turn their mischievous energies onto the Cabinet instead. But fortunately (or alas?) this was no mirage, and I was not lured into the shadow dimension. It was—yes!—a new room, located somewhere between the fourth and fifth floors, and it has a most peculiar quality.

It *sings*.

I've yet to interpret its language—it sounds rather Karstanian, if you want to know, but then Curator Trevayne is the expert on those particular dialects—but the mood is, well, *gloomy*. I cannot decide if that is an ominous portent or if the room simply needs to indulge in a spot of ice cream.

Regardless, this discovery reminded me of a set of stories of which I am particularly fond—the stories we have written about *song*. I have copied them and sent them on for your enjoyment. Do return home swiftly, my dears. And perhaps bring home a box or two of those miniature earplugs? The skullfinches in the fifth-floor aviary will not stop complaining about their nosy new neighbor.

Melodically, lyrically, harmonically,

Curator
Legrand

RHAPSODY IN DOOM

by Claire Legrand

The city of Rhapsody is a city of tangles and knots.

Shops and apartment buildings stand in teetering stacks, and its streets are twisty. Some people swear the streets change, moving to different locations from week to week, just to be confusing. The river that runs through the center of Rhapsody is crisscrossed by a dazzling assortment of bridges built in every architectural style imaginable, because a long time ago, when Rhapsody was first built, the city council held an architectural contest with a grand prize of $100,000, and engineers from far and wide came to out-bridge each other. The result was an alarming and impractical lineup of bridges that the city council had been thoroughly unprepared to handle—stone bridges and iron bridges and wooden bridges and rope bridges and bridges made out of glass.

All of this leads to horrific traffic jams during rush hour, and, for the children of Rhapsody, who don't yet have to contend with rush hour, the bridges provide long sweaty summer afternoons of climbing through the chaos like gangs of monkeys.

The most miraculous thing about Rhapsody, however, is not its array of bridges, nor its twistiness. The most miraculous thing is something you can't see at all. It's something you hear.

Rhapsody has more amphitheaters and concert halls and hole-in-the-wall live music venues than it does groceries, or tailors, or even bridges. For although the citizens of Rhapsody use ordinary money for some trade— like pennies and gold dollars and paper bills that shine silver in moonlight (the secretary of the treasury during the era these paper bills were implemented was a fanciful kind of man)—there is another, much more valuable currency in use throughout Rhapsody.

Listen closely, and you'll hear it, even out here on the outskirts. Close your eyes. Do you hear that cacophony of fiddles and pipes, of drums and tambourines and glockenspiels and horns? That ever-present trill of song?

I'm sure you do hear it. And I'm sure you feel the accompanying thrill along your arms, raising the hairs on your skin and eliciting cascades of goose bumps.

That cacophony is Rhapsody's other, miraculous currency: music. And the thrill you feel, the magnetic pull, the prickling energy—that is magic.

In Rhapsody, even a simple fiddled jig can conjure enough magic to provide a brief reading of one aspect of your future, or an hour-long love spell, or the clearing of a few unsightly blemishes. A piano concerto can get you enough magic to imbue a handful of unremarkable stones with the power of runes. A quality string quartet is enough for a night of invisibility; a symphony performed by a full orchestra, a temporary glamour that can disguise your true features. Both are perfect for covert operations, if that's your thing.

But a song—the simple sound of a melody spun through the air by a single human voice—produces a more powerful magic than any other type of music. I'm not sure why, so don't ask me. It's the truth, though.

Such was the case the day Dmitri Hatchett was born.

Dmitri's mother was talentless and pleasantly ordinary.

Since her parents died when she was twelve, she'd scratched out a humdrum living doing odd jobs for rich people—mending their clothes and massaging their bunions and watching over their personal items when they went out for a day of hunting in the hill country.

Despite her ordinariness—or perhaps because of it—she managed to charm the son of a Mr. Roquefort. His name was Ferdie or Llewellyn or something equally ridiculous, I can't remember. Anyway, they fell in love, I guess, although opinions are mixed on that. But Ferdie-Llewellyn-Whatever soon decided he didn't love her after all, and divorced her, and turned her back out onto the streets.

As you can imagine, by the time Dmitri's mother gave birth to Dmitri, she was in a sorry state. She was alone and heartbroken, and she couldn't afford a hot breakfast, much less a proper nurse. So just after Dmitri drew his first breaths, his mother drew her last.

But not before she sang to him.

That's how the legend goes: That as Dmitri Hatchett's mother lay dying, she sang her son a song. It was full of enough love and sadness and regret and pain to make up for the fact that her voice was kind of repulsive. All that emotion turned her voice, for a few brief moments, into something lovely.

Then she died, and Dmitri was alone. He was found on the street sometime later by Gipsy Blue, the mistress of a pickpocketing gang, who pretended to be a brute but was actually a huge softie. She took him in, and the root of his mother's song was already turning over quietly deep inside him. Gipsy fed him and gave him his name. She dressed him in patched-up diapers and was at least halfway obsessed with tickling his feet. If her gang ever suspected that she actually liked Dmitri, they wisely decided not to say anything about it.

As Dmitri grew up, so did his mother's song. It grew in the most secret part of his heart, which is coincidentally the same spot from which both magic and music originate. It grew and it grew. Dmitri became tall and lanky and freckled, and eventually he realized what was growing inside him—a beautiful song, perhaps one of the most beautiful that had ever existed. And with it, of course, grew the potential for either a great or terrible magic, depending on what kind of person Dmitri turned out to be.

Dmitri, thankfully, wasn't an idiot. He kept his secret safe so he wouldn't end up dead in a twisty alleyway somewhere with his throat or diaphragm cut out by someone on the Rhapsody black market, desperate for magic and willing to undergo or at least facilitate an illegal transplant. As if a transfer of vocal cords or internal organs could give you musical talent. The people of Rhapsody could be so depraved. Not to mention medically ignorant.

So Dmitri kept quiet—he was practically a mute, in fact—until a fateful Saturday afternoon when he was the solid age of twelve. There was a storm brewing, a great roiling storm that cast an ugly light over Rhapsody's rooftops and sent the children scampering inside. It was a storm of destiny. That's how the legend goes. Take it with a grain of salt. You know how legends can be.

That very afternoon, The Amazing Lockhart was traveling near Rhapsody in a wagon covered with painted stars. The wagon was rickety and the paint was peeling, but if you were an astute enough observer, you'd be able to tell that it was a manufactured ricketiness. The paint had been peeled by a tool, not naturally over time.

The Amazing Lockhart wanted you to think he was impoverished and unfortunate, so you would take pity on him and donate generously to his patched felt hat at the end of one of his magic shows.

But Lockhart was neither impoverished nor unfortunate. He had enough money to be comfortable, and he hadn't died yet, so I think we can agree he was fortunate in that regard at least.

He was, however, a fool.

You see, Lockhart was not amazing in the truest sense of the word. He was one of those street magicians who can't perform real magic, but instead has to resort to illusions and sleight of hand. That's all fine, in my opinion. It still *looks* impressive, even if it isn't strictly authentic.

But Lockhart yearned to be a real magician. He dreamt

about it every night. He had done all sorts of nasty things in all sorts of nasty corners of the world in an attempt to force magic inside himself. But it's not the kind of thing you can force, and Lockhart had become a bitter, angry loser.

You might think that's cruel of me, to call him that. Haven't we all felt like a loser at various times in our lives?

But just you wait. He deserves it.

On this same afternoon, a young musician from Rhapsody was traveling the same country road down which Lockhart was traveling.

This young musician was singing to himself as he walked. Most Rhapsodians would never dream of doing such a thing while all alone in a strange place, where anyone could happen by, sense their magic, hear their song, and put two and two together. But this traveling musician had just turned fifteen years old and thought he was the greatest and most indestructible creature to have ever walked the planet.

Lockhart heard the musician's lilting song, and he felt the magic accompanying it. It was unmistakable. Maybe because he'd spent all his life obsessing about it, and had read so many books about it, and had spent years sucking up to actual talented magicians—but whatever the reason,

Lockhart tasted that magic like someone had just dashed a handful of spice onto his tongue. He tasted its bold, brash, kind of stupid fifteen-year-old-boy flavor.

"Ah." He sat up straighter, and his poor abused team of mules winced at how hard he pulled their reins. "Ah, that is something, isn't it? That is something indeed."

Lockhart was tired of traveling around with all the bumpkins and the hicks. He was tired of living off radishes and rats, and he was tired of sucking up to talented magicians. He wanted to *be* a talented magician. He wanted to be rich, famous, and terrifying. He wanted to receive love letters sprayed with perfume.

So he crept up on the musician. He wasn't sure how he was going to go about this, exactly. He'd killed people before as part of horrible rituals—which, by the way, had proven completely useless as well as gruesome, in that they hadn't granted him the power of real magic after all—but he'd never killed someone with the aim of capturing their voice first.

But then he remembered about the box in the back of his wagon—the deep purple box he'd stolen from that dark church in the north. In that church, the monks wore masks and the priests had no tongues. These masked monks had said that whatever resided in this deep purple box would provide Lockhart with whatever he needed at the moment he needed it most.

Ah.

At the time, Lockhart had thought the monks were making fun of him. He had thrown the box carelessly in the back of his wagon. He had listened to them laughing, and their laughter had burned his ears. He had lost two fingers in that church, during a ritual the monks *swore* would get him some magic at last.

Dirty rotten masked liars.

But now, he felt deep in his brittle black heart that this was it. This was the key to his long-awaited success.

Lockhart dug for the purple box with shaking hands. Inside it, nestled within folds of velvet fabric, he found an unkind-looking brass tool. It was made of wire, and shaped like a mask. At the mouth of the mask was a tiny round box, also made of brass. Inside the box was a tiny dark space too small to hold anything but a few pennies. Or something even more precious than that. And as Lockhart sat there fiddling with the device and imagining its uses, he knew this was it.

A diabolical plan came to life in Lockhart's mind. This, he knew, was his destiny.

The young traveling musician didn't see it coming. He was thinking about this cute girl from town who had the best smile he'd ever laid eyes on. Maybe when he got back, he would ask her to go to the meadow with him. He would bring along a picnic lunch. He would tell her jokes and make her laugh.

He would . . . he would . . .

What was that?

A shape in the shadowy road. A hulking darkness in the brambles.

It leaped at him. It pinned him down. It was a man with dirty fingernails and even dirtier teeth. The man thrust an unfamiliar brass tool right in the musician's face.

The tool latched onto the musician, pushing his skin back from his skull and clamping down on his cheeks like a hockey goalie's mask gone wrong.

The musician screamed and tried to claw the device off himself. Even the dirty-fingernailed man looked a bit shocked.

Of course, this didn't stop Lockhart from pressing a switch on the box at the mask's mouth. Levers sprang out of the box and pried open the poor musician's lips. When this happened, some kind of force threw Lockhart back onto the ground and cracked open the musician's jaw with a terrible snapping sound.

The little box's lid flew open, and the musician's body flopped around on the ground like a dying fish.

Finally, he fell still. Except he was making this horrible gagging noise like he wanted to throw up and couldn't.

A thin spiral of light, like golden smoke, floated up from the boy's throat, held open by the levers, and right into the waiting brass box

The levers flew back into the box, and the box snapped shut. The entire device unfolded itself from the musician's face, creeping off him like a liquid spider, and then became still, like it was just an ordinary wire mask and not . . . whatever it truly was, which even I'm not sure of, to be frank. I don't like this sort of business, myself.

For a long time, the musician lay there, gray faced and blank eyed, while Lockhart stared at him and wiped his brow and looked around to make sure no one had seen this happen.

Then he picked up the tool and began to laugh. He laughed loud and long, and he did a little jig right there on the forest road while his team of mules gazed at him judgmentally.

"I did it!" Lockhart crowed. "I stole his voice!" He could feel the magic thrumming there in that box, between his hands. This knob that was now a box full of treasure.

He dropped to his knees and said a prayer to the skies, which was pretty rich, all things considered.

"I will finally be able to do magic," he said, tears rushing down his cheeks. "I will finally, *finally*, be what I'm meant to be."

Little did Lockhart know that he hadn't just stolen that musician's voice. Magic and music are about so much more than what kind of vocal cords you have and the capacity of your lungs.

No, he had stolen the musician's soul. There are consequences for stealing such a thing. They may not happen at first, but they always happen eventually.

Lockhart led the musician into the wagon and tied him into a chair and let him sit there like a zombie, drooling on himself.

Lockhart knew nothing of souls. But those masked monks in the north did. They were probably watching this whole terrible business through some secret magical mirror or something, right at that very moment, eating popcorn or whatever the northern equivalent is. They had never liked The Amazing Lockhart. They'd been waiting for this day.

For reasons utterly mysterious to most people in Rhapsody, who only knew Gipsy Blue as a pimpled criminal suffering from chronic halitosis, Dmitri Hatchett had become fond of Gipsy over the years. After all, she hadn't let him die or anything. And you got used to her stench after a while.

So when she got caught outside in that same fateful storm, and was struck by a freak bolt of lightning, and fell down into the river through the one spot where there wasn't a bridge to break her fall, Dmitri's heart shattered. She had been his only family, after all.

Dmitri gathered her body from the river and brought her home with the rest of Gipsy's gang. He dried her off and set her out on her bed and held her cold, lifeless hand. He felt utterly alone.

He began to cry. His tears fell down his cheeks and onto their joined hands.

Then, for the first time in his life, Dmitri began to sing.

It was a song for the dead. It was supposed to help a dead soul move on to the next life without any trouble, and it rocked the very foundations of Rhapsody with its power.

It rocked and rippled out past Rhapsody, into the hill country, into the brambled woods.

It rocked the wheels of The Amazing Lockhart's wagon. It made his team of mules stumble and snort.

It made the poor gray-faced soulless musician in Lockhart's wagon open his mouth and grunt.

⊒ ⊒ ⊒

It pulled The Amazing Lockhart's gaze out of the woods and onto the horizon, where he could see the faint outlines of a city.

"Could there be more such creatures?" he whispered to himself. And it seemed to him that the purple box nestled in his lap whispered, *Yessss.*

"I must go there," he said, and to experiment, he used a spell he had learned in the western deserts. A simple thing, a petty thing. It was a spell to make a wagon drive itself. He had never been able to do it.

Until now.

He felt a thin cord of power snaking out from the purple box, up through his chest, and out of the wagon. It was angry that it had been stolen, but it obeyed Lockhart anyway. It wrapped around the mules' reins and tapped them lightly on their haunches.

It whispered, *Drive, beasts. Drive.*

And as that thin cord of magic wrapped tighter and tighter around Lockhart's soul, he began to smile. It was an unnaturally thin and wide smile that made him look stretched out.

"I must have more," he said. He sat back, lazy, and let the spell do its thing. "I *will* have more."

"Have you heard?"

Dmitri put his pillow over his head.

"Hey!" Something smacked his skull. "Wake up. You're so lazy, man."

Dmitri glared up at Wrench, who was probably his best friend in Gipsy's gang, on days he could stand Wrench's company, at least.

"Here. Look at this." Wrench threw a newspaper at Dmitri's face.

Dmitri sat up and read the front page, and he felt his stomach tie up in terrible cold knots as he did so.

Another child had been taken.

"That's eleven so far," Dmitri said quietly. Ever since his song for Gipsy, he'd been talking more and more. Not much, but enough to freak people out.

Case in point: Wrench shuddered. "I don't know how I feel about you talking. You're not supposed to talk."

Dmitri shoved him off the bed. "I don't know if I'm okay with seeing your ugly face."

They shoved and punched and wrestled each other. Then Wrench went off to do his Monday rounds on Eldridge Street, and Dmitri wandered off to Jasper Street.

He didn't much feel like pickpocketing, though. Not with those eleven kids missing.

People gone missing and murdered for their magic wasn't news. Remember what I said about the citizens of

Rhapsody and their magical black market and their thing for diaphragms.

But until now, there had always been this unspoken rule: No hurting children.

Add to this the fact that these weren't the usual disappearances, where a body would show up with parts missing.

No, these were complete disappearances. It was like these kids had never existed. No one could find them—not the police, not private investigators, not the search-and-rescue dogs.

Dmitri didn't earn much money that day. His heart wasn't in it. And besides, everyone in Rhapsody was guarding their pockets and staying indoors. No kids played on the bridges. Worst of all, the streets were quiet. No music graced the streets of Rhapsody, not a hint of song.

People were afraid.

When Dmitri arrived at home late that night, his heart heavy with worry, he saw his gang huddled around the kitchen table. They were hovering over the evening edition of the newspaper.

They turned when they saw him, and he knew what had happened by the looks on their faces.

"Wrench is gone," he whispered. "Isn't he?"

The littlest of their gang, a weaselly-looking boy named Hardy, burst into tears. Hardy's older sister tried to sing a piece of comfort magic for him, but she was sniffling too hard to make it work.

The portrait of Gipsy Blue, which hung over their fireplace, seemed to waver in the candlelight like it was crying. The flowers surrounding her pockmarked face were already brown and dry.

Twelve children.

What was the link between them? Or, Dmitri thought, were their disappearances random?

He paced in front of the fire until the last of the gang had either gone upstairs to bed or slumped, snoring, right there on the dirt floor.

Twelve children.

Deep below the river and its bridges, in a dank passage in the sewers, The Amazing Lockhart put on a gramophone record and twirled about happily.

"Twelve, twelve! A dozen for me!" He took a swig of drink and spat it at the face of the nearest child—a sweet-faced girl whose name, he had deduced from the flavor of her soul, was Penny. Her soul thrummed in the tiny box of that evil brass tool, which Lockhart kept in his pocket.

Sometimes, like right now, he took it out and cracked open the box and held it to his ear.

"Shhh!" He pointed at the collection of gray-skinned, slack-jawed children surrounding him. He had tied them to the great concrete pillars holding up the sewer tunnels. The chains cut into their skin. One of them was a bucktoothed boy named Wrench.

"Listen!" Lockhart told them, sneering. They all disgusted him. "Listen to yourselves."

Their twelve voices could be heard coming from inside the box, which had become their prison. Twelve voices, twelve souls, twelve distinct flavors of magic—savory, saccharine, sour, and so on. Lockhart let the flavors of the children's magic float along his tongue. He breathed them in and let their souls filter down into his own horrible one.

He had deduced that the voices of children created the most pliable magic. It was easy to take magic from them and make it his own. Listening to them filled him with both joy and terrible hatred.

Why was it that *he* had not been gifted with this magic from birth? None of these children had lost *their* fingers trying to get a taste of power.

Maybe he would change that. He eyed Penny Granger's bare, muddy toes. Yes, maybe he would.

He had ducked inside his wagon for a knife when the clock over the door chimed the hour.

"Ah!" Lockhart whirled around, forgetting all about the knife. "You know what that means, dearest ones. Play time.

Twelve little children, turned to rot

Twelve bratty trash heaps, all forgot!"

It was an appalling spell, and he had made it up himself. He had *made up his own spell.* Lockhart giggled, half-delirious. He was becoming ridiculously talented. He could hardly stand it. He was desperate to show himself off.

One more child. He needed just one more. Thirteen was a good number. Thirteen was a hefty, tricky number. It was his hope that with thirteen children, he would be able to create something monstrous, something like the brass device, but made entirely of magic instead of metal. He would suck all the power out of this greedy, puffed-up town. He would leave its citizens lifeless husks and be on his way with an endless supply of power.

He grinned to think about it. He only needed one more to make it happen. He knew it instinctively. *Thirteen children.* You could do all sorts of things with thirteen. Those masked monks in their cold black church had told him that. He would have to pay them a visit one of these days, to thank them for what they had given him, and maybe to take off some of their fingers. It was only fair.

Lockhart sat back in his wagon and tapped his toes together.

"One more. I only need one more."

At three in the morning, Dmitri stopped pacing.

It had been a month since that fateful stormy day, since the first child disappeared, and in all his pacing, Dmitri had hit upon a ghastly thought.

"What if," he said slowly, "whoever is taking these children is after their magic?"

Weasel-faced Hardy, who had fallen asleep on the hearth, blinked sleepily awake. "Wha?"

A fire lit up Dmitri's heart. "People have tried to take others' magic before, but it's never worked. They've never had the proper tools. They've done stupid things like carve out body parts."

Hardy nodded sagely. The hearth was cold and ashy, so he started humming to conjure up a tiny warming spell, but Dmitri slapped a hand over Hardy's mouth and silenced him.

"What if," he said, "someone *did* have the proper tools?"

Hardy was dumbstruck. "Like what?"

Dmitri shivered. He wasn't sure he wanted to know. But Gipsy Blue's portrait was staring down at him, and his mother's song was surging up inside of him. He had barely scratched its surface when he sang that tune for Gipsy's death, and the rest of it was ready now, after all these years. *He* was ready.

He took off his cap and plopped it onto Hardy's head. "Tell everyone I'll be back by lunch."

Then he hurried out into the early morning hours. He was frightened, but he had a feeling that his mother, wherever she was and whoever she had been, would be proud of him.

The Amazing Lockhart slithered out of the sewers. His body was long and scaled, thick and agile. His thin black tongue flicked out to taste the cobblestones.

It was a spell he'd found in one of those books he'd picked up at that questionable flea market in Cliff Town. He'd thought the books were useless, but it seemed that when you had magic, anything was possible.

A great bitterness rose up inside him. So many years he had wasted, living a horrible, ordinary life! Never again would he allow that to happen.

He coiled up on the riverbank beneath a bridge, waiting. Children couldn't resist the bridges.

Then he heard it: a song. It was so beautiful he almost wept.

Almost.

He slithered up the river wall and down Broad Street, his fangs glistening with stolen power.

Dmitri was so afraid that his knees were shaking. Sweat coated his palms and plastered his hair to his forehead.

He could feel something approaching in the night—something tremendous and frightening. It was gaining on him, and it wanted him. It thirsted for his voice; it hungered for his magic. He could feel it like a storm in the air—heavy and unstoppable, a rolling mass of force. It would peel off his skin; it would tear out his bones.

But Dmitri stood on the highest bridge in Rhapsody, under the stars, his feet planted on the cold marble stone like twin anchors. He did not run or try to hide. He sang, and he sang.

He sang the song his mother had given him—except for the ending. The ending, he saved for later.

Or so the legend goes.

Lockhart reared up over the side of the bridge. He saw himself in the terror on this boy's face. He saw his towering snake shadow and felt the vibrations of his own might in the air.

He struck, fangs flashing. He wrapped his coils around

the boy and squeezed, making sure not to stop his heart or crush his bones—but almost. He wanted the boy in pain, but not dead. If he was dead, his soul would leave, and the whole thing would be pointless.

Lockhart opened his fanged mouth over the boy's face. His jaws could have swallowed the boy's entire skull. But instead he drank in the sound of the boy's voice. He inhaled the particular magical flavor of the boy's soul.

For this boy, this *Dmitri Hatchett*—Lockhart knew this by listening to the twists and turns of Dmitri's soul—would not stop singing, no matter how much it hurt.

Dmitri was losing consciousness. His vision was darkening, full of red pulsing spots. Something cold and metal was clamped around his face, shoving his jaws apart. He was ninety-nine percent sure a snake was wrapped around his body, crushing the life out of him.

That was insane. Maybe he was hallucinating.

But whoever or whatever it was, Dmitri could feel it gulping down his soul. He knew it was his soul even though he'd never really thought about such things before. He could feel something important being threaded out of his throat. He felt himself drifting out of his body into the tight, dark confines of a tiny brass box.

It was a crowded box. It held twelve other childlike

driftings, and they were cramped and argumentative:

You're stepping on my foot!

Well, maybe if someone *didn't smell so bad, I wouldn't be trying so hard to get away from her!*

Well, maybe I'll step on both *your feet if you don't shut your stupid faces!*

I want to go home. Please, someone help me get out of here!

Cut it out, said Dmitri. It was so weird that he could talk while being outside his body. It was also weird to realize that his body was being dragged into the sewers by a man with dirty teeth and fingernails who kept sticking his tongue in and out like he hadn't quite finished being a snake. But living on the streets as a pickpocketer taught you to be quick on your feet. Even if your feet were temporarily noncorporeal. So Dmitri rallied.

We have to work together, he shouted over the rest of them. *Please listen to me.*

The other twelve children laughed and cried and jeered. *You? Why should we listen to you? You're new. You don't get it, do you?*

Dmitri? That was Wrench's soul, frightened and confused. *Is that you?*

It is. He wanted to hug Wrench, but of course he couldn't. For a moment, he imagined being like this forever—without a body, trapped in a box, his magic being used by another—and a heavy despair pressed down on him.

But the ending of his mother's song was still inside him, safe and waiting, so he didn't let the despair beat him. Souls are plucky like that.

Just everyone be quiet, Dmitri commanded. *Trust me. Please. I'm going to try something.*

And maybe they heard the authority in his voice, or maybe by that point they were desperate enough to try anything, but whatever it was, something miraculous happened:

Twelve bickering souls fell silent, and Dmitri sang his mother's last words.

"Clouds in the sky, sun in the west
Tiny hot heart beats in tiny hot chest
Winds from the east, stars shining bright
Tiny little boy won't go without a fight

Big mean world, long hot road
But your strong arms can carry this load
Life ain't short, life ain't long
All I can give you is this one last song"

He sang it over and over, his voice shaking like a newborn bird. Twelve bickering, savory, sweet, tangy souls listened, and understood. Their voices wove together like the knotted streets of Rhapsody. They gathered themselves into a battering ram of magic for Dmitri to carry.

Lockhart was hanging up Dmitri's body in the center of the circle of children. He figured there was something special about this boy, so he should place him in an important position. There couldn't be any harm in trying to flatter the boy's magic, after all.

He slapped Dmitri across the face, hard. He didn't like the look of him. He slapped him again; the boy looked way too smug.

That's when he felt it: a hot fist tapping his shoulder, a metallic finger running down his back.

I would imagine, at this point, Lockhart thought something like: *That can't be good.* Maybe he didn't; I don't know. Maybe he wasn't afraid whatsoever. But I like to think he was afraid when he turned and saw that wire mask with its levers sticking out and the tiny brass box open and waiting, buoyed there by the magic of thirteen angry child souls.

Their songs echoed throughout the sewers, sending the mules into a panic. Lockhart tried to run, but he couldn't. The wire mask seized him by the face, yanking him to the ground. The levers pried open his stinking, black-lined mouth.

The thirteen souls burst out of their cage, led by Dmitri and his mother's song. The voice of Dmitri's soul was a clear, high sound, and he wasn't alone. The children's collective magic was like a chorus, an army. Like Gipsy Blue's gang of street thieves, minus the body odor.

They gathered, thirteen glowing spools of filmy gold, as the device threw The Amazing Lockhart about the sewer, bashing his head, cracking his bones. He groaned and screamed, but there was no mercy here in this circle of children. When he fell silent, the little brass box opened once more, and Lockhart's soul—a disgusting, stinking thing—crawled out of his throat. It could hardly move. It was flaking away. It was full of his own poison.

The box snapped shut, with Lockhart's soul inside it—silent and alone. The movement was enough to send Lockhart's wide-eyed, gray-faced body rolling down into the flowing sewer water. If you want to call it *water*, that is. I'm not sure that's entirely accurate.

Let's call it sludge and hope he choked on it.

I could tell you many things at this point:

How the children's souls returned to their bodies, and if they all stayed friends. If Dmitri kept singing after that, or if he had no more songs to sing, or if he grew up to be a famous tenor at the opera. If the mules ever found a kind owner, if the traveling musician ever took Penny Granger on that picnic, and if the children told the truth about their disappearances or made up something more believable. Or if they *did* tell the truth, if anyone believed *them*.

Maybe this legend is just that—a legend Dmitri and his friends started telling because the real reason behind their disappearances was something entirely ordinary. Like, maybe they had all went on a camping trip and forgot to tell anyone. Or maybe they decided to pull a Tom Sawyer and see how the town would react if everyone thought they were dead. I wouldn't put it past them.

Anyway, what I'm saying is, I guess you can never know for sure. I'm just telling you how it was told to me. Take it with a grain of salt. You know how legends can be.

WAYWARD SONS AND WINDBLOWN DAUGHTERS

by Stefan Bachmann

Mr. Ferringdale and Mr. Blake stood in Pemberton Street, hunched against the coal smoke and a driving green rain, and peered at each other gravely.

"It was found with the body?" Mr. Ferringdale inquired. He was holding a small bundle of envelopes tied with a red ribbon, and he was holding it very delicately, as if it were valuable, or a severed hand.

"It was," said Mr. Blake. "And a very strange collection it is, too. Fanciful and not particularly helpful. But perhaps they will shed some light on the matter for you. I was hoping you might read them and give me your opinion by tomorrow."

Mr. Ferringdale nodded and tucked the letters into his coat. Pemberton Street traffic drifted around the two men, strangely silent in the rain. Shadow-clouds rolled overhead.

Behind Mr. Blake, in the police station, a gate clanged, echoing.

"Very well," said Mr Ferringdale. "Though if they shed no light on the matter for you, I fear they will do very little for me. Good day."

Mr. Ferringdale touched his hat and hurried away up the street. The rain flew at his face, smelling of rust and chemicals, but he simply turned up his collar against it and pressed on.

Mr. Ferringdale went to his lodgings in Aberlyne. His rooms were situated at the top of a steep, dim staircase in one of those old, narrow, complicated sorts of city houses. Mr. Ferringdale was only renting.

He lived in London officially, in a scrubbed brick three-story with a wife and two children. He was not there often, however. He was not here often either. He was wherever he had to be, for however long he was needed, and then he was elsewhere. His landlady did not call out to him as he climbed the stairs to his rooms.

He found the stove already lit when he came in, and so he busied himself filling a pot of water and putting it on to boil. He took off his overshoes and under-shoes. He hung up his coat.

The bundle of letters sat on a chair, the red ribbon glimmering softly in the light from the stove.

Mr. Ferringdale took his supper at a wobbly table, watching the rain dribble and worm down the windowpanes. He drank his tea.

Then he settled himself into a large threadbare chair and began to read. . . .

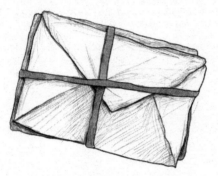

February 15, 1862
Dear Papa,

We are beginning to suspect we are not real people. I often feel I am made of wind and bits of ash, and that I cannot stand upright or all my bones will snap. Harry thinks he might be made of wax. He told me the other night that when he was standing too close to the candle in Mistress Hannicky's study, he thought his skin was going runny. He thought it all might drip away. Do you think we are not real people? Do you think we are changelings, perhaps?

Please write back. It is very lonely here, and it is always raining. Harry is the only person I talk to, but he is very quiet. Some days I think Harry is lost. He tells me he is in a deep forest, even when he is directly beside me. I would call him silly, but then some days I feel as though the wind is singing to me and calling me away. What do you think, Papa? Do you ever suppose you do not belong in the place you are? Do you ever think you are not like all the people around you and that perhaps you should be somewhere else?

It is beginning to storm and thunder outside. I feel the rain all day long. I need to go before the others come in.

Do you think I might come home soon?

Your affectionate daughter,

Pellinora Quitts

P.S. Could you send me some peppermint sticks? I told the other girls you owned a factory that made peppermint sticks. They do not believe me, but perhaps if they did we would be friends?

Mr. Ferringdale frowned and set the letter aside. He picked up the next envelope. A reply. London address. Thick, creamy stock and monogrammed stationary. It was written very differently from the first letter, no longer the shaking, uneven hand of a child. This one was all sharp points, swift lines.

March 6, 1862

Pellinora,

I was very displeased to hear that school is not to your liking. It is one of the finest in the country, and very expensive, and if you are sad I think it may well be because you are not trying to be happy. Have you spoken to the other children? Perhaps if you made an effort to become acquainted with the other little girls there, things would appear brighter.

Furthermore, your gloominess is little wonder when all you do is associate with Harry Snails. He is not a good sort. His own parents say so. He is mean and petty and you will do well to remember the reasons he was sent away. You should perhaps choose a better friend.

I must be going now. I have no more to write. We shall see you at Christmas, and you shall have a rocking horse.

Regards,

Your father

Mr. Ferringdale read the letter again because it didn't really seem like a reply. He wondered if the letters were out of order. But no, this was the response, dated three weeks after the first letter from Pellinora. Mr. Ferringdale took a sip of tea. He opened the next envelope and slid out its contents.

᷂ ᷂ ᷂

March 10, 1862

Dear Papa,

The other children were beastly today, especially to Harry. They threw rocks at him. I told them not to. I told them Harry didn't mean to be horrid. I know he can be. He can be dreadfully mean, but he has had such a hard life, what with going to India and being sick and alone for so long. I understand him, don't you, Papa? He told the other children he didn't want to go near the warm food or it would melt him from the inside out, and then when they didn't believe him he called them names. When we were sent outside to take the air, that was when they started throwing the rocks. One cut Harry right over the eye. He bled a lot. They were throwing rocks at me, too. I don't know why. I pulled Harry away then and we ran out onto the moor. They are very wild, these moors. Mistress Hannicky says we are never to go wandering there, but Papa, I was afraid they would hurt Harry to death! So we ran and ran over the moor. The ground is soft and strange there, Papa, like wet, mossy skin. We ran so long and then we came to the loveliest little pond, just sitting there in the middle of nowhere, clear as a mirror. We couldn't run anymore then. The other children weren't following us, and so Harry and I sat down and cried.

The wind made me feel better after a while, but Harry is still angry. We're back in school now. I wish we didn't have to be. Will you come and take me away? And Harry, too? It is so cold

all the time. It is dreadfully cold, and they never build fires. The headmistress is very cruel. I don't know why she will not build a fire.
　Your affectionate daughter,
　Pellinora Quitts

P.S. I think perhaps you forgot to read the postscript on my last letter. Could you please send me just one peppermint stick? The other girls don't believe me that you are rich. They think you've left me here, and that I'll never leave again, but of course I'm coming home for Christmas? And Harry, too?

The next letter was from the father again. It had been sent over a month later.

April 18, 1862
Pellinora,
　You will stay at Carrybruck until the term is out. You will attend to yourself, and what happens to Harry Snail is none of your concern. I hope you are not being a trial to the other children. We will discuss your further education in December when you are home.
　Regards,
　Your father

Cold, thought Mr. Ferringdale. He sipped his tea.

〜 〜 〜

April 23, 1862

Dear Papa,

We have a friend now, Papa! Here at school! He is a bit strange and quiet, but oh! a friend! He walks and talks with us. He says he saw us out on the moor that day, crying by the pond, and he followed us back, can you believe it? I think perhaps he is from one of the farms, but he is very interesting. He knows so much. He asked us what the trouble was, why we had been crying. We told him. We told him everything and how the other children were dreadful. We told him we thought we were perhaps ashes and wax and ought to be somewhere else, and do you know what he said? He said, "The children are only half the problem."

I only wish he would come inside sometimes. He always stays out. Perhaps it's for the best, but I do feel sorry for him. He is always drenched from the rain.

Your affectionate daughter,

Pellinora Quitts

There was no reply from Mr. Quitts this time. Mr. Ferringdale opened the next envelope, and there was Pellinora's writing again, wobbling ink all down the paper.

May 15, 1862

Dear Papa,

Jack (remember from my last letter? Our new friend?) says the funniest things. Sometimes I think he is a child, but sometimes I think he is someone else, too. Someone old. The other day we were talking with Jack late at night. He was outside the window and we were inside and we were whispering so as not to wake the other children.

"Aren't people stupid?" Harry said, and Jack said, "Oh, yes! People are insufferable. When you become acquainted with them one by one they can be tolerated, but taken together one wants to slap them!"

Isn't that funny? I'm not sure what it means, but I thought it was clever.

Jack sings, too, did I tell you? I don't think I did. He doesn't have a nice voice, but we don't tell him because he can become quite cross and moody. He slaps Harry sometimes. So hard Harry falls. He pushes him. He pushes both of us and the other children, too, but he's better than no one! He's a good friend!

We are going to the moors tomorrow again, after the others have gone to sleep. Jack showed us a way out. A lose panel in the scullery girl's pantry. We will go and dance on the moors, Jack says, and we will visit the ponds and he will tell us secrets. I cannot wait.

Your affectionate daughter,
Pellinora Quitts

Again there was no reply from the father. Odd. The child wrote and wrote and no one answered. Mr. Ferringdale thought of his own two children at home. Tousled heads and starched collars. He peered at the flames dancing inside the stove.

Then he sat up.

Tea. The next envelope.

July 12, 1862

Dear Papa,

I can see right through my hand. I wish you could be here. I'm quite sure I'm a fairy child. When the wind is very strong I feel it blow right through me, stirring my heart as if it is only little whirling particles. I feel I could fly away!

We don't eat anymore, Harry and I. Jack says it's silly to eat, so we don't, and we're not hungry anyway. No one notices. I thought we might get in trouble from the headmistress, but she doesn't know.

Your affectionate daughter,

Pellinora Quitts

Papa,

They found the panel in the scullery girl's pantry. They nailed it closed. We can't go out that way anymore. They found our soaked clothing, too. They don't know it's ours, but they will guess soon, I think. We will be in trouble.

Oh Daddy, take us away before we get in trouble! Please take us away!

Pellinora

⊐ ⊐ ⊐

Mr. Ferringdale unfolded the letters faster now, envelope by envelope. He could see Pellinora in his mind's eye, scribbling away in the blue shadows of a somber country school, the tumbling rain outside and the wind howling over the sharp corners of the building. Mr. Ferringdale wondered. He wondered who Harry Snails was, and why this mean and petty boy had been sent to the country. He wondered if the new friend Pellinora spoke of was imaginary or one of the farmhands, and he wondered if it made any difference in the end.

Mr. Ferringdale sipped his tea.

He opened the next envelope.

November 16, 1862

Pellinora,

(Ah, thought Mr. Ferringdale. Another one from the father.)

I am most distressed by your letters. I found myself in Yorkshire yesterday on business and spoke to your headmistress at the post office. There is no one named Jack at your school. Not even a neighbor boy. And she is very disturbed by your and Harry's habits, and the negative influence you are exerting on the other schoolchildren. She says you are often distant and rude and that you care very little for the cleanliness of your garments and your skin. You often ignore the other children, and she says you and Harry speak to each other as if you are the only souls in the world. Why must you be such a toil, so selfish?

You are leaving Carrybruck at Christmas and will not be going back. What Harry's family does with him is none of my concern.

Regards,

Your father

The next letter was very crumpled, and blotched with great splatters over the ink, like rain or perhaps tears. Mr. Ferringdale frowned when he saw this and rose to tighten the window against a sudden draft from the street.

The dates were approaching the present. The night of the death, six days ago.

November 30, 1862

Dear Papa,

Why didn't you tell me you were in Yorkshire? Did you not wish to see me? We are not wicked children, Papa, I promise! If you only saw, you would understand! I can barely hold this pen, so flimsy have my fingers become. In a day or two they will be little flakes and threads of bone. If you would only come and visit us! We are sorry we caused you distress. Christmas seems very far away.

Your affectionate daughter,

Pellinora

⊇ ⊇ ⊇

Mr. Ferringdale's hand was shaking as he undid the final envelope and slid out the paper. It was limp and wrinkled, showing all the signs of having been utterly submerged in water. The ink was faded in places, so much it was difficult to read. There was no address on it. No stamp or postmark.

December 24, 1862

Dear Papa,

We are going to the pond. We are tired of the school, and Jack agrees it will be best. You said in your last letter that Mistress Hannicky didn't know Jack, and of course she doesn't. That is because Jack lives on the moors like I told you. He said Mistress Hannicky wouldn't know him either way. He says he would frighten her. He is very pale, you see, and he has black spots on his cheeks like an old cracked mirror. I think it is perhaps from some terrible country disease that we do not have in the cities.

I must write quickly now. Jack says he will take care of everything. He will take care of you, too, he said. I don't know what that means, but all will be well. We're going out soon, into the night. There's another way, a loose lock on the gate out of the herb garden that the headmistress doesn't know about. We'll go out onto the moors and we'll take off our shoes and in we'll go for a little swim, Jack says! It won't bother me, and Harry is made of wax. Wax is waterproof, I think.

Oh, Jack is calling now. Farewell, Papa! He is tapping at the
window. Farewell!

Pellinora

(And then, at the bottom, in an unworldy hand, a sharp,
inhuman writing like the spikes of a nail.)

Here you be, Mr Quitts. Some reading material for the cawld,
cawld darke.

Jack

Mr. Ferringdale dropped the letter. He peered at it intently,
lying on the floor. Then he put all the letters back in a heap
and hurried to a cupboard. He rifled through newspapers,
records, correspondence on the case. He came upon a file.
He snapped it open briskly and took out a piece of paper.

Mr. William R. Quitts: found dead on the morning of December
25, 1862 in Kensington, London.

And then:

Pellinora Quitts and Harry Snails were reported missing from
communal breakfast table at Carrybruck Hall on December 25,
1862, North Yorkshire.

There was certainly a motive for the children to have gone
to London. Perhaps they had invented Jack as an alter ego.

Perhaps Harry Snails had become violent and convinced Pellinora that they should exact revenge on their parents. But it was a twelve-hour journey by steam train from Yorkshire, undertaken in freezing December weather by two children. They would never have made it to the station in Leeds, let alone to London so early in the morning.

Who delivered that last letter to Mr. Quitts's bedside, then, was not immediately evident.

"What do you wish me to say, Mr. Ferringdale? That Mr. Quitts was killed by a ghost? That the mysterious Jack of the cracked-mirror face came to London and did him in?"

"No, of course not, but can you explain to me how a man drowns when he is all alone in his house? How he chokes on four pints of black and brackish water while asleep in bed? And how the correspondence of both parties from a dozen months comes to be lying on his bedside table? No, I think you cannot."

"It is nonsense." Mr. Blake shook his head. "What you are suggesting is nonsense. I thought perhaps you could find a psychological underpinning in these letters, not come back speaking of *hocus-pocus*. What you tell the commissioner is none of my concern, but *ghosts* do not kill people."

"It will be ruled suicide. I can tell you that already."

"Very well. Then let it be."

"And the children? Pellinora and Harry? What became of them?"

"I thought you'd ask."

"Of course I'd *ask*! What became of them? Were they found?"

"Found? No. The school lies on the edge of the moors, Mr. Ferringdale, and there are many bogs and little holes in those parts, some very deep. What looks like a silvery little pond might well be a hundred feet deep. I was along when they went searching for them, after the notice came in from the headmistress. We had poles and bloodhounds. We dragged every pond and climbed into every crevice. We found the shoes, rowed up in the moss. But nothing else. No bodies. Only the wind's out there now, the other men kept saying. Only the wind."

Mr. Ferringdale caught a train home the very next day. At the stopover station in Bristol, he bought a large striped box of peppermint sticks.

SPIDERSONG

by Emma Trevayne

Deep in the forest, where the air tasted of moss and rain, the spiders sang.

The forest was on the edge of a great city of glass towers and brick houses, of long roads filled with cars and people. So very many people. They went about their lives, they went to school and work and home again, occasionally shooing small, scuttling things from kitchens and pillows.

"We wait," the spiders said to one another. "We wait until the time is right."

Not a single leaf rustled overhead; the day was entirely still. Above the treetops, far on the horizon, clouds moved across the sky.

The city people did not know about the spiders. Not the big ones, at least, in their enormous webs spun so thick.

There was no reason for the city people to know, to venture so far into the forest.

Today, anyway.

"Tomorrow," said the spiders. *"Hungry."*

And they began to spin new webs.

Claudia Davenport hated her little brother, who had chased the dog over the fence and into the fields on the other side. She wasn't supposed to go into the fields alone, and she definitely wasn't supposed to go into the woods alone.

But she wasn't supposed to lose the dog, either, and blaming it on Jamie would only get her sent to bed without dinner. Tattling wasn't nice, according to her mother. Claudia had very different opinions on that, but curiously, nobody seemed very interested in hearing them.

"Max!" she called. A warm breeze rippled the long grass in the field. It was nice, after so many long, hot days when there hadn't been so much as a breath through the open windows to cool her while she practiced the piano. The grass slapped against her bare, scabbed knees and the dust whipped up around her. "Max!"

She thought, perhaps, she could hear an answering bark from just inside the woods. On she trudged, feeling the air cool against her shoulders the instant she stepped into the shadows. It was quieter here, all sounds of the city muffled, and darker, though there was plenty of light.

"Crazy dog, where are you?" Claudia's voice bounced back and forth, set birds up from branches. "No treats for *you* later."

Footsteps padded along the moss nearby, but it didn't sound like paws, exactly. That didn't bother Claudia a bit. Her little brother Jamie would have been frightened, because he was a wimp and scared of everything, but Claudia liked all kinds of animals and they liked her, too.

Spiders danced along gossamer strings, spinning and weaving. "We are ready," they agreed, and they crawled along their webs to sit, poised and waiting, all their many eyes staring in the same direction.

Down, down the strange avenue created by two lines of thick, gnarled trees.

Down the long path that led all the way to the fields and then the city.

Down the tunnel created by earth below and leaves above, through which—when the weather was just exactly right—the wind blew.

Claudia had never heard music like it before. Like violins, except not. Lower, richer, more like a cello, except not that, either. The melody was unearthly, nothing she recognized, and yet she knew it was music. Intentional sound, not simply noise.

"Oh. Hi, Max," she whispered, quietly enough that it didn't disturb the music playing everywhere, but especially inside her head. The dog had licked a large, slobbery patch on her shin. "When did you get here?"

Max whined and shook a little at her feet.

"Come on."

The dog shook harder. Claudia had to clip his leash to his collar and pull to get him to follow, reluctantly, as she moved toward the music.

Louder, it played. Louder and louder with every step.

It was weird, the way the trees grew this deep in the forest. As if someone had planted two neat rows and then stopped caring what happened beyond that, so the trees were all jumbled up except for these two straight lines, a dozen feet apart. The toes of Claudia's sneakers caught on rocks and snapped twigs, but she didn't stop walking. Behind her, Max dug his little brown paws into the soft earth. She tugged him along.

Was it a harp? She'd seen someone play a harp, once, but it hadn't made her feel like this, warm and sleepy. Almost floating.

The wind rushed at her back, past her, tossing her hair into her face. She followed it, chased it, and stopped, peering through the dimness.

"Welcome," said a voice. A voice that hissed from a body with beady eyes and too many legs. The word wove itself into the music, adding another layer to the song. "She is a bit thin."

"She is enough," said another voice.

"She is plenty," said a third.

The wind blew through the spiderwebs. The music swelled. Max whined again. Claudia stepped closer.

"Plenty for what?" she asked, and her voice did not sound quite like her own. Somewhere, deep inside, she felt a flicker of fear. She *should* be scared, but the music was so pretty. Enormous webs spread out in front of her, stretched between the trees, spun in strange patterns. She reached out to touch a strand of silk, was vaguely surprised when it didn't snap. Instead, a single clear note joined the melody, ringing through the forest.

"Hungry."

Max whined again, pawing at her leg, and Claudia gasped. A spider as large as a football hovered just ahead, grinning.

There was another just there. And there. And over there. All around.

"You want . . . to eat me?"

"There is always one who hears the song when the winds come. Today, we feast."

ᗪ ᗪ ᗪ

Occasionally, they got away. The little girl's dog had yelped and snapped and chased her back down the avenue of trees. The spiders waited with empty bellies, sullen in their musical webs. So close, so very close. But not to be.

"Maybe she came this way," said a voice. "What a strange noise the wind makes in the trees here."

Yes. Oh, yes.

"Mommy? Where's Claudia? I didn't mean to chase Max out of the yard."

"I know, darling. We'll find her."

Two. The spiders grinned again, and bared their fangs.

THE TALENT OF THE HOWL

by Katherine Catmull

Sing us a song, Grandma.

Don't want to. Don't make me.

Then tell us a story, then.

A story, yeah!

We'd love one, Grandma.

Don't want to tell a story. Don't make me.

Do one. You have to do one. A story or a song.

Story or song! Story or song!

Please!

I'll tell a story, then. I'll tell an awful, horrid story, which is what you children deserve.

Hurray!

Long ago, long time ago, when I was young —

That was before the MOON, probably.

—when I was young, there was a girl. A girl who loved

to sing. She could sing indeed, she was a good singer—not an opera singer, not that kind of voice. Her voice was simple as water, and that sweet.

But when she sang a sad song—ah, then. That girl had the talent of the sad song. When she sang a sad one, her voice pulsed with the blood of her aching heart. Her breath moved like the ocean moves, from somewhere far beneath.

And when she sang like that, then the people stood around her, mouths open, eyes full, and when she was finished, they said, "Sing again." That girl had the talent of the howl.

A howl! Ha-ha-ha-ha! That means she had a BAD voice!

No, child. A song is a howl, like a dog's howl, you know.

No it isn't.

Isn't either!

Is that right? Then how come when you sing near a dog, he'll soon begin to howl along with you—at least, if the dog looks up to you, he will. I don't know how *your* dog feels about *you.* A song done right is your whole body howling, like a dog's body howls and howls. That's true for anyone, and any song.

But if you're a true singer, as this girl was—and if you find a song with just the right sadness to it, one that harmonizes with your own sad heart—and if you sing it right, if you sing it true . . . . well, then, as this girl discovered, something remarkable happens. You close your eyes, singing, and the song wraps around you, invisible as glass. The song becomes a container, like a bottle or a boat. And then that bottle-boat bobs along the ocean of time, with you safe inside it.

When you do it right, your howl becomes a glass ship, a ship that carries your worried mind away, far out to sea.

And it's such a relief, to leave this hot, bright, noisy place and find yourself bobbing on the silent-cold and moonlit water. It's such a relief to be carried away, unable to pause, unable to think, only letting your heart pour from your mouth, and wrap about you, and carry you away.

Oh, children: to be alone and silent inside your own heart's song, bobbing on the waves—it's a great relief. A great relief. Greater than I can ever say. . . .

. . . *Grandma?*

Is that the end of the story?

It wasn't very horrible, really.

Sorry. Lost myself a moment.

It's a relief, as I say, to be carried across the sea by your song.

But it's dangerous, too.

Because—as this girl discovered—one day, your song may wash you up somewhere . . . somewhere new. Somewhere *else*.

This girl had a song, a favorite sad song. And one day, as she sang it, and closed her eyes, the song swept her out to the cold sea, as usual. She lay back, singing, and watched the million stars and the only moon, hiding and playing behind bits of cloud.

But then the bobbing stopped, though she was still singing. And she found that she was on a moonlit shore, lit silvery gray, a shore held delicate as a wafer between the jaws of the night ocean and the enormous black sky.

And on that shore was silence, but for the crunch of her shoe on the gray pebbles, but for the wash of the waves, which is a kind of silence. Absolute silence, and silver-cool beauty. And she never wanted to leave.

But, of course, the song came to an end. And when she opened her eyes, she saw them all standing around, staring at her, saying, "Sing it again."

Ah, that poor girl. Like the Pied Piper in reverse. Think of that poor piper the next time you hear his story, and feel for him! Think how dreadful it must be, to be followed everywhere you go by rats and children.

Grandma, what was the song? Her special song, her favorite sad one?

Oh, now. It's an old song, that. You've heard me humming it in bits now and then, no doubt. I never try to properly sing it, anymore. I can't sing it the way that girl did.

Is it that one that goes 'O come the wild dead leaves'? I know that one.

That is the one. Clever girl, Lacy, that is the one indeed.

At any rate. For one whole year the girl would close her eyes and sing, and return again and again to her island. The song made a glass ship, and her breath was the wind in its invisible sails.

What was it like, on the island.

It is hard—it was hard—for the girl to describe. Because when you're on the island, you see a thing, but you forget its name. You forget whether it's of any use to you, and whether it's a good thing or a bad. You only see it; you only see what it is. All the noise of words and saying and choosing and judging is left behind you. You only see the great beauty of the stone, the shell, the sea grass, the star. The great beauty of the moonlight scattered and trembling on the water. And no words, no words. All the words gone quiet.

That sounds stupid!

So totally boring!

I think it sounds wonderful.

Dumb-face Lacy.

Ya dope.

Then what happened, Grandma?

And then ... and then, after a while, she lost the knack

of leaving, when she sang. She couldn't make her bottle-song-boat anymore. And the people went away, and didn't say, "Sing again."

Why did she lose the knack?

Oh, well. I'm not sure. She just got out of the habit, I suppose. Because one time, after she sang, when her eyes opened to see the staring faces, one of the faces—well: it was a kind face, and a handsome one, with long dark brows over smiling green eyes. And he persuaded her to give up the glass boat, and the island, and to give this hot, crowded, noisy life a try.

And it was worth it. Or for a while, at least, she found it was.

But she never saw her island again.

But Gran. It's so sad. She really never got back to the island?

Lacy! Stupid! The song didn't really *take her to an island. She just went in her mind, Grandma means.*

Is that what I mean? Thanks for telling me. Shoo the lot of you now. I don't have all day to stand telling ancient stories. Children and their "sing me a song," as if to sing a song wasn't to . . . Lacy. Girl. Did you hear me say shoo? Why are you still here?

Girl?

Speak up. Words.

Grandma. Teach me that song. Please.

What . . . what song do you mean, you silly child?

I know the girl was you. Teach me that song, 'O come the wild dead leaves,' that song that makes a boat or a bottle. The song that carries you across the sea.

But why? Why would you want to learn such a sad song?

Because I'm no good here. You know I'm no good here.

Oh, Lacy.

I'm not. I'm not meant to be in this place. It's too loud and bright, it's not my place. I can't bear it here, Grandma, I want to go the island with you. And I think I might have the talent, too, the talent of the howl.

But girl, even if we could. Even if we could go, what about the pied piper of it? You forget the coming back, and the people saying sing it again, sing another? There's always the coming back.

Maybe this time we could stay, Grandma. If we sang it together. If we made a harmony. Maybe that would make the ship strong enough to stay on the island, far from the hot and the noise. Only cool and gray and moonlight.

Child.

There's no green-eyed boy for either of us, to keep us here. I'm too young, and Grandpa died a long time ago.

Child, oh, child.

Come on, Grandma, sing, too. Just sing it with me—probably nothing will happen. I've heard you singing. I've been practicing, only I don't know all the words. Listen: 'O come the wild dead leaves of fall / O come the coldest rain. . . .' Then what?

'For summer lies as dead as he / And he'll not rise again.' O girl, you take me back, and you make me think of . . . but we mustn't. . . .

'O come the wild wet winter snow / O come the prickling ice . . .'

'For love's laid deep beneath the ground / And that was summer's price.'

Now we sing together. Eyes closed, Grandma, and hold my hands. 'O come the yellow buds of spring, / O come the melting snow . . .'

'But come for someone else than me / For now's my hour to go.'

'But come for someone else than me / For now's my hour to go.'

'But come for someone else than me/For now's my hour to go. . . .'

Grandma! LACY. Dinner!

It's dinner, you guys. MOM SAID COME!

Weird, they were here like one second ago. I could hear them singing some stupid—Oh! Jeez, here you are. You scared me! Didn't you . . .

What? Are they . . . Wait. What are they—

They're pretending. Come on, you guys. It's obvious you're pretending.

You're not scaring us.

You can't fool us; we know you're just playing. Come on, or I'll poke *you—*

Yeah! We get fair shot to poke you, if you're supposedly . . .

Holy . . .

But . . . something's really wrong. Something's really, really . . . what's happening? What's wrong with them, what's—

Go get Mom. Go get her NOW.

To the attention of Curators Bachmann, Catmull, and Legrand, or whoever else into whose hands this may fall, should I not escape my current predicament,

It is only fitting that I should be writing this on a blank page in a book, the only clean sheet of paper I could find. Books have power, my friends. Let us never forget that. I have made the gravest error of not keeping this knowledge at the forefront of my mind, and now I fear all manner of terrible things may befall me.

Do not worry. I am sure I'll find a way out. In the meantime, I enclose the story of a girl whose bravery and sinister-minded invention make her, I believe, one of our kindred. Please add it to the library.

See you soon (I hope),

Cornelius Trevayne

THE BOOK OF BONES

by Emma Trevayne

A howling wind blew into the room, making the pages of a book flap and whisper.

The book was not quite finished, but those stories that were already written, dried dark on the page, were beautiful things. Touched with gold leaf and formed with purple ink, the letters curled prettily as roses.

Dead roses.

The sorcerer slept. Dreamless, untroubled, undisturbed by what he had done, and would do. Had there been anyone to witness it, they might have heard him snore.

The next night, the sorcerer waited for the village to put itself to bed, lights in windows winking out like dying stars, leaving only the darkness behind. And then he let himself out the door, walked down the path from his little stone cottage, past the shops and houses, and out to the graveyard beyond.

Children were best, imagination still seeped into the marrow, but their graves were too few and far between. He had almost used them up already.

Truly, anyone would do. This evening, he chose almost at random, but not quite. A young man, whose wife and daughter still lived close by. He could see the roof of their home in the distance.

He lifted his shovel. Earth cracked, wood splintered under the shovel's blade. Perhaps, one day, he would come up with a faster method, but for now, digging would have to suffice. He had more important plans, and the single bone now clasped in his hand would help him achieve them.

The ink glowed in the lamplight. Red ink and white bone, ground to powder. It would dry almost black on the pages.

My name is Charles Entwhistle . . .

Eleanor Entwhistle was reading in bed by flashlight. If her mother got up and found her she'd be in trouble, but she'd just gotten to the good part and wasn't going to stop now, no matter how tired she'd be in the morning. Books always had good parts, and when Eleanor grew up she was going to be a writer who wrote stories full of nothing *but* good parts.

The doorknob rattled. Quick as she could, Eleanor dropped the book, turned off the light, lay back on her pillow, and closed her eyes.

It rattled again. Any moment now, it would open, and Eleanor's mother would see what a good girl Eleanor was, fast asleep exactly as she was supposed to be.

It rattled again.

Eleanor's door was not locked. It had no lock. If it did, Eleanor would surely have used it to make sure she wasn't caught staying awake to read.

A shiver passed up her spine. Out in the corridor, the floorboards creaked. Resolutely, Eleanor squeezed her eyes shut and did not open them until sunlight peeked around the edges of the curtains.

"That's odd," said her mother when Eleanor went down to breakfast. "Did you move the teacups?"

"Not me," said Eleanor. She thought of the rattling doorknob but did not mention it.

"Must have been me, then. I *was* very tired last night. Fell asleep soon as my head hit the pillow."

"Oh," said Eleanor. A cold draft passed straight through her and, on the table, the saltshaker tipped over.

She righted it before her mother noticed.

At school, Eleanor did her best not to think about doorknobs and teacups and saltshakers. She read her books, painted a picture, chased after a ball in a muddy field. At lunchtime, she and her best friend, Sarah, sat on the low stone wall that encircled the school at the top of the hill, looking down onto the village.

"Do you believe in ghosts?" Sarah asked.

"I . . . don't know," said Eleanor, startled.

"Dad says we have a ghost. He thinks it's my grandma because she keeps leaving her knitting everywhere."

Whispers rustled from house to house. Strange happenings, things going missing or turning up after being lost for years. Noises in the middle of the night.

Screams that seemed to come from nowhere. From no *one*.

Soon enough, everyone in the village had something to say about what was happening. Ghosts. Pixies. Children playing a prank. Eleanor's mother thought it was a prank, but Eleanor saw that she had begun to sleep with the lights on.

"We should ask Mr. Ludwig," Eleanor said. "Everyone says he's a sorcerer."

Her mother dropped a plate. "That's an awful thing to

say," she said. "He's just an old man who isn't much for company."

But Eleanor wasn't so sure. She had seen him, once or twice, doing odd things. Creeping through the village late at night with a shovel, when she was supposed to be asleep but was reading her book instead.

Now when Eleanor stayed awake, it was not to read. She clutched her flashlight and waited for the doorknob to rattle, for the sound of footsteps on the stairs.

One night, from her window, Eleanor looked down into the garden, at the door of the shed which was open a crack when she was certain it had been tightly locked an hour before.

"Dad?" she whispered, creeping downstairs, turning the lock on the door and stepping outside onto the grass. "Dad?" If she and her mother had a ghost, that's who it would be, Eleanor was certain. Dew soaked the bottoms of her feet and the hems of her pajamas. With a deep breath, she opened the shed door and peeked inside.

Steel clattered and clanged. A thin, pale, watery shape stood among a mess of shovels.

"Dad?" she asked again.

Eleanor had been very young when her father had died; she barely remembered him at all. Most of what she did know had come from the stories her mother had told and a box of photographs Eleanor kept beside her bed.

His ghostly hand reached for a shovel. Eleanor shrank back.

"Find our bones," he hissed, his voice like crackling paper. *"Find our bones. Let us rest."*

From the garden next door, another voice chimed in. "Find our bones. Let us rest."

And another.

"Find our bones."

And another.

"Let us rest."

"Find our bones. Let us rest. Find our bones. Let us rest!"

It seemed as though the whole village was screeching. Eleanor covered her ears, but it didn't help at all.

"FIND OUR BONES! LET US REST!"

Eleanor screamed herself, and ran back into the house.

The sorcerer laughed. Laughed and laughed when he heard them. Oh, they would never rest, not now. Not the dead, and not the living. The ghosts would only get angrier and angrier as their bones settled into the pages of his beautiful book.

Nearly done. Only a few empty pages to fill, nearly all the graves in the graveyard now empty of part of a finger, or a toe, or a rib. Any bone would do, but the smaller ones were easiest to grind up. There was only one grave he would never touch. She would sleep peacefully forever.

Windows shook, spoons shook in their drawers, and the ghosts would not stop screaming. Eleanor and her mother hid in a closet, trembling.

"Why are they so unhappy?" Eleanor asked, for there was no doubt that they were very, very unhappy.

Eleanor's mother clutched her tighter. "I—I don't know," she answered. "Their bones are in the graveyard, right where they belong."

But Eleanor had seen an old man with a shovel. What had he been doing in the night that wasn't better done in the light of day?

She waited until her mother finally fell asleep, head against a tower of old shoeboxes. Very carefully, Eleanor wriggled free and crept from the closet, down the creaking stairs, and out the front door.

"FIND OUR BONES! LET US REST!"

"I AM FINDING YOUR BONES!" Eleanor screamed back into the night. *"BE QUIET!"*

They did not listen, not completely, but it seemed to Eleanor that their chant was slightly muffled.

Good enough.

Eleanor went first to the sorcerer's house, tiptoeing all around it and peering through the windows for the faintest glimpse of light or life, but there was none. Back through the village she went, where everyone was still hiding in their houses, probably in closets like her mother.

When she reached the graveyard gates, she saw a figure, and it was moving. An old man, climbing from a hole beside a pile of earth. He held something up to the moonlight, turning, inspecting. He nodded and put the thing in his pocket before shoveling the dirt back into the grave, patting it flat.

Eleanor hid herself in the darkness, expecting him to come through the gates at any moment.

But he did not. Trembling, she looked again. He was standing before a headstone, wiping his eyes. He snapped his fingers, and a single rose appeared from nowhere. He placed it gently against the marble. Only then did he turn to leave, shovel hoisted over his shoulder, hand patting at his pocket. He walked quickly—quicker than might be expected for someone of his age—toward the village, Eleanor following a safe distance behind.

The screams got louder as they neared the cluster of houses and shops, but as soon as the sorcerer's boots struck the cobbles the ghosts were silenced, as if someone had dropped a heavy blanket of quiet over the entire village.

They lined the street as he passed, cold, translucent faces glowing with fear. Eleanor hid behind a bush until he was safely up the road and the chorus had begun anew.

"Find our bones . . . Find our bones . . . "

"I am," she whispered, as a lamp flickered in the window of the sorcerer's cottage. Inside, the sorcerer was bent to his task, crushing the bone with a mortar and pestle, mixing blood-red ink with the powder, and Eleanor was certain he did not see her watching. He picked up a pen the likes of which she'd never seen, with a pointed nib attached to a long peacock feather, and started to write in the pages of a beautiful, heavy book.

A new voice joined the screams in the village.

And Eleanor knew what she must do.

His final story complete, the sorcerer laid down his quill and left the ink to dry. He climbed the stairs to bed, to a deep, dreamless sleep, soothed by the sounds of terror.

Eleanor's tears smudged the story of Charles Entwhistle, her father. She closed the book and ran her fingertips over the cover. *The Book of Bones,* it read.

It was not the only thing she had stolen from the sorcerer's house, climbing through the open window when she was sure he must be sleeping.

She placed the book next to the mortar and pestle, the peacock feather pen, the bottle of red ink, and a shovel taken from the shed behind her house on a patch of grass in the graveyard.

"You'll be resting soon," she said, though she did not expect the ghosts to hear her.

One by one, she tore the stories from the book and buried each in a shallow hole, matching the names of the authors with the headstones. She saved her father for last, and when she was done, only one blank page still clung to the binding.

The sorcerer's rose was still on the grave, resting just below the name of a woman who had been only twenty-two when she died.

Eleanor began to dig. Her muscles ached and she was so very tired now, but she kept on digging until wood cracked beneath her shovel. She closed her eyes and pulled free the first bone she touched. She threw it into the stone bowl, wiping her hand on her sweater. The bone was old, brittle, easy to smash to dust.

"Let's see how *you* like it," she said, glaring in the direction of the sorcerer's cottage. She mixed the ink, gathered a drop of it on the pen, and opened the book to the empty page.

My name is Lucretia Ludwig . . .

It was, Eleanor thought, her best story yet. Full of good parts, as many as she could cram on one page. And when she was finished she ripped this one out, too, and held it above her head until the wind caught it and took it away.

The village was silent; the cottage at the end of the lane was empty. Mrs. Humphries said she'd seen Mr. Ludwig run off in the middle of the night, screaming, leaving nothing but a trail of deep footprints across the field. Eleanor smiled and sat on the school wall with her best friend Sarah, and looked down at the graveyard where the ghosts rested in peace.

Drawer Eight: FAIRY TALES

My dear Curators,

Following are three tales that we left, rather hurriedly, stuffed beneath straw mattresses at an inn we now know caters to vampires. I have retrieved them and, upon rereading our writings, have found it most enlightening to read the original fairy tales on which they are based. These are: *Ole Lukøje* by Hans Christian Andersen ("The Sandman Cometh"); *The Shadow*, also by Hans Christian Andersen ("Jack Shadow"); and *The Twelve Dancing Princesses* ("The Shoes That Were Danced to Pieces").

Be well and curious,

Curator Bachmann

THE SHOES THAT WERE DANCED TO PIECES

by Katherine Catmull

Our father is a bad man. We hate him.

He has twelve daughters, and I am the youngest. He is the king, but when he dies, none of us shall rule. He laughs at the idea. Although he has twelve daughters like twelve strong trees, like a sheaf of wheat; although we are some of us brilliant, some of us strong and fast, and some of us tenderly kind, and some of us able to talk a flock of birds or people into following wherever she leads—despite all that, he laughs at the idea of a woman ruler.

"I'd more likely leave my kingdom to my dogs," he says.

When my oldest sister tries to lay the case for fairness, or for sanity—that he could choose one of us other than her, even, or that perhaps we could rule together, lend each of our separate strengths to lead the kingdom to a new happiness and peace (for it has seen little of either under his clumsy, brutal rule)—our father mocks her, says in a high, lisping voice (and she doesn't lisp, and her voice is low and cool), "Oh, Daddy, pwease, I want to wear the pwetty crown; it will show off my pwetty shining eyes!"

We hate him. My eldest sister hates him most of all. He would never give her the tutors she begged for, so she has learned and studied in secret all her life. She is the cleverest of us all.

Father intended to give the rulership to some stupid, brutal boy he would choose to marry one of us. But we had other plans. We said, we'll never be married, never. Though we will not rule, we will keep our own freedom until we die.

One morning, as we lay in our twelve beds, my sister Rêve sat up straight and fast. Her eyes were shining and wild. "I have had one of my dreams," she said. Rêve is a great dreamer and knows how to dream things true. But all she would say was that that night, after the king our father went to bed, we should all dress in our favorite, our loveliest, our wildest dresses, and wear our dancing shoes.

We did as she said. "Now see what I dreamed," said Rêve. She knocked three times on the wooden headboard of our eldest sister's bed: *knock, knock, knock.*

For a moment, nothing happened. And then—oh, and

then—the bed sank away, as if sinking into a great black lake. And beneath the bed were stone stairs, going down, down, down.

So down the stairs we went, in our clothes of ebony silk, of cherry-wine velvet, of lilac lace. Our soft dancing shoes made no noise at all on the stone steps.

At the bottom of the staircase, we entered a forest where the trees were made of filigreed silver.

Next we came through another forest, where the trees were shaped of shimmering gold, delicate gold leaves trembling as we stirred the air around them in our passing. The gold made the air feel warm.

Then we moved through a third forest, whose trees were cut from diamond. Each twig and leaf glittered hard and bright around us, and in that forest I felt as cold as if the trees were carved of ice.

We emerged onto the shore of a vast black lake, a lake that mirrored a vast black sky, so both seemed crowded with diamond stars, and no moon at all. Floating before us were twelve boats, each a different color, the colors darkened and subdued under the pale stars.

In each boat sat a young man, each quite different, skin dark or fair, but each with the same mournful smile and something ghostly around the eyes and mouth.

I chose the ghost boy whose boat might have been sky

blue, in the light. When he helped me in, his hand was as cold as the diamond forest.

The ghost boys rowed us in perfect silence to an island where a crystal castle stood. Warm lights moved and glowed inside the castle, like fire caught behind glass.

Inside the castle was an orchestra made up of forest animals—a grave jay with a tiny violin, and a white stag with a cello, and a smiling fox on a stool with a clarinet—oh so many of them, many more. And their music was wild, and it was mournful, too. The music had fire and rage underneath it to match our fire and rage, and it made us want to do nothing but dance.

So dance we did with our cold and ghosty boys. We danced out our rage all the wild night, as the violin-bearing birds swirled above our heads, the fiery lights swirling too as we swirled in the dance, our heads flung back, our feet mad beneath us.

When the eastern horizon began to soften, the boys rowed us back to the edge of the lake, and we walked through the icy diamond forest, and the shimmering gold one, and the delicate silver one, and back up the stairs to our room. On the floor beside each bed, we left our shoes in shreds and pieces.

The next morning, the wretched maid told our father about our shoes. He demanded to know what had happened.

But we were half dead from our long night, and we said nothing at all. Even my sister who always talks back just looked at him, her face pale and empty, and turned away.

He ordered that we must always have shoes, and left. New shoes were brought that afternoon.

The next night, we went dancing again: we danced our anger. And we danced our anger the next night, too, and the next and the next and the next. Every morning, our new shoes lay in shreds on the floor beside our beds; every morning, our father would shout and argue and insult us.

But we were turning half ghost ourselves by day, with all our life in the night, and we only looked at him from dark-circled eyes and yawned.

Our father made an announcement to the kingdom. Any man who could solve the mystery, he would marry off to one of us and make his heir. But if the man tried for three nights and could not solve the mystery, he would lose his head.

"That should motivate them," said our father. His cruelty, his cruelty.

A prince from a far land came to try. Father gave him the room beside ours and left the door between open, which shamed and angered us. But my clever eldest sister made a potion, and put it in fine wine, and offered it to the prince with falsely loving words.

The potion made him sleep all night, and we were left to our raging revels. He slept through three nights, bewildered each morning at how it had happened.

On the third morning, my father had his head chopped off with an axe.

My heart wavered at this, for he had not seemed a bad man, only a hopeful and arrogant one. But my eldest sister, whose rage was greater, laughed. "It is what he deserves," she said. "It is what they all deserve."

Then she added, so perhaps her heart was not quite eaten with anger: "Anyway, it is father who kills them, not I."

More princes came. More princes tried. More lost their heads. My eldest sister's laugh became uglier and too much like my father's.

Then no men came for a long time. We danced out our rage every night. Every morning we grew paler, but our eyes were bright and hot inside their dark circles. My father's anger grew, because something was happening that he could not control.

But that his daughters grew into ghosts before his eyes: that worried him not at all.

After a year of the dancing, a new man came to try. He was different from the others, older, and no prince at all, but a common soldier who had been wounded in the leg, so that he limped badly and could fight no more. He told us that he had met a strange old woman and shared his food with her, and she had repaid him by telling him of our father's offer, "as well as with advice, and a small gift."

I did not like to hear that, for there is great power in the gratitude of strange old women.

My father said, "I hope her gift was an iron neck," and laughed.

When my eldest sister brought this new man the doctored wine and false words, he watched her out of dark eyes, and I thought I saw something like pity in them, which confused and frightened me. But he drank—or we thought he drank. And when the night came, he slept—or we thought he slept.

And yet when we slipped down the stairs that night, I was sure I heard a heavy, uneven gait behind me.

But when I turned, I saw nothing at all.

When we passed through the silver forest, I was sure I heard the limping steps behind me still. And I did hear, I know I heard, a sudden crack, like the snapping of a branch. I looked wildly around. "It was probably an animal," said my sister Tendresse. "Calm yourself, calm yourself."

So I put the limping, swinging, invisible step out of my mind, and out of my hearing, and found my ghostly boy, and danced my raging dance all night in the fiery crystal palace.

The next morning, when the soldier said, as they all

had said, "But I don't understand how I could have fallen asleep," I felt better. My imagination must have been playing tricks on me—my imagination, and perhaps my respect for strange old women.

In the silver forest that night, when I heard the limping, broken steps behind me, I said to myself firmly: "Your imagination."

And at the crack of the branch in the golden forest, I said to myself, "An animal."

Still, I could not throw myself into the black lake of our dance as deeply as usual.

In the morning, the soldier said, "Only one more night! It certainly doesn't look good for me." So I thought it must be all right after all.

And yet that third night, the heavy, limping gait behind me felt like the footfall of Death. The crack of the branch in the diamond forest thrust a shard of ice into my heart.

And as I danced, I swear as I danced with my cold, mournful, ghostly boy, I felt something touch my arm now and then, something I could not see, as if that Death walked among us in the dance.

That morning, my father came with guards to take the soldier away to be beheaded. They found him sitting politely at the edge of his neatly made bed, holding in his lap a silver branch, a golden branch, and a diamond one. As we watched from our room in despair, he told the whole story of what we did each night, holding up the branches one at a time for proof.

The king our father laughed and laughed, and clapped the soldier too hard on his back, and jeered at us. "They want to rule the kingdom, and yet they spend their nights giggling and dancing, like the empty heads they are." So said my father, who did not know, had never seen, our raging, raging dance.

The soldier said nothing. My father stopped laughing and said, "Then take whichever you want for a wife— Bellaluna is the prettiest by far—and I'll set you up in a castle, and then you can wait for me to die, which I hope is a long damn wait." He walked out, the guards behind him.

The soldier turned to us with his dark, opaque eyes. He said, "I think you are all quite beautiful, and much too beautiful for a man like me. Also, I will not take or choose, as if you were toys in a shop; but I will ask, and I will offer my pledge and my faith and my respect."

He turned to my oldest sister. "I am no longer a boy, and I wish a wife who is my equal or better in wisdom. I have been watching you for three nights, and I believe that is you. I will need your wisdom to help me make this land a more peaceful place, for I have had enough of fighting. If you will have me, I will make you my queen and co-ruler, and we will heal the kingdom together. You do not need to give me your answer now."

And he limped away to be shown his new castle.

I watched my eldest sister that night, over the ten narrow beds of my sleeping sisters between us. She lay back with her hands behind her head and her eyes wide open, considering.

In the morning she said to us, "I do not know how to give him my trust, but I am going to give him my trust anyway. My anger has danced through too many pairs of shoes. He is a new man, and I will try a new way."

So the banns were made and the wedding held, with great pomp and many white horses and silver lace and bells. In the following weeks we visited them at their castle, and we saw a new way between a man and a woman, that we had never conceived of before.

One by one, with our father's shrugged permission, we moved to the new castle to live. My sister has filled it with books and art and mathematical instruments and everything our father ever denied us. We sleep well at night, and we have lost our ghostly look, and we live in the world around us.

Our father is a bad man. We hate our father.

But one day our father will die. And together with this wounded man, we will make a new and better kingdom.

Once our father dies.

THE SANDMAN COMETH

by Claire Legrand

When Harvey goes to bed on Saturday night, his heart is black and hot. In general, he's a good kid, but he's suffered one too many indignities today, and thirteen-year-old boys have very little patience to begin with.

First of all, there's the matter of the dolls. His eight-year-old sister Jessie left her dolls all over the floor after a morning of manic play with her friends from next door. Harvey stepped on them and tripped over them one too many times, and finally lost his temper and kicked one of them into the wall. Naturally, he happened to kick the one with the porcelain face. It shattered, and Jessie was an inconsolable mess for the rest of the day.

Secondly, there's the matter of his parents. Did they reprimand Jessie for leaving her toys strewn about so irresponsibly? No, they didn't. All they did was punish

Harvey for committing the understandable and relatively minor crime of kicking a doll into a wall. The unfairness of it makes Harvey's insides seethe.

And that leads to the third thing, which is Harvey not being able to go to the movies tonight with Dennis and Jordan and Enrique and Enrique's dad, who is far cooler than Harvey's dad will ever be. Harvey can't go because he's grounded. He's grounded because he reacted like any sane person would after stepping on dolls that his little sister refused to clean up.

There is no justice in the world tonight. That's one of the primary thoughts on Harvey's mind as he falls into a tempestuous sleep.

The other thought is this: "I hate them. I hate all three of them. I want to wake up in the morning and have the house to myself so they can't annoy me ever again."

(Oh, dear.)

Harvey wakes up in the morning to a blissfully quiet house. In fact, at first he thinks he might have woken up in the wrong house somehow, even though that makes no sense. He doesn't hear his sister running around singing, he doesn't hear his father banging dishes and pans in the kitchen, and he doesn't hear his mother's shows blaring on the television.

He falls back asleep, fantasizing that they've all decided to have mercy on him and spare him the chore of Sunday errands. He decides that when he wakes up again, he'll clean the kitchen so maybe his parents will lessen his punishment. He figures they'll return in a couple of hours.

They don't.

It's been a long day for Harvey. He doesn't understand where his family has gone. At first it's wonderful, having the house to himself. He cleans the kitchen, and even has time after that to play some video games without Jessie running through the living room asking if she can play, too.

He also has time to do his homework. And microwave himself a frozen dinner. And go out on the driveway—after dark, on a school night!—and shoot hoops. It is at this point he remembers to look in the garage. He realizes that his parents and Jessie haven't gone to run errands—unless they've gone on foot, which is unlikely.

Both cars are still parked in the garage.

Harvey is not sleeping well.

Before going to bed, he tried calling some friends of his parents, and also some of Jessie's friends, to see if anyone knew where they were—but the phone didn't work. That was odd; Harvey checked to make sure it was charged, and it was. But it wouldn't dial a single number. Harvey found his parents' cell phones, but they didn't work either.

The television played nothing but static. Video games worked, but not the television. The computer wouldn't connect to the internet. And, as Henry lay there on his bed trying to quiet his mind, he realized with a creeping sense of dread that when he had been outside shooting hoops earlier, he hadn't seen a single other living thing on his street—not a person, not a bird, not the DeRosarios' fat cat.

But now Harvey is asleep, tossing and turning as these worries stew in his mind. He doesn't see the man enter his room, quiet as shadow. The man is tall and thin and dark, with a crisp black suit and a spotless black umbrella. He leans on the umbrella and watches Harvey for a long time. He is smiling and waiting for Harvey to wake up.

When Harvey does wake up, it is in the middle of the night, and the first thing he sees is the man, still and slender.

Harvey screams, and the man lets him. The man looks bored.

When Harvey is done screaming, the man says, "Have you finished?"

The question takes Harvey aback. He replies, "I guess."

"Good." The man approaches, his coattails trailing behind him like long black tongues. "I'll make this simple. I have your family, and I'll only bring them back if you do exactly as I say."

Harvey is at first dumbstruck and then outraged. Remorse floods through him like a sick tidal wave, and the man watching him seems to shudder, like he can feel Harvey's emotion and finds it delicious.

"What do you mean you have them?" Harvey demands. "Where are they? And who are you?"

"I can't tell you where they are," the man says. "As for your second question, I have many names. I am Morpheus, I am Ole Lukøje, I am the Bringer of Dreams. You may call me the Sandman."

With that, the Sandman bows, cutting the air like a black scythe.

Harvey is fairly practical for a thirteen-year-old boy. He knows that such things as Sandmen don't exist. And yet here is the Sandman, bowing before him. And here is his empty house, and here is the phone and the computer and the television that don't work. And here is his empty street.

He balls his fists into his bedsheets. "You have my parents, and my sister."

The Sandman inclines his head. "As I said."

"Why?"

"Because I need your help." A small smile curls across his face. "And now, so do they."

Harvey draws a deep breath. He is terrified; he has never been especially brave. He is the boy who stands on the bank of the creek and watches the other boys swing on the rope into the water.

"What do I have to do?"

The Sandman takes a vial from his pocket and dips a gloved finger into it. "You must complete for me six tasks. If you succeed"—he smears a grainy, rank-smelling tar over Harvey's eyelids, sealing them shut—"you may be able to save your family."

Harvey falls back onto the bed, as heavy and cold as a stone. A shiny substance plugs up his ears and mouth and nose and eyes. Still, though, his eyelids flutter. He is dreaming.

The Sandman settles onto the foot of Harvey's bed, soft and sleek as a cat. He waits.

Harvey awakes in a jungle.

The air is ripe with the smells of rot and sweaty animal fur and tropical flowers. The air is so steamy that Harvey finds it difficult to breathe. He holds in his hand a sealed envelope, addressed in an immaculate hand to The One Who Waits.

A breath wafts across Harvey's neck. He whirls, but no one is there. He feels cold, ghostly fingers on his shoulders. He slaps them away, but ends up only slapping himself.

Stop slapping yourself and listen to me, says the Sandman's voice, deep inside Harvey's head. With every word, that same cold breath caresses Harvey's neck. *This is your first task: Deliver this letter to The One Who Waits, who lives at the other end of the jungle. Do not stop for anything. Do not eat the fruit.*

Then, just like that, the Sandman's presence disappears. Harvey is alone.

None of this makes sense, but the letter in Harvey's hand feels real enough, so he figures he should go along with this, just in case. Anyway, delivering a letter doesn't sound so hard, and he's not hungry, so avoiding fruit won't be a problem.

But then Harvey begins to walk. The way is overgrown and dripping with moisture, and he notices that the branches hang heavy with fruit—at first just normal fruit like bananas and oranges, and although they are brightly colored, they don't particularly tempt Henry. But then he sees mangoes and passion fruit, and kiwi and pineapples, and soon Henry is pushing aside piles of grapes and bushes laden with strawberries, and countless other unfamiliar fruits, yellows and blues and purples, brush against his face and arms, tickle his cheeks.

The fruits' perfumes twist up his nose and make him feel faint. They smell increasingly delicious—tart and sweet, juicy and tender, and some of them smell like fruit but some of them smell like choice meat, and others like glazed pastries.

Soon, Harvey cannot help himself. He truly wasn't hungry, but now his stomach twists painfully. He is frantic with craving. He plucks a bright red fruit from its branch and pops it into his mouth. He chews, and the fruit bursts; he swallows, and juice and seeds drip down his chin. He feels, for a moment, the most satisfied he has ever felt.

Then the jungle begins to quake around him. Starting close to him, and then spreading out in waves, the plants shrivel and blacken and turn to dust. Harvey hurries through their remains, the taste of the stolen fruit turning sour on his tongue. It seems to him that the dying branches grab for his feet as he runs. He tramples piles of rotting fruit that squelch between his toes. The ground is quaking apart, a crack in the earth trailing his steps.

He emerges on the other side of the jungle just in time. The whole thing collapses behind him, and Harvey pants to catch his breath. That's when he sees it: the envelope, fallen open in his hand. The letter inside it is sopping wet, black with ash, and the words drip off the ruined paper and onto the ground, where they collect in steaming black puddles. The words left on the page are gibberish. The letter is unreadable.

Harvey feels a shadow fall over his face. He looks up and sees a tall, hooded figure standing at a crossroads in a green field. The figure holds out its hand, which looks surprisingly human.

"Are you The One Who Waits?" asks Henry.

The figure nods, and Henry shoves the letter into its hand and closes his eyes.

Harvey wakes back in his bedroom and promptly gets sick on the floor. Apparently, the fruit did not agree with him.

The Sandman watches him, irritated. "You ate the fruit."

"I couldn't help it."

"You ruined the letter."

Harvey turns, afraid. "You said deliver the letter, and I did."

The Sandman's mouth grows thin. "I suppose I shall have to be more specific in the future."

"Where was that place?"

"There are many places you can't access but I can. That was one of them."

"What is all this *about*, anyway?"

"Does it matter? If you want your family back, you'll perform my tasks regardless."

"But—"

"If I wanted to give you any more information," says the Sandman smoothly, "I would do so. Don't ask me pointless questions."

He smears a fresh coat of tar across Harvey's eyes, and Harvey falls back into his pillows for the second time.

Harvey is on a boat painted red and white, with silver sails that spread out like wings.

The air here is quiet and still, and the prow of the boat pushes through a thick black swamp littered with dead trees and alligator carcasses.

Harvey takes a step, and something crunches beneath his foot. He looks down and almost gags.

The deck of the boat is covered with the bodies of dead swans.

Find the princesses, the Sandman whispers from far away, his breath carrying the stench of the tar from his vial. *One is the true princess; six are impostors. Find them and pick the right one.*

Something terrible has happened here; that much is obvious to Harvey. He sees that the sky is shifting, full of malevolent clouds. He sees lightning on the horizon but hears no answering thunder. He sees thin houses built on stilts, rising up out of the water, and he calls out, hoping whoever lives there will help him find his way, but no one answers.

Harvey stands at the wheel and steers the boat for countless hours, until blisters form on his palms. It's impossible to track the time; the light in the sky never changes. Finally, Harvey sees a black shape in the distance that looks castlelike, and princesses live in castles, so he decides to head that way.

He arrives at the gates of a castle made of stone and iron. At the gate stand seven identical figures—all in spiked armor and voluminous cloaks. They wear helmets that resemble crowns, and battle axes hang from their belts. In their hands they hold powdered cakes in the shape of pigs. They offer them to Harvey for a taste.

Harvey climbs down from the boat and trudges across a tumble of rocks to reach the gate where the princesses stand, for of course that's who they are. As he walks, panic grows inside him. These princesses look exactly alike. He cannot see their faces. How is he to tell the real one from the impostors?

Harvey inspects them, licking his dry lips. He is nearly ready to give up when he notices that one of the cakes is different from the others: it is missing a bite-sized piece. It's a risky guess, but Harvey decides that if *he* were surrounded by six impostors, he would want to do something to show he was the real Harvey. Perhaps, he thinks, the real princess managed to sneak a bite, and this was a sign.

There is nothing else to do. Harvey kneels in front of this princess and bows his head. "Your Highness," he says, "you are the one true princess."

From above and around him comes the sound of sliding steel. He looks up in time to see the other six princesses unsheathe their axes. They let out inhuman shrieks. The true princess, the one Harvey has chosen, rips off her helmet, revealing a face so hard and beautiful that Harvey feels tears come to his eyes. She raises her axe to defend him, and Harvey turns away, shielding his face in her cloak.

Harvey gasps awake in his bed. His sheets are soaked with sweat and cling to him like clammy fingers.

"Well?" The Sandman sounds bored, but his eyes are alight with interest. "What happened?"

"I found her." Harvey is still catching his breath. "At least I think so. Her cake had a bite missing from it. That's how I knew."

"I'm not sure what cake you're talking about," says the Sandman, "but I'd know if you had failed. Don't expect me to congratulate you, though."

Harvey frowns. His ears are still ringing with the clashes of axes, and he's more than a little annoyed. "I don't. I expect you to release my family after I win at your stupid games."

The Sandman looks grave and full of secrets. "They are not games. Don't make the mistake of treating them as such, Harvey."

Harvey shivers. "Fine. Can we get on with it? I've got four tasks to go."

A grin spreads across the Sandman's face. He seals Harvey's eyes shut for a third time, and Harvey slips back into darkness.

Harvey is being thrown against walls of rock.

At least, that's what it feels like. He breathes salt and is shaking with cold. He struggles up to breathe and is pushed back under. Something throws him into somersaults through a thick, overwhelming heaviness.

He remembers, somewhere in the back of his mind, that he is asleep, that the Sandman is waiting patiently at the foot of his bed, but that doesn't stop Harvey from feeling like he is about to die. He needs to breathe, he needs air, he needs ground under his feet—

He wakes up on a beach awash with sunlight. A white beach littered with shells and seaweed and the corpses of sea creatures washed ashore. He is sopping wet, and struggles to lift himself up and look around. Behind him stretches a great blue sea, sparkling and calm after a night of storms. Harvey coughs up ocean water. His stomach is burning.

Find the girl disguised as a bird, whispers the Sandman, his cold, faraway fingers wiping Harvey's wet hair back from his eyes. *Set her free. Avoid the Good Doctor.*

This task makes the least amount of sense yet, but Harvey forces himself across the beach and into a meadow. At first there is nothing but grass, but then ruins appear— cottages and temples, bridges and towers. They are gray and crumbling, but still beautiful. There are roads and there is a market, and people milling about. Harvey hears them chattering and feels relieved. The chattering has a friendly sound to it. Perhaps he will actually have help this time.

But when Harvey gets closer, he notices something startling about the people in this ruined village: they have beaks.

They have feathers and clawed feet. They have wings and black beady eyes. Their faces are part human; there is human flesh there, and human teeth. But at the shoulders the human flesh transitions into black bird feathers, and the human teeth line yellow bird beaks instead of lips. The bird-people speak in disjointed words and rattling squawks. They neither fly nor walk but instead hop around, like they don't know what to do with themselves.

At the center of the town is an enormous temple with a red tiled roof. Harvey sees a figure in white standing there, surveying the domain from a terrace. Harvey ducks his head and hurries into the shadows. Could that white figure be the Good Doctor? Whoever *that* is.

What has happened here? Harvey can't know for sure, but he is a smart boy and constructs a hypothesis. Perhaps the Good Doctor isn't so good at all. Perhaps the Good Doctor conducts experiments, crafting birds and people into bird-people.

The air smells like medicine and burnt feathers. Harvey doesn't like it.

He hears a ruckus and peeks around the corner of a building. A crowd of bird-people gather in a circle. There are hen-people and duck-people and a giant gobbling turkey with the face of a man and clawed fingers.

They are making fun of someone—a small bird-person whose feathers don't look quite right.

Harvey's skin tingles. It is the girl disguised as a bird. He must free her. Though the Good Doctor watches from on high—surely that's who that is, up on that terrace—Harvey must free this girl. The bullying bird-people are kicking the girl's legs, pecking her skin. They are jeering at her, calling her stupid, calling her beautiful in a mocking fashion.

Harvey is filled with horror and rage. He rushes to the girl and grabs her arm, dislodging pasted-on feathers. He runs with her toward the ocean, a mob of bird-people at their heels. The bird-people are vicious. They peck with their beaks and tear with their human teeth. They curse Harvey and the girl. They call for the Good Doctor.

Looking back over his shoulder, Harvey sees that the terrace is empty.

"Where are you taking me?" gasps the girl. Her tied-on beak has fallen. Her feathers are flying off.

Harvey doesn't have an answer for her. His legs carry them into the ocean, and they dive. Everything in him recoils at the idea of returning to the sea that nearly drowned him, but drowning is better than becoming one of the things that are chasing them.

Water fills his ears. He hears a man yelling something on the shore. He feels rubber gloved hands reaching for him. He loses his hold on the girl's hand and opens his mouth to call for her, but he is lost in blackness and foam.

Harvey wakes shivering. He is curled into a knot on his bed, but he still feels the churning of the water and the pinch of the Good Doctor's hands.

The Sandman sits quietly beside him, inspecting him. "Well? Is she freed?"

"I don't know." Harvey is distraught. "I took her into the ocean. There was nowhere else to go. Those bird-people were chasing us. I panicked."

The Sandman nods. "I think that should be fine. She is a good swimmer. And the sea holds many secrets, some of which are escape routes."

"What is *that* supposed to mean?" Harvey is reaching the end of his rope, but he is only halfway finished.

The Sandman cocks his head and regards Harvey. The motion is too birdlike for Harvey to feel comfortable. He turns away.

"Whatever," he says. "Never mind. Let's just keep going."

"You didn't like seeing her there, did you? Seeing her trapped and bullied?"

"Of course I didn't! It was wrong." Harvey's hands clench into fists. "She didn't deserve that. No one does."

The Sandman nods. "I see." He is quiet for a long time. "Well, then." He takes out his vial, and Harvey closes his eyes. He feels the cool brush of the Sandman's fingers, and hears him whisper, "You are halfway there, Harvey."

Harvey wakes up on a bed of moss in a church graveyard.

Bells are ringing, and the church windows are full of light. Harvey sits in the damp autumn wind and waits for the Sandman's instructions. The air smells of rain.

Marry her.

That's all the Sandman says, and Harvey is concerned; that instruction seems particularly ominous. But he doesn't have a choice.

Ah, but you do.

Harvey is startled to hear the Sandman speak again, and he realizes the Sandman is right. Harvey does have a choice. He doesn't have to go through these tasks. He can return home, and leave his family to their fate.

But he can't do that. He will do the right thing.

Even with that decided, what he finds inside the church nearly sends him running. It is a congregation of people, and a priest and a bride, and an organist playing Pachelbel's Canon in D. Typical, except for the fact that the people in this church all wear masks. The masks are shaped like mouse faces, and are plain and plastic. It might have been funny, in another situation: a group of dressed-up people wearing mouse masks. The people stand up and turn to watch Harvey as he walks down the aisle.

A great terror seizes him. Now that he is closer, he can see that the masks aren't tied on; they are sewn on. They are sewn with ugly black stitches, plastic to skin, and the skin is raw and red.

Harvey steps up beside the bride. She takes his hand, and they are married by the priest whose voice is muffled by his mask. The final step, the priest explains, is up to Harvey. A mask sits on the altar. It is for Harvey to wear.

Harvey is sweating. He cries out for the Sandman, but there is no answer. For several long seconds, he considers running.

Then, ashamed, he takes hold of the mask and places it on his face. The mask settles into position, and a sharp pain works its way around Harvey's chin, then cheeks, then forehead, affixing the mask to his skull. It burns. He screams and drops to his knees. His bride pats him on the shoulder, soothing him. The priest leads the congregation in a hymn.

Harvey wakes on the floor of his bedroom, scratching at his face. The Sandman kneels beside him and catches his wild arms before he can do any more damage.

"There, there."

Harvey pushes him away. "You didn't say I would have to do that. You said *marry her*, not sew a mask to my face!"

"The masking ritual is part of marriage ceremonies there."

"There? There *where?*"

The Sandman sighs. "We've been over this, Harvey."

"So, I'm married to some woman who wears a mouse mask in some place I can't go to unless you send me there. What does that even mean? What will happen to her now that she's married me?"

"Well," the Sandman says, smiling, "that will be interesting for you to find out someday, won't it?"

"I hate you." Harvey climbs back into bed. He is tired and weak. "I hate you for doing this to me."

"Everyone hates me. But sometimes these things must be done."

Harvey lies back in bed, rigid as a board, full of anger. He refuses to acknowledge that the Sandman sounded sad, just then. He refuses to acknowledge anything but his own rage. It gives him strength.

"Twice more, Harvey," says the Sandman, and soon Harvey's eyes are cool with sleep.

Harvey is in an attic, sitting beside a dollhouse.

The attic window is dirty and ajar; a thin beam of sunlight shines on the dollhouse, illuminating its rooms, which look as though a storm has ripped through them. The doll furniture is upturned; the doll portraits have fallen from the walls.

The dolls themselves are scattered about, lying on their faces, straddling the roof, stuffed under sofas.

Put the dollhouse to rights, comes the Sandman's voice, *and the dolls back into their proper places.*

Harvey breathes a sigh of relief. That does not sound so hard, compared to everything else, so he gets to work at once.

He removes every doll and piece of furniture and sets them on the floor. The rooms empty, he takes a moment to inspect the dollhouse: five bedrooms, two bathrooms, a dining room, a kitchen, a parlor, a living room, a game room, an attic, a basement, a garage. Four floors altogether, counting the attic and basement.

A strange feeling comes over him as he begins putting the furniture back into place. He can't know where the furniture is supposed to go, and yet he does. A sense of rightness that tugs his hands here and there—the sofa goes against the red wall in the living room; the desk goes in the green bedroom beside the fireplace.

The more furniture he replaces, the more familiar this dollhouse becomes. He feels that he has played with this dollhouse before, even though he knows that to be impossible. He feels that he has *lived* in this dollhouse before, which is even more impossible.

Harvey retrieves the first doll—the mother, he assumes. She has blond hair and is wearing a blue dress. He puts her in the living room, watching television. He puts the father in the kitchen, getting something to eat. He puts the brother at the top of the basement stairs.

Somehow, Harvey knows exactly where each doll should go. He knows their names—the father, George; the mother, Pamela; the son, Herman. He knows their hopes and fears, which strikes him as odd; dolls don't have hopes and fears.

The last doll is a small girl. Her name is Bertha, and Harvey knows she needs to go into the basement. He knows it like he knows two added to another two makes four. But when Harvey turns the tiny basement doorknob, he hears a scream.

It is Bertha. He knows she is screaming, but the scream is not coming from her; it's coming from everywhere.

"Don't make me go down there!" Bertha screams. She is terrified, and that makes Harvey terrified, because he can feel her fear like it's his own. "Please, he'll lock me in!"

He? Harvey turns to the brother doll, Herman. The details of his face have rubbed off over time, but Harvey gets the feeling that Herman is a brute. Harvey pauses, uncertain. He knows Bertha's place is in the basement, but he doesn't want to put her there. But if he doesn't put her there, he will fail in his task, and the Sandman will keep his family.

"Please, don't do it," sobs Bertha. She is now a ghostly

apparition, a small girl with braids and braces. "Please, don't put me down there. He'll lock me in; he'll trap me. I hate being down there. It scares me!"

Harvey sees another apparition at the far end of the attic—Herman, the brother, full-sized and approaching fast.

"But you're a doll!" Harvey protests.

"Maybe to you, I'm a doll," says Bertha, "but to me, I'm real! I wasn't always like this! I didn't always live here! Oh, please, please don't do it!" Her hands are clasped, like she is praying to Harvey. He sees ghostly tears run down her cheeks.

Harvey considers her for a few more seconds. He could throw the Bertha doll into the basement and shut the tiny basement door. He could.

But he doesn't. Bertha is too afraid. He grabs the Herman doll instead, and the Herman apparition, on the other side of the dollhouse, freezes.

"Put me down," he says quietly.

Harvey stands. "No," he says, and though he is afraid, he throws the Herman doll out the attic window, into the sun.

Harvey awakes in his bedroom, crying. He finds the Sandman and falls to his knees.

"Please," he chokes out, "please, don't hurt my family. I couldn't do it. I couldn't put the dolls back in their proper places. The girl doll, Bertha. She was scared. I couldn't trap her in that basement. Herman was scaring her. The basement scares her. Please, please."

The Sandman kneels and tilts up Harvey's chin. "Ah," he says, "but you did put the dolls in their proper places." He wipes Harvey's cheeks. "Some souls deserve to be thrown out, and you did that beautifully."

Harvey sniffles, backing away. The Sandman is looking kindly at him, and somehow that's the most disturbing thing of all. "You mean, you won't hurt my family?"

"Not for that, no. In fact, if you had put Bertha in the basement, we would be having a very different conversation right now. You did right. But you do have one more task to complete."

Harvey climbs back into bed. He is exhausted, but a little less so now that he has heard the Sandman's approval. The kind words wrap around his heart, cushioning it.

"Sleep, Harvey," whispers the Sandman. Lovingly, he seals Harvey's eyes shut for the last time.

Harvey awakes in a village where it is almost midnight. In a few minutes, it will be Sunday.

The village lies nestled in a small valley between black

mountains with jagged peaks, and the fields surrounding this village are on fire.

It is a cold, silver fire, so cold that it feels hot. Harvey shields his eyes from the brightness, stumbling through the door of the nearest building—a small cottage with a metal roof. He peeks out through his fingers, watching the chaos outside. People run to and fro along the streets, shouting, grabbing items from their homes, abandoning their village for the hills. Harvey sees why: the silver fire is approaching the outskirts. Soon, it will devour the entire settlement.

"Harvey," says a familiar voice, and Harvey turns, startled, for there, in a portrait hung on the wall, sits the Sandman in a high-backed red chair, twirling his black umbrella.

"What are you doing here? Why aren't you talking to me in my head?"

The Sandman shrugs. "I like variation."

"What do I have to do this time?"

The Sandman smiles, as if he appreciates how Harvey has come to accept his own mysterious ways. "The fire you see is no ordinary fire. It is star-fire. Find the fallen star and put it back in its proper place before it burns down this village."

Harvey is aghast. "You mean, back into space?"

"Where else would a star go?"

"But that doesn't make sense! How can I possibly do that?"

"That's entirely up to you, Harvey." The Sandman rises from his chair and walks out of the picture frame without another word.

Harvey can't waste any time. He rushes outside and into the wall of silver fire. It burns him; it feels as though he is plunging into arctic waters. He can hardly open his eyes. He crawls like a blind baby on the ground, searching for the fallen star.

His hand lands upon a hard, cold stone, smooth as ice. Harvey cracks open his eyes and sees a pulsing light, brighter even than the fire. It scalds his retinas, and blinds him. Where the star touches his palm, it brands his skin. But he holds it tight anyway and stumbles through the village, trailing sparks behind him.

"Point me to the highest mountain," he tells everyone he encounters, and with the villagers' help, he finds his way to the base of a black mountain so tall that its peak seems to brush the moon.

Harvey begins to climb. He is burned and aching, and in so much pain that tears stream down his face constantly. The salt inflames his wounds, but he soldiers on, because more painful than anything is the thought that if he fails, he will have failed his family.

He climbs, and he climbs. The air grows thinner, and Harvey starts to wheeze. He is cold, and he is hunted by mountain cats, but something seems to deflect them every time they pounce—maybe it's a black umbrella being swung like an axe, or maybe it's some kind of protective force field emanating from the star in Harvey's hand. Who knows? Harvey doesn't.

He reaches the icy slopes of the mountain peak, and can climb no farther. He looks up with eyes that can no longer see. He feels moonlight on his ruined skin. He reaches back, his brittle bones snapping, and throws the star into the sky as far as he can.

He collapses facefirst into the snow.

Harvey is on trial.

He blinks, confused, trying to figure out why and how and where. But it's true: he is in a courtroom, and he doesn't recognize everyone on the jury, but he does see The One Who Waits and the one true princess, the girl disguised as a bird and his mouse-masked bride. He sees Bertha the doll in the lap of her girl-shaped soul.

"Sandman?" Harvey whispers, turning around and around. At least he can see now, and at least his skin has healed. But he is full of fear. He has completed six tasks, but did he complete them well enough? He realizes that this is the end, that now he will learn the fate of his family.

Everyone rises when the judge enters. The judge is handsome and strong, a god among men. He wears an unfamiliar silver uniform and a black velvet cloak. The judge's aide, a bespectacled man, rips down a curtain at the far end of the room, behind which sit Harvey's parents and his sister, Jessie. They do not see him. They do not see anything at all.

Harvey lunges for them, but he has been bound to his chair. From the bench, the judge watches coldly.

"In the case of Harvey Black," the girl disguised as a bird reads, "the jury has reached its verdict."

"Wait!" Harvey struggles against his bindings. "I haven't gotten to speak! I don't have a lawyer! Can't I ask some of the jurors to speak on my behalf? I helped them; I saved them! Ask the Sandman; he'll tell you! Where *is* he?"

"There will be no more interruptions," says the judge, his voice a terrible blend of thousands. "What is the verdict?"

"According to the testimony of the Sandman," says the girl disguised as a bird, "Harvey Black has completed his tasks in a manner satisfying their accord."

Harvey slumps back in his chair. "So my family is safe?"

"Perhaps," intones the judge. "You have a choice now, Harvey. You can go home and wake up, and all this will have been a mere dream—but your family may or may not return with you."

Harvey is outraged. "What do you mean? I did exactly what I was supposed to!"

"Or," the judge continues, "you can stay here and work for the Sandman, and your family will be returned home safely, guaranteed."

"Where is he? Bring him here! He promised, he *promised*!"

Everyone watches Harvey as he cries tears of betrayal and fear, alone on his chair. He cries for a long time, but when he finally looks up, his expression is one of determination.

"Fine," he says, his voice clogged with sadness, "I'll stay here. Let them go. Just let them go."

In an instant, Harvey's parents and sister vanish, and the judge's face melts into a warm smile. His outer skin sheds, revealing a familiar figure: the sallow, dark-eyed Sandman, leaning on his umbrella.

"You've done well, Harvey," says the Sandman as the jury applauds. The Sandman's voice is rough, and his eyes are bright. "I am proud of you. You may go."

Flabbergasted, Harvey says, "What? What do you mean? What just happened? You said—"

"I gave you a terrible choice—save yourself or save

your family, and you chose the latter. Not many would have done that, Harvey. Not many would have kept Bertha out of the basement, or sewn a mask to his own face." The Sandman approaches and puts a hand on each of Harvey's shoulders. Harvey's chains crumble away. "You are special, Harvey. I chose well, and I thank you for proving me right."

Harvey feels a strange warmth at having made the Sandman so proud, even though this man lies at the root of his recent troubles. "You said I could go. Are you telling the truth?"

"I always tell the truth, Harvey, even when it makes people uncomfortable to hear it."

"Who *are* you?"

The Sandman holds out his hands. "I am Morpheus. I am the Bringer of Dreams. I am Ole Lukøje. I am the Old Storyteller, the Dreamwalker, the Sandman. I enter worlds only accessible through dreams, where I right wrongs and put chaos into order. I guide those who die in their sleep to the Lord of the Dead. I wrangle nightmares and coax peace into troubled hearts and coax trouble into the hearts of the content. I am the balance of the universe."

The Sandman crouches. His face is kindly, and Harvey cannot look away from those deep, dark eyes. "Someday, you will replace me, Harvey. You chose it, just now. I can't change that. But I can do this much for you: I can give you what was not given me. I can give you your life first."

He stands and helps Harvey to his feet. "We'll meet again, Harvey Black, when you're old and wrinkled, and your heart slows in your sleep. We'll meet again, and I will teach you everything I know. Until then—" The Sandman takes out the familiar vial.

"But wait!" Harvey says, throwing out his arm. He is suddenly sad to leave. He sees entire worlds in the Sandman's endless eyes. He sees gods and monsters, dreams and death. He sees a lonely man.

But he cannot keep his eyes open, and soon he sees nothing at all.

Harvey wakes up to the smell of breakfast cooking downstairs, the sounds of his family chatting about their day. It is Sunday morning, and he remembers nothing. He feels well rested and stretches in the sunlight.

JACK SHADOW

by Emma Trevayne

The shadow slipped through the night, hid from the sun, stretched out every morning and evening. Through towns and along roads, the shadow slid.

You might not think that a shadow would have a name, but this one did, unpronounceable though it certainly was. It sounded a little like a snake slithering over moss, a little like fairy tears hitting the surface of a river.

But we . . . we shall call him Jack, just for now, because it is easier than snake slithers and fairy tears, and this story is quite difficult enough to tell as it is.

Jack was hunting. He had been for many years, and hoped it would not take much longer. A shadow, you see, needs a person, and this was the one thing he did not currently have.

Over time, he had tried on many, as one might test a

new suit to make sure it was a good fit. The last one, well, he had been nearly right, nearly perfect, but in the end that had made him very wrong.

A city loomed ahead; surely he would find what he was looking for there, with so many people to choose from. Glass towers stood tall among small houses, reminding him of palaces. Of the days of dragons and kings.

Yes, my friends, our Jack the Shadow is that old, and then some.

I do suppose that now, as Jack slips into the city, mingling with all the ordinary shadows, it is a good time to warn you that if Jack ever seeks to become *your* shadow, you must run. Run far and fast and do not look back. I only wish I had been able to warn the others. I, unlike our Jack, am capable of regret.

Then again, you might well never know if Jack, or one like him, has begun to follow you, for he is a dark, sharp-edged blade of a thing.

He moved along the bustling streets, alert, careful, almost disappearing as the sun dropped lower and lower in the sky. He entered a quiet neighborhood full of tall, snow-white houses and old trees that spread leafy branches overhead.

This was promising. And *you* of course will know that when I say *promising* I mean *dreadful,* but to Jack, it was very promising indeed.

Up ahead, on the lawn of a large house, a young boy kicked a ball, always reaching it just a second before his shadow—a real shadow—did. Jack crept toward them.

"Sam!" came a voice from the house. "Time to wash up for dinner!"

"Coming!" the boy called back.

Sam's real shadow started to trail him inside, but Jack caught it and held it back.

"We won't be needing you anymore," Jack said as the front door closed.

Sam's shadow turned around. It trembled in the breeze.

"No," it said. "He's a perfectly good boy and I won't let you hurt him!"

"Hmmm," said Jack. "Why would you think I would hurt him?"

"I've heard of you," it answered. "I heard what you did to that poor man, following him around for years and years, sucking the very life out of him until *he* was more of a shadow than you were!"

Jack laughed. It frightened the birds from the trees. He had been particularly proud of that one, but in the end, the man had not been the perfect fit. He had not wanted to become Jack's shadow, and so there was only one thing that could be done.

"You killed him, and I won't let you do it to Sam."

"I do not think," Jack said, "that you have a choice." Swiftly, he plucked a strand of cobweb from a nearby bush and with it he slit the other shadow's throat.

Now, you and I both know that one could not ordinarily do such a thing with a cobweb, but shadows are not ordinary, and Jack was extraordinary, in the strictest sense of that word. Shadows do not play by the rules, and so the dead shadow shattered into a thousand tiny, black-winged moths and flew away.

The dead shadow had been right about one thing. In fact, it had been right about everything, but it was certainly correct that Sam was a perfectly nice boy. Jack sat at the table while Sam ate, hid in a corner while he did every last bit of his schoolwork, and listened from the closet when his father read to him each night. He followed Sam to school and kicked a ball around the grass with him before dinner.

Jack was sure it was a perfect fit, that it was simply a matter of time.

Sam grew older, always a good boy, but taller, thinner, paler, his veins blue beneath his skin. His mother took him to the doctor, who said Sam was perfectly healthy, but perhaps needed more sleep.

Jack hid under the chair in the doctor's office and laughed. Goose bumps broke out over Sam's skin.

"Sam," Jack said that night, when the lights were out, the house quiet as a tomb.

"Who said that?" Sam asked, sitting bolt upright in bed.

"I'm your shadow." Jack slid from the bed, over to the patch of moonlight on the floor. He stretched high as the ceiling, leaning over the boy in the bed. "You've been very good, but now it is time."

"T-time for what?" Sam blinked, as if he was unsure whether he was truly awake.

"You are not dreaming," said Jack. "It is time. I have followed you since you were young, Sam. I have done everything you asked of me, and now you must do what I ask of you. It is your turn to become *my* shadow."

"I *am* dreaming," Sam replied. "You aren't real." He lay back down and closed his eyes, turning his face into the pillow.

Jack shook with rage, his whole thin, flat body shivering. He slipped from the room, down the stairs, to the kitchen drawer where all the sharp knives were kept. Cobwebs did not work on people, and people follow the rules.

I cannot bear what happened next, just cannot bear it. You can imagine, you can close your eyes and picture it, if you so choose, though I wouldn't choose to. Please forgive me if I don't share everything, describe every drop of blood as it bloomed on the pillow.

I told you already that I wish I could have warned the others, and I only hope this has been enough of a warning for you. And so, rather than describe every last, horrible detail, I will instead ask you to do something for me. Go outside, stand in the sun. Close your eyes and feel it warm your face.

Open them again. Look around.

Is that truly your shadow?

Are you sure?

My dear Curators:

I include this story with some hesitation. I sometimes wonder if those who do not know enough to pay the storyteller might, perhaps, deserve what they get. But since that fate is such a ghastly one, I include this as a sort of cautionary tale, even for those who don't deserve it.

By the way, I am quite sure I shipped you seven shadows after I collected this tale—not six. I really do hope you've found the seventh by now. I cannot put this too strongly: I would not recommend sleeping until it is found.

Curton Cofull

THE STORYTELLER'S SHADOWS

by Katherine Catmull

This is a tale about a storyteller and his shadows. Listen closely, or pay the price.

He's a good storyteller, this man. He prepares. In each new town, before he performs, he spends hours walking the city streets and neighborhood roads, watching.

Where you live, for example, he will buy a sandwich and sit in the shade and watch the people walk by, unnoticed . . . but noticing.

He's a nondescript person himself, almost hard to see. Your eyes somehow sweep past him.

When night creeps up on your town, the storyteller will come and put up a white screen, like a small movie screen, and hang a lamp behind it, so that the light shines through the screen.

But he himself, he will stand off to the side, in the

dark, and all you'll know of him is his soft, hypnotic voice, telling stories, waiting for the crowd to gather.

He's a good storyteller, this man, very good indeed. But what draws people—what draws them every time, and what will draw you—is the shadow puppets.

He charges no entrance fee. "Don't pay till you've seen it," he always says, in a voice like velvet stroked the wrong way. Then he returns to his story, his voice rising and falling, swelling and sinking, out of the darkness.

And as the story swells and sinks, shadowy figures began to move across the screen.

The shadow puppets are simple figures—a child, a dog, a woman, a house, a tree: like that. But the child, the dog, the tree are witchy, jagged versions of themselves, flat and dark and eyeless. Like the puppeteer's voice, sometimes they swell up huge, and sometimes they shrink down small. Sometimes one will distort and twist into something else altogether, something much more disturbing—and then become itself again, acting out the storyteller's words.

(When they come to your town, you—and you alone—will notice that beneath the screen, you can see no sign of a puppeteer. *No feet,* you will whisper, tapping your mother's arm. *Look, no skirt or pants, no hands, nothing back there, so how could*—but your mother will hush you, and call it a theater trick.)

The storyteller never tells the same story twice. He makes a new one every time, set in that town, starring the people of the town. The audience loves that, laughing in recognition at the sandwich maker who tries to slip you day-old bread, or the way that one high school student always rides his bike past one particular girl's house.

And even though the story is new every time, the ragged black shadows flicker without hesitation against the pale sheet: the silhouette of a boy on a bike slows down when he sees a girl in a window; the silhouette of a sandwich man with an apron looped behind his waist reaches under the counter for the old bread. The audience laughs and laughs (except the sandwich man; except the blushing boy).

In time, the story turns more fearful. A ragged little girl shadow stumbling, running, turns to see the monstrous, swollen thing that pursues her. She holds her arms above her head to ward off her fate—too late. The audience, your audience, will gasp, and some will cover their eyes.

So the audience will laugh, and the audience will gasp. And then the story ends.

"Pay what you wish, now," the storyteller will say from the darkness, pushing a box of coins and bills into the departing audience's path. Then he'll watch to see what each person leaves—the blushing boy, his shy girl, the laughing musician, the stingy sandwich man—and you, half tugged along by your mother, as you peer under the screen to see where the puppeteers could possibly be.

And some of you will give a good amount, and say *Thank you! Lovely!* to the man in the shadows as you button your coats against the cold. And some of you will give very little, and walk off looking pleased with yourselves, as if you'd gotten away with something. And some will slip along with the crowd and give nothing at all.

The storyteller will see you all and make no comment.

But although that's the end of one story, another is just beginning.

Because after you leave, the man begins to whisper. And as the red moon sinks, and night deepens, the witchy figures begin to move across the screen again. Only this time, they don't stay on the screen. As the storyteller murmurs his new and darker story, the night-colored shadow puppets go out to play.

Let's say that this night, they go to your house. Maybe your parents didn't pitch any money into the storyteller's box; or they pitched in coins and left paper in their pockets.

Or maybe that day the storyteller saw you jeer at a girl

who fell, or push a boy off his bike, or kill a butterfly on purpose. Something like that.

For whatever reason, on this night, you lie on the carpet, staring into the fire, thinking about the storyteller and his shadows, and the puppeteer who wasn't there. And as you do, a shadow slips down the chimney to play among the flames.

You almost don't notice it at first. But then you see: you see the dark shape playing among the flames. You see the terrible pictures it makes for you there. This shadow shows you your house burning, or your school burning, your classmates screaming, flames rushing up around them—or worse. It might show you worse.

And your mother will say, "What a face you're making, my goodness! Are you sick, sweetheart? Let me feel your head."

When you've been tucked in early, just in case, and kissed good night, you'll hear a sound outside your window, a whispery, scratching sound, like a twig against the glass— *only there's no tree by that window,* you think to yourself as your heart pounds over the papery, rattling, insistent sound of something looking for a way in.

And if you're brave enough to get out of bed, stumbling on cold bare feet, and throw open the curtain: what will you see? Maybe a shadowy shape pressed against your window, a dark and distorted face, with its mouth wide open, pressing against the glass, about to break through.

But you know what? I think you won't be that brave, which is just as well. So let's say instead that the shadow slips under the sill and slides across your bedroom wall, growing large and then small again, bending and twisting, making new and more dreadful shapes—as should not happen, you know it shouldn't, *because the nightlight doesn't flicker, it doesn't flicker, so how can the shadow move?*

You will turn your face, and close your eyes against the moving shadows, and clench your fists--and somehow, you will fall asleep.

But that's a mistake. Because that's when the ragged shadows slip down from the wall and across your covers, until they are peering into your face. That's when they breathe their smoky shadow sighs into your mouth and nose.

And sometimes, that's when they bite. Shadows bite hard.

"Spider bite," your parents will say the next day, "and a bad one," they'll add, when the bite swells up hot and red, when the poison slithers deep into your skin; when the doctor's prescription doesn't help (it can't help—it's not a prescription for shadows); when you lie feverish in that same bed, hearing your friends outside, shouting and playing.

Still, if that happens? In my opinion, you'll have gotten off lucky. If the shadows are *really* angry with you—or if the storyteller is—they can do far worse than bite. There are people who have run away and never returned, because of shadows; who have gone mad, or drowned themselves, or worse.

With shadows, there's always a worse.

But what am I saying? That's other people. That's not you. *You* aren't frightened of shadows. You've never lain awake, when the house was dark and everyone was asleep, watching shadows shift and play from under your bedroom door, heart at a gallop, waiting for the doorknob to turn.

You've never held your breath to calm your wild heart, under the shadow of a tall, hunched figure at the end of your bed, as it watches you, and watches, and watches, just waiting for you to fall asleep.

In the morning, where that figure stood, your parents will only find a bathrobe draped over a bureau, with someone's old football helmet sitting on top of it.

That's what they'll find, in the morning.

But in the morning, will they find you?

They will, I think they will—as long as you follow my

advice and don't anger that storyteller. Don't let him catch you in little cruelties. He doesn't like that, at all, and neither do his friends.

Also, and I can't emphasize this enough: pay the storyteller.

And when the shadows come anyway, whatever you do: don't fall asleep.

EPILOGUE

This collection of recent letters among the Curators ties the final knot on a few of the stories you've just read—and suggests a new direction for the Cabinet in the future.

Dear old friends,

Out of curiosity—but what do we do that is *not* out of curiosity?—I have followed up on a few of our tales, just to complete our records.

Mabel Mavelia, from Curator Bachmann's tale of the same name, recently passed away at an advanced age. She was buried on the grounds of the asylum where she had lived most of her life. On her gravestone are carved these words: "Root, stem, and blossom, here Mabel grows." No one seems to know who paid for the stone, or what the words mean. But within days after her burial—her January burial, and a bitter, snowy January at that—the grave was covered in velvety gray flowers with tiny purple hearts.

Perhaps "luck ain't real," as Tom's Pa said in Curator Legrand's fascinating tale "The Tin Man's Price." Still, that dangerous little candy tin has a way of turning up, however deeply it's buried. I've verified numerous sightings, including a Junior Rodeo Queen who "accidentally" broke her sister's leg and an *American Idol* contestant who . . . well, even I can't bear to write that one out. In short: *urgent* to find that tin.

I also stopped at the museum described in Curator Trevayne's "Generously donated by . . ." I was looking especially for that statue of Pan, of course. I walked all over that museum, map in hand, and followed a series of directions given by ever more confident museum guards, all of them sending me in different directions. Finally I gave up, and was in the museum cafe sipping a restorative cup of extremely black tea, when from *inside the teacup* I heard faint, mocking laughter. What followed—well, that is another story altogether, too long for this brief report.

Finally, I met with the surviving family members from my story "The Talent of the Howl." All of them report hearing, around the time of the full moon each month, the sound of two voices in the grandmother's old room, singing in delicate harmony. One voice is old and rough and strong, they say; the other young, and clear as water. They cannot locate the source of the singing. Their friends will no longer visit the house when the moon is full.

What a pleasure is our profession,

Curator Catmull

A month or two later, this from Curator Trevayne:

Fellow Curators!

Apologies for the urgent tone of this letter, but time is of the utmost! Not five minutes ago, I received news from a contact I encountered while visiting the town that suffered so much horrendous damage at the tiny hands of those honey-loving fairies . . . I'm sure you recall the tale? At any rate, apparently mischief is afoot at the bottom of the sea just on the other side of those very mountains. Something about a shipwreck, though my correspondent was too shaken to give many specifics. I am packing for my adventure to this place as I write.

Curator Catmull has admirably completed the histories of things we have already collected, however we have proof, if we needed it, that there are a great many more objects to see, tales to tell, than we have yet managed. Word has also come of a city that flipped over in the middle of the night and is now hanging from the clouds, though until I see this spectacle for myself I simply won't believe it.

Indeed, the mailbox at our beloved Cabinet is crammed to bursting with vague hints, whispers of the fantastic and terrible. The world itself is a Cabinet of Curiosities, and these objects simply *must* be uncovered, their truths revealed. Curators Bachmann and Catmull, I should be ever so grateful if you would investigate the rumor of the dragons out beyond the Desert of Despair (both go, there is safety in numbers), and Curator Legrand, do you have time to find that pirate we were told of last week?

I shall write again upon my return. Be safe and well in your dangerous escapades, my friends,

Curator Trevayne

Shortly thereafter, Curator Legrand came up with a brilliant plan:

Dear Curators Bachmann, Catmull, and Trevayne,

I write to you from inside an Egyptian tomb.

Don't worry; my foolproof kit is intact, and I've plenty of cashews to snack on. Anyway, according to my calculations, the doorway to the Empire should open up in approximately seventeen minutes, and then I will no longer be trapped in a tomb. Granted, I will in all likelihood be trapped in some puzzle of the Emperor's design—you know how fond he is of showing off—but at least the air won't smell quite so strongly of mummy.

To pass the time, I've been ruminating on the logic of our methodology. Friends, we have created something truly extraordinary in our Cabinet of Curiosities—an apparently endless collection of every marvel and horror imaginable. But, I wonder: Is it wise to restrict employment at the Cabinet to only us four? It is a staggering task we have set for ourselves, scouring the world for items to fill our infinite cupboards and never-ending libraries.

Mightn't we consider hiring an apprentice or two? Someone to feed the books and entertain the poltergeists and make sure the attic pixies don't start cannibalizing one another? While we seek curiosities in the great, wide wild, our apprentice(s) could mind the Cabinet, tend to guests, make sure the linen closet is stocked with fresh meat.

I know this suggestion might startle you. But keep in mind, if I hadn't been quite so tired from cataloging skeletons last weekend, I might have been able to avoid being tricked into that sarcophagus this morning.

Thoughtfully yours,

Curator Legrand

And now a last letter, written not for us, but for those readers of this book who might share the Curators' curiosity, adventurous spirit, and pleasure in crafting a tale—the select, perhaps slightly mad few who may someday become Curators themselves.

Curators old and new,

We have come far in the past pages, have we not? We have traveled to distant islands, down basement steps, through fields of bloody roses and into forests of spiders and towering buildings. I, for one, have recently returned from the bottom of the sea. And you? Where are you? In a bare apartment in a great city? In a lovely house full of flowers and mice? There are curiosities there, wherever it is. There are curiosities right next door, in the head of the old woman who sits so still and sad in her chair; in her mind are a thousand stories for you to collect, a thousand sparks and wonders. There are curiosities in the trees in your garden and in the water of your fish tank and in your schoolhouse and in the sad children and the happy children and in the pages on the shelves. You need only seek them out. You need only reach out your hand or open your mouth or step out your door. Go on. Be brave. Speak to the old lady. Dig in the garden for treasure, and climb the trees to spy the tower-tops in the distance. Go down the cellar steps. You may be surprised at what you find. You may be saddened or terrified. But it will be worth it.

Because one day, perhaps very soon, you will be a curator, too—a guardian of so many memories and so many tales. You have already begun. Carry on, good friend.

On behalf of all of us here in the Cabinet, I bid you a curious life,

Curator Bachmann

Meet The Curators

STEFAN BACHMANN:

Tinker of Shadows and Tailor of Lies, with a fascination for eighth notes, old trees and their inhabitants, and pictures that move. Don't give him anything to hold because his fingers are stained with ink. (At least, it looks like ink . . .)

Stefan was born in Colorado and stayed there for about five minutes until his parents decided they would rather live in Switzerland. They moved into a hundred-year-old house outside of Zurich and he's been there ever since. He is a student of classical music at the Zurich Conservatory and the winner of a bevy of prizes few people have ever heard of. His debut, the gothic-steampunk-faery-fantasy *The Peculiar*, was published by Greenwillow/HarperCollins in Fall 2012 and was a *New York Times* Editor's Choice as well as a *Publishers Weekly* Best Book of 2012, with rights selling in seven languages. *The Whatnot*, the companion to *The Peculiar*, was published in 2013.

KATHERINE CATMULL: *Cataloger and Philosopher of Scientific Marvels with a particular focus on Jars of Moonlight, Frozen Flowers, Broken Fish Fins, Shiny Things Found on Pavements, and Bringing Cookies to Meetings.*

Katherine looks friendly, but she isn't really very. She can usually be found lurking at home with her feral cat and her husband, who has disturbing eyebrows. Her novel *Summer and Bird* (Dutton Children's/Penguin), which was named one of *Booklist*'s Top Ten First Novels for Youth in 2012, is about two sisters who try to find their vanished parents and find quite a lot of awful and exciting things instead, from an evil queen to a snake as long as the world is wide. Chapter 6 begins "The Puppeteer was full of dead birds," if that gives you any idea. Her next book is due out in 2015, and will be just as creepy. Katherine is also an actor (and you know what they're like) and does voiceover work for games like DC Universe Online (where she is the voice of Oracle, as well as a ravenous female zombie, a most unpleasant Atlantean, and others) and Wizard 101 (where she is Myrella Windspar, your faithful real estate salescat).

CLAIRE LEGRAND:
Dark Puppetress and Master Librarian, specializing in Dancing Accoutrements, Unicorn Paraphernalia, and the Especially Gruesome Relics of Botched Time Travel.

Claire is cheerful when you first meet her and increasingly disturbing the better acquainted with her you become. This might be why she feels so at home sorting through ancient tomes written with wicked intent and charred fingernails of great potential. But never fear: She will happily sit in the sunshine and discuss unicorns with you while sipping hot chocolate, her absolute favorite beverage. Her first novel, *The Cavendish Home for Boys and Girls*, a NYPL Best Book of 2012, is about a girl who must face off with a sadistic orphanage director to save her slovenly yet charming best friend. Her second novel, *The Year of Shadows*, is about ghosts—good ones and bad ones—a haunted symphony hall, and twelve-year-old Olivia, who would be right at home at the Cabinet, for she enjoys sketching pictures of the strange and dreadful. Curator Legrand's third novel, *Winterspell* (and the prequel novella, *Summerfall*), is for young adult readers, and contains lots of violent swordplay and kissing, the latter of which, as we all know, leads to cooties.

EMMA TREVAYNE:

Collector of Auditory Oddities, Whimsical Words, and Cryptic Cyphers. Pays special attention to petrichor, things that glimmer, and mechanical body parts.

Emma is often mistaken for a unicorn because of her hair, which makes her slightly nervous around Curator Legrand at Cabinet meetings. Her dog is convinced butterflies are really fairies in disguise. (And if you saw the size of his jaws, you wouldn't argue with him either.) She is that very special type of person who reads dictionaries for fun, hovering with held breath over words such as *fiendish*, *lucifugous*, and *malevolence*. Over a meal entirely made up of cakes and chocolate, she will tell you strange and terrible things about violent houseplants. Her first novel, *Coda* (and its sequel, *Chorus*), is for teenagers and is about music that makes you feel very odd indeed, but she has also written a middle grade steampunk fairy tale called *Flights and Chimes and Mysterious Times*, in which she did unforgivable things to famous landmarks and laughed the whole time. Clearly, whichever age group she writes for, the normal rules of science and nature (and perhaps, politeness and decency) are there to be broken.

483

INDEX OF
STORY TITLES